THE DRESSMAKER OF DRAPER'S LANE

Liz Trenow's family have been silk weavers for nearly three hundred years, and run the oldest family-owned silk company in Britain, one of just three still operating today. Liz worked as a journalist for regional and national newspapers, and on BBC radio and television news, before turning her hand to fiction. She lives in East Anglia with her artist husband, and they have two grown-up daughters.

Find out more at **www.liztrenow.com**, like her Facebook page at **www.facebook.com/liztrenow** or join her on Twitter **@LizTrenow**.

Also by Liz Trenow

The Last Telegram
The Forgotten Seamstress
The Poppy Factory
The Silk Weaver
In Love and War

LIZ TRENOW

The Dressmaker of Draper's Lane

PAN BOOKS

First published 2019 by Pan Books
an imprint of Pan Macmillan
20 New Wharf Road, London N1 9RR
Associated companies throughout the world
www.panmacmillan.com

ISBN 978-1-5098-7981-6

1 3 5 7 9 8 6 4 2

A CIP catalogue record for this book is available from the British Library.

Artwork © Hemesh Alles

Typeset by Palimpsest Book Production Limited, Falkirk, Stirlingshire
Printed and bound by CPI Group (UK) Ltd, Croydon, CRO 4YY

Visit **www.panmacmillan.com** to read more about all our books
and to buy them. You will also find features, author interviews and
news of any author events, and you can sign up for e-newsletters
so that you're always first to hear about our new releases.

This book is dedicated to Elsie, Fox and Gil

PROLOGUE

She is unaware of her legs moving beneath her, of one foot taking a step and then another, except for the fact that the great gates in the distance seem to be drawing ever closer.

Her mind is blank. She keeps her eyes lowered to the ground, passing silently through the crowds on Gray's Inn Road like a spectre. No one notices her and she dares not allow herself to look at her surroundings nor even to think, for if she did she would surely turn and flee. The only notion in her head is that where she is going offers the sole hope of saving her child's life.

The bundle in her arms is still and silent now, having ceased whimpering some hours ago. The baby is too feeble to cry any more. It is of no matter to her that she has not eaten for several days except that it has caused her milk to become thin and weak.

This child is the single most precious thing she has ever known. How can she bear to give her up? Yet how can she bear to let her die?

At first the solution seemed simple. She would end both of their lives together, so they could never be parted. Several times she has returned to Blackfriars Bridge, watching the dark, cold waters swirling below and trying to summon the courage to jump. But first she must climb onto the parapet, which means freeing her hands by laying down the bundle on the edge of the bridge, and even this momentary separation seems too dangerous to contemplate. What if the child should slip into the river without her? Who would hold her tight as she fell, whispering reassurances that although the water would be cold and the journey difficult, everything would be fine when they reached the other side? Would she even have the courage to follow her?

Each time she has left the bridge feeling foolish and tearful, trudging the weary path back to the city, still no clearer about what the future might hold.

Until they told her about the Foundling Hospital. It's a place just opened up, where they will look after babies until their mothers can go back for them, they said.

Now she is aware of passing a long brick wall to her right-hand side and a building, the gatehouse, flanked by two brick sentry boxes. A man gives her a cursory glance and nods her through. She emerges onto a wide gravelled driveway with well-trimmed lawns either side. In the far distance, or so it seems to her, is what looks like a palace; a vast building of many windows, more than she can count. Two wings of this building reach towards her and, as she walks, start to surround her like a funnel drawing her inexorably towards her fate.

Ahead is surely the main entrance, although it looks more like a temple than a home for children. Leading up to it is a wide set of steps on which, as she now approaches, she can see gathered a group of figures, maybe a couple of dozen; bedraggled, bewildered women, their faces hidden by shawls, all carrying bundles in their arms. Women like herself.

She joins the throng – it is too untidy to be considered a queue – and waits. No one knows what they are waiting for and no one talks to each other. The group is silent save for the occasional heart-rending cry of a child, and the sound of muffled weeping. Hunger and heat cause her to hallucinate: she is waiting at the gates of heaven and they are about to open. She and her child will live in the light of God's goodness forever. But this blissful illusion is shattered by the sound of the wooden doors being unbolted, and a man shouting: 'Form an orderly queue, ladies, please. Don't push. You will all be seen.'

Despite his exhortations the women press forward, holding out their bundles, pleading: 'Take my baby', 'Please, save my child', 'He is a good lad and strong, take him.'

The man stands firm, insisting that he will not allow anyone inside until they have obeyed his instruction. 'You know what a queue is, ladies? One at a time. Yes, that's it, get into a row.' At last they are formed into an orderly line of which she takes up the rear. She is about to give up and turn away, thinking that surely they will take the first babies first and she has no chance, when he calls out, kindly. 'Come back, dearie. Didn't I promise that everyone would be seen? That includes you, if you're prepared to be patient.' She falls obediently back into line and shuffles forward as the queue moves through into a large hallway, and then into a high-ceilinged room grander than any she has ever seen before.

Even more surprising than the grandeur of the place is the number of well-dressed ladies and gentlemen in this room. She cannot imagine what they are doing here. They stand and sit around the walls of the room, chatting among themselves and regarding the line of ragged mothers with a mixture of interest and dismay, as though they are viewing a cabinet of curiosities. The room is warm and one or two are fanning themselves; another is holding a handkerchief to her nose.

Suddenly aware of her own odour, she wraps her shawl more firmly around her waist. She cannot remember the last time she took more than a cursory rub down with a damp flannel, and she has worn the same clothes for weeks. The presence of these onlookers disturbs her; she turns her face to her child, but the sight of the little sleeping face is like the stab of a dagger, a reminder of the betrayal she is about to commit. She raises her eyes. All around are oil paintings in gilt frames, mostly of ships and classical scenes. But just above, to her right, is a large portrait of a kindly-looking man with wild grey hair and a red jacket. He has charts on the table beside him and a globe at his feet, but he is taking no heed of these. Instead, he seems to be smiling directly at her. She smiles back, and it cheers her.

One of the ladies follows her gaze. 'That is Thomas Coram, our founder,' she says. 'A very great man, for whose beneficence you must be truly grateful.'

She has no idea what beneficence means, but she senses that he must be a good man, the sort of man you would want to have as a father if you were lucky enough to have known one, which she was not.

Someone pushes past her so roughly that she is nearly thrown off-balance. It is one of the women she saw in the queue ahead, still carrying her bundle, only now she is wailing so loudly that some of the babies begin to cry in sympathy. As she rushes for the door she throws down a small, shiny black object which rolls across the floor towards the ladies. One of them stoops to pick it up, and passes it back to a man holding a large calico bag. She watches this man and sees that he invites each mother, as she comes to the head of the queue, to reach into the bag and pull out a ball. Some are red, others white or black. Ahead of her in the queue two women start to whisper, and she can just about make out what they are saying.

'Poor cow, got the ruddy black ball,' one says.

'They won't take her baby?'

'Thass what 'appened to us last time, didn' it, sweetling?' the woman croons to her child.

'What about the red ball?'

'Waiting list.'

'Then you have to get a white ball, or they won't even take the baby?'

'Yup. If the doc says it's healthy.'

'After we've waited all this time.'

''Cos they got more'n they can manage.'

The brief exchange makes everything clear: the future of herself and her baby lies in a lottery of little coloured balls. She waits in line, dully, devoid of emotion. She doesn't even care about the stares of the smart ladies and gentlemen any more. What will happen will happen. It is out of her hands. Obediently, she reaches into the bag and pulls out a white ball that seems to sear her eyes with its cruel, unearthly brightness.

Only later, as she leaves the hospital through the hallway, out of the door, down the steps and out into the bright sunlight, does the numbness wear off. Her arms are empty. The full horror and finality of what has just happened, of what she has so calmly acquiesced to, hits her with a scorching pain so powerful that she cannot breathe, nor see, nor speak.

She staggers and falls to the ground, wishing for nothing except to die.

LONDON 1768

I

Gown: a full-length, sleeved garment with a fitted bodice and skirts cut in two basic variations: the English Gown (also nightgown or robe à l'Anglaise) and the Sack Gown (negligee, sacque or robe à la Française).

> *From Miss Charlotte's glossary for the instruction of apprentice seamstresses*

It is a charming tableau, tinted in my memory with the glow of innocence, a light wash of gold or pink such as a painter might use to impart a spirit of contentment to their composition.

Two young women are taking tea by the fireside in a modest parlour, its grey-painted panelling hung with a few indistinct prints. Long white cambric curtains are pulled aside to reveal, on a rail in the background, a kaleidoscope of silk gowns, petticoats and waistcoats that over the coming months will be worn at society events all over London and even further afield.

They themselves are dressed simply and unadorned in plain taffetas, their sleeves without lace, their heads uncovered. They are friends, in informal company. The fairer one, her nose and cheeks dotted with freckles, rests back in her chair. 'Of all the women with whom I am acquainted, you are surely the one who knows herself the best,' she says. 'You seem so confident, so secure in your place.'

Her companion, smaller and darker with a serious demeanour and neat, contained features, raises her eyebrows and shakes her head modestly even though, in this moment, she does indeed feel truly blessed. She grows increasingly confident in her work; she has family, friends and enough money with which to enjoy a comfortable life. She is beginning truly to know herself. Or that is what she thinks.

But she is wrong. The artist takes up his tubes of grey and brown with just a tint of purple, and mixes up on his palette the colours of thunder clouds that, now that we study the canvas more carefully, we can see lurking on the horizon. For the truth is that she knows herself barely at all.

The two young women are, of course, myself and my dearest friend, Anna Vendome.

'I have always envied you, Charlotte, ever since we first met,' she said. 'Remember that day when Aunt Sarah brought me for my first gown fittings? I was so nervous and confused. I didn't know a thing about fashion and nor did I really want to, at the time, but you helped me through it.'

How could I forget? Miss Butterfield, as I then knew her, had been shy to the point of being almost monosyllabic, but I could already sense the strength of character beneath that subdued demeanour. 'And your aunt so determined to turn you into the model of a young society lady.'

'A hopeless task, as it turned out.' She guffawed in the

most unladylike manner. It is true, with her long back, large hands and feet and that unruly hair; she has never fitted the mould. Which is why we get on so well, I always think. In some ways, we are both outsiders.

'You were so confident and so professional. I was in awe of you. Still am, a little.' She held up her palms, wide-eyed, feigning fear.

'Don't tease. I'm just an ordinary woman trying to make her way in the world.'

'Ordinary? I don't think so.'

'Look at you, too. People flocking to your door.' In just a few short years Anna's designs for flowered silks have already become in such demand that they have needed to hire an additional half-dozen journeymen to weave them. Henri told me himself that his business would be only half as profitable without his wife's artistic talents.

'Men recognise you, Charlotte, for the businesswoman you are. That's the difference. They always ask for Henri first, even though it is my designs they're after, and I'm often taken for the servant. They just don't seem to believe it is possible for a woman to know what she is talking about, or indeed that she could, in some fields, have greater expertise than a man.'

The inequity between the sexes is a recurring theme of our conversations.

'But you have created all of this on your own,' she went on, waving an expansive arm in the direction of the garment rail. 'Here you are with your name above the door, with some of the wealthiest of society ladies calling for your services. You make your own money and you pay your own bills. You employ several skilled seamstresses who all seem to admire you. And you are beholden to no other, man or woman. Just to yourself. It's a remarkable achievement.'

She is right, I suppose. After a particularly unpromising start, and as an unmarried woman of no society pedigree or fortune, I have managed with the help and generosity of friends to fashion a decent life for myself, a life that I imagined would serve me well for the rest of my days.

But what Anna said next would set in train a sequence of events that would rock those foundations to the core.

'Oh, I nearly forgot to give you this.'

Pulling on her cloak – the midnight-blue velvet with the ruby hood lining – Anna reached into her pocket and pulled out a notice printed on cheap paper, the type of flyer handed around to advertise plays, concerts or those tonics that promise to cure all your ills.

FOR SALE BY AUCTION
DUE TO BANKRUPTCY

The ENTIRE stock of the finest silks,
satins, damasks, brocades,
and other top quality tissues &c. &c.

At The Red Lyon Inn, Spitalfields
Upper Rooms
On Tuesday the 22nd day of September 1768
Viewing from one o'clock, sale begins two o'clock

EVERYTHING MUST GO

'It's not your uncle, I hope?' I said. The merchant Joseph Sadler and his ne'er-do-well son William had been through difficult times in the past few years, and might

have overstretched themselves by moving to grander premises in Ludgate Hill.

She laughed. 'Thankfully they seem to prosper, despite
Will's best efforts to sink them. But about this auction.
Will you go with me?'

'You plan to go? Whatever do you hope to find there,
my friend?'

'I am curious, dearest. You never know what might turn
up. Perhaps even some French silks fit to tickle the fancy
of a society lady at half the cost of new?'

'How can I leave the shop for a whole afternoon?' I was
still unconvinced.

'It's a Tuesday, Charlotte. Early closing day.'

There was a great press of bodies outside the Red Lyon
as we waited for the auction rooms to open and as the
only women among a crowd of men we attracted a fair
few stares and muttered comments. The sky was overcast,
threatening the first rains of autumn, and I was on the
point of giving up.

'Come on, it will be interesting, dearest,' Anna said,
tightening her grip on my arm.

At last the doors opened, and we made our way up the
long flight of wooden stairs to a capacious room stretching
the width of the building above the alehouse. On three
sides trestle tables sagged under rolls of fabric, dozens of
them, fat and full. With holdings like these it was little
wonder the merchant had gone bankrupt; they must be
worth hundreds, even thousands of pounds. Even so, none

were of any real interest to me: fashions are so capricious; I never require more than a couple of dozen yards for any one outfit, and have little storage space.

Anna headed directly to the other side of the room where a table was laden with folded cloths, short pieces and reel ends, all carefully labelled with specifications and dimensions. She picked up a bundle of mixed silks tied with a ribbon, pulled out a corner and peered at the back of the weave with her pocket magnifier.

'I swear it's a Leman, or perhaps a Baudouin. Henri would know,' she muttered, almost to herself. 'Such brilliant designers. D'you know, Charlotte, some of these silks have more than a thousand threads in every inch. It could take weeks to weave just a couple of yards. They used to fetch premium prices.'

These heavy silks with their rococo patterns are of only passing interest for me, being too outmoded for my fashion-conscious clients, but Anna has an inexhaustible curiosity for the design and technicalities of weaving, especially those of the French masters.

'They're such rare examples. I'd really like to have them, Charlotte. I can't imagine many others would be interested in such small swatches, can you?' she said, checking the label. 'Lot two-six-one.'

'Have you ever bid at an auction before?' She shook her head. 'It cannot be too difficult, can it?' I said.

At two o'clock the auction got under way and we retired to the rear of the room to observe.

The auctioneer skilfully drummed up an atmosphere of urgency, filling the room with feverish energy, and the sale proceeded swiftly. Larger lots went for what seemed like bargain prices and before long the crowd had thinned and tables emptied as successful bidders carried away their spoils, hefting the rolls onto their shoulders with triumphant grins.

Anna fidgeted beside me, shifting from foot to foot, adjusting her shawl and bonnet. The auctioneer's eyes turned towards us, eyebrows questioning. 'Are you in, young lady?' A dozen heads turned and a titter of amusement rippled through the room as she shook her head, blushing fiercely.

'Your head is much cooler than mine, Charlotte,' she whispered. 'Will you bid for me?'

'I'd only end up bidding against myself. It was your idea. You do it.'

'I have but two pounds,' she said. 'Please, just have a go.'

By now there were five people left in the room: myself and Anna, the auctioneer and two scruffy characters who looked like pedlars.

'Two-six-one. Short pieces of brocade and damask,' the auctioneer announced. 'Who'll give me a guinea?' Surely everyone could hear my heart thudding? 'Ten shillings then?' he barked irritably, as though we were wasting his time. I pinched my lips.

'Five?' One of the traders raised his hand, the other followed swiftly afterwards. The two vied for bids, raising a shilling a time.

'Ten shillings,' he said. 'Ten shillings. Going, going . . .' Anna nudged me. 'Eleven,' I squeaked.

The traders glowered and bid again until it reached fifteen shillings. 'And sixpence,' I heard myself saying. My head was in such a spin that when the hammer went down

I could not be entirely sure whether it had fallen in my favour.

'Fifteen shillings and sixpence to the lady. Name, please?'

Anna's cheeks were flushed with triumph now. 'Bravo, Charlotte,' she whispered.

'He wants your name, Anna.'

'My name?'

'For the sale. So he can record what you owe.'

It was only a bunch of silk pieces too short to be of much use, bought for a few shillings, but it felt as though we had won a great prize. Little did I know then that, far from being a prize, this little bundle was like Pandora's box. Much anguish would result from the opening of it.

2

Open robe: a gown whose skirt encircles the back and sides but is open at the front, allowing the petticoat to be seen.

The Vendome house feels like home. It is not overly large or grand; like most houses in this part of London it doubles, as does my own, as a business premises, lively with the comings and goings of customers and suppliers as well as the family who live there. Besides Anna and Henri there is his master Monsieur Lavalle, now mostly retired, and his pretty daughter Mariette, who seems about to become engaged to her silversmith sweetheart any day now. A drawboy sleeps in the weaving loft and the apprentice in the basement beside the kitchen.

We are usually greeted by the thud of small feet and the cry of 'Maman', but little Jean is only two years old and needs his afternoon rest. I assumed that was where he must be, with his grandmother watching over him. Everyone had quietly hoped that Henri's mother Clothilde and Monsieur Lavalle might make a union to comfort each other in their declining years, but it was not to be. Although they are the best of friends she remains living in rented rooms nearby, coming each day so that Anna can work. A cook feeds this crowd with endless patience and good humour. She certainly needs it – the numbers at table, and their times of arrival, are always unpredictable.

The house was quiet that afternoon, save for the comforting thud of looms in the weaving loft above. Monsieur Lavalle no longer weaves, complaining that the ladder is too steep for his creaky joints, but Henri will work up there for at least half of each day, instructing the apprentice and the drawboy. It is the sound of industry, and I love to hear it. My own business is largely silent save for the snip-snip of scissors and the low conversation of the seamstresses.

Just as at my own shop, two rooms on the ground floor are dedicated to business, with a showroom at the front and an office at the rear filled from floor to ceiling with samples, workbooks, ledgers for accounts and customer details, with barely a space to squeeze between the desks. Anna works there when she can to keep abreast of business affairs but complains about the disorder and poor light, often resorting to carrying her pencils, paints and point papers up to the front room on the first floor that serves as a parlour for the family.

Here, the sun floods through tall windows and seconds are counted out in the measured tick-tock of the tall grandfather clock in the corner, Monsieur Lavalle's pride and joy. On chillier days like this one there is always a cheerful blaze in the fireplace and plentiful tallows burning in the sconces, their light reflected in the looking glass above the fireplace and glinting off the dark wood panelling. An old harpsichord sits in the corner; a decorative piece much neglected by Mariette, despite her father's exhortations. Anna claims her neglect is a blessing, for the girl has no aptitude nor any ambition to improve, and her clumsy attempts are tiresome on the ear.

By the fireside is the master's old chair, high-backed against the draught, its red leather faded and worn. No one else sits there, certainly not when Monsieur Lavalle is at home. He is the kindest man and I have never heard an angry word from him, but he likes his routine and can be stern with those who cross him.

A glass-fronted case on the far wall holds dozens of porcelain ornaments, elaborate scenes of shepherds and milkmaids and the like, which it was the pleasure of the late Madame Lavalle to collect. In a private moment I once watched Monsieur Lavalle unlock the doors to take out a precious item, whispering to it as he dusted it off, as though communing with his beloved wife. Even though he will never admit to any sadness, it is obvious that his heart is still in mourning.

It was to this room that, in our exultant mood, we brought our auction spoils.

'Come,' Anna said, clearing books and papers from the table by the window. She untied the ribbon and laid out the pieces of fabric – twelve in all – and immediately began to examine more closely those she believed to be by the masters she so revered: Leman, Baudouin or Dandridge. These men – many of them refugees to London from persecution in their own countries – are long dead now, but we who work in the business owe a debt of gratitude for their sophisticated designs and ground-breaking techniques. It is at least partly due to them that Spitalfields silks are now renowned throughout the world.

I busied myself inspecting the other swatches, lifting and unfolding each in turn to see whether they could be of any use. A design of oak leaves and brown acorns against a light blue ground caught my eye.

'That's pretty,' Anna said, glancing over. 'Would you have a use for it?'

'It'd make an interesting lining for a gentleman's jacket,' I said. 'For pockets, cuffs and facings. Let me give you some money for it.'

'Don't be silly. These are the only ones I wanted for myself. The rest are yours if you would like any of them.'

I placed the oak leaf design to one side and continued my investigation. None of the other fabrics were of any interest, until it came to the last. Just as soon as I unfolded it the back of my neck seemed to prickle, and I felt a sharp pain in the palm of my hand.

The silk, brocaded in the most brilliant reds, purples and greens on a pale ground, showed a small oriental building like the follies so beloved of the aristocracy, settled among oversized lotus flowers and a gnarled, twisted tree from which an exotic bird, quite unlike any in this country, seemed to sing. I had seen similar silks before: Chinoiserie designs, inspired by porcelain imported from the Far East, were all the rage a few decades ago. But this was different. Interwoven through the brocade were the finest threads of silver.

'What is it, Charlotte? You have turned so pale. You poor dear, in my excitement over the Leman silks I have neglected you. Let me call for tea and something sweet.'

'It's this silk.' My hands shook as I passed it to her. Something caught in the back of my throat. It was the scent of dried lavender, such as we use to deter moths.

'It is unusual, I grant you, I have never seen anything like it before,' she said, after a moment. 'A bit gaudy, don't you think? Not in the most subtle of tastes. It must have been designed for someone who needed to impress.' She scraped the tarnished metallic thread with a fingernail and took out her glass for closer inspection. 'It is real silver, all right; must have cost a pretty penny or two. The customer will have been well-heeled, that is certain.'

As she held the fabric up to the window it seemed to shimmer and shift, as though it was alive. Bright dots of sunshine reflected off the silver threads and began to spin around the room with increasing speed; a dazzling, dizzying whirlpool of light that burned my eyes and roared in my ears.

'Oh! Charlotte.' I felt Anna's steadying hand on my arm. She pulled up a chair. 'Here, sit down. Take deep breaths,' she ordered. 'Don't try to talk.'

After a cup of tea and two of cook's delicious almond biscuits, I began to recover. The silk still lay on the table by the window and although a few reflections still peppered the walls, at least they were not moving. The roaring in my head had abated, the pain in my palm had disappeared.

'What came over you?' Anna asked.

'Truly, I cannot say,' I said. 'All I know is, that silk is both strange to me and yet oddly familiar.'

'But to make you feel so faint?'

'Could you not smell the lavender?'

'What lavender?' she asked.

Had I imagined it? I shook my head, trying to plumb the depths of my memory, but there was nothing save for the disquieting feeling – an intimation, if you will – that this silk had once been of great significance to me, long ago.

On my way home that late afternoon I came upon a beggar, a young woman in rags sitting at the edge of the roadway at the junction of Church Street with Paternoster Row, where the wheels of carts and carriages passed perilously close as they rounded the corner. As I approached she held out a bundle. At first I thought she was offering goods for sale and prepared to shake my head, as usual, without slowing my step. Street pedlars can be the very devil if you show the slightest interest. More than once have I been followed almost to my door by a seller desperate to offload his wares before nightfall.

As I drew near, she spoke. It was more of a whisper, barely audible, but in those few seconds there was a lull in the general hubbub of the street, so that I heard every word.

'Madam, take him, please.'

Normally I would have hurried on. There are just too many beggars in London to help. If I stopped to offer a farthing to each one I would empty my pockets within five minutes of leaving the front door. But she was different, her face and hands a dark mahogany colour, unusual even in this part of London with its immigrations and shifting populations, where you are just as likely to hear other languages as your own. And she looked so young, a child almost.

Again she offered the bundle. 'He is a good boy, madam. Take him, I beg of you.'

The bundle began to whimper as she pulled the rags away to reveal its face: a baby no more than a few days old, its cheeks paler than hers, sallow even, but just as thin. At that moment a carriage rounded the corner at speed, and only the fast actions of the coachman saved us from being trampled to death by his horses.

I grabbed her arm and pulled her to her feet. 'It's not safe here. Come with me.' People gaped, of course. I would have done the same: whatever was a young lady dressed in silks doing with a dark-skinned beggar girl? But I didn't care. Something about the desperate expression on her face had touched my heart.

We stopped at a food stall and purchased a hot meat pie and a glass of milk.

'I cannot pay, madam,' she said, shaking her head. 'I have nothing to give. All I wish is for my child to live.' She looked down at the baby lying silently in her arms, tears leaving pale streaks on her cheeks.

'I want nothing in return,' I said, passing her my handkerchief. 'You are clearly famished, so please eat. Then we can talk.'

She wiped her face, took the pie and devoured it in four great mouthfuls, as though she had not eaten for days. Then she took the milk and gulped it down, wide eyes darting nervously around all the while. I returned the mug to the stall.

'Now you must explain. Whose is this child?'

'He is mine, madam. A fine boy, as you see. But I cannot keep him.' I did not ask why, for the reasons were all too evident. She could barely keep herself, the poor child. Although well-spoken she had clearly fallen on hard times, most likely as a consequence of misplaced faith in a white man's promises. She may have been in service, just as I had been, and been dismissed when her condition became obvious.

She burst into tears once more. 'All I want is for him to have a good life.'

'Have you tried the parish?'

'The priest sent me packing,' she sobbed. 'I am not married, you see . . .'

The parish was supposed to help women in her situation, but I knew they were overwhelmed.

'Have you heard of the Foundling Hospital?' I asked.

She shook her head.

'They may take him,' I said. 'It is worth trying.' What I did not tell her is that the Hospital itself is also swamped with mothers desperate to give their babies a chance in life. I had heard they ran a kind of lottery: depending on the colour of ball you picked up at the entrance, you could be turned away or allowed in. Then, only if your child passed the medical examination would they be accepted.

'They will care for him and give him a good education,' I said. 'Then if at some time in the future your circumstances improve, you may go and reclaim him. They will ask you to leave a token, the half of something which you will keep so that you can prove you are his mother.'

As her face brightened it became even more painfully obvious how young she really was, probably no more than sixteen. How much my heart ached for her.

'Where is this place?' she asked.

'You can read?' She nodded.

I begged a slip of paper and a pencil from the stallholder and wrote *Lamb's Conduit Field, Bloomsbury* and then, below, *Miss Charlotte, Costumière, Draper's Lane.*

'Here is sixpence for the coach,' I said. 'Let me know how you fare.'

She tucked the slip and the coin into her bodice. 'How can I ever repay you?' she sniffed.

'There is no need, child,' I said. 'I wish you well.'

As I watched her walk away, a shiver went down my spine.

That could have been my mother.

3

Stomacher: a triangular panel placed between the bodice edges of an open robe. It may be boned and is often elaborately decorated and sometimes laced across the upper border.

Each day after that I waited, expecting to see her face on my doorstep with the child in her arms, but when after a week she had not returned, I dared to hope. Perhaps, just perhaps, she had taken a white ball, and the child had passed the Hospital's medical inspection. With luck he would be placed with a good, kind foster mother who knew how to keep young babies alive, and then at the age of five he would return to the Foundling Hospital.

There, even though he would never know the love of a family, he would at least be fed and clothed, and taught the skills he would need for the apprenticeship he would take up at fourteen. And if the people caring for you did not show you much affection, at least you had the company of your fellows. I often wonder how my best friend from those days is faring now, recalling how she and I would climb into bed with each other to keep warm on the coldest nights, how we shared our food and stood up for each other against unfairness.

Perhaps, just perhaps, he would survive and go on to live a good life, as I have done. He might grow up into a fine young man and if he was lucky, he would meet his love and have a family of his own, for that is the best we can hope for in this precarious life of ours. But would he ever see his mother again? Would he find himself looking in the glass, as I do, trying to imagine what his mother was like?

I wonder whether my mother had a little mole on her chin, like mine, and whether she was dark-haired and brown-eyed; or are those traits I have inherited from my father, whoever he was?

I ponder, too, what brought her to such despair, twice, that she had to give up both of her daughters? These questions lurk at the edges of my mind and I usually try to fend them off for fear they will drag me into a morass of introspection. But my meeting with this young woman had brought them tumbling back, irresistible as rain.

Just after my fourth birthday, the foster mother with whom the authorities had placed me, and who I loved with all my heart, told me that I would shortly have to go back to the Hospital to join my fellow foundlings. Older 'brothers and sisters' who lived with us had mysteriously disappeared when they reached that age, but for some reason I had never imagined that it could happen to me.

'But why?' I'd howled, clasping her skirts as though I could hold onto her forever.

'I would keep you in an instant, sweet child, but you must return because I am not your real mother.'

'What is a real mother? Who is she?' I wailed. When you are a child, the person who provides you with the constancy of love, along with warmth, food and comfort, *is* your mother.

'We do not know,' she said. 'And nor will you ever know, like as not, because you were given up as a foundling.'

'What is a foundling?'

'A foundling is a child with no mother or father to care for them,' she explained patiently.

'Where have they gone? Are they dead?' The concept felt remote.

'Perhaps. Or it may be that for some reason they could not keep you.'

Although I asked again and again, she was never able to satisfy my hunger, and hanging over me was the deep well of fear and sorrow of knowing that someday soon she too was going to give me up. Was I not good enough to have a proper mother? Even though I behaved impeccably from then onwards, always helping as best I could with the housework and with the other little ones, the day inexorably approached. I was torn from her arms and returned to the Hospital, where I became just a number, a child to be controlled and moulded into an adult, a child not worthy of a mother's love; and where such misery and homesickness engulfed me that I felt sure I must die from it.

Our hearts ached for what we had never known. Not a day passed without my imagining how my mother would arrive to claim me. I dreamed about it: how she would sweep into the driveway in a coach and four and recognise me immediately before whisking me away with promises of new clothes, delicious sweetmeats, the most comfortable feather mattress and a pretty coverlet on my bed.

Yet still, after all these years, I know so little about her.

But at least I have my sister, Louisa. Without her, I would be nothing. Had she not found me when she did, I might not even be alive.

Our circumstances could not be more different, of course. She lives in a spacious, well-ordered vicarage, performing to perfection the role of a clergyman's wife. She has no need to earn her own money, nor would her husband ever contemplate allowing her to do so.

In a few short years she has managed to befriend and endear herself to the squire of her village and his family and I feel sure that it is partly due to her efforts that they have endowed the parish with the greatest of generosity: new kitchens for the workhouse, the extension of the almshouses to accommodate growing numbers of elderly and infirm, the restoration of the church bells. It is she who ensures that when the bishop comes to tea the most delicious of cakes are on offer, containing none of the dried fruit that gives him heartburn, and the tea served in the best bone china.

She prunes the roses in the churchyard, visits the sick and elderly and runs stalls at fetes and fairs, all the while providing a comfortable home and the best education available for Peter, who, at just ten years old, is growing like a young sapling and seems equally gifted at mathematics and drawing. He is rather handsome these days, with the dark hair and neat features Louisa and I share, but the ready smile and amused glint in his chestnut eyes he must have discovered for himself, for lightness of heart is something that both my sister and I strive to find, at times. Anna frequently chides me for looking too solemn. Life is a serious business, I generally retort, trying to smile just to please her.

Louisa's husband, the Reverend Ambrose Fairchild, is an industrious and well-respected vicar who sets about his work with a zeal that would be the envy of many a parish. An older man, tall, overbearing and somewhat stern, he is overly pious for my own taste and wont to threaten the wrath of the Lord upon the heads of those who do not meet his high moral expectations. At times I find him terrifying, although Louisa appears content. At least, that is what I assume, for she never speaks ill of him.

When he was about eight, Peter asked me what I thought hell was like. He was convinced that he would end up there, because he had stolen another boy's conker. I tried to reassure him, but he was not convinced. 'Father says that however small the sin, God will know.' His little chin began to tremble. 'I don't want to burn in everlasting fire, Auntie.'

I pulled him to me. 'Dearest boy, God knows that you are sorry. You must look for another prize specimen and give it to your friend.'

'But then he will suspect something.'

'So you must acknowledge your mistake and apologise.'

Whether he followed my advice I will never know, for it was never mentioned again.

But I must not cavil about Ambrose, for it is thanks to him that Louisa and I have been reunited after so many years of separation. I am always invited to the vicarage for special occasions: Christmas and Easter, my birthday in June. In between these times she will bring Peter to London, and more often than not these visits coincide with her need of a new gown, some breeches or a waistcoat for Peter or Ambrose. Or some mending, for she has never learned the art of needlework for herself and claims there is no one in the village who does it so well. I never ask her for payment, for I owe her far too much already.

We have become a proper family, and this is the rhythm of our lives. I have much to be grateful for, and it is all thanks to Louisa.

It was mid-October and she and Peter were due to arrive in London in a few days' time. The nights were drawing in, and even here in the city I could smell the scents of autumn. Each morning would rise with a gentle concealing mist, each day the sun would break through with a golden syrupy light. London wears its charms most brightly in spring and autumn, and I was looking forward to showing my country relatives the many pleasures it can offer.

Although their visits are always much longed for, the preparations are exhausting. I must make up my own bed with clean linen for Louisa and a pallet for Peter. I will sleep on the floor of the cutting room. Peter's favourite foods must be purchased and prepared in my tiny kitchen. In anticipation of their visit the modesty of my accommodation becomes all too apparent in my eyes, so to compensate I clean and tidy until my fingers are worn to the bone, and spend more than I can afford on flowers and other little touches.

Why do I feel such a need to court my sister's approval in this way? She has never shown anything other than complete affection towards me, never remarked upon any perceived shortcoming nor been seen running a sly finger along a mantel or window frame. Perhaps it is my own approbation that I seek: to prove that I am worthy of the life she has helped me find?

It had been four months since our last meeting and when the day finally arrived I was, as usual, on a knife-edge, thrumming with anticipation. At the coach stop they emerged, white-faced and stiff-limbed from their long journey and, as ever, Louisa and I fell into each other's arms, pressing our faces into each other's necks. The ferocity of our embrace and the sweetness of that familiar warmth takes me by surprise each time.

How I yearn to do the same with my boy: to gather him into my arms and hold him, to kiss his cheeks, nuzzle my face into his sweet neck, to tickle the tender places around his waist as he once used to love. But he believes himself to be so grown-up these days that he will submit only to the briefest contact; an arm over a shoulder, or the shake of a hand. Perhaps later, after we have taken something to eat, he will come to sit beside me on the settle and rest against me.

At supper I tried not to interrogate him. I would have liked to know every tiny detail, to learn about every sniffle or chilblain, the ebb and flow of his friendships, the winning or losing at sport, his achievements in school and the songs he has learned to sing in his sweet treble voice. But the best I can usually hope for is that this information will be volunteered, slowly trickling out over the course of the few hours we have together without too much prompting.

Instead, I began to chatter away about Christmas. It was still two months away but already my thoughts were turning to gifts, in particular for Peter.

'Heavens, Charlotte, it is not yet November. Let us not

begin to consider those things so soon,' Louisa said. 'We've Advent to get through yet.'

'I will need time to sew something,' I countered. 'Let me take some measurements while you are here and you can look at some silks. You are growing into such a tall young man.'

He blushed sweetly, embarrassed by the attention, but after a few moments did allow that his best jacket was a little tight. Even before Louisa had time to indicate with a nod that she approved the notion, my mind was already spinning ahead: what colour fabric would I use, what design, what small details might I add to make the garment distinctive for my special boy?

I cleared away the plates and stoked the fire. This is the best time of all, when they are recovered from the rigours of the journey and we are able to relax in each other's company once more, settling into the informal ease you can only find between family and close friends. How would they like to spend the following day? I asked. Would it be a walk down to the Thames to see the great ships unloading, or a visit to St Paul's Cathedral? Peter favoured the former, Louisa the latter. I declared that they would have to decide between themselves. It was their visit, after all. I could enjoy these wonders at any time.

While they were discussing the merits of each activity my mind turned again to Peter's new jacket, and recalled the oak leaf fabric we'd found at the auction. I went next door to the showroom to retrieve the parcel Anna had wrapped for me.

I untied the string and took out the oak leaf silk, holding it up for Peter's approval.

'Oaks are my favourite trees,' he said. 'The very best for climbing.'

So absorbed were we in our discussion of the jacket design that I barely noticed the brown paper wrapping that had slipped to the floor. Louisa gave a small gasp.

'Wherever did you get this?' In her hands was the short length of Chinoiserie design that Anna must have included in the parcel. Now, as the silk unfolded, its silver threads began to shimmer as before, glinting and reflecting the firelight. And, just as before, the room seemed suffused with the scent of lavender.

I was about to explain when she gave a harsh little 'oh' as though she had been pricked by a needle, and dropped the fabric to her lap.

'Did something hurt you?' She shook her head, but there was something wrong. I went to her side and just as I reached her she fell against me, heavy as a log.

'Quick, Peter, take her other arm.'

For a second he seemed too shocked to move.

'Come on. She's taken a faint.'

Taking one arm each, we laid her down as best we could on the rug in front of the fire. I placed a cushion beneath her head and began to fan her with a fold of the wrapping paper.

'Run to the kitchen and bring a cup of cold water.'

By the time he returned, her eyes had begun to flutter open.

'What . . . where?' she muttered.

'Just rest, dearest, and see if you can take a sip of this,' I said, putting the cup to her lips.

To our great relief she was soon able to sit up. We lifted

her to a chair, where she slowly regained her colour and her appetite: two home-made shortbreads disappeared in quick succession, washed down with a cup of my best tea.

'How are you feeling now?'

'Much better, thank you. What happened?'

'You cried out as though you'd been hurt. Did something in the silk prick you?'

She looked at me vaguely. 'The silk?'

I pointed to the table, where Peter had thoughtfully placed it. 'This one, with the silver threading.'

'Don't fuss, Charlotte. It is nothing. Just a touch of exhaustion from the journey. I shall be right as rain in the morning.'

'Listen, Louisa. I believe it *was* something to do with the silk. It was the same for me, when I first saw it. I feel sure I have seen it before somewhere, but however hard I try, I cannot remember.'

'Ooh, that's weird,' Peter interjected, in a silly voice. 'Is it haunted? There's a house near us where they say . . .'

'That's enough,' Louisa cut in sharply. 'You know your father forbids you to talk of that place. Any mention of ghosts is an abhorrence to God. They are the fabrication of the devil, he says, and if you speak of them you are pandering to the devil's ways.'

He gave a sulky frown and took up the poker, prodding the log till the flames began to flicker up the chimney once more.

'It's nothing to do with ghosts or hauntings,' I insisted. 'It's just that you and I obviously both have some shared recognition of this silk. I'm curious, that's all.'

Her face was closed now. I knew that look: not in front

of Peter. I put away the silk, wrapping it once more in the brown paper. I would save my questions for later.

After supper Peter went off to read and I took out the small bottle of port kept especially for these occasions. There is never any alcohol at the vicarage because Ambrose is so fiercely opposed to it, but Louisa often enjoys a little tipple with me when they visit.

I told her about the young woman I had met in the street a few weeks previously. 'She was trying to give me her baby. I bought her some food and gave her the address of the Hospital,' I said. 'Let us hope they were able to take him. It broke my heart, seeing her walking away like that,' I went on. 'It made me think about how our mother must have felt when she was forced to give us up. I still can't help wondering what happened to her.'

Louisa seemed deep in thought. 'We can never know, Agnes. What is done is done, dearest.'

'Maybe so, but it doesn't stop me wondering. Tell me again what you remember about her.'

She sighed. 'I recall so little of those days, and it pains me to dig up the past.'

'Having such scant knowledge of her feels like an empty space in my heart. Even just a little information would be better than nothing,' I said.

She took a breath, as though she was about to say something, but fell into silence again. At last she began. 'They are not happy memories, dearest sister, which is why I have always sought to protect you from them. I think I have already told you that I was only three when I was taken from our mother. It was a cottage, somewhere in the east of the city.'

'Do you know where?'

'Not precisely, for I was still young; but it was towards Stepney Green, as I recall. All around, clinging in the air, was the foul smell of human waste, because it was close to a place where they removed clay for making bricks and as soon as the holes were dug, the night-soil men would empty their buckets into them. I have no memory of our father, nor was I ever told what happened to him. All I know is that for some reason our mother had encountered great misfortune and had become destitute, spending what pennies she could get on gin to ease her pain. So she sent me to live with her sister.'

'What do you remember of that?'

'At first it was like paradise, because at least there was food on the table.'

'I suppose our mother wanted the best for you?'

'Our aunt was not a bad woman in her heart, but she already had five children, two of them sickly, and soon enough she was fit to burst with a sixth, which died almost instantly. She was worn out with grief and her husband, who was a journeyman, was short of work. So I became a skivvy, an unpaid servant, and I was determined to get away. My plan was to find a paid position in a prosperous household, but I tried and tried with no success. That is when I heard that Ambrose was seeking a maid. You know the rest, dearest.'

Soon after we'd been reunited, Louisa had told me how, as she put it, Ambrose had 'rescued' her. After hearing tell that the new vicar, lately moved to the parish, was seeking staff for the vicarage, she had gone to apply. At first she was taken on as a maid and then, when the old housekeeper became too infirm to work, he'd offered her the post.

That very first day, he asked her to do some shopping and dictated a list so long that she could not remember them all, so that she returned without several important items. Falling into a rage, he asked why she had not written them down, and she was forced to admit that she could neither read nor write. From then on he'd made it his mission to teach her the basics needed for her job.

It was during one of these lessons that he'd astonished her by declaring, without preamble, that he was determined to seek a wife, and would Louisa consider it? He is a decade older than her and she had always been a little afraid of him, but he had been so patient over the reading and writing that she didn't hesitate. They were married just as soon as the banns were read.

'Whatever happened to our aunt, do you know?'

'We lost contact. To be honest, she never showed me much love, so I wasn't overly concerned; but I did go back once, after we were married, only to find that she had moved. She disappeared without trace. But none of that mattered to me any more, because we found out about you.'

'You didn't even know that I'd been born?'

'How could I? You have to remember, dearest, that I was sent away when I was only three and my aunt would never speak of her sister. All she would say was that she'd been a disgrace to the family.'

Whatever had happened in those years, I wondered. If our mother had been destitute, what was her life like, having already given up one child? I refilled Louisa's glass.

'But however *did* you find out about me, if you were already estranged from our mother and our aunt?'

'It was one of Ambrose's parishioners who told us,' she said.

'She knew of your connection?'

'I don't believe she ever explained, but she must have been in touch with our mother, somehow, because she told us that she'd given birth to another child – that was you – who she'd taken to the Foundling Hospital. And that soon after that, she'd passed away.'

'Were you sad?'

She shook her head. 'To be honest, I remember so little of our mother that I felt almost nothing. Far more important was learning about you. Ambrose agreed that I could write to the Hospital, and that is how we found you.'

'And I am so pleased that you did, my dearest,' I said.

She looked up and smiled. 'Now look at the pair of us. We might have had a rocky start, but we've both survived.'

'More than survived,' I said. 'We found a family.'

4

Petticoat: a garment covering the lower body, often decorative and flounced, designed to be seen beneath an open robe.

Peter's choice of activity prevailed and the following morning we set off for the Tower of London and the wharves of Tower Docks, just forty minutes' walk from my shop. The weather was dry and bright, just as I had hoped, although a chilly breeze whipped off the water once we arrived. We found a place on a small mound below the Tower from where there is a vista of the dockside and the business of sea trading that continues day and night, through every season of the year.

The tide was reaching its highest point and out on the river we were treated to the magnificent sight of three square-riggers arriving in full sail. On their decks sailors scurried about, hauling on ropes and lowering sails as their captains manoeuvred the vessels with great skill despite the sprightly winds.

Once moored, these great ships seemed to loom over the wharves, tall as church towers and wide as palaces. Below them the dockside was a hive of activity, colour and noise: cargoes of all description being offloaded, winched up into the sky on ropes as thick as a man's thigh before being deposited onto one of the many carts and carriages waiting below. Further cartloads of goods waited, ready to be hauled into the emptied holds.

Peter's eyes were wide as saucers. 'Where have all these ships come from?' he shouted over the great hubbub of shouts, the creak of ropes, the crash of crates and clatter of wheels on cobblestones.

'From the Americas, many of them, or the Far East, and also some shorter journeys from the shores of Europe,' I said.

'And what is it they are bringing?' Louisa asked.

'Cotton, silk, tobacco, sugar, all kinds,' I said. 'We make it into finished goods such as woven cottons and silks, and then sell it back to them.' What I did not mention was that many of the ships would take return journeys via Africa, where they would collect hundreds, even thousands, of labourers and take them to work in the New World on farms and plantations. From time to time I have read articles in newspapers decrying the trade as human slavery, and calling for it to be abolished. Yet nothing will ever be done to stop it, Henri says, because the rich and powerful in this land depend on this labour for their accumulation of wealth.

Just then we spied below us a group of around thirty navy men, marching in formation below the Custom House, their officers and the captain in his bicorn hat bringing up the rear. What a glorious sight they made: the sailors in their blue shirts and wide trousers, the officers in darker blue frock coats and pure white breeches, the gold of their buttons, braids and shoulder tabs glinting in the weak sunshine.

My eye was caught by a single sailor, different from the rest by merit of his dark skin: mahogany-coloured like that of the beggar girl's. I wondered whether there could be any connection before dismissing the notion as idle speculation. This man held himself tall and proud as the rest of his fellows, in contrast to the ragged soul I had encountered in the street. He was no servant or slave.

Their destination was a great warship moored to the right of us, away from the scruffier merchant ships, its bulwarks studded from bow to stern with rows of small square windows behind which, I assumed, lurked dozens of deadly cannon. The sailors stopped, forming a line either side at the base of the gangplank. A high-pitched pipe whistled from high on the deck above as the officers and men passed between them.

'How fine they look,' Peter whispered. 'How old do you have to be to enlist, Auntie?'

'Don't you go imagining that we would ever allow you to join the navy, my boy,' Louisa said. 'It is far too dangerous.'

'But would you not be proud of me, dressed up like that?'

'We would not be so proud to hear that you had drowned in some terrible storm, been shot by natives or died a lingering death of some dreadful tropical disease.'

'But I would be fighting for my country. Is that not an honourable profession?'

'You are not going to join the navy, Peter. I forbid it, and that is final. Come, let us walk.'

'When I am twenty-one I can do as I wish, you know. That is the law.'

My sister flushed, buttoning her lip and walking onwards even more briskly than before.

Anna arrived for luncheon. She is always cheerful company, joshing Peter in the same way as she teases her little sister Janey, and he seems to take it in his stride. She can ask questions about his schoolwork or his friendships that would appear overly curious, coming from me.

'If he mentions joining the navy, make discouraging noises,' I whispered as we collected from the kitchen plates of bread, butter, cold meats and pickles, and Peter's favourite, the stewed apple and custard tart that I had so lovingly prepared the previous day.

'For why, pray?'

'We went to the dockside this morning and saw the men embarking on a warship. He is much struck with their uniforms,' I said. 'When Louisa chided him, saying it was too dangerous, he gave her a bit of cheek.'

Anna laughed. 'A bold-spirited boy, that's what I like. Leave it to me.'

Under Anna's innocent questioning Peter happily divulged that he'd been told he would be singing the solos in the Christmas service at church, and that he had a new friend, the son of a curate recently moved to the parish. Gabriel had taught him a game called chess, played with pieces in the shape of knights, bishops, kings and queens, all of which must make different moves.

'Ambrose doesn't approve of board games,' Louisa said. 'He says they're the next thing to gambling. But chess seems to be different; it is complicated, and I like to see them having to use their brains in such a concentrated manner. Besides, they have such fun I cannot bring myself to tell them off.' She added, 'Tell us what happened when you and Gabriel "borrowed" a rope from the farmer to make a swing across a river.'

'We are all ears, Peter,' I urged. Hearing of his exploits always brings the simultaneous emotions of joy and envy that he is able to enjoy such a carefree childhood in the countryside, such freedoms never allowed to us Hospital children.

He laughed. 'We had the idea that we might be able to jump off onto the other bank but neither of us wanted to go first, so we drew straws, and of course Mr Muggins here picked the short one. I was sure it would work, because when we swung the rope it reached easily across, but I just ended up swinging like a pendulum over the water, shouting to Gaby to pull me back, but he was laughing too much and my arms got so tired I couldn't hold on any more.' The obvious outcome had us all chuckling long before he'd finished the tale.

'What a sorry sight you were on the doorstep, dripping with waterweed.'

'Have you have no pity, Mother?' he said. 'I could have drowned, or died of pneumonia.'

'Talking of which,' Anna said, ever so casually, 'did I tell you about the body that got washed up in the Thames the other day?'

Louisa frowned. I know that expression; it means 'stop now'. But my friend took no notice.

'They couldn't tell anything from his face, 'cos it was all gone. But they knew he was a navy man, on account of the uniform. Turns out he died in battle and was buried at sea, which means his body was dropped over the side of the ship. But somehow he did not get eaten by sharks, and he's arrived home, or at least his uniform has.'

'How horrible,' we choroused, sharing glances. Peter's appetite seemed to disappear after that. He refused a second helping of pie, and asked to be excused. Louisa gave Anna a private smile of thanks.

❀❀❀

Time passes too quickly on these visits, but the bells of Christ Church cannot be denied. Each of the three tolls felt like a further wrench, signifying that there was just an hour before they had to leave to catch the carriage returning to Essex. Two long months would pass before I could see them again. In this last precious hour I busied myself with a tape, taking Peter's measurements for the new jacket, all the while allowing myself a stroke of his hair, a touch of his hand, a moment to inhale his sweet boy-child smell. Over the years, I have learned to treasure these small intimacies, storing them away in my mind for succour on cold nights or long, lonely Sunday afternoons.

'Thank you for coming. I hope that the journey is not too uncomfortable,' I said, helping Louisa on with her cape.

'It is but four hours. And I have my boy to keep me company.'

Although she does not mean it, her words can sometimes cut me like a blade.

5

Robe à l'Anglaise: *a gown with a false waistcoat sewn to the lining of the inner bodice, often closed at the top and sloping away to the sides.*

'Penny for them, Charlotte?' Anna asked, as we walked back from the coach stop.

'Oh, nothing much. I'm always sad when they leave.' I found my finger rubbing the spot on my cheek where it had been touched by Peter's lips. The prospect of returning to an empty house was suddenly unappealing. 'Have you time to come in for a little while?'

'Of course. I'll help you clear up.'

We are so easy together, the two of us. Neither having enjoyed the benefit of maids or cooks in our childhoods, we are both accustomed to taking on domestic tasks. Tidying, washing up, making the tea, we move around each other in a kind of co-ordinated dance, always anticipating the other's need, taking up an activity where the other leaves off until the tasks are swiftly completed.

'Peter is such a handsome lad these days,' she said, drying the dishes as I washed them. 'All the girls of the parish will be after him, mark my words.'

Then he will be even further lost to me, I thought. But what I said was, 'He is growing out of his jacket – I have measured him for a new one as a Christmas present, and plan to use that oak leaf design as a lining.'

'Didn't I say it would be useful? What about that other piece, the one you took against so? The silvery pagodas?'

My hands stilled in the sink, recalling Louisa's pallor, and her faint. Surely it could not have been the silk; perhaps she was suffering from some ailment she'd chosen not to share.

'Charlotte?'

'It was just . . .'

'Just?'

'It is the strangest thing. I don't quite understand it myself. You know how odd that silk made me feel? When Louisa saw the silk she took a faint too. In fact, we had to catch her to stop her falling.'

Anna's eyebrows lifted. 'She actually fainted?'

'More or less.'

'Did you ask her afterwards?'

'No, she dismissed it completely. I thought perhaps she might be sickening for something.'

'She looked perfectly well to me, and in an exceptionally good humour, I thought,' Anna said. 'I shouldn't worry; it was probably just a coincidence.'

Upstairs in my private room we lit the fire in the grate, the first of the season, and sat back, watching the flames. 'You are very fortunate to have such a lovely sister, my dearest,' Anna said. 'I wish I could see Janey as often, but it is so far, and she is not strong.'

'I am fortunate indeed.'

'And there seems to be such a special bond between yourself and your nephew,' she went on. 'No, really. It is a delight to behold.'

It was on the tip of my tongue, but I held back. We have promised, the three of us, that no one, especially not Peter, will ever know.

She peered at me. 'Did I say something wrong?'

I shook my head. 'No, nothing. I am just a little sad now they have gone.'

Sometimes she reads my thoughts. 'He's the very image of you, did you know that? Anyone could take him for your son, you are so alike.'

'I have promised. Oh, Anna . . .' I could say no more, because my breath was overtaken by a powerful sob, as though the bonds of that secret had been fatally stretched and all the hidden truths were set to burst out. I felt her arms around me, stroking my hair, whispering soothing words.

'Take a sip of water,' she said, bringing the glass from my chamber next door. I wiped my eyes, took a few deep breaths and drank. 'Promise or no promise, it may help to tell someone.'

'But the promise is that I must not tell.'

I looked up and she gazed back, directly into my eyes. 'Forgive me, Charlotte, but I believe I know your secret.' I held my breath. 'Peter *is* your son. Am I right?'

The tears began afresh, of course, but somehow it was not so painful now and I allowed them to flow unchecked. She stayed beside me until I composed myself.

'You know you can trust me, don't you?' she said.

I hesitated, even now.

'Why is your son living with your sister?'

I did not tell her everything, for we would have been there all night.

'You know that I went to work in a big house at the age of fourteen?' I began.

'And that is where you learned your seamstress's craft.'

How could I describe the agony of those months? It was my first position, and I had been happy at first, keen to learn and to please, grateful for a modicum of freedom after the constraints of life at the Hospital, and the opportunity to earn money for myself. The Major and his wife were quiet souls who did little entertaining, and their two sons were already grown up and had left home, so the work was light. The house was not over-large but beautiful, four-square and built of soft yellow stone, set in wide rolling countryside. It was not so far from the city of Gloucester and on my days off I could cadge a ride from a carter to walk the quaint little streets and even, once or twice, to visit the cathedral.

I began as a laundry maid and quickly progressed to housemaid. By the time I was fifteen I was trusted enough by the housekeeper, Mrs Baxter, to deputise for her on her days off. It was on one of those days that I was summoned to the chamber of the Major's wife.

When she saw me, her face fell. 'Where is Baxter?'

'She has been given leave for two days, ma'am,' I said, making my best curtsy. 'To visit her mother. She has asked me to stand in her stead.'

She looked doubtful, even displeased, although she had always appeared content with my services in the past.

'Whatever am I to do, then? My best gown is ruined,' she cried. As she took up the beautiful green silk *robe à l'Anglaise* that had been resting on the bed, I saw that the bodice had somehow sustained a long gash. 'We are due for tea at the bishop's palace this afternoon. The major has told me I must look at my best, as he wishes to ask a favour of the diocese regarding our church. And now look what has happened. Mrs B. would have fixed it in an instant, but Alice is hopeless with a needle. Whatever am I to do?'

I did not suggest that she might consider wearing another of the many silk gowns hanging in her dressing room, nor did I hint that she should consider replacing miserable Alice, the lady's maid who considered herself so superior that she would never even pass the time of day with the junior staff.

Instead I found myself saying: 'I can mend that for you, madam. You will not even see the join.'

She looked at me uncertainly. How was she to know that since the age of six I had been learning to work with a needle and thread? Reading and writing, singing and needlework; these were the skills the Hospital ensured that all girls learned, equipping us for a life in service.

'You? You know sewing? You are just a housemaid.'

'I was a laundry maid before, ma'am,' I said. 'And I have been mending clothes in this household as part of my duties for nearly two years now.'

'But this is silk.'

'I know silk,' I said, as confidently as I could. In fact I had worked with the fabric only a few times, enough to know how treacherously fine and slippery its threads can be; how some of the looser weaves can unravel in an instant and how the slightest of perspiration on a fingertip can mark the delicate dyes. Perhaps it was youthful bravado, but I felt certain that this rip could be invisibly mended and might earn me, just perhaps, a small bonus.

'Very well, then,' she said, handing it over. 'I shall give you a chance to prove yourself. But if you make a mess of it, I may have to invite you to consider your position.'

It was a hot afternoon and I had the idea of taking my work into the dairy, the coolest place in the house, to reduce the danger of sweating over my task. I took a chair in the corner and laid out a sheet to protect the gown, half-listening to the dairymaids gossiping and giggling as they churned the butter.

Their main topic of conversation was the imminent arrival of the Major's younger son, Captain Tobias, known to the family as Toby, who was lately returned from the Americas, where he had been serving in the English army. He had been slightly injured and had taken this opportunity to resign his commission, planning to marry his betrothed – the daughter of a good family in Bristol – and help his father run the estate. Apparently Toby was handsome and bold, liable to steal a kiss from any girl who took his fancy. 'Or even more, if you're not careful,' one said, causing her companions to shriek with horror.

I did my best to ignore their chatter, trying to work out how to mend the gown. I could not steal any of the bodice fabric for a new seam, since I was aware that the Major's wife had put on a few additional pounds and it was already a little tight. Instead, I took a strip from the hem and used this to interline the rip, ensuring that the nap of the fabric lay in the same direction and piecing it together with the tiniest of stitches. It took several hours, but I felt pleased with the result.

When I returned the gown my mistress reached for her pince-nez. 'Well, well. I do declare that your work is even better than that of Mrs B. I can barely see the mend,' she said, looking up with a smile. Later, when I went to call them for the carriage, she took me aside once more. 'You have worked a miracle, young lady. This gown feels so much more comfortable than before. You deserve an extra shilling in your wage this month. And be assured that should a more senior position come up, you will certainly be considered.'

A shilling! It was a fortune, almost half of my week's wage. This was when I began to understand the power of the needle, with the realisation that a perfectly fitted gown is a sure way to the heart – and the purse – of a wealthy lady. My happiness knew no bounds, for a while at least. Until Tobias arrived.

The milkmaids were right: he was handsome enough, but so arrogant that I disliked him on first encounter. When I brought tea for the mistress he told me off for bringing too few biscuits.

'Do you think we are mice, that you bring us crumbs?' he bellowed, guffawing at his own joke and glancing around to ensure others were doing so too. When I returned with an additional plateful – having survived cook's displeasure – he winked at me. 'That's a pretty blush you have there, young miss.'

I tried to avoid him whenever possible but a housemaid has little power over her own destiny. He took to calling for me by name: 'Charlotte, bring more logs for the fire,' I would hear him shout. And when I arrived with them, he'd stand right behind me as I placed them in the hearth. 'So I can appreciate your sweet little rump,' he said, in an oily tone that made my skin crawl.

When his betrothed arrived at the Manor his behaviour with her was impeccable. She was a pretty thing, vapid but polite as pie to me and the other servants, and I felt sure she had no idea what sorrows married life would bring her. When she and the rest of the household had retired to their chambers and he was left alone with the brandy bottle, Tobias would roar like a rutting stag, calling for his slippers, his pipe, his waistcoat, whatever he could think of to keep me scuttling around till well after midnight.

Each time I entered the room it was like running the gauntlet, doing my best to remain calm and polite while trying to avoid the hands reaching for my chest, my thighs or my backside. When he missed, he'd just laugh. It was a sport for him, a battle of wits. 'You're such a little tease, Charlotte,' he'd slur. 'But I'll get you one day, mark my word.' Once or twice he actually caught me but he was so clumsy with drink that I managed to slip away, although my uniform was ripped and I had to stay up half the night trying to mend it by candlelight.

He might have considered it a game, but for me it became a struggle for survival. I went to Mrs B. for advice, but she chided me as though it were my fault for encouraging him. 'Once he's married and she becomes mistress of this house, he'll have to think twice about his carrying on,' she said. 'But in the meantime it is your responsibility to avoid him. There's nothing I can do to protect you, so you'll have to look after yourself. Never approach too close, never catch his eye, lock your door at night. And never even think of complaining to madam, or you'll be out of this house in an instant. He's the apple of her eye.'

For a few weeks I tried to follow her advice, until Boxing Day, when all the staff went out to welcome the hunt. Even cook had gone, taking pastries to the gathering crowds. Believing I had the house to myself, I went into the pantry for a piece of bread and cheese – it was hours since my breakfast and would be several more before luncheon. I was starving.

I heard the clump of boots on the servants' stairs and quickly pulled the pantry door behind me. The footsteps passed and I allowed myself to breathe again. They seemed to be heading for the cellar, but soon returned, closer and closer. As the pantry door was flung open, it was all I could do not to cry out. Tobias was clutching a bottle of brandy.

'You!' His face was bright with triumph. 'You're not stealing food, are you, pretty miss?' I cringed against the shelves until my back felt bruised.

'No, I am allowed . . .' I began, but of course his mind was already set.

'So, I found a little tart in the pantry.' He smirked, pleased with his own humour. 'And I declare that I am so hungry that I shall eat you up.' He held his arm tight around me, pulled me close and covered my face with his disgusting wet lips. The other hand was ripping at my skirt as he hitched me up onto the shelf, forcing my legs apart. The crocks fell to the floor around us, and even in my terror I found myself wondering how to explain to the breakages to cook.

Even the worst of my childhood beatings had never

caused such intense pain. I must have cried out, but his hand covered my mouth and anyway there was no one nearby to hear. It was over in an instant: he snorted like a pig and then pulled away, panting as he re-buttoned himself and reset his wig.

'Hah! What a delicious little tart,' he crowed. 'I shall take another bite whenever it pleases me. If you ever breathe a word I shall tell cook how I caught you stealing from her pantry. And you know what that means.'

He grabbed his brandy and left.

I hobbled to my room and did my best to wash as well as I could with the water left over from the morning and the sliver of soap we were allowed once it was worn too small for the mistress. But however much I scrubbed I felt dirty, inside and out. I was sick in the bowl more than once.

The other servants were returning from the hunt reception, and the house filled with sounds once more. There was a knock at my door, and Mrs B.'s voice: 'Wherever have you been, Charlotte? Hasten yourself. You have chores.'

The days passed, somehow. When Tobias went away for a few weeks I breathed easily once more. For whole hours at a time I managed to forget. But when he returned I knew at once from the glint in his eye that he had not forgotten. Sure enough, late one night there was a knock on my door. Before I could answer the handle was already turning. I had locked it, of course, but he hissed: 'Open up, missy, or I'll break down the door. And you know what Mrs B. does to thieves.'

I had no option. He was just as brusque this time but it wasn't so painful, and I managed not to cry out. 'I think you're beginning to enjoy it, you little hussy,' he said afterwards, with a greasy smile. 'Which is just as well, for I plan to have you as often as I like, now I know where to find you. *Bon soir, ma petite.*'

These days I often use French terms, since this is the language of the silk weavers and of their craft, and is often applied in fashion. But even now, the memory it evokes can sometimes make me shudder. When Tobias affected the French, I suppose because to his ears it sounded romantic, it left me feeling bleaker than ever. I was desperate. Once, on a dreary February morning, after a night when Tobias had demanded that he must have me twice, and took his time about it, I even considered walking to the lake and drowning myself.

He had me trapped, like a fly in a spider's web.

6

Polonaise: an overskirt hitched up by interior or exterior loops, buttons or tassels to create swags of fabric at the sides or back of the dress, often worn with ankle-length petticoats and high-heeled walking shoes.

Anna listened in attentive silence. I'd summarised, of course. Even the best of friends should not have to bear the more intimate details.

'My poor, poor darling. I would run that brute through if I ever got hold of him. Why didn't you tell someone?'

'He would have reported me for theft, and what was my word against his? I'd have been sacked without a reference and little chance of finding another position. I could have ended up on the streets.'

'Could you not have turned to Louisa for help?'

'The thing is . . .' How could I explain the complicated turn of events that had led to the discovery of my sister? 'At that time, she had not even found me.'

'Found you? Whatever do you mean, dearest?'

'We did not know of each other's existence.'

'How on earth . . . ?'

'It's a long story, Anna. Have you got time to hear it?'

'I have all the time in the world, dearest. So how old were you when you found your sister?'

'Sixteen. To the very day.'

It was my birthday, and Mrs Hogarth arrived at the Manor asking to speak to me. My joy was beyond bounds. She usually wrote to me on my birthday, but I had not seen her since leaving London. To behold that dear face again, that gentle, affectionate smile, was a salve to my poor misused soul – it was all I could do to stop myself weeping with happiness.

Jane Hogarth is the most motherly woman in the world; it seems so sad that she and William were never blessed with a family of their own.

Their story was the most romantic I had ever heard: they fell in love at first sight, and married in defiance of her parents' wishes. Her father was the eminent painter Sir James Thornhill and did not approve of the young print-maker yet to make his mark on the art world. Of course the rift was soon healed; only a fool could fail to see how talented William was, and how much he adored Jane.

Although she never spoke of it, I am sure that their inability to have their own children was what led to William taking to his heart the work of the Foundling Hospital. He agreed to become a governor and busied himself with organising exhibitions of paintings to raise money, and Jane was involved in her own way, volunteering to inspect the foster homes where babies were placed in their early years and even fostering a few of them in her own home.

I first met her when we were being prepared for a life 'in service' and she came to the Hospital to give us a talk about how we should comport ourselves in a grand house: instructing us to be obedient at all times, hold our tongues and express no opinion, to choose our friends and allies carefully, and always to work to the best of our abilities.

Her advice stayed with me and stood me in good stead, in the main, but what she did not include was how to fend off the likes of Tobias. I have never told her of the ill that befell me at his hands, for the events of those few months still fill me with shame.

After her talk we Hospital girls handed around tea and biscuits to the assembled governors. As I passed, she detained me. 'I watched your bright eyes as you listened, young lady,' she said. 'I am sure with your intelligence and enthusiasm you will make a very successful life for yourself.'

'Thank you, ma'am.' I curtsied as we had been taught, but as I did so a couple of biscuits slipped to the floor. She took the plate and placed it on the table, then leaned and picked up the broken pieces, deftly slipping them into the pocket of my tunic. 'Share them with your friends later,' she whispered, putting her finger to her lips. My mouth watered – we were always hungry.

'Now, Miss Bright Eyes, what activities do you enjoy the most?'

'Needlework, ma'am. And singing in the choir.'

'Singing will never make you a living, but needlework most certainly could, if you are really determined and dedicated,' she said. 'My husband's sister Ann is a fine example: she even has her own shop.'

A woman, owning a shop? The idea was unimaginable.

'I will take you there one day,' she said. 'Would you like that?'

The suggestion was astounding, beyond my wildest dreams. 'I would like that very much, ma'am,' I stuttered.

'Then that's a promise. Tell me your name, child.'

'Charlotte Amesbury,' I said.

'Charlotte. I shall remember that name.' She winked and gave me back the empty plate. 'Now you had better get back to your duties before matron catches us.'

And now here she was, having travelled all the way from London to Gloucestershire to wish me happy birthday. Mrs B. allowed us her office and, on learning how far Mrs Hogarth had come, sent a pot of tea and two large slices of her best poppy seed cake.

'They seem very nice here,' Jane said.

'I am content,' I said, guarding my words. 'The Major and his wife are most kind, and she appreciates my sewing skills, which is flattering.' It was on the tip of my tongue to say more, to beg her to rescue me from the nightmare in which I found myself. But before I could speak further she pulled an envelope from her pocket, and passed it to me. I assumed it to be her usual birthday missive, a note which sometimes contained a small financial gift, but this one was not in her writing.

'I bring the most remarkable news, Charlotte,' she said. 'But take your time. Read it carefully.'

The letter was written on heavy vellum in a careful yet slightly unsteady hand, as though by someone for whom writing was a skill recently learned. But in my excitement I didn't notice this at the time. It was addressed to the Foundling Hospital.

Dear Sirs,

My husband, the Reverend Ambrose Fairchild, and I are seeking information about a child deposited with you nearly sixteen years ago, recorded name of Agnes Potton, whom I believe to be my sister. Only recently have we learned of the child's existence and how through unfortunate circumstances our mother was forced to give her up.

I pray you will be able to help us find out what happened to her. We are of good standing in society and have the means to welcome the girl into our family if, God willing, she has survived.

Yours &c.

Louisa Fairchild

The Vicarage, Westford Abbots, Essex

I looked up into Mrs Hogarth's expectant eyes. 'But what has this to do with me?'

She smiled like a magician about to reveal a posy of flowers, or a rabbit, from a hat. 'Because, my dearest girl, you are that baby, Agnes Potton.'

'But my name is Charlotte Amesbury.' I shook my head, confused.

'That is the name given to you by the Hospital, Charlotte. It is their policy to give each child a new identity, a new start. I have been shown the records and have seen with my own eyes, in black and white, and there is no doubt in my mind that you are indeed that same girl, Agnes Potton.'

Still I struggled to comprehend. 'You mean . . . I am not Charlotte Amesbury?'

Her voice was kind and low. 'You are of course still our

dear Charlotte and always will be, if that is what you choose. But your birth name was Agnes Potton, and this is important, because it means that you have a sister, Louisa Fairchild, who has been looking for you and would like to meet you. Read her letter again: she is offering to take you into her family, if that is what you would like.'

The words swam before my eyes, but their meaning slowly began to sink in, like blessed rainfall softening a crust of parched earth. A *sister*? A sister who lived in Essex. I had no idea where that was, but it scarcely mattered: after all these years of believing myself to be entirely alone in the world, I now had a family.

Blissful visions tiptoed into my mind: the pretty young wife of an upright, honest clergyman, living in a clean, ordered vicarage in a charming village, doing good works and earning the respect of the community. Perhaps they even had children of their own, this couple, who would be my little nieces and nephews. I had a sudden, urgent need to know these people, to prove they were not just a mirage. 'Can I meet them?'

'I recommend that you write to Mrs Fairchild at once, telling her about yourself. You can broach the question of whether she would like to visit you, or for you to visit her. I have no doubt that she will invite you at once,' Mrs Hogarth said. 'You have their address, and as your birthday present I am going to give you the fare for the stagecoach.' She produced another envelope and pressed it into my hands.

'How far is Essex?'

'A long way from here,' she said. 'You will need to go via London, which is two days, and take a new coach the fol-

THE DRESSMAKER OF DRAPER'S LANE

lowing day. Westford Abbots is probably just half a day from London.'

'Three *days* just to get there? It is impossible. I cannot take more than a day's leave at one time.'

'Nothing is impossible, dear heart.' I longed to throw myself into Jane Hogarth's arms, to press my cheek against that comfortable, well-upholstered breast. She had been the closest thing to a mother for me but her physical affections were always a little constrained, as though she was being careful to avoid too much intimacy, for fear, I suppose, that I might become overly dependent.

But now I had a sister. A real sister. My mind scampered ahead, allowing myself to imagine that, in time, I might discover my *real* mother too.

Jane stood up, smoothing her skirt. 'I shall go immediately to visit your mistress, and I will inform her that this is a matter of such importance that she must give you at least two weeks' leave,' she said. 'I shall use my greatest powers of persuasion. You shall meet your new family within the month, that I promise.'

7

Pinner: a type of hair covering for women consisting of a decorative piece of fabric pinned to the top of the head with a ruffle around the sides and front and sometimes with lappets.

I left the Manor on a windy day in late June. Clouds scudded across the sky like galloping horses urging me onwards at the greatest possible speed towards my new family. Louisa's reply had arrived promptly.

Dearest sister, (the word caused my heart to turn several somersaults)

    It was with great excitement that we received your letter. God has truly blessed us that we have been able to find you, and that you are alive and well. I am consumed with impatience to meet you, to welcome you to our house and into our family. Please come as soon as you are able, and stay as long as you wish. I enclose two pounds to cover the cost of your fare. Just send us a quick note to give us your date of travel.

    In joy and love
    Your sister, Louisa Fairchild

By the time we reached Westford Abbots I was almost delirious with exhaustion and hunger, having endured three long days of being jolted around in the coach and two nights in dirty, noisy staging inns. I paid only for basic accommodation, which meant slops for dinner and a bed in a room with half a dozen others. When I alighted from the carriage and saw walking down the street towards me a woman who could have been my double, I thought it must be a hallucination.

We gazed at each other in mutual astonishment and delight. There was no doubt that we were sisters. How could we not be, being so alike, with only the subtle differ ence of a few additional years? Her modest height and slight figure were just as my own, she had my straight brown hair, chestnut eyes sparkling beneath an arch of dark eyebrow, a heart-shaped face with a button nose, strong chin and a shy smile. It was like looking at myself. In an instant her arms were around me, and it felt as though there had never been a time when I had not known this embrace.

Throughout that day, and the days that followed, we delighted in discovering small things which only served to strengthen that conviction: we both loved cheese, rhubarb, gooseberries and plum pudding. She would bite her lip when thinking, as I did. She brushed her hair back from her forehead with the same movement as my own. Her forehead crinkled in two little vertical frown lines between her eyebrows, just like mine.

Her husband, the reverend, declared that he could not tell, from another room, whether it was she or I speaking, for we had the same tone and the same inflections. He did not appear amused at our likeness – indeed for much of the time I felt as though he considered me something of an inconvenience, an interruption to his daily life.

For all that, I could never have imagined that being a sister could bring such infinite pleasure.

She insisted on calling me Agnes but I quickly grew used to it, feeling myself to be in very heaven, delighted by the space, the peace, the freedom and the plentiful food at the vicarage. For the very first time in my life I had a room of my very own, at the front of the house, and was told that it could be mine for as long as I wished.

While my gown and petticoat were being laundered Louisa allowed me to borrow some of her clothes. We were perfectly the same size, and as I twirled before the looking glass in her chamber I had the first vision of myself as a proper young lady and not just a servant girl, a taste of what I hoped to become in the future. She lent me books, although I was entirely unaccustomed to the notion of having all the time in the world to read without being interrupted by someone else's demands. There was never any need to worry about the candle-end burning out. In this well-provided house there was always another, laid beside the stick.

We walked in the orchards and she told me all about the different types of apples, which ones made good eaters and others good cookers, and how the bees kept in the beehives along the hedgerows were so important for fertilising the flowers. The tree she loved more than any of the others was an old, gnarled apple in the corner of the vicarage garden. As we ran our hands over the rough, broken bark, she told me how Ambrose had threatened to cut it down for firewood, but she had pleaded for him to spare it. After that, whenever I felt lonely or confused, I would go to sit under that tree for comfort.

She taught me about birds, too. How the robins and blackbirds would fight each other for their territories, but the starlings would happily crowd into a puddle together to splash themselves clean. She especially loved those with the brightest plumage: robins, blue tits, goldcrests and woodpeckers.

We talked and talked. It turned out that she was seven years older than me, but had been fostered with an aunt and had lost touch with our mother; that she too had felt very alone in the world, with no brothers and sisters, until she met Ambrose.

'He rescued me.' I longed to ask more: from what had he rescued her, and how, but she refused to elaborate. 'The past is the past. Let us look forward to our future,' is all she would say. For a while I was content with this. How could I not be, with all my dreams come true? Yet as the days went by it seemed that finding a sister had ignited an intense desire to discover more about my past, so I urged her to tell me more.

'I never knew our father,' she said, solemnly. 'I believe he died young.'

'But you must have known our mother. What was she like? Did she look like us? And why did she have to give me up? Did she not love us?'

'I am sure that she loved us very much, dearest, but she fell upon misfortune and her life became so difficult that she fostered me to an aunt. I was very unhappy there, she treated me badly, neglecting my welfare and using me as an unpaid servant. I longed to return to our mother but they would not help me. After a while I realised that all I could do was try to put her from my mind.'

However much I pressed, she seemed unwilling to tell me more. 'It was a very unhappy time,' was all she would say. 'Forgive me, I prefer not to dwell on it.'

So I let the subject drop, willing myself to be content with my extraordinary turn of good fortune.

Louisa's husband the Reverend – he insisted I call him brother, or Ambrose, but neither fell easily from my lips – was often out visiting the sick and needy, or attending meetings of the diocesan high-ups. When at home he would join us for an evening meal but his presence always made me feel on edge, and conversation flowed so much more easily when he was not there.

He was a good few years older than Louisa, more like an uncle, a stern, imposing figure, broad and tall, with a white wig always perfectly powdered and dressed all in black – cassock, breeches and stockings – save for the stiffly starched white cravat at his neck. His eyes were dark and slightly terrifying beneath heavy brows, his lips a thin straight line rarely relieved by a smile. He appeared remote from everyday life, his mind elsewhere in the lofty realms of faith and intellect.

I thought him rather devoid of emotion until that Sunday when we went to church. As he preached his whole person became illuminated by a fierce internal flame.

His frequent absences meant that Louisa and I had much time to ourselves and I deduced that, for all her charitable engagements, she found life a little lonely in this small village. We were taking tea the afternoon before I was due to return to my post.

'Do you have to return to Gloucester?' she asked. 'Could you not stay with us instead?'

Was this really happening? I hardly dared to take a breath for fear that I would wake to find it was a dream. I heard my voice responding: 'Of course I should love nothing better than to stay. But I must return to work. I have no other means of supporting myself.'

She smiled, fondly. 'Dearest sister, do you believe I would let you go so easily, now that I have found you after all these years? Ambrose and I have already discussed it. He says you may stay while we seek another position nearby, so we may see each other as often as we like. With your permission, I shall write to your mistress tomorrow, asking her to free you from your position forthwith and that we expect a good reference.'

I ran into her arms. 'Oh thank you, thank you. I shall be the best sister in the world.'

It was the day on which I was due to start work as a ladies' maid at the big house next door that I woke feeling sicker than I had ever known. My body was racked with spasms and it was all I could do to haul myself from the bed to the bowl. Louisa was calling, but I could barely summon the energy to respond. Then she was in the doorway, her face aghast. 'My dearest, are you not well? What can I do?'

'Water,' I managed to croak. Once I had taken a few sips she helped me back to bed.

'You are white as a sheet,' she said, 'and definitely not fit for work today. I shall send a note to Westford Hall at once.'

Several days passed, stretching into a week. I could not eat more than a crust of dry bread without the vengeful sickness returning, and I became weak and unable to stand without support. When after two weeks I did not seem to be recovering Ambrose called a doctor, who questioned me in detail, took a pulse and listened to my heart. He asked my sister to leave the room and, when she was gone, sat down beside me, his face solemn as a graveyard.

'I understand that you are not married, young lady?'

I shook my head. What did that have to do with my sickness?

'Then it is with regret that I must inform you that you are with child.'

Once I had finished weeping and cursing my misbegotten fate I asked to speak to my sister, alone. I had no choice but to tell her. How else could my sickness be explained? My condition would become apparent soon enough.

Louisa's reaction was cool at first. 'This man, Tobias. Why could you not have resisted him?'

'I would have lost my post at the Manor.'

'You'd have lost it anyway, in this state.' She sighed. 'Whatever are we to do with you now, Agnes?'

I spent the next twenty-four hours paralysed with terror, fearing that any day I would be cast out of paradise. Surely Ambrose would send me packing? With his high moral standards, how could he possibly allow a fallen woman to remain in his house? That night I overheard loud conversation from their chamber, but it was too indistinct for me to make out what was being said. Nonetheless I felt certain that this was the end.

All of my good fortune was lost. My new family had been just a mirage. I barely slept that night for the dismal scenarios that paraded through my mind: of me being sent packing, walking the streets of London with my few belongings, starved of food and forced to sleep under bridges, and all the while trying to keep my baby alive.

When Louisa called me into the drawing room the following day, I felt sure they were about to give me my marching orders. She and Ambrose were formally seated at the table and tea was being served in the best china, with delicate sugar biscuits on the side. Was this some exquisite kind of torture? Had they been set there deliberately to emphasise what I was about to lose?

My hands trembled as I took the cup. At last, Louisa began. 'Ambrose and I have been giving your situation much thought and prayer.'

'I understand . . .' She silenced me with a finger.

'Wait until I have explained. We have a proposal.' She glanced at Ambrose, who gave the slightest tilt of his head. 'I think you would agree that it is most unthinkable for you to have a child out of wedlock?'

Blood smarted in my cheeks.

'And you will probably appreciate that it would cause us considerable embarrassment for you to stay here, once your condition is evident?'

I turned my eyes to my lap. Here it comes, I thought, steeling myself. I would leave with dignity, I would not cry.

But no. The greatest surprise was yet to come.

'It has for a few years now been our dearest wish that we

should have children of our own but God has not seen fit to grant us this blessing, and we had almost given up hoping.' I could not fathom what all of this had to do with my situation, but she had not yet told me to pack my bags, so I remained silent.

'God has now brought you to our house and now, it seems, He has blessed us in an unexpected way. He has brought with you an unborn child.' She paused a second. 'A child, I think you would agree, that you cannot keep for yourself.'

My head whirled. I had not thought beyond the fact of my pregnancy, nor of my situation as being anything more than a burden I fervently desired to be rid of. I had not considered what might happen to the baby.

'But which, if you are willing, Ambrose and I could raise as our own. What do you think of that, Agnes?'

My mind struggled to understand.

'Agnes?'

I tried unsuccessfully to stutter something. 'It . . . perhaps . . .'

'This child is my flesh and blood, too, after all,' she continued. 'He will likely look like you, and thus like me. So how would anyone know if we reversed our roles and I were to be his mother? You would be his aunt. We are all family, after all. He will grow up in a comfortable, loving home and you can see him whenever you want.'

Now, at last fully comprehending her meaning, I fell into stunned silence.

'What do you think, Agnes?' This was Ambrose, curt with impatience.

Stupidly, the only question I could think of was, 'What if it is not a boy? Will you still want a girl child?' I stuttered.

'My darling, of course. We should love a girl just as much.' Louisa leaned across the table to take my hand. 'Oh please say yes, dear heart, I implore you. You will make us the happiest parents in the world.'

Of course, in the end and after much heart-searching, I agreed. I was in no position to refuse. And that is how I gave up my child, much as my mother had done.

8

Damask: a silk stuff with reversible pattern woven with one warp yarn and one weft yarn, usually with the pattern in warp-faced satin weave and the ground in weft-faced or sateen weave.

The two months before Christmas are the busiest of the year in my shop, with clients demanding reassurances that their gowns will be ready for the round of balls and other social gatherings that seem to be necessary to celebrate the birth of Christ. What He would have made of it, heaven knows, but it keeps my coffers well filled and for that I am most truly grateful.

Not that I need much for myself, other than to pay the rent and my own modest living expenses, but I am pleased to be able to pay my seamstresses generously for their overtime since many of them are raising families on their own, or have the disadvantage of useless husbands. When I hear their unhappy tales it makes me glad that I only have myself to worry about. We cannot all be so fortunate as to find a love like Anna's.

In my few moments of spare time, often late in the evening, I began work on Peter's jacket. There were a couple of yards of dark blue damask remaining from a customer's order that she had allowed me to keep. I measured it out carefully, and then measured it again, to make absolutely sure that it would be enough. It was the perfect shade for a young boy and I chose the latest style, of course; for although Ambrose might disapprove of him looking too fashionable, Peter was already beginning to take pride in his appearance. I wanted him to feel special, proud of what my expertise could provide.

As I cut and pieced, tacked and sewed, every stitch seemed to hold my love. If I slipped – for when you are tired it is so easy to make a small mistake – I would unpick it, for there could be no covering up, or making do. A mother's love is unconditional, it should never be perverted or distorted, and this embodiment of my own devotion must be perfect too.

What Louisa had told me had revived my curiosity about our mother. Although the information was still vague and incomplete, at least I now had something to work with. That evening, I wrote down:

She probably looked like me and Louisa
Her surname was Potton
She lived near the 'night soil' grounds close to Stepney Green
People thereabouts might still remember her

The following Sunday I took a coach eastwards. It was surprising to discover that so many more new houses and manufactories had been built between Spitalfields and Stepney Green that it was no longer a separate village, but an extension of London. The weather was chilly and grey, the streets quiet and all of the traders were closed.

I walked the length of the main street imagining my

mother to be here, walking this same route, stopping to chat with people she knew. I had planned to stop one or two of the elderly residents to ask whether they might have known her, but few people passed. Only after several minutes did I realise that most of them would be in church.

That gave me a better idea: I could ask the vicar. I could see a church tower in the distance and headed for it. It was a fine, proud flint stone building, set in a wide acreage of churchyard crowded with headstones, the dead of centuries past laid out here. From inside there came the joyful sound of singing – a service was under way.

I began to walk between the graves, my eyes scouring the inscriptions on the stones. What a story they told: the plague must have hit this hamlet especially hard, for I counted numerous stones dating from those times, sometimes many dozens of names with the same date of death. Other stones were decorated with anchors and fishes, clearly the graves of sailors, dating back centuries. By the time I heard the final hymn being sung my legs ached and my eyes were burning. I must have read hundreds of names, but none of them was a Potton.

At last the congregation began to emerge. It took an age, for they all wanted to pass the time of day with their vicar, a fresh-faced youthful-looking fellow who seemed to have a glad word for every soul in his care. If anyone in this village had known my mother, it would have been him, or his predecessor.

He caught my eye and smiled. 'I've seen you waiting, miss. Can I help you?'

'I have a question, sir,' I said.

'Ask away,' he said.

'I am looking for any information about my mother. She lived hereabouts.'

'What was her name?'

'Potton. I have no Christian name.'

He frowned, and shook his head. 'It is not a name I recognise. Is she still alive, do you know?'

'I'm afraid she died some years ago,' I said. 'But I have searched your graveyard without any luck.'

'Do you know where she lived?'

'All I know is that she was very poor, and lived close to the night-soil pits.'

'Ah, yes. Those pits are long gone,' he said. 'You will have seen the new houses being built? That is where they were. People tell me there were many poor souls squatting in those parts, but the builders threw them off the land, some ten or fifteen years ago, this would have been, long before I arrived here.'

I must have looked crestfallen because he added brightly, 'But if you have a few moments, miss, I can let you look through our parish records, the births, marriages and deaths. It is possible that you may find what you are looking for there.' He led me into the church and then through into the vestry, a dark, dusty-smelling room, lined with shelves on which were lodged dozens of leather-bound volumes.

'Can you give me the approximate date when your mother lived here?'

'I was born in June 1741, so perhaps around then?'

He searched for a few moments, running his fingers along the spines, before taking down three ledgers and placing them onto the table. 'Births, marriages and deaths 1740–1750,' he said. 'Feel free to take your time.'

The first was titled *Births, January 1740–December 1749*. I turned to June 1741: John, Margaret, Jethro, Sarah, Susan, Marshall, Job, Lancelot, Henrietta, Iris and plenty more babies had been born in that month, but no Agnes. It seems that I was never registered, at least not in this parish.

I turned to the next: *Marriages, January 1740–December 1749*, and scanned page after page in hope of discovering whether I had a father. No Potton appeared.

Finally, I turned to *Deaths, January 1740–December 1749*. The lists made melancholy reading, especially because they included the names of so many babies and young children. How rare it was to find anyone who lived to the full three score years and ten that was promised to us in the old psalm. I turned each page with renewed optimism that I might discover at least when my mother died, and whether she had a grave somewhere. But there was not a single Potton among these pages either.

An hour and a half later I reached the last page of the final ledger, shivering with the cold and wondering whether my mother had actually ever existed. She seemed to have left so little trace of herself. Perhaps my sister had mis-remembered the name of the parish, and her records were elsewhere? Or she had another name altogether? Would I ever discover anything about my mother?

Tuesday afternoon is a half day for the seamstresses, and early closing for the shop. I was tidying the sewing room when I heard rapping at the front door.

At first I thought it might be the beggar girl, who had

been in my thoughts these past few weeks, but squinting out of the window into the street below I saw a capacious lady standing on the doorstep, heavily wrapped in cloak and shawl against the weather. I would barely have recognised her but for the basket: the one in which Mrs Jane Hogarth carries the elderly pug dog that was the constant companion of her dear late husband, and now cannot be separated from his mistress. She comes into the city less frequently since being widowed, which makes these visits all the more precious.

'Dearest Charlotte,' she said, beaming beneath the hood and shawl. 'I hope this is convenient?'

'Of course. Come in. I am always delighted to see you,' I said. 'Let me take your cloak.' As she put down the basket to disrobe, the dog raised its head and gave a disgruntled growl.

'It is a pleasure to see you too, Pug,' I said. 'Will you take tea, Jane? I have a fire in my room, if you think you can manage the stairs?' She is broad of beam and close to her sixtieth year.

'I'm sure I'll manage. I was only planning to collect my new gloves and muff, but if you are not too busy, a cup of tea would be most welcome.'

By the time I returned with the tea she had puffed her way up the two flights of stairs and was settled into my most comfortable chair, with the dog nestled contentedly in her lap. 'I hope you don't mind me bringing this old thing? I find it a great comfort, you know, like having a part of him with me.'

In his later years William had rarely left their country retreat, claiming that he could not leave his precious dog.

'Hates the noise and the cobblestones in the city, poor old boy,' he used to say. I did not realise it then, but William had become increasingly melancholic after a very public row over one of his satirical prints, and was already beginning to suffer ill health. Since his death, Jane had rented out the London house and retired almost permanently to the countryside.

I poured and she took a sip. 'Hmm, this is delicious tea.'

'It's a Pekoe. A present from my sister.'

'What a generous gift. And she has good taste, too.'

'Ambrose buys from a special trader he met working in the London parish.'

'Indeed. Vicars have to drink a lot of tea,' she said, laughing as she accepted a shortbread biscuit – another gift, this time from a satisfied customer.

'I have missed you, Jane. How is Chiswick?' I said.

'All is well, dearest,' she said. 'We love it there. I only come up to town to shop. But today I had a few hours to spare, so I also dropped in to the Hospital – they persuaded me to take William's place on the committee, you know, and they do such good work.'

I nodded. It may have been a hard childhood, but I knew they had probably saved my life.

'When I arrived, I found a baby on the step – we often do, you know. When mothers aren't lucky in the draw and get turned away, they are so desperate they just leave them.'

'The poor things,' I said, thinking of the young woman I'd seen in the street.

'It was alive, just about. And when they unwrapped him, they found this.'

As she reached into her pocket, took out a scrap of paper

and handed it to me, my heart jumped in my chest. It read: *Lamb's Conduit Field, Bloomsbury*. And then, below, *Miss Charlotte, Costumière, Draper's Lane*.

'You don't think . . .' I began to gabble. 'It's not mine, you know?'

'Of course I know that, you silly,' she said. 'But I assume you are somehow acquainted with the mother?'

'It was a young girl I met in the street some weeks ago. She was so desperate. I told her about the Hospital and gave her my address so that she could tell me how she got on.'

'Well, her ploy worked. The baby was skinny but otherwise healthy, so I persuaded them to take him in and he'll be sent to a foster mother for feeding up. With a bit of luck he will survive.'

I hugged her. 'Thank you so much, Jane. Oh, I would so like to be able to tell her that her baby is safe and well.'

'She knows where you are. Perhaps she will call in one day, when she has recovered from her sorrow.'

How could I explain that giving away your child is something from which you never recover? Although I had agreed to the arrangement for Louisa and Ambrose to adopt my baby – there being no other option – I had never really acknowledged in my heart that I would, quite literally, have to 'give him up'. I was sent away to a convent to give birth and from the very instant of seeing him, my love was utterly overwhelming and he never left my arms. Those first few days were perfect, just him and me in our own little world in the sparse cell, the nuns bringing me food and drink. I had no thoughts of the future. The present moment was all that mattered.

Handing my baby over to the wet nurse sent by Ambrose

to collect him four days later felt like having a knife thrust into my heart, a genuine physical pain that I still experience even now, whenever I think about that day. There was nothing the nuns could do to console me. My empty belly remained round as though nature was mocking me, my breasts burned with unwanted milk. Returning to my cell without him was the purest agony, and the only relief to be gained was through the distraction of exercise. For three whole days and nights I walked, almost without ceasing, along the gloomy cavernous convent corridors, until one evening they found me collapsed and half-frozen in a remote, unfrequented corner.

In my delirium I believed that my baby was back in my arms once more. I crooned to him, sang him lullabies, put him to my breast. Perhaps in an attempt to bring me back to reality, the nuns read me Louisa's letters, in which she described how well he was faring and how grateful they both were for my allowing them to adopt him as their own. Slowly I began to recover my physical strength, but my mind was broken. I had no idea who I was any more.

❦

'This has been most pleasant, dearest Charlotte,' Jane said. 'But it is already growing dark and I must be on my way.' She gathered her shawl around her shoulders and bent down to retrieve the dog, who growled sleepily as she lifted him into his basket.

'I have your muff and gloves parcelled up, ready. Please send my best wishes to your sister-in-law, Ann. I hope you will call again before too long?'

We made our slow way down the first flight of stairs to the landing, where she paused to look into the sewing room. 'It is so reminiscent of Ann's shop, it makes me quite nostalgic,' she said. 'But how well I recall our first visit here. We were all so excited for you.'

Just a few days after the shop had opened, Jane and her sister-in-law Ann had arrived with orders: a brand new waistcoat for William and a cape for Mary Lewis, her dear cousin and constant companion who lived with them, as well as some garments for alteration.

'You were my first real customers. I was so excited.'

'William cherished that waistcoat until the day he died,' Jane said. 'In fact, we buried him in it.' The sorrow etched on her face turned to a sweet smile. 'I have known there was something about you ever since I first met you as a little girl, Charlotte, but I never imagined that you would have your very own business, and at such a young age.'

When her own business closed, Ann had given me the addresses of three seamstresses, with wise words that have stayed with me ever since: 'Never scrimp on staff, Charlotte. Choose good people whom you trust, and pay them well. They will reward you with fine work and bring customers back again and again.'

'Mrs Taylor is still with me, also Elsie and Sarah.'

'The redoubtable Mrs T.,' she laughed. 'Ann will be pleased to hear it. She has instructed that I must not leave without finding out how your business fares.'

'I could not manage without her.' I put a hand on her arm. 'I could never have done it without you. You have been like the mother I never had.'

'And you the daughter who was never truly mine. We are

all so proud of you.' She placed her hand over mine, pressing it affectionately. What good fortune had brought me to this place, and surrounded me with the best of friends.

We continued downstairs to the showroom where, as I retrieved her parcel and her cloak, she went to examine the gowns on the dressmakers' dummies in the window – 'what charming styles they wear these days' – and then turned to embrace me. Then something made her halt, her eyes fixed to the counter where I lay out silks for inspection. In the corner lay the pagoda silk.

'Great heavens,' she said, with a little gasp.

She went to the counter and took up the silk, unfolding it and examining it, the silver threads glinting in the last rays of light from the windows, looking at it for a very long time without a word.

'It *is* that silk,' she murmured. 'Wherever did you get it from, my dearest?'

'It's just a short reel-end my friend bought at auction, and there is something about it that makes it familiar to me,' I said. 'But perhaps it was at your house?'

'My dear,' she said, gently. 'I have *indeed* seen this silk once before. There is something I need to explain.'

9

Sackback: a formal style of open gown worn over a hooped petticoat with box pleats stitched at the neckline and allowed to hang free from the shoulder to the floor, often with a slight train.

'My dearest Charlotte . . .' Her eyes were lowered, uncharacteristically, for Jane is the most direct person I know. 'You ask me whether I might have seen this silk before.'

'You have?'

She nodded. 'Yes, Charlotte. I have indeed seen it before.' Her voice was soft as though she did not want anyone to overhear, even though there was no one else in the building.

'And . . .' My stomach fluttered with anticipation.

'My dearest, it is a matter of much delicacy. You must promise never to divulge what I am about to tell you, for fear that it might bring the memory of my dearest William into disrepute.'

'Heavens, what mystery is this, Jane? Please, tell me at once before I die of curiosity. My lips will be sealed on the matter, I promise.'

She refolded the silk and placed it carefully back onto the counter, smoothing it with her hand. 'You know that you were a foundling, delivered to the Hospital as a new baby? And that they gave you a new name – Charlotte Amesbury – when your birth name was Agnes Potton?'

'I learned this on meeting my sister.'

'The governors believed that being a foundling could bring shame to a child, and that this could be washed away by giving them a new identity.'

'I never felt any shame, just sorrow,' I said. 'And confusion, as though I am two people in one.'

'It is done for the very best of reasons, believe me, and the hospital has a system for ensuring that the child's original identity is secretly preserved, just in case.'

'And what is this system you speak of?'

'You already know it, dearest, for you told your young beggar woman. The tokens that the mothers leave are attached to the paper records the Hospital keeps on each baby, the birthdate, the sex and size, their birth name, the names of parents or relatives and any distinguishing marks.'

'This was how Louisa . . . ?' I imagined her turning up at the hospital, waiting at that grand gate with Ambrose by her side, so full of hope and anticipation.

'Exactly so,' Jane went on. 'William knew you were a favourite of mine so when it looked as though you were about to be reunited with your family, he told me, in strictest confidence. Then, when I was with him at the Hospital one day, he showed me your record and the scrap of fabric your mother left as a token.'

The scrap of fabric. Could it have been . . . ?

'Are you going to tell me?' I faltered, hardly daring to hear the answer.

She nodded slowly. 'The token held with your records

was a piece of silk with a pagoda design brocaded in silver. I have never forgotten it, for it is one of the most distinctive in all of the records.'

The information was dizzying. It all seemed so unlikely. Questions crowded my mind. 'Did my sister bring a matching piece?'

'William did not relate exactly what happened. She may have had other forms of proof. But she would have seen it pinned to your records when she came to claim you.'

'My mother was destitute. Wherever did she get hold of a piece of that valuable fabric? When I showed it to Louisa she denied all knowledge,' I said, still struggling to make sense of this curious revelation.

'You will have to ask her. It may just be an interesting coincidence; who knows? But I beg you, please do not divulge what I have told you. William always impressed on me the confidentiality of the records, and he was most adamant that no one must ever know that I had seen it.'

'I just fear she is protecting me from something . . .' I couldn't imagine, let alone put into words, what that might be.

'She's a good and honourable woman, Charlotte, who went through much to find her sister. She's shown you nothing but kindness and generosity and it is perfectly plain that she loves you, so I'm sure there is a simple, rational explanation.'

She bent down to pick up her precious pug. 'And now I really must be on my way. I wish you and your family a very happy Christmas, and you must come to see us in the country in the New Year, dear girl. You look a little pasty-faced, if you don't mind me saying so. The fresh air would do you good. Don't work so hard, and make sure you eat enough, please?'

❦

After Jane left I tried to return to my work, but the light had gone. I made myself a plate of bread and ham for supper but I could taste nothing. Her news had thrown my thoughts into disarray.

As she told it, the story seemed straightforward: my sister gained proof of my existence and sought to find me. This was perfectly natural; anyone would have done the same, and the story had a happy ending when two sisters met each other for the very first time.

But now, sitting here in the gloom of the evening, I recalled the silk unfurling, my sister's face turning deathly pale. Why had she denied recognising it? What could possibly be so mysterious? She had described almost everything else about the circumstances leading to my discovery. Was she not also curious about how our mother had come by such a precious piece of fabric? What shame could there possibly be from sharing the truth, now we had experienced the good fortune of our reunion?

My imagination began to invent wild scenarios: what about the rest of her story? If she chose to be so secretive about the silk, what else was she hiding? There was no sign of a Potton anywhere in Stepney. Had she, for some unknown reason, decided to claim me falsely? I could not imagine why, for she and Ambrose had been so generous, with little else that was obviously to their advantage.

Except, of course, they had gained Peter, my son and now theirs. For a few horrifying moments I imagined that they might have planned everything this way, before pulling myself together, berating myself for such ridiculous fancies. I had not even known that I was expecting until several weeks after we'd been reunited, months after they came looking for me.

I went to bed and must have drifted off to sleep, for I woke remembering that I had dreamed of vividly coloured birds flying through forests of misshapen trees. Again, there was a distant memory I could not quite pin down: like grasping for a soap bubble that bursts as soon as your hand touches it.

In the kitchen, I set a fire and boiled the kettle. The presence of everyday things was reassuring: all was still in its place and the world had not turned upside down. Warmth and candlelight brought me to my senses: there was bound to be a simple explanation. I would be seeing Louisa in a few weeks' time. All I needed to do was ask her.

10

Pocket: *single or paired pouches of fabric tied with tapes around the waist beneath the petticoat or gown, accessible through hidden slits in the seams of the overgarments.*

It was the day before Christmas Eve, and the carriage was packed with people travelling to join relatives for the festivities. Happily I had, as usual, paid in advance to secure a seat. Nonetheless, being squeezed in with nine other adults – all of them amply built and carrying large quantities of luggage, or holding babies and small children on their knees – never makes for a restful journey.

Since I first took the journey to Westford Abbots much of the highway has been paved, so it now takes just four hours. Louisa and Peter always wait at the cross to greet me, and that first embrace with my boy erases in a moment the discomforts of the journey. Then we walk the two hundred yards along the street to the vicarage, past the butchers and the bakery, the marketplace and the Moot Hall, and climb the small hill on which the church sits, on the site of the old medieval abbey, standing proud over the otherwise flat Essex landscape.

Lining the gravelled pathway to the church and the

vicarage are ancient yews that creak and groan like old men, especially in high winds. Ambrose told us that because they are evergreen and do not lose their leaves in winter they are considered by the Church to be a symbol of the Resurrection. They were probably planted when the Abbey was here, six hundred years ago, he said. I find it almost impossible to contemplate this span of time, but those trees give the place a reassuring sense of permanence. It will always be here.

Along one side of the churchyard is a high red brick wall and a gate through which you can glimpse the imposing frontage of Westford Hall, grander even than the Manor in Gloucestershire. The Pettisford family have lived there for generations, they say, having been granted the Lordship by Queen Elizabeth. The latest Lord P. is a go-ahead man, keen to introduce the latest farming techniques that, although not always popular with his workers and other village folk, certainly seem to be successful in improving his fortunes. Craftspeople have been busy at the Hall and throughout the village ever since I first began coming here.

All these scenes were running through my mind as we travelled the last few miles until, at last, we arrived at the Cross. As we pulled to a halt I peered through the window, feverish with anticipation. Louisa was there, but alone.

Fear clutched at my throat. 'Where is Peter? He is not unwell, I hope?'

'It is nothing to worry about,' she said. 'Probably just a chill. It is such a bitter day Ambrose said he must stay in the warm.'

Although he was cheerful enough when he greeted me, he appeared very pale and at dinner displayed little appetite.

Louisa sent him to bed early, and for once he did not complain. After the meal was over I climbed the stairs to wish him goodnight, but he was already fast asleep. As I kissed him, his forehead felt strangely hot and clammy.

'It's that time of year,' Louisa said, trying to reassure me. 'It's only come on in the past day or so, nothing to warrant calling the doctor. He'll be better in the morning.'

I slept poorly again, tossing and turning with dreams of silk and loss, but the following day she was proved right. By the time I rose, stiff and aching from the rigours of my journey, Peter was already up and dressed, with a great deal more colour to his cheeks, impatient to get on with the important business of the day.

For Christmas Eve is when we bring greenery into the house, to decorate the hallway, drawing room and dining room. Ambrose disapproves, claiming it to be a heathen custom, but the parishioners seem determined to decorate the church in the same way, so he has decided not to oppose them. Besides, Peter enjoys it, and Ambrose finds him difficult to deny. It has become a tradition for the pair of us to venture out, whatever the weather, gathering holly and ivy. It keeps us out of mischief, as my sister says, while she and cook are about their labours in the kitchen.

The weather was grey but not so cold as the previous day. We donned coats and hats and went via the gardener's shed to collect a sack, a pruning knife and two pairs of sturdy gloves. There is nothing better than setting about a joint task to help ease the flow of conversation. As we searched for holly with its berries as yet uneaten by the birds, Peter talked about how his team had triumphed in the school rounders tournament. And then, stripping long strands of ivy from the trunks of oaks, he told me about how, after hearing raised voices from Ambrose's study, he'd seen the church warden marching out, slamming the door, never to be seen since.

'Is this the father of your friend, Gabriel?'

His face was sadder than I'd seen for a long time. 'I keep hoping he will come back.'

'Perhaps he will, some time. Perhaps your . . . Ambrose' – I could not bring myself to call him 'your father' – 'and Gabriel's father will make up their differences.'

'I hope so. I miss him.' My heart yearned for the boys, their new friendship and their chess games ended so abruptly because of an argument between two bull-headed men.

But Peter was soon distracted. As we cut some handsome stands of glossy laurel he told me about going with his mother to Westford Hall, and how the youngest daughter of the house was the prettiest girl he had ever seen. When I asked whether she was likely to be in attendance at church for the Christmas Eve service he reddened to the tips of his ears.

By the time we got home the house was filled with wonderful aromas of baking and spices to which we added the smells of resinous pine and the aromatic rosemary plucked from the bush that grows so abundantly by the back door.

That afternoon we exchanged gifts, and I held my breath as Peter unwrapped his new jacket and went immediately to try it on. It fitted a little loosely on account of the growing room I had allowed, but he declared himself delighted. He would wear it to church. When I pointed out the oak design of the linings Ambrose quoted the old saw about 'mighty oaks from little acorns grow', and Peter squirmed with embarrassment.

Later, as his sweet voice reverberated through the church, singing the first verse of *While Shepherds Watched* unaccompanied by choir or band, I found my eyes filled with tears of joy and pride. Christmas was truly here, and as I climbed into my bed that night, my spirits could not have been higher. Thoughts of broaching with Louisa the subject of the silk were far from my mind.

Christmas morning brings more churchgoing, followed by the usual delicious dinner of goose and plum pudding, after which we clear up and take a brief rest before visitors from the parish arrive for tea. It was already gone seven by the time everyone had gone home, and I felt exhausted from making small talk with strangers, neighbours, parishioners and diocesan folk, and handing out drinks and the small savoury delicacies and cakes that Louisa and cook had managed to produce in almost endless supply.

I added another log to the fire in the living room and collapsed into a chair. Louisa joined me, sinking onto the chair opposite and pulling off her lace cap with a long, satisfied sigh. She looked as exhausted as I felt.

'What a successful day, sister,' I said. 'You are a very generous hostess.'

'I think Peter enjoyed himself too, do you not? That jacket is your best yet – I overheard him receiving several compliments.'

'Sewing is the best way I know of showing my love for him.'

'He deserved it. He's a good lad,' she said, fondly.

'He is lucky to have such a loving family,' I said. 'It is my good fortune, too, Louisa.'

She leaned across to the small side table, retrieved her part-knitted mitten and began to untangle the wool.

'Indeed, that good fortune was brought home to me only the other day,' I went on. 'You know I told you about that young woman I met in the street, who was offering me her baby?'

She twisted the wool around the needle and turned a stitch. 'Did you ever find out what happened to her?'

'Not exactly,' I said. 'But Jane Hogarth told me they had found the baby on the steps of the Foundling Hospital, and taken it in.'

'How did she know it was *that* baby?'

I told her about the note. 'Anyway, I was very relieved to hear that the baby was safe. I hope that one day she will be able to go and retrieve the child.'

Louisa nodded and continued her work. The fire crackled in the grate.

'Jane said it reminded her of something William told her one day, when he came home from one of his meetings at the Hospital.' Louisa twisted another thread, hooking it with practised fingers. 'She said the mothers left tokens to prove their parentage, in case they wanted to claim the baby back later. It made me wonder what kind of token our mother left for me.'

The fingers stilled now, and she seemed to be studying the ball of yarn in her lap as I gabbled on. 'Of course, when you went to find me they'd have known you were my sister at once without any such proof, for we're like two peas in a pod, don't you think?' My words came out all wrong, nerves getting the better of me. 'Really, dearest, I'm just being silly. It doesn't matter. What Jane said made me curious, that is all.'

When at last Louisa raised her head, her dark eyes were burning. 'We surely owe Mr and Mrs Hogarth a great debt of gratitude for helping to bring us together,' she said in the slow, deliberate tone of one trying to control their anger. 'And I know that she has long been a great friend and patron of yours. Being reunited with you has brought me the greatest happiness in the world, Agnes, and perhaps it would never have happened without her. But I wish she would stop interfering.'

'She was not interfering, she was just . . .' The words dried in my mouth.

'It is none of her business, Agnes. Remember that.' She gave me a look that could have sliced through stone.

'My life would be nothing without you, Louisa. I love you deeply.' My voice sounded brittle, over-bright, and I could feel the tell-tale prickle of tears already forming at the back of my eyes. 'Had you not come to find me, I would probably have been fending for myself on the streets, and heaven knows what I would have done with Peter. He might even have ended up in that terrible place too.'

She started, as though stung. 'Was it so terrible? I thought you were well treated there? At least you were clothed and fed, and received an education. Better than I ever knew.'

'Of course, they did their best for us,' I said, relieved that the conversation had moved on, her anger diverted. We had talked about my early years in the Hospital before, of course, shortly after being reunited, but never recently. It felt like firmer ground. 'In many ways we were fortunate; it was better than being abandoned or left for dead, like so many others. But our hearts ached for love.'

'It breaks my heart to hear you speak so.'

'But I was one of the lucky ones. Luckier than I could ever have imagined. You came along and found me. We found our love for each other.' She smiled and turned back to her work. The storm had calmed and I should have stopped there, grateful for the reprieve; but something compelled me onwards.

'Don't you wish, too, that you could have known our mother better? I mean . . .' I avoided looking up for fear that her expression might stop the words in my mouth. 'If she was so destitute, where did she get hold of that silk?'

'What silk? You are talking in riddles, dearest.'

'The silk she left as a token. It is exactly the same as the silk I showed you at the shop, remember, when you last visited?'

It was clear that my words had caught her off guard. 'What . . . ? How do you know . . . ?'

'It was something Jane told me . . .'

Louisa stood suddenly, putting aside her knitting and moving over to the mantel, turning her back to me. 'I really don't know what you are talking about, Agnes. Why do you persist in asking such questions? How am I expected to remember any details from all those years ago?'

She began to snuff out the sconces between finger and thumb, careless of the burn it must have caused. 'Why is it so important to know every wretched detail of our past? Can you not be content with the life you have, the family you have? You have us, you have your shop, your independence. Many would be envious of your lot.'

I tried to adopt what I hoped was a conciliatory tone. 'I'm just curious. About the coincidence, that is all.' I had goaded her to anger twice, and could not risk it again.

'Coincidence?' she scoffed. 'More likely a mix-up at that wretched Hospital. You should not be so credulous, Agnes. Jane Hogarth should stop her meddling. Can you really trust what she says about something that happened so many years ago? Old women become forgetful, you know.' She lit two chamber sticks that had been left on a side table and handed one to me before extinguishing the remaining sconce with a decisive puff. 'And now I am going to retire. There is much to do in the morning. We shall not speak of this again.'

I followed her meekly up the stairs. At the landing, she turned away before our customary goodnight kiss, and I went to my room with a heavy heart.

✹

My candle soon burned away, and lying in the cold bed in the dark lent me plenty of opportunity to berate myself. What a fool I was, so anxious to solve every mystery of life. Why had I pursued my questioning to the bitter end, antagonising my dearest sister? And, in the end, to no avail.

She was right. I enjoyed a life many would envy: why did I need more? I must leave it be, for now. My relationship with Louisa was too precious to jeopardise.

I was drifting off to sleep when I heard voices.

At first I believed them to be coming from outside in the street; men returning from the inn, perhaps, a little worse for beer. But it was a woman's voice, followed by an anguished cry that made me sit up and then climb from the bed, taking the few short paces to the window. Outside, the street was in darkness, no torches or movement, all still.

The man's voice came again, a deep rumble that I now realised emanated from inside the house. I ran to the bedroom door and opened it as silently as I could. Listening further, it became clear that it was Ambrose.

'. . . you know perfectly well. Do not anger me further, wife.' Something banged, like a book thrown to the floor, so suddenly that it made me start.

A pause, and then Louisa's voice, pleading. 'But Jane Hogarth . . .'

A chill draught seemed to creep along the landing. They were talking about me.

'What if . . . ?'

'That is my final word. Otherwise I will not be held responsible for the consequences.'

They must have moved further into the room, for the conversation became muffled and inaudible, although his voice was still raised. A second later there was a second banging noise, followed by a harsh squeal.

And then nothing. What was going on *now*?

I listened into the silence until my ears burned. I longed to run along the corridor to find out what was happening, and had to engage every muscle in my body to hold myself back. After several long minutes I managed to persuade myself that I must not interfere.

Closing the door, I retreated to my bed once more. But there was to be no sleep for me that night. What had she told Ambrose that so angered him? What was it that he was so adamant I should never know? My wretched curiosity had already tested her patience and resulted in an ill-tempered exchange with her husband. Why had I been so weak, and meek, and not rushed to the aid of my sister? But there was nothing more I could do now, for fear of causing even further upset.

It was already dawn when I finally fell into a deep sleep, and by the time I woke the household was silent. I guessed that Ambrose was already out on his rounds. My sister was chopping vegetables in the kitchen. I glanced at her, covertly checking for any sign of bruises or scratches. But there was no indication of injury, nor did she seem to be suffering any pain as she moved.

'You have missed breakfast,' she said calmly, as though nothing of the previous evening had taken place. 'I hope you are not unwell, dearest?'

'It is nothing, thank you. Just a little disturbed in the night.'

Her knife paused a second, before resuming its work. 'What was it?'

'Probably just some voices in the street.'

'Those men spend every evening at the inn. It is a mystery how their wives tolerate it.' She retrieved a pot and lifted the chopped vegetables into it. 'Cook is seeing her family today, and I must prepare this so I can get the meat on to broil. Help yourself to bread and butter. There's cheese in the larder, or preserve if you prefer. The pan is on for coffee. We can walk after luncheon if that suits, once Peter is home from his friend's?'

It was as though the previous night's events had never taken place. As time went by I became more convinced that my imagination had run away with itself, heightened by anxiety and the darkness of the hour, and the noises I'd overheard were easily explained: simply the banging of a door and the closure of a squeaky drawer.

Even so the uneasiness remained, along with a feeling of guilt for having caused discord between my sister and her husband. I sensed that raising the topic may have put her in danger, and I must never ask again.

I marvelled at the way she could resume such a normal, easy tone, regardless of the fractiousness between us just a few hours before. How I blessed what appeared to be her infinite capacity for forgiveness. Perhaps that is what happens, in families.

A few moments later we heard the front door and Ambrose entered and, without taking off his coat, slumped heavily onto a chair.

She went immediately to his side. 'My poor dear. Let me get you a cup of something? Hot milk, perhaps?'

He brushed her hand away a little too brusquely. 'Leave me be, wife. I don't need you fussing.'

The room fell into an uncomfortable silence. At last she ventured, 'And who have you been visiting this morning, dearest?'

He sighed. 'Old Chapman.'

'His lungs playing up again?'

'Not this time. He has a high fever and a rash. I called for the doctor and waited for his visit. He says the old fellow may not be long for this world.'

'Oh no! Poor Mr C. Whatever ails him this time?'

Ambrose lowered his voice. 'The doctor fears it may be the typhus.'

II

Mob cap: also known as a 'bonnet'. A hair covering made of round, gathered or pleated cloth (usually linen) worn for undress under a linen caul, with frilled or ruffled brim and lace lappets to either side of the face.

The word snatched at my heart. *Typhus*. A terrifying scourge that seems to have no pity, sparing no one in its path, whatever their age or circumstances.

Louisa went deathly pale. 'But I thought that was one of the reasons we left the city, Ambrose. How can typhus come here into the countryside, where the air is so healthy?'

The disease is common in prisons, of course, and no one is overly concerned about the deaths of a few villains. But it is no respecter of status; it was said that a judge and a lawyer had died of it only a few years ago. It has also been known to occur in quite ordinary small towns and villages far from the city. No one can understand how it travels so fast and attacks so indiscriminately.

Ambrose shrugged. 'Chapman said there was a lad loitering around the cross not so long ago. Word was he'd been in gaol and was trying to trace his family around these parts. Perhaps he brought it with him.'

'I hope he's been sent packing?'

'He hasn't been seen since.'

'My darling,' she said. 'You must not visit the Chapmans again, please. Will you promise me?'

'It is my duty.' Ambrose straightened his back, lifting his chin and rolling his eyes to the sky as he does in the pulpit. 'Jesus commanded us, remember? "Is anyone among you sick? Let them call the elders of the church to pray over them and anoint them with oil in the name of the Lord." We shall know soon whether it is as the doctor fears but until then, dear heart, there is no need to distress yourself. The Lord will protect us.' He rose from his seat. 'There is nothing further to be done today except for commending Mr Chapman and his family in our prayers.'

Panic threw my head into confusion. I had been planning to return to London the following morning, for there were two important clients booked, both requiring urgent alterations to the gowns they planned to wear for the prestigious Twelfth Night ball at the Inns of Court. But how could I leave my precious boy in danger?

Ambrose retired to his study, and we were alone again. 'I've been thinking, sister. Why don't I take Peter back with me, to keep him safe?'

Her brow puckered in puzzlement. 'Are you fully in command of your senses, Agnes? School starts next week. Why would he want to go to London?'

'Just for a few weeks. I cannot bear him being in danger of the typhus.' Peter has my blood running in his veins but I have never been able to mother him, not in the truest sense. The burden of grief and guilt weighs heavily, every moment of every day.

She snorted. 'And you think he would be safer in the middle of that stinking, disease-ridden city? We don't even know yet what Mr Chapman is suffering from, but if we discover the worst I will absolutely ensure that Peter stays away from company, from school and church and out of danger until the crisis is over.'

I ignored the insults about my city. 'But I love him so much, Louisa.'

Now she turned fully towards me, a saucepan lid in one hand and an empty pot in another. Pink spots of anger stained her cheeks. 'And you think *we* do not love him? That's the trouble with you, Agnes. You seem to assume that you have the prerogative of love for the boy, that no one else could possibly feel for him as much as you do.'

I should have backed off but instead found myself saying those forbidden words. 'I am his mother, after all.'

'For heaven's sake!' The lid flew across the kitchen, narrowly missing my head and landing with a clatter in the corner by the stove, where the cat was sleeping. The animal yowled and disappeared in a blur of fur. 'You have not nursed him, rocked him to sleep, fed and cared for him all day and every night, for ten years. I *have*.' With each phrase Louisa hammered the pot on the table, like knocking nails into my heart.

She drew breath, waving the pot in my direction and I ducked instinctively as she dashed it to the floor. 'You would do well to remember our agreement, Agnes.' She stomped out of the kitchen, slamming the door behind her. The unspoken words 'Or else . . .' hung in the air. Or else what? Or else she would refuse to let me see him?

There was no time for wondering, for I heard a voice at

the back porch and just had time to wipe my eyes before the door opened and Peter entered.

His cheeks were rosy from the fresh air, his face lit with the sweetest smile. 'Guess what, Auntie Aggie? Gabriel is back. They were only away for Christmas. He's coming tomorrow to play chess, so you can meet him.'

How I wished to stay, to be with him, to witness for myself the happiness he clearly felt at the return of his friend, to watch the boys at their game, their minds developing and learning as they worked out the complexities of their moves.

'Alas, I must take the coach tomorrow back to London.'

His features clouded. 'I don't want you to go, not yet. Stay a bit longer. Stay for my birthday.' I buried my face in his hair and wished that this moment could last forever.

The kettle began to whistle and Louisa came back into the room. 'We'd better get on with luncheon or we won't have time to walk before it gets dark,' she said, briskly.

The journey the following day provided ample time for musing upon our spat. It was uncharacteristic for my sister to be so tetchy with me, and my heart quailed as I recalled the noises I'd heard in the night. Why hadn't I kept my silly mouth shut? By raising the topic of the silk what should have been a joyful family celebration had turned into a horrible coldness between us, and caused an ill-tempered argument between Louisa and Ambrose.

She and I are so alike, but there has always been an undercurrent in my relationship with my sister, something that I cannot define. Anna and I have differences of opinion like most friends, but neither of us seems to take it personally and any irritation disappears in an instant. But Louisa and I seem to be touchy with each other quite often, unable fully to explain our feelings in a calm, measured manner. Perhaps that is what it is like, being sisters, especially for sisters who had such difficult beginnings, who never knew each other as children?

Her memories were of being an unwanted, unpaid servant in a family that considered her a burden, just another mouth to feed. Mine were of the Foundling Hospital where, well-meaning as they might be, the staff considered us empty vessels to be instructed, little souls to be saved. There was never anyone to make me feel special. So while I have never doubted the love that Louisa and I feel for each other, and the fact that both of us adore Peter, this business of being a family is something we are still, even now, learning to master.

There was little more to be done. On reaching home I forced myself to focus on the week's work ahead, putting my sister's words to the back of my mind and trying not to worry about the typhus. The days after Christmas are often like this, I told myself: disappointment that the festivities are passed, saying goodbye to our families, facing a long January with all its gloomy weather. I would write to thank her for their hospitality, and she would return my letters with news of their lives.

It was the day after Boxing Day, and tomorrow the seamstresses would return, ready for work. There would be customers to see, suppliers to contact. I was pleased to be back, ready to get on with normal life.

Throwing off my cloak and shoes, I began to wander through the rooms, as though reacquainting myself with the place I know so well. It is always a source of delight to be reminded that this is my very own shop, my own business. I have my own loyal customers and make enough profit to pay the wages of three seamstresses as well as supporting myself. I live modestly, but want for little.

Louisa wrote the following day to tell me that the old man had died that very evening. The typhus was never confirmed because the doctor failed to return to his patient.

Ambrose, whose faith renders him more selfless than a saint, continued visiting to the last but happily has shown no ill effects whatsoever, thus far. So fear not, dear Agnes, all is well here in Westford Abbots. Even though the weather is harsh Peter is bursting with energy. School begins again shortly and his arithmetic is improving by the day. He sends his love, as do all of us. We hope business is going well?

Thus reassured, I turned my attention to the shop. For the truth was that business was not going well. Not well at all.

12

Muffs: worn for keeping hands warm. May be cylindrical, or boxy, compact or (increasingly fashionable) long and draped, made of padded, embroidered silk decorated with lace, or (for more practical use) made of fur such as coney, lined with silk.

In some ways a lull in trade just after Christmas is to be expected. After the hectic period of preparation for the festivities, the months of January and February are usually quieter, and this can be a blessing, for the hours of daylight are short and thus, usually, the working hours of my seam-stresses.

In previous years we seemed to manage: sometimes the cold weather brings in orders by the dozen for new cloaks, muffs and gloves as well as old winter garments for repair, all required, of course, for 'tomorrow'. I might then, as dusk drew in, have found myself pleading with the seamstresses to continue their work, even though they disliked sewing by candlelight and I was fully aware that any profits would be sadly diminished by the additional costs of candles and overtime wages.

But this year the orders seemed to dwindle and then, for whole weeks at a time, cease altogether. I longed to hear the tinkle of our front door bell heralding the arrival of a new customer with orders for new gowns, petticoats, cloaks or muffs, but it remained painfully silent. The seamstresses worked more slowly to eke out our existing orders, but it was only so long before I would have to restrict their hours – something I hated to do, for I knew that none of them had menfolk at home bringing in the wages. They and their children were utterly dependent upon the money they earned from me. If I could not pay, they would starve.

Ever since the very first days I have never taken our continuing trade for granted. Thankfully I pay a peppercorn rent thanks to the generosity of a man to whom my brother-in-law once provided succour at a difficult time in his life. Draper's Lane, nestled between the wealthy City of London and the concentration of silk weavers in Spitalfields and Bethnal Green, is perfectly situated for a *costumière* needing to attract ladies of the best pedigree.

That evening I wandered about my premises, racking my brain for ways of generating more trade. It would break my heart to give it all up, after working so hard to make a viable business. This place is my little empire, created by my own hand, and my home besides. It is all I have ever wanted. On the ground floor is the showroom, the shop-front, with its shelves of beautiful silks and displays of hats, sashes, muffs, shoes and other accessories. A couple of mannequins wearing the latest designs for men and women stand in the bow window.

At the rear is the fitting room, which doubles as a parlour. Over the years I have gathered items of second-hand furniture to furnish it with what I like to think of as modest elegance: an old but serviceable Persian carpet, a few inoffensive prints to relieve the eye, a small table for serving tea and four blue velvet-upholstered chairs set either side of the fireplace. This is where I bring customers for more detailed discussions of their needs and then, for measurements or fittings, I can draw the white calico curtains across the far side of the room to preserve their modesty.

Up the narrow staircase are two further rooms decorated simply in white with cream-painted floors, which I insist must be always swept perfectly clean. One, lined with shelves of fabric, rolls of squared and tracing paper, shears, chalks, pencils and rulers, has just two wide counters on either side. This is the cutting room.

The other is the sewing room, the true heart of the business. At its wide windows, south-west-facing to catch the longest hours of daylight, are set chairs for the seamstresses and small tables holding baskets of necessities personalised according to the task in hand: scissors, needle books, pincushions, thimbles and threads of the required colours. All around the walls are shelves and drawers containing yarns in cotton, linen, wool and silk of every imaginable colour, beads and buttons of every size and design, embroidery silks, hooks, thimbles, clamps, reels of lace and ribbons.

Sometimes of an evening after the seamstresses have left I like to spend time in this room. Hung on wooden pegs are part-constructed garments of every kind, gowns, sleeves, petticoats, bonnets, waistcoats and breeches. It is tempting to examine the progress of the day's work and the quality of the workmanship, but I try to resist: this is the responsibility of my chief seamstress, Mrs Taylor. A widow in her middle years with a name that surely made certain of her career, she has worked with me from the beginning and I rely on her entirely.

Sometimes, when the day's work is done, I will sit quietly for a few moments at one of the chairs, breathing in the musky aroma of silk, the lavender oil that Mrs T. applies to ease the pain in her finger joints and, especially in hot weather, the lingering smell of perspiration. I imagine echoes of the day's companionable industry resonating around the walls, the seamstresses' cheerful banter, their laughter and shared secrets, their exclamations of frustration or triumph.

I treat them well, counting myself fortunate to have such reliable workers, for I depend on them entirely. Whatever else is happening, while I deal with awkward or demanding customers or attempt to keep my patience with the excuses of weavers for whatever it is that has caused the tardiness of their delivery, work in this room must continue, for it is the fulcrum around which all else revolves.

But usually, when six o'clock comes, I turn the notice on the front door to 'Closed' and retire to my two private rooms high in the attic. Only here can I take off my mob cap, loosen my stays and relax.

Did I say 'relax'? The truth is that running one's own business allows for precious little relaxation. There is always a mountain of paperwork: chasing up unpaid bills, issuing new invoices, stock-taking, ordering, ensuring that there is enough cash to pay the wages. One room is my chamber, the other a private sitting room that doubles as a work space. At one end is a large table beneath the eaves, which is my designing space, where I do my drawing. This is the most special place of all, the place where I can exercise my imagination.

Pinned above the table on the sloping rafters are my designs for gowns, sleeves, petticoats, waistcoats, bonnets, cloaks, hats, gloves and even shoes. Fashion changes so rapidly these days – from simplicity to extreme elaboration within a few years. Should it be sackback or simple, buttoned or hooked, lace or ruffles, hoops or pads, wide skirts or trains? The trick is in knowing which way it will swing next year.

My friend the printer and stationer over the road shows me the plates produced for the frontispieces of ladies' pocket books, illustrating what purport to be the latest dress trends. 'We could put these all together in a magazine entirely dedicated to fashion, Miss C.,' he tells me. 'With all your lovely designs and drawings, I would set and print it. It'd sell like hot cakes. We'd make our fortunes.'

Since the early days of my apprenticeship with Ann Hogarth I have, for my own instruction, kept a notebook containing a glossary of styles to accompany the folder in which I keep all my sketches. Of late I have considered that it might one day be useful as a booklet for the instruction of apprentice seamstresses.

But what my friend does not seem to appreciate is that fashions change so quickly that any such publication would fall out of date within just a few months. Besides, I am not entirely convinced that my customers would appreciate being thus directed. While all ladies quite naturally aspire to be *à la mode*, what they dread above all else is meeting someone wearing precisely the same dress. It is this concern upon which all bespoke fashion businesses depend. Customers describe in the minutest of detail the gown, petticoats, sleeves or capes they have seen in Bath or wherever, and then ask me to design subtle amendments to render the garments uniquely their own.

'At the Inns of Court ball Mrs So-and-so was wearing those square-shaped hoops, my dear, but frankly they gave her the look of a box. Shall we go for something a little more *au naturel*?' I amend my drawing to show a gentler curve to the line of the skirt.

'*Comme ça*?' I will ask. (Speaking French when talking about fashion lends a certain air of mystique. When Ann Hogarth changed her shop sign from 'milliner' to '*costumière*' the customers flooded in.)

They nod enthusiastically, and before long we will have gained another profitable commission.

But now business had never been so slow, and something had to be done. Next day I went over the road to ask my friend if he would print some advertising flyers at cost price. I have done him many favours in the past, keeping an eye on his shop when he needed to pop out, or taking in parcels when he is away. I enjoy his company very much and over a cup of tea we had a most interesting discussion about the best ways of pulling in business.

He suggested offering discounts for new customers; I felt that offering our services more cheaply might look too desperate and perhaps diminish our reputation for top-quality work, and annoy our existing clients.

'Well, why don't you make it for all customers, but only for a limited period, say two months?' In the end I came round to his thinking, and we composed the wording:

HURRY NOW WHILE SPECIAL
NEW YEAR OFFER LASTS!

Miss Charlotte, high-class costumière
of quality gowns, petticoats, capes,
muffs & gentlemen's wear

offers 10% discount on all orders on production of this Flyer
at 38 Draper's Lane, East London

OFFER ENDS 28th FEBRUARY

He set the heavy metal lettering onto a form and
clamped it shut, spreading the ink using a soft leather pad
tied to the end of a stick and covering it with a sheet of
turquoise paper – 'you want it to be eye-catching, or you'll
be wasting your money' – before passing it through a roller.
The result was better than I'd imagined. Two hundred blue
flyers were delivered the following day.

I took them upstairs to show Mrs T., Elsie and Sarah.
'You will all be aware how slow orders have been?' They
nodded, glancing nervously between themselves. 'But I
want to avoid putting you on short time if at all possible,
so for the rest of this week and next you will work in the
shop every morning – if we have no orders we will sew
muffs and gloves to sell as ready-made. In the afternoons,
if you are agreed, I will pay you to deliver these leaflets
anywhere they will reach the eyes of new customers.'

'This is very forward-thinking, Miss C.,' Mrs Taylor said.
'We've been asking among ourselves why trade is so slow.'

'I can only assume that there is more competition from
shops offering goods more cheaply than we would wish to,'

I said. 'But perhaps this will attract more people to sample the quality of our services and our design. Are you all agreed?'

They murmured assent. Of course no one wants to leave a warm sewing room in late January to tread the streets, but they could see there was no alternative. That afternoon I went to our leather supplier and requested four square yards of soft glove leather on credit, and three square yards of coney fur for muffs. Their linings would be made of scraps we had left over from previous orders. This way, I hoped we could muddle through until the warmer weather arrived.

That Sunday, Anna called in to tell me that her father's visit from Suffolk had been postponed because he and her sister were both suffering from heavy colds. She was disappointed but sanguine. 'It is best they do not travel until they are both returned to full health.'

'You look a little pale yourself,' I remarked. 'Are you quite well, dear friend?'

'Do you have a few moments?' she whispered. 'I have something to tell you.'

We climbed the stairs to my attic room, where I had made a fire. For some reason I feared bad tidings, but my friend was smiling.

'So what is it you have to tell me?'

'Jean is to have a new brother or sister.'

'Oh my dear, this really is the best news.' We embraced, and wept a few tears of happiness together. Some time ago she had confided that after the difficult birth of her first-born she feared that she might not be able to bear another child. As the months passed, it began to seem as though her anxieties may have been justified.

'When?'

'Early July, we think.'

I made a quick calculation. 'So it is already well established?'

'We pray so,' she said.

'Have you told Jean yet?'

'He's too little to understand,' she said. 'I will tell him when it starts to show.' She stopped, biting her lip.

'Penny for them?'

'When my mother was pregnant and she told me I would have a little brother or sister, I couldn't believe it,' she said. 'How could there be a baby inside her? And then . . .'

Her mother had died giving birth to Janey. 'My dearest, you must not dwell on that. It will go well, I am sure.'

'Yes, I am sure you are right. I should stop worrying. Oh, I nearly forgot to tell you. That silk we bought . . . ?'

'The pagoda silk?' I'd been so busy since Christmas trying to get the business back on its feet that it had slipped to the back of my mind.

'Monsieur Lavalle confirms my view that the design is by Leman, or possibly Dandridge, woven by someone called Walters, who was a highly respected English master. It could even have been a royal silk.'

'Good heavens. For Queen Charlotte?' Wherever would my mother have got hold of a piece of royal silk?

'No, this was more than thirty years ago. Wouldn't it have been Queen Caroline at that time? They were very keen on Chinoiserie back then because Chinese porcelain had become so fashionable. Hence the pagoda and the dragons.'

'Dragons? I never noticed the dragons.'

'Here.' She pointed to the twisted, malformed trunk of a tree in the landscape behind the pagoda. On closer scrutiny I could see that coiled around the trunk, looking like part of the tree itself, was a fantastical scaly creature, a wild-eyed lizard.

'Whoever could want dragons on a dress silk?'

'They're a symbol of power, are they not?' she said. The idea that it had been woven to a royal order made me even more apprehensive. These commissions are usually handled with the utmost confidentiality, so how on earth had my mother got hold of it?

'I suppose we'll never know,' I said.

'I'm not giving up yet, though. There are so many questions. Weren't you going to ask Louisa about it, over Christmas?'

'I did, and she brushed me off, told me not to meddle. And then we had a spat about Peter.'

'Oh, my dearest. I'm sorry. What went wrong?'

I found myself telling her about the typhus and my suggestion that Peter might come to London. 'She was furious and told me never to mention it again.'

'She is your sister, and she loves you and Peter as much as you love them. Take heart, sweet one. All will be well. Life will continue as before.'

On her way out she espied the pile of blue flyers resting on the counter, ready to be distributed the coming week. 'What is this?' She took one up to read it. 'Oh Charlotte, is trade so slow that you are having to discount your services?'

'I'm afraid so. It is very difficult at the moment. I have to do something, or lay off my seamstresses, and I cannot bear to do that.'

'Then I am sure you are doing the right thing,' she said. 'But if I may take a few, I will get Henri to deliver them to his merchants and mercers. They can pass them on to their customers.'

'That would be very helpful, thank you.'

'I am sure trade will pick up before long. It always has, in the past.' She patted her stomach, smiling. 'Anyway, I've been thinking I should get my order in early for a new gown to accommodate this one. So maybe I can take advantage of your generous discount.'

A week later I received an invitation: *Come to tea. My father and sister have recovered, and are arriving on Saturday. We would love to see you for tea on Sunday.*

Had I known my father, I would wish him to be the very model of Anna's. Although they are both Church of England vicars he could not be more different from my brother-in-law, and if there is a God I certainly prefer the Reverend Butterfield's version. Ambrose's faith is severe, leading him to extreme and fixed opinions, but Theodore seems to believe that the Almighty has an all-embracing, all-forgiving nature, like his own.

We first met nine years ago during those worrying weeks when Henri was in gaol, wrongly accused of causing affray.

On receiving news of this calamity I had written at once to Anna asking whether she knew of anyone who might come to his aid. That they were in love was already plain to see, although I knew that her uncle and aunt, her guardians in the city, would be utterly opposed to any such relationship.

When she disappeared suddenly to Suffolk without mentioning a word of it to me, I feared their opinion must have prevailed and she was nursing a broken heart, so when she turned up at the shop just a few days later, in response to my letter, I could not have been more delighted. With her was a tall, stooped man with grey hair and beard flowing untidily onto his shoulders, wearing a clerical collar.

'Charlotte, please meet my father,' she said.

'Sir, it is a pleasure,' I said, surprised by his informal appearance. 'Anna never told me you were a man of the cloth. How should I address you?'

'Theo,' was his reply. 'That is what everyone calls me.'

And that, in a nutshell, is the measure of the man: he is modest, thoughtful and self-deprecating, with an economical mode of expression in which a few words can convey layers of meaning, at home with any level of society and so utterly dedicated to his flock and his family that you cannot help but love him.

Anna's sister Janey is the sweetest-natured girl you could ever hope to meet although, on account of a difficult birth, she is a little lame on her left side, struggles with her words and cannot always be trusted to remember things. Yet for all this she has not a hint of shyness about her. We developed a strong bond when, together with Mariette, we were both bridesmaids at Anna's wedding. Janey took her duties very seriously, and we made sure that she caught the bouquet tossed into the crowd after the ceremony. She loved the dress I'd sewn for her and had worn it every day thereafter, at least for the three subsequent days of my stay.

Now, on this chill February day, I looked forward to renewing my acquaintance with Anna's family, with the cheering prospect of good food and conversation. It must have been more than a fortnight since I'd enjoyed the company of any but my own seamstresses and customers, and my heart was light on setting out along the route that has become so familiar, the route that seems to represent the powerful bond of friendship between myself and Anna. I pray that it will never be broken.

Here in that cosy parlour were gathered Anna and little Jean, her father and Janey, Henri and his mother Clothilde and Monsieur Lavalle, master of the house, as well as his daughter Mariette and her fiancé Philippe, a French silversmith with a growing reputation for ornate filigree designs.

'Come and see Mariette's magazine. We are looking at the latest fashions,' Janey cried, taking me by the hand and pulling me to a seat between her and Mariette, who had little Jean on her knee. On the other side of the room Theo, Monsieur Lavalle and Philippe appeared to be debating the impact of new scientific discoveries on our understanding of God. Henri was telling his mother about the new spinning machines he'd seen advertised.

'They'll soon be putting you out of work,' he said, since she is a silk throwster, spinning the silk by hand as she prepares it for the loom.

'The sooner the better,' she replied, with the gentle smile that smooths the lines of hardship and sorrow etched upon her face. Clothilde is increasingly frail these days and Henri would like her to give up work and come to live with them, but she is still fiercely independent. Perhaps the arrival of these machines will tip the balance.

Firelight glowed on the wooden panelling; a table was laid with plates of cakes and biscuits and the fine porcelain tea set usually kept in the glass cabinet, now twinkling in its new freedom. Anna was looking exceptionally well, her eyes bright, her earlier pallor disappeared. Once she'd finished handing around tea and cakes she came to sit at my side.

'Have you told everyone yet?' I whispered.

I had not reckoned on Janey's sharp ears. 'Tell us what?'

Anna laughed. 'Well, we planned to say something this afternoon, so this seems as good a time as any.' She leaned forward and tapped a teaspoon on her cup, bringing the company to silence. 'Henri and I have something to announce,' she said.

You could have heard a pin drop.

'Go on, then,' Henri urged.

'You tell them.'

He came to Anna's side, putting his arm around her shoulder. 'We are expecting a brother or sister for Jean,' he said, blushing crimson. 'In July. Not long to wait now.'

The room erupted. Janey shrieked and jumped up to throw her arms around Anna, knocking a plate onto the floor, where it broke with such a crash that little Jean began crying.

Clothilde kissed Anna on both cheeks. 'Another grandchild,' she said, wiping her eyes. 'After all the losses of our lives you have brought us so much happiness, my dear.' I was reminded of how her two daughters and husband had died, fleeing persecution from their homeland of France.

'This deserves something stronger than tea,' Monsieur Lavalle said, bringing out a bottle of port and a tray of glasses.

The burn of the liquor in my throat was a welcome distraction. For all the overflowing of happiness in the room there was a matching sadness silently drowning my heart, a sorrow born of envy, although I would never allow myself to show it. I missed my own child so deeply. How joyful it would have been to raise him as part of a lively extended family such as this. And yet one of the bitter truths I have learned in my brief years of being part of a family, and of knowing motherly love, is that although it may bring heights of happiness you could never have anticipated, it can also bring pain that cuts like a blade, and cannot be assuaged by any medicine.

13

Cloak: an outerwear garment made of wool, velvet or silk cut in a half-circle pattern, sometimes with a collar or hood and tied at the neck. Lengths vary, usually ending at or below the waist.

The weather turned colder yet, with occasional snowflakes floating down from a leaden sky. I prayed it would not fall in any great amount, for few customers will willingly brave slippery cobbles and the slush of London streets. I was peering out of the shop windows when the post arrived; a pleasant distraction, especially since it included a letter from Louisa. I ripped it open eagerly, keen to discover whether she was confirming the dates for my visit at Easter, now just a few weeks away.

Reading the words 'Dearest sister' still gives me shivers of happiness, but best of all is when she includes a letter from Peter. All of the notes he has ever written are stored in my chest upstairs, bound with a blue ribbon. I sometimes get them out to read them anew or simply to hold them in my hands, to cherish them, observing the steady improvement in his penmanship and vocabulary, from the scribbles and simple stick figures of the early days to the complex sentences in which he now expresses himself.

This time there were just two sheets, both in Louisa's childlike hand:

Dearest sister,

I write with sorry news. Ambrose says we must cancel all visiting plans for the next month or so as it is unsafe for you, or indeed ourselves, to travel on account of the typhus which, you may have read in the newspapers, has spread throughout our part of Essex.

There have been one or two cases here in Westford Abbots but please be assured that we are perfectly safe and are taking every precaution to remain so. Peter is staying home from school and church, and is allowed only one or two special friends to visit him here at the vicarage.

I have dropped all my visits and invitations, as have most of our acquaintances. Ambrose says he must continue his duties, of course. Though he chides me for being overly anxious I urge him daily to keep a distance from members of the congregation to avoid their vapours.

It is very dull here as a consequence and I long for your company, but believe Ambrose is right that we should be cautious, at least for the moment.

We hope this finds you well, despite the terrible chill.

Your loving sister, Louisa

Typhus, again, threatening all those I hold dear with its creeping, invisible, deadly evil? How could I bear to think of the two people whom I hold most dear, my son and my sister, exposed to the dreadful threat lurking in their parish?

Being so far away left me feeling helpless and my first instinct was to pack a bag and rush at once for the stagecoach, but reason prevailed. Ambrose would be furious and might even turn me away, perhaps with good reason; for although no one knew how, the disease was known to spread from person to person. What if I should find myself sitting on the stagecoach next to someone already infected, and then bring it into the house, all unknowing?

The solution was obvious. I wrote immediately:

Your letter fills me with great fear, dearest sister. You must come away as quickly as possible. We can hire a private gig for you and Peter, and you shall come to stay with me until the threat has passed.

After two anxious days and sleepless nights, I received her reply.

Thank you for your kind offer, but Ambrose says we are safer staying where we are. After all, most cases of the typhus occur in London, and we would not wish to find ourselves, as he puts it, leaping from the frying pan into the fire.

Perhaps it was my state of anxiety about the business and the typhus threat, coupled with little sleep, but her letter seemed to exasperate me beyond reason. 'Ambrose this, Ambrose that,' I muttered, crumpling the paper into a ball and tossing it into the fire. 'That wretched man has an opinion on every matter under the sun. Why will she never challenge him? Does she have no mind of her own?'

She was right, of course. There was disease in the city too. But among the many hundreds of thousands living here the relative danger is tiny compared with a small village like Westford, where there were already two cases of typhus in a population of a few hundred. In the full flow of my fury and frustration, I dashed off a reply.

> *Dearest sister,*
> *Has Ambrose taken leave of his senses? I cannot understand how anyone can possibly believe that remaining in a disease-ridden parish could be safe for yourself and my son. Please, reconsider my offer and come to London immediately.*

Of course I should have waited until I was calmer, when better judgement might have prevailed. But the post-boy arrived just then, so I sealed the letter and gave it to him.

Two more days passed, then four, then a whole week of fevered anticipation.

How could I have been so foolish? Telling my sister that her husband must have lost his senses and transgressing so blatantly, on paper, the unwritten rule that I should never, ever, refer to Peter as 'my son'? How I regretted that hasty letter, and wished so dearly that I could have retrieved it. But now I had to wait, hoping that she would understand that it had been written in a state of great anxiety.

I began to fear the worst, imagining, in my darkest moments when I woke in a cold sweat in the early hours of the morning, that all three of them had succumbed to the disease. The newspapers were full of wider concerns: John Wilkes expelled from Parliament again, and the war in the

American colonies. An outbreak of typhus in Essex was never going to make the headlines.

I wrote again:

*Dearest Louisa, please forgive the hasty words of my
previous letter. I am desperate to hear from you. Please
write to let me know that you are all well. I long to
visit you, and each day without knowing is like a knife
in my heart.*

Easter was just under a month away, and normally I would have been making plans to visit. The weather had at last turned a little warmer, hinting at the arrival of spring, but it was winter in my soul. Two further weeks went by without word, and each day I forced myself to resist the temptation to leap onto a coach. Each day, reason prevailed. Just wait, I told myself. Her letter will arrive soon, and all will be well. At last a letter arrived, addressed in Ambrose's spidery hand.

He had almost never written directly to me before and I tore it open, fearing that it must surely bear grave news about Louisa.

Dear Agnes,

*It pains me to write thus, but your sister and I were
much distressed by the personal insult in your letter and
the insinuation that we are acting in a way unsafe for
ourselves and Peter by allowing him to remain in 'a
disease-ridden parish'.*

*May I remind you of the generosity and hospitality
we have extended to you over the years, and that your*

business depends on the very reasonable terms I have
negotiated for you? After all of this, you have the
temerity to question whether I am in full possession of
my senses, and to cast doubt on our ability to raise your
nephew in a right and proper way.

I must reiterate our earlier insistence that you may
not visit until you are invited, and that will only be
once we are completely certain that the threat of typhus
has fully passed.

Yours &c.
Ambrose Fairchild

The next I knew was Elsie's hand on my arm.

'Miss Charlotte? Are you unwell?'

The seamstress was crouched on the floor beside me. I
allowed her to help me to my feet and lead me into the
parlour, where she sat me down and brought a glass of
water.

'You're terrible pale,' she said. 'I hope it is not bad news?'

Her sympathy weakened me, but it would not do to cry
in front of the staff. 'It is nothing, my dear, but thank you for
your concern. I will rest in my room for a while, if you don't
mind.' She helped me up the two flights of stairs. 'You just
call for me, if you need anything. Promise?'

Once she had left the room I wept freely, cursing my
own stupidity. My letter had been crass and thoughtless,
and I deserved his anger. Had I not been so impatient and
hasty, had I read through my words more carefully and
considered how they might be received, this upset might
never have happened. It was obvious that Louisa shared her
concerns with her husband and since she never denied him

anything, would be certain to abide by his instructions. That was the way their marriage worked. There was little to be done except apologise.

Raising myself from the bed, I completed my morning ablutions and put on a day gown, then sat at the table and, after several drafts, perfected to my satisfaction what I hoped was a truly penitent missive.

> *Dear brother-in-law,*
>
> *Your letter filled me with remorse. How could I have written so carelessly when you and Louisa have shown me nothing but love and generosity? My only excuse is that my deep concern for all of you must have muddled my brain. Please believe me that I never meant, in all the world, to imply any failure on your part, nor of your care for your son.*
>
> *Please accept my sincere apologies. I long to see you all again, so please let me know when I can visit, soonest.*
>
> *Your loving sister-in-law, Agnes*

Now my fate rested entirely in Ambrose's hands. Although the fear of rejection and the terror of being denied contact with Peter – and indeed my sister – was agonising, apologising left me feeling a little better. All I could do was hope the apology would be accepted. Even then, I knew it would take a while to recover good relations and Louisa would feel constrained from writing to me once more until her husband had decided to forgive me.

As usual I threw myself into work, cutting out, sewing and embroidering at such a fevered pace that Mrs T. felt compelled to say something: 'Forgive me, Miss Charlotte, but if you continue this way we shall be sitting here idle-handed.'

But little could distract me from my fears. My relationship with Ambrose has never been an easy one. It is entirely one-sided; I am wholly dependent upon his will. Louisa appears to adore him even though he is often unkind to her. He is powerful and unforgiving, and has always held my fate in his hands.

The truth is that I owe the man a great debt of gratitude. Were it not for him, I would never have been able to set up this shop, nor would I be running the business as it is today. I would probably still be a lowly seamstress, working for another. But what I had never anticipated even in my most fearful moments was that he would, without warning, decide to call in that debt.

That very afternoon I received a visit from my landlord, Mr Boyson, with shocking news that threatened to throw all of my dreams, and the past years of hard work, into jeopardy.

14

Feather stitch: a variety of chain stitch resembling a bird's feather commonly used for decorative borders.

Seed stitch: a good filler stitch which looks like small pills, or seeds.

Yes, I have worked hard to build my business, but luck was on my side, too. I would never have achieved it without the help of others. It is almost impossible for a young woman to gain an apprenticeship or to run her own establishment, unless she inherits it. So it was my extraordinary good fortune to have not just one, but two mentors: Ann Hogarth, to whom I was apprenticed, and Ambrose Fairchild, my brother-in-law, who would help me set up in this shop.

Eleven years ago, in those dark days in the convent after the baby had been taken from me, a wise old nun spent much time with me in my cell; or, as I recovered and if the weather permitted, walking in the grounds. She was too old and frail to take part in the domestic activities of the house, the cooking and cleaning and gardening, so instead she had become the counsellor, the *confidante*. In that low voice, tinged with an accent – French, or Belgian? – she posed gentle questions. Then she would listen to my rambling answers without interjection, simply affirming with the gaze of her kind brown eyes that she understood.

She had lived in the convent for many years, but her knowledge was surprisingly worldly. The wisest advice she gave me, which I treasure to this day and to which I frequently return when feeling sad, is that the best way of recovering from low spirits is to start making plans. As I waited out the lonely, painful weeks after Peter's birth, she brought pen and paper and told me to write to anyone who might be able to offer me employment.

The notion of returning to service filled me with despair. But I recalled what Jane Hogarth had told me about her sister-in-law Ann, how she ran her own business as a *costumière* in London. I'd had to ask what a *costumière* was, and she had promised to take me there one day. She had shown me a leaflet with an ornate masthead that William had designed for his sister:

Ann Hogarth, costumière, it read.
At Little Britain Gate at the sign of the King's Arms. Ye
best and most fashionable readymade frocks, suits of fustian,
ticken and holland, stript dimmity and flannel waistcoats,
blue and canvas frocks, and bluecoat boys drawers.
By Wholesale or retale at reasonable rates.

Now, following the nun's advice, I wrote to Jane to ask whether her sister-in-law might be in need of a good seamstress at her shop? Almost by return, she replied that although Ann had no vacancies at present, I should come to stay with her in London and we could visit the shop. Although nothing could dull the agony of giving up my baby, at least now I had something to look forward to.

Meeting Ann Hogarth was a revelation. Her rather plain appearance – short and round, like her brother – belied a powerful personality. Although possessed of little natural beauty, she radiated confidence and charm along with a warmth of character that must, I thought, have stood her in good stead dealing with customers and suppliers alike.

She showed us around her premises, on which I have modelled my own: showroom on the ground floor, workshops on the first, and her personal apartments in the attic. When a customer called, Jane and I were left to chat with her senior seamstress, Mrs Taylor, who spoke of her employer in respectful tones: both kindly and fair, she said, informal in her dealings without being overfriendly, and always expecting the highest of standards of work. So it was a dream come true when, just a few weeks later, I received a letter from Ann to say that one of her seamstresses was retiring, and would I consider taking up the post?

Although Louisa tried to persuade me that a job in service would be more secure and that I would be able to visit them more frequently, the thought of being a housemaid for the rest of my life was more than I could bear. The prospect of starting a new life in the city was thrilling; the sorrow of leaving Peter eased by the thought that, in time, I would earn enough to buy him little luxuries I had never enjoyed.

As a novice, the work assigned to me at first was relatively dull, consisting usually of straightforward cutting out and sewing simple utility garments, one much the same as the next. But before long Ann was giving me more complex tasks: cloaks, for example, were in great demand that cold winter, and soon I was allowed to measure up, cut out, piece and sew a beautiful brocade for a gentleman's waistcoat. It took me an entire fortnight, often working into the night, but I was determined to make sure that it was as perfect as possible, the stitching so tiny that it was barely visible, the seams so strong that they would never part even after too many large dinners.

My customer was a man of the middling sort in his middling years, not so arrogant as some of the young bloods tended to be. Trying on the finished garment after just a single fitting earlier in the week, he beamed from ear to ear.

'This is utterly charming, my dear,' he proclaimed, turning from side to side to regard himself in the long glass. 'Perfection. I do declare it makes me look slimmer and younger than I have felt for many a year. My dear wife will be astonished. I shall persuade her to attend here in future rather than the establishment she currently patronises, where even a bonnet seems to cost a small fortune.'

The pride that I felt in that moment, the realisation that I had accomplished something worthwhile, something of quality, was entirely new and unexpected. As a foundling and as a domestic servant, you are expected to do your duty but no one compliments you on the quality of your work. Now, my skills had earned a customer's genuine respect, and given him pleasure. All at once it was clear what I wanted to do with the rest of my life.

It was after I had been apprenticed to Ann Hogarth for eight months, and had finally managed to save up enough to rent my own rooms, that she announced she was closing the business. She invited myself, Mrs Taylor, Elsie and Sarah to put down our work and listen to the important news she had to impart.

'You have all, all four of you, been the best seamstresses anyone could ever have wished for,' she began. We shared glances; she was not usually so free with compliments. 'And you have helped me build up this business from a simple millinery service to what we can now, with great justification, call ourselves: *costumières*.'

She went on, 'However, you are all aware of my advancing years, and recently even what little input I can offer has become too much to manage. In addition, our landlord has just informed me that he wishes to take back the premises for redevelopment and the prospect of moving once more is, as you can imagine, simply too daunting.'

Beside me, Sarah gave a small sigh; we all sensed what was coming, and Ann spelled it out kindly and carefully, watching our faces all the while. She had tried to sell the business as a going concern but it appeared no one could be persuaded that it was a sufficiently profitable venture. The shop would close at Christmas, in just one month's time. We would all be provided with excellent references and she was sure we would experience no problems in finding new posts.

When Ann's shop finally closed, I returned to Westford Abbots with a dreary heart. I had failed to find a new post as a seamstress, and the prospect of going back into domestic service, with long days of drudgery, cleaning and waiting on my employers' every whim, became frighteningly real once more.

Over supper I explained to Louisa and Ambrose my

predicament, describing the difficulty of finding regular employment now that Ann had closed the shop, and how my hopes of saving enough to set up my own business were now well out of reach.

At first, my brother-in-law ate silently with his usual impassive, unreadable expression, and I imagined that his mind was elsewhere as usual, perhaps preparing Sunday's sermon. But once he had emptied the plate he began to ask questions: how much would I need to rent premises in a decent area? How long would I expect it to take before I was making a profit, and was there really enough trade to support a new business? I tried to answer as best I could, but under his grilling it soon became clear how little I knew or understood about the world of commerce. By the time he finished I was close to tears. But as he left the table his words just seven sparse syllables preceded by a grunt – left me with a glimmer of hope: 'Humph. Let me see what I can do.'

'What do you think he meant?' I asked Louisa the following day. We were sitting in her drawing room watching Peter as he scurried about like a large and clumsy beetle, practising his new crawling technique.

'Long ago Ambrose worked as a curate and then as a vicar, in East London,' she said. 'It was a very poor area, but he was much respected there for the work he did trying to help people to help themselves. Perhaps he knows someone.' Christmas was upon us, and nothing more was said until, on 29th December, as I was sitting at the bureau once more penning requests to the housekeepers of large houses and Louisa was building brick towers with Peter, Ambrose burst in with a letter in his hand.

'It's from that old rogue Boyson,' he declared. 'He's come up trumps.'

'Boyson? The man who was accused of . . . ?'

He put a finger to his lips. 'That matter is over and done with, remember? When he was finally released he told me that if I ever needed a favour, I should come to him. And he's responded with a splendid offer, a property near Cheapside which might just make a good location for a dressmaker. In Draper's Lane.'

'What an appropriate name. But what will he charge?' she asked.

'He's offering it rent-free for a year. Rate by negotiation after that.'

Rent-free? I could scarcely believe my ears. According to Ambrose, this Mr Boyson was in the property business and would know what he was talking about. 'If he thinks it's a good location for a dressmaker's, then it surely will be,' he said.

'May I be so bold as to ask why he is being so generous?' I asked.

Ambrose brushed away my question, so I asked Louisa when he'd gone.

'I don't know the detail of what happened,' she said. 'But Boyson fell foul of some crooked businesspeople who accused him of fraud or theft, claiming hundreds of pounds in compensation. The poor fellow was locked up in New-gate facing transportation, or worse, when his wife came in desperation to Ambrose. For some reason my dearest husband believed him and set out to prove that he had been wronged. He laboured over it night and day – that much I knew, because at the time I was his housekeeper. When it came to the trial the judge believed the testimony of a vicar over that of the tricksters, so Boyson was set free.'

'My goodness, he should have been a lawyer.'

'We would be living in greater luxury had he done so,' she said, laughing. 'But that is one of the things I so admire in him: always driven by a strong sense of what is just. But the call of God is too great, and the two vocations are not so incompatible, it seems.'

'Ambrose said Boyson was a rogue. Is it safe to take up his offer?'

'If he says it is so, then it will be so and he will accompany you to visit the place as soon as possible. If you like what you see, then it will be yours, of that I am sure.'

I rushed to embrace her. 'Dearest sister, I am so touched by your generosity, the both of you.'

She held me at arm's length, and looked into my eyes. 'You are the generous one, dear Charlotte. Every day I give thanks for Peter, your wonderful gift to us. This is the least we can do in return.'

Good as his word, Ambrose accompanied me to London to meet the man he continued to call 'that old rogue'. Mr Boyson was certainly old, his face wrinkled like a walnut, his back bent as a shepherd's crook, rendering him no taller than a child. As for the 'rogue' epithet he certainly had a twinkle in his eye, and he appeared to own a number of buildings in the area, so he must have made a fair bit of money somewhere along the line, legitimately or otherwise, but in his responses to Ambrose he was meek as a child.

The location turned out to be ideal for my kind of business, being equidistant between the weavers of Spitalfields and the wealthier sorts living west of Holborn. There were several other shops in the street, but no other dressmakers – or *costumières*, as I had decided to call myself in recognition of Ann Hogarth's aspirations. Although in the meantime they had all secured other positions, Mrs Taylor, Sarah and Elsie agreed to join me, excited to be part of a new venture.

The property sat on the sunnier side of the street, the ground-floor room already sporting a fine bay window from its previous occupancy as a general store. The basement had served as a storage space, but had the elements of a rudimentary kitchen. Boyson remained downstairs, blaming his creaky knees, as Ambrose and I climbed to the two airy rooms on the first floor, both blessed with large windows that made them perfect for cutting and sewing.

But where would I sleep? I couldn't afford separate lodgings. It was then we noticed the small door leading onto a narrow, winding stair and together climbed upwards to discover two smaller attic rooms with dormer windows overlooking the roofs of nearby houses.

'This is perfect,' I said. 'Thank you so much, brother-in-law.'

As he smiled, clearly pleased to have arranged this place for me, there was a glimmer in his eye that I came only later to understand: it was a look of triumph. Ambrose is a man who desires above all things to hold power over those around him and granting favours, appearing beneficent, was one of the ways that he wielded that power.

So, after years of what had appeared to be a perfectly amicable arrangement, years in which I had always paid the rent on time and it had risen each year by mutual consent in line with what I could afford, what Mr Boyson said now came as a blow that threatened to knock me off my feet.

'I feel I must warn you, Miss Charlotte, that I am shortly going to have to impose a significant increase in your rent.' I must have gaped at him in disbelief, for he continued to gabble on for a few moments: 'I'm afraid it cannot be helped, what with the price of everything going up, and the growing demand for properties like these.'

At last I found my voice: 'This is something of a surprise, Mr Boyson. Do we not have an agreement that we would discuss rent rises according to what I could afford? It seems to have worked perfectly well up until now. Was that not what we arranged through the Reverend Fairchild?'

It was not until that moment that I fully understood what must have prompted him to visit. At the mention of Ambrose the old man's gaze slid to the floor, his eyes refusing to meet mine, and I realised with a powerful certainty that this visit was no coincidence. It was a warning initiated by my brother-in-law, a threat designed to bring me to heel, to remind me in whose hands my future lay. He was calling in that debt.

How dare Ambrose resort to threatening me through his lackey? Yes, my letter had been hasty and ill-considered but they were only words, after all, a minor impertinence, a petty sin. And now he was threatening the very survival of my business. Perhaps I should have expected it; so long as everything went his way Ambrose could be perfectly kind and patient, but cross him for an instant and he would exert his power once more.

Anger made my voice tremulous. 'Do you have in mind a sum, Mr Boyson? And when this might happen? Custom has been very slow of late and my business could not sustain any large increase.'

'That will have to be for you to consider,' he said, turning away. 'I shall write to advise you.'

15

Corsage en fourreau: *a flattering design for the fuller figure with the rear bodice seams stiffened with cane.*

Each morning I rushed anxiously to the post, waiting for letters from either Louisa or Boyson, on which my future happiness seemed to depend. Day after anxious day passed with no further news.

To make matters worse, a particularly demanding customer to whom we all referred as 'the dreaded Lady S.' arrived at our door on a Tuesday afternoon, bearing a large parcel. When I tried to explain that it was early closing day she simply barged past me into the shop.

Lady S. was once a client of Ann Hogarth, and had transferred her custom to me when Ann's shop closed. She was wealthy as Croesus and terribly well connected, bringing the custom of several equally well-heeled friends. In no small part had their patronage and valuable orders helped to boost and sustain our turnover in the early years. But she was, to put it mildly, a little difficult to please.

'I demand a refund,' she bellowed, so loudly I feared all my neighbours would hear.

'Do come into the fitting room, Madam,' I said, closing

the door behind her as quickly as possible, and trying to keep my tone calm and low. 'So you can explain what the problem is. Can I bring you a cup of my best Pekoe?'

'I don't want tea,' she said. 'I just want my money back on this shoddy piece of work. I wore it only the once and it simply fell apart. I was so embarrassed that I've half a mind to sue you for loss of reputation as well.'

'I am so sorry to hear this,' I murmured in as obsequious a tone as I could muster. 'Please come through into the parlour and show me what it is that has displeased you.'

'I am not displeased. I am furious.' She tore open the parcel and threw the gown – a *corsage en fourreau* involving much work and many yards of expensive silk satin – onto the floor like a bundle of rags. As lifted it up, I spied a two-inch rip in the bodice, beneath the sleeve. Unlike many gown-makers, we always insist on sewing double seams along the bodice but, despite our care, these rips can happen from time to time, especially if the wearer gains a little weight. The dress had been completed some months previously, and Lady S. certainly looked puffier around the jowls than I remembered.

'Oh dear, I am most dreadfully sorry,' I said. 'This certainly should not have happened, as all the seams are double-stitched' – I tried to show it to her, but she turned her face away – 'but as it is just along the seam, it can be easily remedied. We will reinforce it with an extra strip of calico to ensure that such a thing does not happen again.' She glared at me as I ploughed on. 'Of course there will be no charge at all. Perhaps you might consider trying on the gown once more to reassure us that the fit is still correct . . . ?'

The words were barely out of my mouth when she began to shout once more. 'No charge? No charge? Did you not hear me first time, madam? Of course there will be no charge. I want my money back.'

I was not prepared to relent so easily, for the silk alone had cost a small fortune – thirty pounds or more – not to mention the lacework and beading and the many hours of work my seamstresses had devoted to it. The total invoice had approached sixty guineas, if I remembered it correctly. To refund it would gobble up my profits for a couple of months, which we could ill afford right now.

'Madam, it is a beautiful dress and flatters you so. It would be a shame to give up on it now.'

'No, I will not take it back,' she pronounced firmly. 'The very sight of it distresses me. Since I am determined never to enter this shop again, I shall send my secretary for a refund early next week, Monday or Tuesday. If you refuse me, I will ensure that the reputation of Miss Charlotte, *costumière*' – she spat out the word with disdain – 'is as so much dirt among my circle. And that would see you finished, if I am not mistaken?'

She was right. If her circle of friends were to withdraw their custom we would struggle to survive. She left me with little choice. Much as I disliked the woman, I could not risk losing even more custom.

It upset me, I'll grant that. Although I have learned over the years not to allow the complaints of dissatisfied customers to get under my skin, sometimes it is impossible to remain sanguine. That sort of cash was not easy to lay hands on, but I would have to find it from somewhere.

Next morning I invited Mrs Taylor to join me for tea in the parlour.

Although we carried a great deal of mutual respect, she and I, we did not normally socialise, and I believe she liked it this way. Taking my cue from Ann Hogarth, I try to be friendly towards all of my staff but never let that stray into friendship, in case there should arise a circumstance in which one must be stern.

'Let me guess. It's that dreaded Lady S., if I'm not mistaken,' she said. 'I saw that gown in the parlour, the satin number that took hours of work. What was it this time?'

'She called in yesterday when the shop was closed, of course, barged in and threw the gown on the floor in a temper. The bodice has a split, I'm afraid.'

'Oh Miss Charlotte, I am most dreadfully sorry. Was it not double-seamed? Sarah can be a little slapdash at times.'

'I could find no fault with the needlework, Mrs T.,' I said. 'I think the rip was the consequence of too much strain – she has certainly gained some weight since taking delivery of the gown. However, that is not relevant now. The problem is that she will not accept a mend. She's asked for her money back, and if not she'll tell her friends to blacklist us.'

'She's the very devil, that one,' Mrs T. observed, unhelpfully.

'The problem is that I need to raise sixty pounds by next week, but I've been raiding our savings over the past few weeks trying to keep everyone at work. Have you got any suggestions?'

'It's certainly a tidy sum.' She frowned, biting the tip of a finger. 'But now I think of it, I can recall a similar kind of crisis befell us at Ann Hogarth's. She visited all her creditors in person and explained her predicament, and most of them paid up at once. Then she went to all the merchants from whom she'd bought silks and other fabrics over the years – the larger suppliers, you understand – and asked for credit against future orders. Some of them went for it, as I recall. She had an excellent reputation, of course.' She peered at me over her teacup. 'But then people talk well of you too, Miss Charlotte, even though you're a relative newcomer.'

Newcomer? I'd been trading for ten years. Even so, her backwards compliment cheered me, and the no-nonsense advice gave me heart. I spent the rest of the morning checking the books and listing all our major creditors, and then set out to visit each one, in person.

When I'd first met Ann Hogarth at her shop, she'd invited us into her private rooms and I'd asked her what she most enjoyed about the work. Although she loved to work in silk, she told me, creating fashionable ladies' gowns and gentlemen's waistcoats, the 'bread and butter' income came from more mundane garments: workwear such as men's trousers and jackets and uniforms in worsteds, cambrics and linens. 'Fashion is so fickle. Gown styles go in and out of favour among the society set but workwear is constant, so long as you deliver good quality at a good price, and on time.'

How did she manage in business as a single woman, I wanted to know? How did she gain respect from suppliers, merchants and the rest, most of whom are men? Her reply has stayed with me, all these years.

'I never take no for an answer,' she said, smiling demurely. 'I'm always charming, of course, but clear and persistent about what I want. And if it is not forthcoming

I simply remind them that I can take my business else-where. Feminine wiles may ease the path but I never overuse them, for men are vain creatures and apt to make foolish assumptions.'

Now, as I knocked at the office door of a workwear sup-plier who still owed us after six months for an order of fifty aprons that we had rushed through on account of the great urgency he'd insisted upon, Ann's words resounded in my ears. His debt of eight pounds was the largest owing to us, but despite several reminders he had failed to pay up. This time I would not take no for an answer.

I recalled Mr Da Silva as an imposing character, a tall burly man of swarthy complexion with a heavy untrimmed beard, and was not looking forward to this meeting. But as he answered the door he seemed quite diminished, shorter than I recalled, thinner and rather washed out. Perhaps he had taken unwell, I thought, pasting on my sweetest smile. But I would not let pity deter me.

'Good afternoon, Mr Da Silva. I hope I find you well?'

'Oh, it's you,' he said curtly. 'I can't see you today. Too busy.' He made to close the door but I pushed my foot forward to prevent it. *Be clear and persistent about what you want.*

'Sir, you know full well that you owe me the sum of eight pounds, and despite our reminders this has not been forth-coming for six months.'

'Yes, yes. I'll get it to you next week,' he said, looking at the floor. We were so close that I could smell the foulness of his breath, but still I did not remove my foot.

'Mr Da Silva, I am afraid that I must insist. At your insistence we delivered that order with the greatest of rapidity but you have not seen fit to reward our good service with a timely payment. Now I cannot wait any longer, which is why I have undertaken to visit you in person today, and will not leave without the money that is due to me.'

He sighed and let go of the door, turning into the room behind. I followed him into a dimly lit storehouse with boxes piled high on every wall and, at its centre, a high clerk's desk. He hauled himself with some difficulty onto the bench, pulled a key from his pocket, unlocked the desk and lifted the lid. Standing as close as I could bear given the stench of the man, I could see that the interior was filled with bags of coins and tied bundles of paper money.

He took out a sheaf and peeled off eight grubby, tattered bank notes. For a few uncomfortable moments he held the notes close to his chest, looking me up and down. We were alone in this gloomy room, the door having swung shut behind me, and I found myself suddenly afraid. But then, to my relief, he held the notes out towards me and I took them from him.

'Satisfied now, madam?' he grunted.

'I thank you, sir, and I wish you good day,' I said, turning to retrace my steps towards the door. I felt him following close behind and hastened my step, but he caught me by the arm. He leaned his face close, whispering his foul breath onto my cheek.

'There's more where that came from, Missy. One good turn deserves another, if you get my meaning?'

'How dare you, sir,' I shouted, ripping my arm away and running for the door. Happily it opened easily and I dashed out into the street, breathing the sweet fresh air as I stuffed the notes into my bodice for safety. It was only after I got back to the shop and sat down that I found myself trembling. *Men are vain creatures and apt to make foolish assumptions.* I had learned the veracity of Ann's advice the hard way.

Thereafter, I asked Mrs T. to accompany me on my rounds of creditors. It took up valuable work time, of course, but it was reassuring to have her with me, and we soon collected nearly thirty pounds, halfway to our goal.

There were three major suppliers with whom we had built up a relationship over the years, merchants whom I trusted to source and deliver good-quality fabrics, in good time. Poring over the books, I totted up the total value of the supplies we had purchased from them over the past ten years: they amounted to many hundreds of pounds. Then I worked out the value, as an average for each year of trading, and calculated that if I asked each of them to advance credit against potential orders for the coming quarter-year, and if each of them agreed, we would have almost reached our target for the reimbursement of Lady S.

I set out once more on my rounds, alone this time. I was confident of the good character of each of these men, and each time I was rewarded with a warm welcome. On presentation of my figures each one of them readily agreed to my request, and the sum was soon raised. On Tuesday Lady S.'s secretary arrived and appeared surprised to be handed an envelope containing the cash that she had demanded.

'I shall make sure that my lady understands that you have paid up promptly and in full,' he said, bowing deeply. I felt sorry for the man, having to work for such a harridan, and was glad to see the back of him. That night I poured myself a glass of port to wash away the bitter taste of the whole affair. I doubted Lady S. would come near the shop again – and perhaps that was a relief – but I felt proud of myself for averting disaster, and felt reasonably confident that she would not spread disagreeable rumours to her friends.

No letter arrived from Mr Boyson, and I began to believe that it had just been an empty threat, prompted by Ambrose. And there was further good news too, in the form of a brief note from my sister.

Dearest Agnes,
    Do not fear. We are all still well, and there have been no further cases of the typhus in the village, thank the Lord. But Ambrose feels it is wise to wait a few more weeks before allowing us to travel once more, or to receive visitors. Perhaps all will be clear for me to visit once Easter is passed?

Best of all, there was a note from Peter folded into the letter:

Dearest Auntie,
    I am so bored, not being allowed to go to school or see my friends. Come soon and cheer me up.
    Your loving Peter

There was no mention of Ambrose's missive; perhaps he had never told her of it. But at last I could breathe more easily.

16

Brocade: a silk fabric with a pattern of raised figures, creating the effect of embroidery by the introduction of many-coloured weft yarns, sometimes metallic.

Amid all my concerns the pagoda silk had lain forgotten, but Anna arrived with news that Monsieur Lavalle had persuaded the auctioneer – an old acquaintance – to divulge the identity and address of the merchant who had put his silks up for auction.

'He might remember who commissioned that Chinoiserie brocade,' she said.

'It probably won't solve the mystery of how my mother got hold of it, but let's go and ask him anyway,' I said. 'Nothing ventured, and all that.'

Thus it was on a bright spring day she and I set out for Spital Square. This is the smarter part of Spitalfields, where the wealthier silk masters live and, by coincidence, is where Anna had stayed with her uncle and aunt on her arrival in London.

'It holds many memories, not all of them good,' she said. 'I was very lonely when I first arrived, and then things went terribly wrong for my poor uncle, thanks to that idiot

THE DRESSMAKER OF DRAPER'S LANE

William.' Joseph Sadler had been ostracised by the Mercer's Company because his son, Anna's cousin, had been illegally selling French silks to cover his gambling debts. But happily his problems were now resolved, and their business fortunes revived sufficiently to achieve his wife's dream of a new house in Ludgate Hill, alongside other prosperous mercers.

'But there are happier recollections, surely,' I said. 'It's where we first met, after all, when I came to discuss your new gowns.'

'I was in such a daze, those first few days,' she mused. 'You terrified me, because you seemed so confident, you knew so much.'

'Me, terrifying? I find that hard to credit.'

'Once I got to know you and began to admire you, I hoped you might become a friend.'

'And what good fortune we found in meeting each other,' I said.

As we entered the square she pointed to a low wall under the shade of a large tree. 'Just over there is where I first learned Henri's name. He was sitting there with Guy . . .'

'Poor Guy.' That winter, Henri's friend had become caught up with the Bold Defiance in a raid on the house of a silk master suspected of paying below the *Book of Prices* rates. Along with two others, he'd been arrested, tried and hanged.

'It broke Henri's heart, what happened to him. He didn't stand a chance, poor boy, after falling in with that crowd.'

'But what were they doing here?'

'Just loitering about, so I thought at the time, although later he admitted he'd been making a delivery in the area and delayed his return, hoping to catch a glimpse of me. There was something special about him, even then.'

'And so it proved, dearest Anna. You discovered the love of your life, just sitting on that wall. Someone should put up a plaque.'

Our conversation had left me light of heart but now, as Anna pulled out a scrap of paper to check the address, my sense of foreboding returned. The merchant's house was an imposing four-storey building in red brick with a grand white stone portico.

'How can he still afford to live here if he's bankrupt?' I whispered as we waited for a response to our knock.

'From the results of the sale, I suppose. No doubt we'll find out,' she said.

A tiny old lady answered the door, her back so stooped that she had to twist her neck to look up into our faces. '*Oui?*' she croaked.

'My name is Anna Vendome, and this is my friend Charlotte Amesbury. I understand that Monsieur Girardieu lives here?'

'*Peut-être.* He might.' Mistrust etched the lines on her face. 'What you want with him?'

'We have a simple question about a piece of silk,' Anna said. 'That is all. It should not take more than a few moments of his time.'

'I ask,' the old lady said, and closed the door in our faces. We glanced at each other, wondering whether she would ever return. It took a while, but she did come back, and to our slight surprise we were invited in through a dark hallway and into the front room of what must have been the merchant's business quarters.

'Take a seat, *mesdames*,' she said. 'Monsieur Girardieu will join you shortly.'

Although it was nearly midday the shutters were still closed and we struggled, in the gloom, to find our way across the room. As our eyes adjusted, it became plain that there was in fact nowhere to sit because every chair and table was entirely covered with piles of books, files and paperwork.

Eventually we heard noises in the hallway, the door opened and a tall man entered. 'Why have you left our visitors in the dark?' he barked. 'Open the shutters, if you please.' The hinges squealed in protest as the old lady struggled to haul them open, but before long daylight beamed through dusty windows onto a scene of dusty disorder.

'Monsieur Girardieu?'

'I am he,' he said in lightly accented English, giving a small formal bow. Now that we could see him more plainly, it was clear that he must once have been a very handsome fellow. Despite his age and the stick on which he leaned, he still presented a fine figure of a man unbowed by recent misfortunes. His wig was freshly powdered and his jacket and waistcoat, although old-fashioned in style, were of the very finest brocade. His shirt and cravat were smartly laundered and his boots shiny with polish. He looked somehow familiar, so I assumed that we must have met through business in the past.

'Allow me to introduce myself. I am Charlotte Amesbury, *costumière* of Draper's Lane, and this is my friend Anna Vendome, a noted designer of silk.'

His smile was warm, almost playful. '*Charmant*. And what brings you two delightful young ladies to my door this sunny morning?'

'We are seeking information about a piece of fabric.'

'*Bien sûr*, mesdames. I will do what I can to help.'

As I unwrapped the silk from its parcel and passed it to him, the silver threads glistening and glimmering in the sunlight, he gave a small gasp. '*Bon dieu!* Wherever did you get this?'

'From the auction of your stock. In a bundle of other silks.'

He leaned heavily on his stick, swaying slightly as though a breeze had entered the room. Then he sat heavily on the nearest chair, scattering books and papers onto the floor.

'This . . .' He peered at it again, frowning, incredulous. 'In the auction?'

I nodded. His response scared me. What further revelations could he be about to divulge?

'It should never have . . .' He pulled out a red kerchief, mopping his brow and muttering something unintelligible under his breath. '*Si quelqu'un trouve . . .*'

I cleared a chair and sat beside him. 'Finds out *what*, sir? Whatever is so special about this silk?'

He shook his head emphatically. '*Je regrette que je ne peux pas dire, madame*. I am not allowed.' Dust motes danced in the light and the air smelled acrid, almost choking. Whatever could he mean, 'not allowed'? How could a simple piece of silk be so precious or so secret? And who on earth could be making the rules?

'Sir, we are ladies of integrity,' I said now, urgently needing to know more. 'It is very important for us to understand. Very, very important. And we promise faithfully that we will never repeat anything you tell us. You may trust us implicitly.'

The old man studied our faces in turn and peered at the fabric once more. We waited as the silence lengthened, becoming denser and more heavily freighted with significance with each passing second. My chest felt unpleasantly heavy and it was difficult to breathe the heavy, musty air.

At last, reluctantly, as though the words were being forced from his chest, he began to speak.

'Very well.' He lowered his voice. 'But you must tell no one. *C'est très secret* . . . Leman made me sign *un déclaration*. Even the weaver Walters had to sign, and him an Englishman.'

Anna looked at me, raising an eyebrow. Monsieur Lavalle was right. 'Who was Leman designing for?'

'*Ma mémoire est faible. Mais . . . c'était pour la Reine, peut-être.*'

'A royal commission?' My voice squeaked with surprise. 'For the queen?'

'*Hélas*, it was many years ago.' He rubbed his temple with a forefinger, dislodging his wig, then pulled it straight. 'Perhaps not the queen but one of her household, a lady in waiting?'

Leaning heavily on his stick, he raised himself and limped to the shelves lining the room, running his finger along the leather spines of a dozen ledgers, muttering to himself the while. He selected a volume and carried it with some difficulty to the table by the window, where Anna and I gathered either side of him. With painfully slow deliberation, he began to turn the pages. I was reminded of the registers I had scoured so fruitlessly in the cold vestry of St Dunstan's Church back in November, and hoped that the information he sought here might prove more rewarding.

To the top left-hand corner of each spread was pinned a sample of fabric with all the details of its provenance: the name of the design, the date, the designer, the weaver, the breadth of the fabric, the finished length and number of figures contained within it, a description and weights of the yarns used and the totals of warp and weft threads. In the lower right-hand corner were written details of the customer for whom it had been woven.

I found myself holding my breath, expecting each turn to reveal the pagoda design. About halfway through he stopped at a page containing no sample of fabric. At the top was written: 'Chinese design. Leman. Weaver: Joseph Walters.' It was a large order of twenty yards, including '16oz silvering'. In the bottom right-hand corner, where the customer's name and address would normally have been inscribed, were just four words.

We peered more closely, trying to decipher the faded script.

'*Mr Clairborne, for HH*?' I read out. 'Should that be H-*R*-H?'

The old man sighed and straightened his back. 'Mr Clairborne was the royal *costumière*,' he said. 'It was one of several royal commissions at that time. Alas, when the new king arrived I received no further business from the palace, and I have never seen Mr Clairborne since.' He sighed. 'I can only assume the king brought in a new man. Thus are fortunes made or lost for those who venture into exalted circles.'

He lifted his gaze and peered out of the window with an expression of such intense melancholy that I almost reached out to place a hand on his arm, to reassure him that life carries on no matter what misadventures assail us. Something made me feel sorry for this man. How had he managed to go bankrupt when clearly he had run a highly successful business with very important clients? What misfortunes had brought him down so?

'Sir, do you recall who this HH was?' I reminded him.

He seemed to steel himself, shutting the ledger with a hard thud and limping back to the shelf to replace it. When he turned back, his face was closed once more: 'I am afraid that is all I know, *mesdames*. I can confirm that it was a royal commission but as regards for whom, I cannot help you further.'

It was clearly our cue to leave, but how could we, when he had offered such tantalising information? 'I beg you, sir,' I said. 'You must remember something more about the customer for whom you sourced such valuable and beautiful silk?'

'I remember nothing more. Now, *mesdames*, I beg you, perhaps you will permit me to continue about my business. Good day to you.'

He was standing in the centre of the room. 'Very well, sir, we will be on our way, just as soon as I can collect our parcel,' I said, gesturing to the chair behind him on which the silk lay, silently shimmering. He made no move to allow my way and this time there was a different tone to his voice, colder and more resolute.

'I cannot let you take the silk, I regret,' he said.

'But sir, it belongs to us. We bought it at the auction of

your fabrics last year and can produce the receipt if you want proof.'

'I do not doubt your word, madam,' he replied. 'But I have a request. This was an important commission for me and I wish to buy the silk back from you.'

'Then why did you put it up for sale?'

'It was included by mistake. Now I fear that if it gets into the wrong hands, it may bring trouble.'

'Pray, how could a simple piece of silk cause trouble?' I said, in my most charming tone.

He sighed. 'How can I explain? I signed a declaration of confidentiality, promising that all of the fabric, every scrap, would be signed over to the palace. Clearly, a mistake was made and a piece was somehow retained. I cannot tell what would happen if this were discovered, but I dare not risk it. Please, tell me your price.'

I had no wish to add to his woes, but how could I let the silk go now that I knew how important it was to my own history, how it had been the agent that led to my being reunited with my family?

'Sir, I do not wish to cause distress, but we cannot sell it back to you. This fabric is of great personal significance for me. But you have my word that we shall take the greatest of care not to let it be seen by anyone other than those whom we can also trust.'

I held his gaze to make it perfectly clear that I was in earnest, and at last his face softened into the briefest glimmer of a smile. 'You are clearly a very determined young lady and I am inclined to trust you,' he said, turning to take up the silk and the brown wrapping paper, passing them to me. 'What was your name again?'

'Charlotte Amesbury.' I felt a surge of compassion for the old man, moved by his dignity in the face of misfortune. 'My shop is in Draper's Lane, not far from here, if you ever wish to call by.'

He gave another small bow. 'It has been my pleasure to meet such charming young ladies.'

Did I detect a passing expression of regret, or disappointment? After a long career as a successful merchant, his life must now feel very circumscribed.

Anna gave my arm a gentle tug. 'Thank you, sir, you have been most helpful. But now we must be on our way,' she said.

'*Adieu, mesdames,*' he said, offering his hand to each of us in turn. 'It has been a pleasure to meet you both, but remember your promise, I beg of you. I am an old man with just a few years to live, and dearly wish them to be peaceful ones.'

'We will, sir,' I said. 'And we wish you well. Good day.'

17

Mantle: a fancy short cape of silk, lace or fur, sometimes lined and edged.

'Whatever did you make of all that?' Anna whispered as we retraced our steps home.

My head was full of mixed emotions, and I struggled to compose a coherent answer. I felt sad for the man amid the ruins of his once-successful business.

'I had no idea that dealing with royal commissions could be such a confidential affair.'

'Nor I,' she said. 'I suppose they don't want anyone to copy their designs. There are some orders that Henri has to be very careful with, for the same reason. That's why we weave them in the loft, rather than let them out to journeymen.'

'But now I'm burning to know who HH is, or was.'

'Me too.' We walked onwards. 'Let's go back and ask Monsieur Lavalle if he knows. He was right about everything else.'

'But can we do this without betraying our promise to Monsieur Girardieu?'

'Of course we can. Leave it to me.'

By the time we got back to Wood Street, the earlier sun was obscured by a heavy grey cloud threatening rain. Monsieur Lavalle was in his usual place by the parlour fire, reading his newspaper.

'Come in, come in,' he said, folding the paper and pushing himself up with some difficulty. 'A pleasure to see you, Miss Amesbury. Pull up some chairs to warm yourselves by the fire. What brings you here in this inclement weather?'

'We have a question,' Anna said.

'And you think I will know the answer?' he chuckled. 'Then you overestimate me, daughter.' She was not of course his daughter nor even properly his daughter-in-law, but he called her such out of simple affection, just as he always referred to Henri as his son.

'We have just returned from visiting Monsieur Girardieu,' she began.

'Poor old fellow,' he said. 'He was well respected and successful, but quite suddenly we heard that he was closing.'

'He certainly had plenty of stock,' I said. 'Had he overstretched himself, perhaps?'

'That may have been a part of it, but word on the street was that he may have got himself in trouble in some other way. The word "blackmail" was bandied about among the fellows at the Company.' He meant the Worshipful Company of Weavers, the guild on which he served as a Freeman.

'Heavens,' Anna said. 'Was that anything to do with the royal commissions he handled, do you suppose?'

'I don't think so. That finished long ago, when the new queen arrived. But really, I don't know for sure, but people said it was a personal matter. He never speaks of it.'

'He wronged someone?' I said.

'Could be.' Monsieur Lavalle laughed. 'He was certainly a ladies' man when he was younger. A bit of a dandy, you could say.'

I shivered. These were the exact phrases staff at the Manor had used to describe Tobias, and I'd always thought them falsely flattering. These men who used women because they had power over them were just plain wicked, as far as I was concerned, but Monsieur Girardieu didn't really seem the type.

'Do you know what the initials HH stand for?' Anna asked now.

'Not H*R*H? His Royal Highness.'

'No, just HH. We think it refers to someone in the royal household.'

'Are you being deliberately mysterious, daughter? You will have to give me more clues.'

'Alas I cannot tell you more, for we have promised a confidence.'

'HH, eh? Royal connection? Then let me think.' He took a clay pipe from the rack beside his chair, pulled a plug of tobacco from his pocket and tamped it into the bowl, lighting it with a taper from the fire. Clouds of aromatic smoke filled the room as he puffed it into life.

'This is something to do with Girardieu?'

'Alas, we cannot say.'

'Let me see now. HH? Ah yes, that's it. Probably refers to Henrietta Howard.' He knew much more than he was letting on.

'I've heard the name,' I said now. 'Who was she? Do enlighten us, sir.'

'It was common gossip that the old king kept mistresses, and Henrietta was his favourite,' he said, taking another puff on his pipe. 'She had rather expensive tastes. After she left the palace, she built a great mansion in Richmond or thereabouts, and held salons for intellectuals and artists. She died only a couple of years ago.'

'Good heavens,' Anna said.

'Now you have raised my curiosity,' Monsieur Lavalle said. 'Are you going to tell me why this comes as such a revelation to the pair of you?'

'Forgive us,' she said. 'Perhaps, in time, we may be able to say. But not now.' She rose from her seat. 'And we must go to check on how cook is getting on with lunch.'

'Then if you have no more exciting news for me, I shall have to seek it elsewhere.' He chuckled and took up his newspaper.

My head was in a spin. 'That silk was commissioned by and woven for the king's mistress?' I whispered, as we closed the door behind us.

'That is what we need to find out,' she said.

But how? I wondered. We seemed to have pursued every avenue, and the mystery seemed to have grown ever deeper. Once again it was Jane Hogarth who opened the door – albeit inadvertently – to a way forward.

Dearest Charlotte, she wrote,

Come to Chiswick for luncheon this Sunday if you are free. Ann longs to catch up with shop news and we have a fine joint of lamb too large for just our household. Do say yes, and I shall send the gig at ten o'clock.

The Hogarths had purchased what William liked to call their 'little country retreat' in Chiswick, Jane had once told me, on the back of the success of his so-called 'morality series' of prints, including *A Rake's Progress*, which sold in thousands to the wealthy who piously believed themselves to be immune to the weakness and depravity he depicted. Having been so close to poverty all of my life, these depictions make uncomfortable viewing, but who was I to cavil? William's new prosperity had led to his generosity towards good causes such as the Foundling Hospital, without which I might not have survived on this earth.

Although I had never visited the 'country retreat' before, I had heard much about it from both Jane and Ann. The area was apparently a magnet for many other artistic and literary types drawn by the fresh air and beautiful landscapes of the riverside, offering convivial company and excellent contacts for William's business.

Now I found myself bouncing towards Chiswick in Jane's private gig, eagerly anticipating a delicious luncheon and my spirits lifting as the grey streets of London yielded to vistas of green; the gardens surrounding the Queen's Palace and then, once past the Knight's Bridge, the park of another royal palace, at Kensington. After that it was open fields all the way to the small town of Hammersmith.

We were almost there when I noticed by the wayside a milestone with the words 'Richmond, three miles'. My heart gave a little leap: surely that was where Henrietta Howard built the 'great mansion' Monsieur Lavalle had spoken of? And it was just a bare few miles from Chiswick, a near neighbour for the Hogarths. Was it possible that Jane and William had known her, or even been invited to one of her famous salons for artists and intellectuals? I could hardly wait to ask.

Just a mile further on we turned onto the Chiswick Road, with the great wide stretch of the River Thames unfolding as we approached the village. The carriage slowed and turned into a simple gateway topped with overly grand stone urns. The first thing I noticed about the house was the fine oriel window on the first floor, overlooking the gardens and an orchard filled with fruit trees.

The pug rushed towards me, yapping around my feet as I alighted.

'Come here, you silly animal. She's a friend, remember,' Jane called ineffectually. 'Welcome, Charlotte. Sorry about the commotion. She thinks she's a big dog, ready to fight off all comers.' We laughed. 'I hope your journey was not too arduous.'

She led me through the front door into the hallway, where she took my cape, and then into a spacious kitchen and a lively scene of domestic life: cook working at pastry on a marble-top in the corner, a maid chopping onions and a manservant who leapt from his seat by the fire and put down his clay pipe as we entered. With complete absence of ceremony Jane introduced me to them all, then took the kettle herself to the pump to fill it and place it onto the hob, adding a few extra faggots to the fire.

'Would you take tea or coffee after your long journey?' she asked.

Ann appeared, full of affectionate greetings, and led me up a short flight of stairs to the drawing room, a long room panelled in grey and generously lit from the oriel I'd observed below. Placed in front of the window were a table and chairs with a view beyond the gardens of green fields and, in the distance, a small village and church tower. The pug went immediately to a water bowl beneath the table, slurping noisily.

'He loved to lie at William's feet as he sat here to draw,' Jane said. 'We keep the bowl there to remind us.' At the other end of the room burned a cheerful fire. Ann sat beside me on the chaise, taking my hand. 'It is so good to see you again, Charlotte. I am keen to learn how your business fares. Do you still have the custom of you-know-who, or have you managed to palm her off onto another? And how are Mrs Taylor, Sarah and Elsie getting on these days? Are they still with you? Do they still chatter all day?'

'Give the poor girl a moment to catch her breath after the journey, Ann,' Jane chided her, but we were soon plunged into conversation about customers, including my trials with Lady S. Ann sympathised, telling me that they had encountered a similar problem a few years back, and had also ended up giving her a refund. 'I know it hurts, but you did the right thing,' she said. 'The woman is a beast, but she does wield a great deal of influence among her circle. And as you have done as she ordered, she'll quickly come round, mark my words.'

'Is it worth the aggravation, though?'

'That depends on how strong you feel. My guess is that you will have earned her respect now and she will be a little easier to deal with in future.' She gave me the address of a merchant who would probably lend me the cash as credit should I encounter any further financial difficulties. I thanked her profusely, accepting the cup of coffee Jane now proffered. I was feeling better already.

Long hours in my own company in recent days had left me thirsting for such companionable exchange, and the rest of the morning passed in a flash. We were joined by Jane's cousin Mary Lewis and sweet, round-faced Miss Bere, who also appeared to live with the family, although I found myself wondering where they all slept in this apparently modest house.

The conversation moved easily from business to art, literature, philosophy, current affairs and local gossip, often punctuated with much hilarity. I felt greatly at home in this household of women, enjoying the way they treated each other with such respect, as equals, without deference.

Once we had eaten our fill of delicious roast meats, vegetables and rhubarb fool for luncheon, the company prepared to adjourn upstairs once more, but Jane caught my arm. 'The weather is still fair,' she said, 'and I could do with some fresh air. Let me show you the garden.'

We took our capes and ventured out to the orchard, Jane pointing out the mulberry just about to burst into leaf, the nut walk along which William had played ninepins with the foundling children, and in the corner the stables above which, in the summer at least, he liked to draw and paint. Even now, four years after his death, she seemed to feel his presence everywhere.

Through the gate we came upon the kitchen garden, still bare save for rows of cabbages and leeks that had over-wintered in the dark soil.

'Come, let's take a seat,' Jane said, moving to a bench against the south wall on which were espaliered a variety of trees, their buds already beginning to swell.

'You are looking well, dear Charlotte,' she said, turning

towards me. 'A little less pasty than when I visited you in London.'

'It is a joy to see you all here in your charming country house, Jane.' It was sheltered here and we raised our faces towards the sun, soaking up its unaccustomed warmth. A blackbird somewhere behind the wall joyfully proclaimed the advent of spring.

It was not long before she asked the question I knew was coming: 'Tell me, dearest, were you able to find out more about that silk we discussed last time? I pray you were able to ask your sister without betraying my confidence?'

I had prepared my answer carefully. 'Louisa denies knowing anything, but I have discovered something which I sense will be of great interest to you, since it concerns a neighbour of yours.'

She turned, taking my hands in hers. 'Oh my dearest, tell me at once. I shall die if you keep me in suspense a moment longer.'

'Do you know anything of Henrietta Howard? I believe she lived not far from here?'

'Goodness, child. Whatever has brought this to your mind?'

'I have discovered that the silk was woven by royal commission, for someone with the initials HH.'

She gave a little shriek. 'Good gracious. I knew it was special, but I had no idea . . .' She tailed off. 'But now I think of it, that does sound quite plausible. Henrietta was said to love her Chinoiserie and apparently her house is full of it, although we never got to see it. William was always angling for an invitation to one of her soirées, but I fear he'd fallen out of favour towards the end.'

She fell silent for a moment, and then, 'But dearest, I have an idea. How would you like me to organise a visit to Marble Hill?'

'Marble Hill?'

'Henrietta's house, in Richmond.'

Visit Henrietta's house? 'That would be extraordinary, Jane. But how . . . ?'

'Leave it to me, dearest. I know people who may be able to help. I will let you know.'

I returned to London full of new optimism, daring to believe that finding out more about Henrietta Howard might somehow lead me to the identity of my mother.

18

Décolletage: the French word referring to the upper part of a woman's body, comprising her neck, shoulders, back and upper chest, that is exposed by the neckline of her clothing.

The discount flyers had done their work more effectively than I'd ever dared to imagine. Ten new customers had called on us within the first two weeks, four of whom placed orders totalling nearly a hundred pounds, including a fine Easter day gown and a gentleman's waistcoat in silk brocade. The discount they received seemed a fair price for this new business.

Other callers seemed genuinely impressed by the examples displayed in the shop window, and we sold six pairs of ready-made gloves and eight muffs. At last there was reason to feel more optimistic. In addition, just as Ann Hogarth had predicted, acceding to Lady S.'s demands seemed to have worked miracles. Although she herself did not reappear until a few months later, some of the customers we knew to be her associates returned for new business.

The shop was suddenly busier than ever.

Among our new customers was a Mrs Arbuthnot and her sixteen-year-old daughter Amelia. From their address

I surmised that they were ordinary sorts of people, determined to launch their daughter into high society. Perhaps they had come into an inheritance, or were spending their savings, but it was clear Amelia Arbuthnot must have nothing but the best.

'We are invited to so many exciting events, are we not? And we have simply nothing to wear, do we, Amelia?' her mother shrilled as I measured them for new ball gowns, two apiece.

'There's the May Ball at the Inns of Court, Charles wants to take me to the pleasure gardens now the weather has improved, and his family has invited us to Inworth Court for the weekend in the last week of the month,' her daughter tittered in response.

'And if we are satisfied with these gowns we shall surely return for our summer outfits,' her mother added. 'As we are invited to Bath this August.'

'I could faint with excitement,' her daughter sighed, as we pored over dress designs. Her mother refused to be swayed by her daughter's demands for a revealing *décolletage* following the latest fashions, insisting that the bodice lines should be modest. 'It is better to be demure, dearest. The young men will find you all the more attractive as a consequence.'

To my delight they each chose Anna's new designs for their fabrics, her more naturalistic styles showing real flowers against a white or cream ground, perfect for a young lady of Amelia's simple beauty and charm.

'So appropriate for spring and summer,' I purred.

That evening I reflected on how mother and daughter had responded to each other in the way that friends do, laughing and teasing as they engaged in the important task of ensuring a successful entry into society. While pleased for them, I couldn't help feeling a little envious. What would it have been like to enjoy such a close relationship with my mother, to have had her support as I entered adult life? With no one to advise me, I'd had to learn my lessons the hard way.

To keep up with orders, we interviewed for temporary seamstresses and took on two youngsters, Alice and Abigail, who brought a new liveliness to the shop, to Mrs T.'s consternation. 'Elsie and Sarah know my ways,' she said. 'I like a peaceful workroom. But these two give me a headache with their unceasing chatter.'

'But how is their work? Do they complete their tasks competently and neatly?'

'Oh yes, madam, they are good little seamstresses.'

'Then try to think of their chatter as a sign that they are enjoying themselves. You know as well as I do that everyone delivers their best work when they are happy. This might even have been one of the lessons you taught me yourself when I first came to Ann Hogarth's shop, if I remember correctly?'

She tipped her head, a nod of reluctant acknowledgement. 'But it does not ease the pain in my head, madam.'

'You never know, there might be something of interest in their chatter – tips on the latest fashions, or suggestions for potential new customers, perhaps? And the rest of the time you will just have to shut yourself away in the cutting room, or learn how to close your ears.'

'I do try,' she said, unconvinced.

'Perhaps it will be easier when I tell you that as a

consequence of all the new business we are getting, and for the added responsibilities of managing four seamstresses instead of two, I am able to offer you an additional two and sixpence a week?'

'That will certainly help to ease the headache, Miss Charlotte,' she said, smiling now. She's a good sort, thoroughly reliable and highly skilled. I cannot afford to lose her.

'And for my part I will have a word with the girls, and ask them to chatter a little more quietly.'

'Thank you, madam,' she said. 'And now, about that lace for Lady Fothersgill's gown . . .'

We worked solidly for two whole weeks throughout all the hours of daylight, barely even stopping for mealtimes, to fulfil the rush of orders on time. The sequence of final fittings, one each morning and afternoon for a whole week, was our reward.

These appointments can often be difficult: there will always be one who complains about the shape of the bodice – usually a lady who enjoys too many rich dinners – the scoop of the neckline, the length of the petticoat, or the ruffling on the sleeves, which can result in many hours of extra work for no additional remuneration. Happily, nearly every single customer declared themselves delighted with the results, and there were barely any alterations to be made. One even remarked that my name was on the lips of many in her circle, and that I should expect further orders from her friends in future.

My suppliers were content with the additional custom, and I was soon able to start paying back the credit they had advanced me to pay off Lady S. There was still no further word from Mr Boyson, and for the first time in several months I allowed myself to believe that the business would survive.

I was exhausted, which made Jane's invitation all the more welcome.

Dearest Charlotte,

Remembering what we discussed at your previous visit, I have someone I would like you to meet: an old friend of ours staying nearby who may be able to organise an invitation to Marble Hill. I have invited him and his wife to dine with us on Saturday evening. They are great fun.

I hope you will be free to come and celebrate Easter with us, and stay the night, too.

If you are agreed, I will send our gig at one p.m. on Saturday.

Your ever-loving Jane

I accepted at once.

'Dearest girl,' she said, welcoming me in. 'You are just in time. Our other guests will be with us in about an hour.'

'May I be forewarned of their identity, or is it a secret?'

'Did I not say? It's David Garrick and his wife, Eva Marie.'

'David *Garrick*, the actor?' I said, alarmed. 'I should have worn a smarter gown had you warned me that we would be in such exalted company.'

She laughed. 'Don't you worry, my dearest, you are perfectly attired. They are the most informal people you could hope to meet, and such good friends of ours,' she babbled on as we went upstairs to the parlour. 'William painted a wonderful portrait of him, which he says helped him become famous. Eva is such a beauty, I'm sure my Will was also just a little in love with her.'

'Alas, I know so little about the theatre.' Apart from the fact that I had no money to spend on such diversions, a playhouse was not a place one would attend alone.

'But you will surely know of his reputation, dearest? He seems single-handedly to have turned around the fading fortunes of the great Drury Lane theatre.'

'He sounds utterly terrifying.'

'Don't be a goose. You are my friend, they are my friends. There are no differences in this house,' Jane retorted. 'You will adore them. Eva was once a dancer, in Vienna. We can expect a delightful evening. Now, will you take a small glass of something before they arrive? Port, perhaps?'

David Garrick blew across the threshold of the Hogarths' house like a one-man whirlwind. He is a handsome man, with a face so mobile that it assumes in quick succession the most convincing expressions of sorrow, utmost joy, total confusion, intense curiosity and absolute surprise, so that it is almost impossible to keep up. He stands not much taller than myself, but more than compensates for this slight stature with the size of his personality, which I found, at first, a little overwhelming.

Behind him on the doorstep, like the calm eye to her husband's storm, stood the loveliest woman I have ever met. Jane's description of Eva Garrick as a great beauty scarcely credits such exquisite features, fine bone structure and delicate deportment. Although her fine head of dark hair now showed strands of silver, her skin was pale and fresh as that of a woman decades younger.

I was trying not to gape at this apparition of loveliness when she reached forward to shake my hand. 'We are delighted to meet you, Miss Amesbury.' Dark intelligent eyes met my own, a slight but still detectable accent giving her speech a mildly exotic tone. 'Jane has spoken of you. She is very proud of your achievements.'

My cheeks burned. How could such a fine lady possibly be interested in a simple seamstress, a scantily schooled foundling dragged up by her bootstraps? Yes, I had women of her class among my customers, but it seemed scarcely credible that I could be actually socialising with such educated and wealthy people.

'You are too kind,' I managed to stutter. 'Please, do call me Charlotte.'

'And I am Eva,' she said.

Once upstairs in the drawing room, as wine was being poured, she came to my side. 'Jane tells me you design beautiful gowns,' she said. 'You must give me your card. My dearest husband chides me whenever I order a new gown, and is wont to preach at me about clothing being mere frippery. But how dare he complain, when he is always dressing up for his work? What we ladies wear is just as important as the facade an actor assumes when he is on stage, do you not think?'

Never had I heard of fashion being compared with theatrical costume and now, feeling on firmer ground and perhaps still enjoying the effects of the earlier glass of port, my shyness seemed to evaporate.

'The clothes we wear can indeed be a disguise of sorts,

but I believe fashion is at its best when it reflects an expression of our true selves,' I said. It is a view I had often considered privately but never before expressed in public. 'Those who slavishly follow the latest fads seem to me to demonstrate a level of timidity, and it shows. But a woman who knows herself, a woman of confidence, will trust her own instinct and seek a design which flatters her natural assets but also reflects her personality to the world as she really is.'

Her laugh was a bell-like tinkle that sounded like an expression of pure joy. 'Jane, where have you been hiding this delightful young woman?' she called across the room. 'Do you hear that, husband? My gowns are an expression of myself, whereas your beloved theatrical costumes are a mere facade.'

Before I knew it, everyone – Jane, Ann, Eva, Mr Garrick, Mary Lewis and Miss Bere – was good-naturedly debating the differences between costume and fashion. Even the pug seemed to rise from his slumber, waddling across to be lifted into Jane's devoted arms.

So engaged was the company that the maid, standing in the doorway, had to say it twice to make herself heard. 'Dinner is served, Mrs Hogarth.'

<hr />

The dining-room table downstairs was most beautifully laid with white linen upon which rows of silver cutlery sparkled in the light of many candles. After so many frugal, lonely suppers my stomach rumbled in anticipation of the feast ahead.

Jane bade Mr Garrick sit in the large carver chair at the head of the table.

'But this is William's place,' he protested.

'Tonight you are the man of the house. In fact, the only man in the house.'

'Then it will be my honour to take the seat of one of the finest artists this country has ever known.'

Eva was ushered to her husband's right hand, and I to his left. 'Surely this should be your place, Jane, beside your honoured guests?'

'You are equally honoured, dearest Charlotte. Besides,' she whispered, 'you can ask him about HH.'

Among his many talents, Mr Garrick seems also to have exceptionally keen ears. 'What was that about HH?' he asked, helping me to my seat.

Unprepared for the question so soon, I blurted: 'Naturally, in my profession I take a great interest in silks, sir, and a sample of sumptuous fabric has come into my possession that has piqued my curiosity. All I know is that it was woven for a wealthy customer with the initials HH.'

'Surely that must be Henrietta, dearest?' Eva said, leaning across to join the conversation. 'She also took a great interest in silks.'

'You are right, my sweet,' Mr Garrick said. 'Dearest Henrietta. Such a charming lady, and much missed. I suppose we can surmise why she put up with the attentions of the dreary old king for so many years, for it is well known that his settlement paid for Marble Hill House, so perhaps it was worth it in the end. She was the liveliest hostess and knew so many influential people, but we haven't been back since she died, alas.'

'We went first with the Devonshires, didn't we?' Eva added.

Jane explained: 'They're our grand neighbours at Chiswick House. Where our guests are staying this weekend.'

'And it was the Duchess of Devonshire who introduced me to this disreputable actor fellow.' Eva glanced fondly at her husband.

'Lord, what fools these mortals be!' he proclaimed in a theatrical tone. 'But we have never looked back, have we, dearest? It's been my good fortune to spend the past twenty years with the very best of women and wives.' He placed his hand over hers so tenderly that I was inclined to revise my opinion of the man.

The first course arrived: white veal soup served with elegant slices of toasted bread. Small murmurs of appreciation could be heard around the table as the first spoonfuls were taken.

'And now, Miss Amesbury,' Mr Garrick said. 'You must tell us about this silk of yours.'

'It is a very special fabric . . .' I struggled to find a coherent response. 'A Chinoiserie design with much silvering, I mean silver threads.'

'Dearest Henrietta was a great one for Chinoiserie and has a fine collection of porcelain,' Eva said. 'What a shame you cannot ask her in person.'

The feast now brought to the table was spectacular: roast pork and a chicken pie, a mound of vegetables, two bowls of apple sauce and several gravy boats. Mr Garrick tackled the task of carving the meat with typical gusto, our glasses were filled with claret and the table fell silent as we tucked into the most delicious meal I'd eaten since my previous visit. As the plates emptied, conversation resumed. I hoped it might return to Henrietta Howard, but there were more important topics to be aired.

'Do tell, Mr Garrick, are you still playing Shakespeare?' Ann asked.

'Ah, indeed. Still just a poor player that struts and frets his hour upon the stage, and then is heard no more,' he declared, prompting a short round of applause from the other guests and the cry of 'encore' from Jane.

'Enough, husband.' Eva placed a hand on his arm. 'You will give us indigestion quoting the Bard at the dinner table. Why don't you tell these good people of your latest venture?'

'We are all ears,' Jane said.

He placed his knife and fork beside his plate, and finished his final mouthful. 'I have been in discussion with the good folks of the village of Stratford-upon-Avon about how we might celebrate the anniversary of the great man's birth, you know, to protect his fame for future generations. I travelled there recently to meet a group of doughty ladies who have persisted in ensuring that the plays are performed in his home town, and they have convinced me that there should be a proper theatre with professional actors for this very purpose. We thought we should start with a pageant, of scenes from the plays, music and general revelry, to wake everyone up to the wonders of the town's great heritage. We're planning for September this year.'

'A pageant? How delightful,' Miss Bere whispered from the far end of the table.

'You shall all attend.' He gave an expansive flourish. 'I

have it in mind to stage it again later in the season at Drury Lane, and all in this room shall have tickets if they so wish.'

Murmurs of appreciation followed. The more I observed of Mr Garrick, the more impressed I became. Nothing and no one could halt such a great force of nature; a man like this could rule the world. What vast ambition he had, what extraordinary confidence. If just an ounce of that could be mine, I would travel at once to Westford Abbots and demand that Louisa explain how she came by the silk.

'What I am hoping is that my dearest Eva will perform for the pageant. Indeed, Mr Arne has composed the music for it,' Mr Garrick said.

'They have settled their differences, thank goodness,' Eva said, although nothing further was explained.

'A dance? Is it too soon to have a preview, Eva?' Jane asked, followed by murmurs of support from around the table.

A blush bloomed on those perfect cheeks. 'Oh no. I have not danced in public for many a year.'

'You are among friends.'

'The dance is by no means prepared. Perhaps I could please you with a song, instead?' Of course everyone agreed and after the apple pudding we retired upstairs to the drawing room, gathering around the harpsichord in the corner. Eva opened the lid and played a few notes. 'It is called "The Soft Flowing Avon",' she said. 'About the river on which the birthplace of William Shakespeare is set.'

She now began to sing in the sweetest, most mellifluous voice I have ever heard:

'Thou soft flowing Avon, by the silver stream;
Of things more than mortal thy Shakespeare would dream.

The fairies by moonlight dance round the green bed.
For hallow'd the turf which pillow'd his head.'

There were just two verses, but I was transported by the haunting tune and the eloquence of the poetry. When, all too soon, it was ended, I joined the calls of 'encore, encore', like a seasoned concertgoer.

The rest of the evening passed in a heady blur of wine and lively conversation. Eva recited a poem called 'Where the Bee Sucks' from another Shakespeare play, and Mr Garrick himself gave us a rendering of what he called a soliloquy – which I came to understand to be a sort of out-loud thinking – from a play called *As You Like It*, in which the character bemoans the passing of his years and ends comparing old age to a second childhood, 'sans teeth, sans eyes, sans taste, sans everything'.

It was a sad image that stayed in my mind for many a month.

19

Velvet: a woven tufted fabric in which the cut threads are evenly distributed, with a short dense pile, giving it a distinctive soft feel.

I woke early the following morning to the song of birds claiming their territories, each one seeming to top its neighbour in variety and volume. Of course I had heard the same in Gloucestershire and in Essex, but somehow these Chiswick birds sounded so much bolder. Perhaps – I smiled at the fanciful thought – in Westford Abbots they had been instructed not to disturb Ambrose.

It was Sunday, and after morning service at the nearby church of St Nicholas we went to the graveyard to 'visit William', as Jane called it.

She led me onto a small promontory close to the river, and approached a tall memorial topped with an urn like those on the gateposts of their house. 'It's a bit too grand for my Will, I always think, but his friends insisted it should be impressive to match his stature and the affection in which he was held. And look, Mr Garrick composed this for him . . .' She pointed at the inscription.

Farewell great Painter of Mankind, it began, continuing

in such overblown pomposity for several lines. I could just imagine the actor proclaiming them from the stage. Suddenly, from behind us came the booming voice of the man himself. 'Saying hello to the good old boy, are we? We saw you in church but you disappeared.'

'Good morning to you both,' Jane said.

'Now, Miss Amesbury, we were talking of Henrietta Howard last evening, were we not? How do you like to accompany us to Marble Hill House this afternoon? The duchess has offered use of her coach.'

'Oh, you simply must come,' Eva said. 'So you can see her Chinoiserie wall painting, and the porcelain. Her nephew lives there now, and will probably show us around.'

'So-called nephew,' Mr Garrick muttered.

'Hush, dearest,' she chided. 'Come now, we must not keep the duchess waiting. Is it convenient if we collect you at half past two?'

When David and Eva Garrick arrived in the Devonshires' coach I had to pinch myself. Stamping their hooves in impatience were four splendid white horses, their blue-dyed feather plumes matching the coachmen's uniforms. Never before had I even seen the inside of such a splendid machine, let alone travelled in one. The interior was the size of a small room, opulently upholstered in buttoned cornflower-blue velvet with gilt trim, with feather cushions fluffy as clouds.

I was excited at first – who wouldn't be, experiencing such luxury? – but soon began to feel like an imposter, especially when we saw men doffing their caps and their womenfolk curtsying as we passed. Had they known my own humble origins they would soon have ceased their deference.

David Garrick explained the afternoon's arrangements: 'John Howard, Henrietta's nephew, regrets that he will not be at home this afternoon. But her young niece will show us the state rooms.'

'This morning in the graveyard you referred to him as her "so-called" nephew, David,' Jane asked. 'May I perhaps indelicately ask, are you hinting at what I suspect you are suggesting?'

Eva exchanged a glance with her husband. 'It is but a rumour.'

'A bit more than that, I'd have thought,' he countered.

'You must not keep us in suspense like this, dearest David. You are among friends, after all. Our lips are sealed.'

'Well . . .' He paused for dramatic effect. 'The king was a dreary old soul, but you wouldn't expect a decade of intimate relations to result in no issue, would you? It is rumoured that both John and his sister Dorothy, who were brought up as the children of Henrietta's brother and sister-in-law, were in fact her own, and the king their father. It was said that from time to time she took leave from the palace and returned sleeker in appearance than when she left.'

'How wonderfully scandalous,' Jane said. 'Does she have any children acknowledged as her own?'

'Just a son from her first marriage, I believe, who died young, so these two would have been her natural heirs in any case. But it is a rather unusual arrangement, is it not?

The king made sure Henrietta had enough money to live in style after she left court, so as soon as she married her second husband, old George Berkeley, bless his soul, young Dorothy and John came to stay, and spent most of their childhood there, as has Henrietta's great-niece, named after her, who will be greeting us this afternoon.'

I listened with both fascination and a growing sense of unease: children adopted by a sibling – a situation mirroring my own. But the difference was that a king's mistress would have sufficient wealth and influence to keep them close while shielding herself from scandal.

'Indeed, one might assume that if there were two illegitimate children, there could very well be others. I suppose we'll never know,' Eva added.

The carriage slowed and passed through a grand gateway. A little further along the gravelled driveway the house came into view and I found myself gaping with astonishment. This enormous, startlingly white building of perfectly classical proportions with a high portico and tall pillars was more like a palace than a house.

Had I been an artist I would have taken out my paints and easel at once but, as I am not, memory must serve as my canvas. Standing high on a small hill, the house overlooked swathes of lawn that reached uninterrupted to the banks of the wide, glistening Thames. It was difficult to believe that this perfectly tranquil river could be the same waterway we visited a few months ago in the city, its waters dirty and chaotic with vast ships and skiffs manoeuvring in and out of dock, its shores a cacophony of cargo, cranes and men.

Here, the only activity was a barge being drawn slowly

along the further bank by two heavy horses on the towpath, a couple of smaller boats drifting with sails only half-filled by the gentle breeze and two rowed skiffs making greater speed. A fisherman sat with his line in the water apparently without expectation, his head lolling sleepily beneath a wide-brimmed hat. In the meadows on the far side a group of horse riders trotted by, their joyful laughter amplified across the water.

We were welcomed by a butler into a cavernous hallway floored in black and white marble chequerboard and with more pillars than I've seen in any church, before being led through to a formal reception room where Mr Garrick drew our attention to the large gilt-framed painting hung above the fireplace: 'Here she is, the lady herself, as a young woman.'

The sitter was a sweet young thing, open-faced, innocent and even vulnerable, dressed informally in a gown of unadorned pink satin with only a hint of lace around the neckline, her hair loose and falling over her shoulders. The image could not have been further from the painted, coiffed sophisticate I'd envisioned; the wealthy, worldly character who bedded a king and enjoyed the company of artistic and literary types, the sort of lady who might commission a silvered Chinese design for one of her gowns.

It was hard to imagine the young woman in the portrait creating such a house for herself. The reception room in which we waited was designed to impress, the décor in glittering cream and gold with much fancy plasterwork. All around were elegant tables and cabinets of highly polished mahogany and intricate inlay, but there was nowhere comfortable to sit. It did not feel like a home in any sense of the word that I understood, more a place for entertaining and showing off.

After what felt like an interminable time the butler returned, bowing deeply. 'Miss Henrietta has asked if you will wait for her in the dining room. Please come with me.'

This space was much more intimate, with none of the ostentation of the reception room. But what immediately caught my eye – and Jane's too, for I heard her gasp beside me – was the wallpaper, hand-painted with the most elegant Chinese design of plants, trees and birds, covering all four walls from the dado rail to the ceiling.

'Goodness,' I mouthed.

'No pagodas,' she whispered back.

'But those flowers, I could swear they are the same . . .' Just as I leaned forward to examine the pattern more closely, a young girl entered the room.

'Mr Garrick,' she piped. 'My favourite actor! And Mrs Garrick. What an honour. I am so sorry my uncle is not here to welcome you and . . .'

'Our friends Mrs Jane Hogarth and Miss Charlotte Amesbury,' Mr Garrick said.

She may have been only fourteen or so, but she comported herself with the practised manners of a society lady and was the very image of her great-aunt; or was it her grandmother? The fresh face and high forehead, the dark, wide-set eyes and brown hair tied back with a green ribbon matching the silk damask of her simple gown were so reminiscent of the lady in the portrait that I could barely take my eyes off her.

'I am Henrietta Hotham and you are all most welcome.

Will you take tea?' she said, pleasantly. 'Do take a seat. My governess Miss Brown will join us shortly.'

As we took our places and the conversation flowed around me I had a further opportunity to study the wall painting. The gnarled trees and tall plants with wide leaves and pink petals were indeed very similar to that depicted in the silk but, as Jane had observed, there were no pagodas.

When Miss Brown arrived and began to pour the tea I noticed that the pot, cups and saucers were of the finest Chinese porcelain, decorated with a twisted tree and a dragon. These stylised subjects were so commonly used in oriental design, I told myself, that much as I wished it they proved nothing.

After tea Henrietta offered to show us around the house and led us through the green room, the gold room and the library, all hung with numerous portraits, several of them featuring her ladyship. Each time I hoped to see her wearing the pagoda silk, but each time was disappointed. As our visit drew to an end the evidence that I craved, proof that the silk had been woven for the king's mistress, seemed yet more elusive. Although her love of Chinoiserie was in evidence everywhere, there were no silvery pagodas to be seen.

When Jane enquired if she might 'freshen up' in readiness for our homeward journey, I asked to join her. The butler seemed to demur for a moment. 'I am afraid that the facilities are under restoration at the moment, madam.'

Young Henrietta interrupted, 'Can she not use my aunt's facilities, Marshall? They are good friends, are they not?'

'Of course, Miss,' he said. 'My apologies.' He directed us up a sweeping stairway to what was referred to as 'her ladyship's dressing room'. This turned out to be a dedicated room for bathing such as I had never seen before, covered floor to ceiling with pink and cream tiles. A large marble bath stood in the centre, a table with a beautiful decorated porcelain washing bowl and matching jugs to the side. In front of a gilt-framed looking glass was a dressing table with brushes and bottles of make-up still in their places, as though the mistress had just left the room.

'Ah, here it is,' Jane announced, opening a small door camouflaged as a painted panel. We peered inside at the throne set upon a dais, with a wooden seat under which rested a highly ornamented chamber pot. 'This is where the honourable lady once sat,' she said, laughing. 'And I shall do the very same.'

All my life people have warned me that curiosity 'kills the cat', but I firmly believe it helps to expand one's know-ledge. So while waiting for Jane, I took the opportunity to explore further. Each wall of this room held a door. One led to the currently occupied 'throne room', another into her ladyship's chamber with an enormous bed at its centre curtained in glorious blue and gold damask. A third was locked.

But the fourth opened into just what I was hoping for. It must have remained untouched since her ladyship's death and as my eyes adjusted to the darkness I could see that this was no ordinary wardrobe. It was the size of a small room filled, from floor to ceiling, with garments of every description: shoes, capes, hats, gloves and muffs, petticoats and stays. An overwhelming smell of camphor and sweet perfume overlaid the sour odour of old perspiration.

'Where are you, Charlotte?' came Jane's voice. 'It's your turn on the throne.'

'I'm in here,' I called. 'Come and see.'

Her shadow darkened the room as she stood on the threshold. 'Whatever are you doing, my dear? They are waiting for us downstairs. Should you even be in here?'

'Probably not, but just see what I have found.' I indicated a rail covered in white sheeting, and raised a corner to reveal a treasure trove of dresses – at least a hundred, I guessed, although there was no time to count. 'We've got to find out if there's a gown made from the pagoda silk, Jane. It may be my last chance to discover whether it really was commissioned for her.'

'And what will that prove, dearest?'

The truth was that I didn't really know, but I couldn't leave without looking. 'Please, it will take but a few minutes if we work together. I'll start at this end if you start by the door.'

I could scarcely believe the variety of gowns before my eyes, plain and brocaded fabrics in every colour of the rainbow: red taffeta, cerise satin, yellow cambric, a stunning blue/green shot silk, black for mourning, emerald twill, cream organza, showy rococo swirls, simple floral motifs, geometric figures and elegant curves.

How must it feel, I wondered, to have such a choice of heavenly garments to wear? Did she ever tire of such riches and wish to wear a simple calico day dress? There seemed to be no such thing in this collection.

As we began pulling out gown after gorgeous gown I couldn't stop myself exclaiming: 'Heavens, look at the beading on this one', and 'Oh, I could die to wear this, just the once.' At the other end of the rack Jane herself gave the occasional gasp: 'My, I've never seen such beautiful silk embroidery', or 'This is just extraordinary'.

All too soon we heard the voice of the butler calling from the hallway: 'Mrs Hogarth, Miss Amesbury, I have been asked to enquire if you are both quite well.' We looked at each other, muffling giggles with hands over our mouths.

'We are perfectly well, thank you,' Jane called back, managing admirably to control her voice. 'But we may be a little longer, so please give our apologies to those who await us.'

We continued our search a little more quickly, though I truly wished there was all the time in the world to examine the fabrics, the design and the workmanship here in this cupboard. The collection contained a thousand lessons in our craft – my seamstresses would have been thrilled to see it.

Jane and I were working towards each other and fast approaching the centre of the rail. I was about to give up hope when, with pounding heart, I saw it: the pagoda silk. As we pulled the gown free for a clearer look we could not help gasping, before falling into silent admiration. Although the silvering had tarnished and the dimly lit room offered no give-away glimmer, it was undoubtedly the very same silk, made up into an astonishingly beautiful gown, perhaps the most remarkable I have ever seen.

The skirt was so wide that it must have been designed for the enormous hoops fashionable a few decades ago, the sleeves loose below the elbow so that deep ruffles of lace could be tied beneath, the bodice lavishly and elaborately decorated with thousands of silver sequins. On closer inspection, I could see that the stitching throughout was so delicate as to be almost invisible. Whoever had sewn it was an extraordinary craftswoman.

'My goodness. That really is a dress to impress,' I said, finding my voice at last. 'Wouldn't it be fun to try it on?'

'Oh, you are such a naughty thing,' Jane said. 'We shouldn't even be in here at all, snooping like this, and we certainly don't have time for a fitting session.'

'But is it not extraordinary, Jane? Such a thing of beauty. I have never seen anything like it before. It must have been made for a very special occasion.'

'Come, dearest,' she said. 'You will just have to treasure it in your memory, for we really must return to our friends downstairs, or they will think we have come to a misadventure, perhaps drowned in that enormous bath.'

Reluctantly, I eased the dress back onto the rail and pulled the protective white sheeting into place. Jane took my arm and I followed, closing the door on my treasure with a heavy heart. I would never see it again.

'Well, at least you have your proof now,' she said as we descended the great staircase. 'That silk your mother left for you was definitely woven for Henrietta Howard.'

The rest of the day passed in a blur: the return journey to Chiswick in that luxurious coach and four, saying our farewells to the Garricks, then a quick glass of water and a biscuit to fortify myself for the return to London in the Hogarths' only slightly less comfortable gig.

It was much later that evening, after I had retired to bed, that I had time to mull over the extraordinary events of the past twenty-four hours. And yet, even though we had proved that the pagoda silk was woven for the former king's mistress, this knowledge only heightened the mystery of how this precious fabric had come into the possession of my poor mother.

What if she had stolen it? The theft, if that was what had happened, would not have been discovered until after I was born and taken to the Hospital, when my mother offered the piece of silk – probably her only possession of any value – as a token. But what then? What if the theft was discovered and she was sentenced to transportation or, worse, execution? Then, another astonishing thought: could she actually still be alive, transported to somewhere on the other side of the world? Were records kept, and where could I find them?

I must have slept for a while then, because I woke suddenly, just as dawn was breaking, recalling the conversation in the coach about the 'so-called nephew', and Mr Garrick's words: 'There could very well be others. And whatever happened to them, we wonder?' If she had borne other illegitimate children why had she not kept them close, just as she had with John and Dorothy? She had money aplenty, after all. Or perhaps the king, fearing scandal at the arrival of further 'nieces and nephews', had simply insisted?

The Foundling Hospital, with its rules about giving inmates new identities, would have provided the perfect cover. Anyone wealthy enough to make a sizeable donation – at least £100, Jane had told me – was assured a place for their unwanted offspring. Despite her privileges, had Henrietta, like myself and so many others, suffered the agony of giving up a child?

And then, as my mind wandered, it invented a scenario so chilling that it seemed to grip my chest like a vice. How else to explain how a silk so precious, so rare that the merchant had been sworn to secrecy, had ended up as my token? It was a thrilling, terrifying thought, and the more I considered it, the more convincing it became. The portrait of that sweet young woman proved it, surely: we had the same colouring, the same wide forehead and dark eyes. Could Henrietta have been my mother? And then, a further preposterous thought that brought me out in a clammy sweat: if she was my mother, then was my father the old king?

But if I was really the daughter of Henrietta Howard, where did Louisa fit into the picture? Was she just an earlier offspring of the king and his mistress? If so, why had she created that elaborate story about the straitened circumstances of our mother, about being fostered to an aunt and treated like a servant?

I sat up in bed, and slowly my heart calmed. It was an absurd notion, the notion of a madwoman. It could not possibly be true. Yet the coincidences were so compelling that I could not entirely dismiss it from my mind.

20

Bays: a coarse, open wool fabric with a long nap; very hard-wearing, often used for workwear or outerwear.

I had not seen Anna since our visit to Monsieur Girardieu several weeks previously, and there was so much to tell.

The family were still at the table finishing their supper, but I was welcomed in and invited to join them for a bowl of flummery. 'It's cook's new recipe,' Anna said. 'Do try.'

I tucked in, savouring the delicious flavourings of cinnamon and nutmeg. Monsieur Lavalle and Henri were in full flow, discussing the most recent controversy among members of the Worshipful Company of Weavers while the two apprentices listened silently. Anna seemed unusually quiet as she nursed little Jean on her knee, feeding him oatmeal from her own plate. I noticed that despite her enthusiasm for the new recipe she ate barely a scrap of it for herself.

When she told the little lad it was time for bed he lurched from her lap and toddled towards me, demanding to be picked up. Always glad of the opportunity to cuddle the boy, I gathered him into my arms. 'Tell you what, Jayjay. Would you like me to tell you a story?'

'Are you sure, Charlotte? He's such a heavy lump these

days I struggle to carry him up the stairs.' Anna patted the now obvious bulge of her belly.

'There is nothing I'd like more, and I know your routine well enough.' I stood, resting him on my hip. 'Kiss Mama, Papa and Grandpapa goodnight.' Upstairs, I washed the little boy's face and hands with a sponge. The water was cold but he did not complain. I tied him into his soft cambric nightgown and gave him a drink from the cup of milk Anna had given us before starting on the story.

There is nothing more comforting than holding a sleepy child on your lap, breathing in the sweet, sugared-almond smell of their hair, feeling the weight and warmth of their little bodies. The bundle of energy that usually wriggled free now rested, relaxed and heavy in my arms, as I recounted the tale of how Tom Thumb arrived at King Arthur's court and how, as a reward for killing the ogres, Arthur granted Tom the hand of a princess. The idea of a tiny man seems greatly to appeal to children. It was certainly one of Peter's favourites and it is a joy for me to repeat it now that Jean is old enough to understand.

He was already rubbing his eyes when I laid him in his cot beside Anna and Henri's big bed, tucking the quilt around him, and I could not resist kneeling beside him for a few moments, stroking his hair and crooning the lullaby that I'd sung to Peter on the few occasions I was allowed.

As I left the room, I found Anna seated on a chair at the turn of the stairs.

'I hope you weren't listening to my squawking up there?'

'Your voice is very sweet,' she said, patting the stool beside her. 'Is he asleep?'

'Soundly so.'

'Then come and join me. The others are in the living room still arguing about politics, but I sense that you have news.'

'Yes and no,' I said. 'But first, you must tell me what was so preoccupying you at supper that you ate not a taste of that delicious flummery.'

She sighed. 'I feel so weary much of the time and my feet are already swollen. I would dearly love to visit my father and Jane in Suffolk before the baby arrives but I fear I may have left it too late. The thought of spending two long days in a coach is just too much.'

'Could they not come here again?'

'I cannot ask him, Charlotte. His curate wrote recently that father had been laid low for several weeks since his last visit, and unable to preach, which makes him very grumpy. It does worry me.'

In the shadows, the blue bruises below her eyes appeared deeper than ever.

'Is there anything I can do, dearest?'

'I don't believe so, not at the moment. I thank you for your concern. But where have you been? We have barely seen you since Easter. How is business faring these days? Did your flyers have the desired effect?'

'Oh indeed, and I thank you and Henri for your help. The shop is busier than ever and we've even had to take on new seamstresses.'

'I am so pleased. And did you go to Essex for Easter?'

'Sadly no, but I went to Chiswick instead, and Jane organised a visit to Henrietta Howard's house. And guess what?'

'How can I guess? She was mysteriously raised from the dead and claimed you as her long-lost daughter?'

'Don't joke, it's not so far from the truth. We found the silk.'

'What do you mean, *the silk*?'

'We went with David Garrick and his wife. And we found the gown.'

'*David Garrick?* The actor?' she cried. 'And HH's gown? Heavens. I cannot keep up with this. I urge you, start again. Tell me everything, from the beginning.'

By the time I'd finished, she was laughing. 'What a brazen pair, rummaging in her ladyship's wardrobe. But at least you have your proof.'

'But how on earth did my mother get hold of the silk, unless . . . ?'

'Unless what, dearest?'

I explained how it was widely believed that Henrietta had fostered two of her illegitimate children – fathered by the king – with her brother. 'Don't you see? That is just what I was forced to do with Peter?'

'I can see the parallels, Charlotte. But what are you getting at now?'

'It is also rumoured that she bore other children. So where are they? What if . . . ' I hesitated to voice my darkest thoughts. 'Could they have been raised in the Hospital, like me? What if – oh Anna, this sounds so stupid, saying it out loud.'

'Say it. I promise not to laugh.'

'Could it have been her who left the silk token?'

'Henrietta Howard?' Her face crumpled with the effort of trying to maintain a serious expression. 'Are you seriously suggesting that Henrietta was your mother? And the king your father? Oh Charlotte, forgive me, but this sounds like you've made up something from a fairy story.'

'I don't know why you think it so absurd,' I muttered, mildly defensive.

'For a start, wouldn't she have been too old?'

'I don't know, how old was she?'

'You said yourself she died two years ago, and I remember people talking about how lively she had remained to the very end, even though she was deaf and had reached nearly threescore and twenty years. She would have been in her mid-fifties at the very least when you were born.'

But Louisa is seven years my senior. Perhaps *she* was Henrietta's daughter?

'And didn't you yourself say she built this beautiful house on the Thames with money given by the king, and she left court to live there when she married her new husband?' Anna went on. 'And that's where she brought up her so-called niece and nephew?'

I nodded.

'When did she leave court? Did Mr Garrick say?'

'A few years before the queen died.'

'Queen Caroline died before we were born, Charlotte. But Monsieur Lavalle might remember the date. Let us ask him.'

'No, please don't, Anna. It's a silly notion. Why don't we just forget it?'

'Silly or not, you will always wonder unless we prove it to be impossible.'

'Very well, then. So long as you don't tell him why we're asking.'

'Don't be a dolt, of course I won't,' she said, standing up with a little groan. 'Sorry, it's my legs. I cannot remember them hurting this way with Jean.'

'You must take it easy, my dearest,' I said, following her down the stairs. 'You have still three months to go yet.'

'Don't remind me. I wish it could be born tomorrow.'

Downstairs in the parlour the men were still making merry with a bottle of port while arguing about the rights and wrongs of the new acts that Parliament had passed to protect weavers' wages. We waited patiently for the right moment to speak to Monsieur Lavalle.

'Anna and I were having a discussion about the olden days,' she started. 'Can you remember when Queen Caroline died?'

'What, another royal query? Whatever kind of mischief are you up to, the pair of you?' The old boy's eyes twinkled as he put down his glass. 'However, since you ask, I remember precisely when it was. 1737. The funeral was at Westminster Abbey on the seventeenth of December, the very day that I married my dearest wife. I remember everyone joking that we'd married just in time to go into mourning, and thinking that business was going to be tough, weaving only black crepe.'

'Why did you want to know?' Henri piped up.

Anna gave him a fierce stare. 'Oh, nothing. Just wondering.' She took my hand. 'Come, Charlotte, let's check whether that naughty lad is still asleep.'

'So, when were you born, Charlotte?' she whispered, once we were out of earshot.

'1741,' I said. 'In June.'

'Four years after Queen Caroline died. Henrietta left court long before that. She couldn't have been your mother.'

'But she could have been Louisa's,' I said. 'She is seven years older than me.'

Anna paused. 'That is a remote chance, I grant you. Henrietta had illegitimate children, and Henrietta was the person for whom the silk was woven. But that does not mean she was your mother. You must give up these foolish notions before you are sent to the madhouse, dearest.'

'But if HH is not our mother, then who? And how did she get hold of the silk?'

'There is nothing for it, dear friend. You will have to ask your sister.'

21

Cambric: a fine, lightweight French cloth of linen or cotton often used for shirts, handkerchiefs and ruffs. The thread is also used for lacemaking and needlework.

The opportunity came even sooner than I'd hoped. Louisa's letter arrived the very next day, with an invitation to visit the coming weekend.

But my delight and excitement were tempered with anxiety: how would I be welcomed by Ambrose, whose character I had impugned and whose motives I still mistrusted? How would Peter have changed, after all this time? And most of all, the question with the highest stakes: how to raise the subject of Henrietta Howard with my sister?

All my concerns slipped away when I alighted at Westford Abbots and saw Louisa waiting at the cross with Peter. Yes, it really was my boy, although he seemed to have grown so much that I had to look twice to be certain. He was turning into a young man before my eyes.

'It's been far too long,' my sister said as we embraced, so warmly it was as though nothing harsh had ever passed between us. 'We have so much to catch up with.' Indeed, I thought to myself. More than you can imagine.

Peter collected my bag and we began to walk. 'How are you, Peter? Are you enjoying being back at school?'

He muttered something inaudible, face to the ground.

'Reply politely to your aunt, Peter,' Louisa prompted.

'Yes, thank you, Aunt Agnes,' he allowed.

'You wrote about the apple blossom. I hope you will come with me to show me the brightest displays.'

Louisa filled the silence. 'Of course we shall walk. The blossom is a joy to see, after this long horrid winter,' she said. 'And the weather is set to be fair for the next few days, so the farmers say.'

'I have school tomorrow, Ma,' he said. 'In case you have forgotten.'

'I do not appreciate this new tone of yours, Peter,' she said, sharply. 'We shall walk after school, if the weather permits, and you will join us. What do you say?'

'Yes, Mama.'

Not even this uneasy exchange could dampen my spirits. My baby was no more, nor even the little boy who enjoyed hugs and stories and who I could entertain with drawings or castles built of wooden blocks. But what a fine young man he was becoming.

As we passed the marketplace a group of young women ceased their gossiping, their heads turning. One called, 'Good afternoon, Master Peter,' while the others giggled.

He responded with a smile so flirtatious, a mixture of bashful and bold, that it jolted me to the core. For the first time, I saw in his face an unwelcome resemblance to another charmer with dark, dancing eyes. Pray God that Peter would not also inherit Tobias's arrogant, brutish nature.

As we waited for Ambrose to arrive home that evening, nerves seemed to make my stomach curdle. I'd been contemplating the best way of handling our first encounter and decided that a quick, simple apology would help to clear the air right away.

'Please forgive the hasty words in my letter,' I said, when he had taken off his coat.

'Think no more of it, sister-in-law. Consider that to be in the past.'

For all his piousness and pomposity and for all that I feared him, Ambrose's behaviour was never less than that of a perfect gentleman, which only made my knowledge of his darker side even more chilling. He was the model of affability throughout supper, tendering polite enquiries about how the business was faring and listening with great attentiveness. The words 'landlord' or 'rent' never passed our lips. Convinced that he had engineered Mr Boyson's visit as some kind of warning, I was all too aware of how vulnerable it had left me. It would have been very unwise to mention it.

'And did you have a pleasant Easter weekend?' Louisa asked, as we sat down to supper. I described my Easter jaunt to Chiswick, meeting the Garricks and our visit to Marble Hill House.

'She built that house herself?' Peter asked.

'Not with her bare hands, I don't suppose,' Louisa said.

'But it must have cost a fortune to build a palace like that.'

'Some people are so rich they cannot think what to do

with all their money,' I said, hoping that he would not ask how Henrietta had made hers. Of course I made no mention of the gown. I was saving that until Louisa and I could be alone.

After the meal, as usual, we retired to the drawing room, Ambrose to his study and Peter to a game of chess with his friend. Louisa took up her handiwork – she'd moved on to making socks for the deserving poor.

'I hope I am properly forgiven now,' I began. 'In my haste I wrote words that were ill-considered, and even disrespectful.'

'Think nothing of it, dearest,' she said. 'My husband may be quick to anger, but he is also quick to forgive.'

'I was so relieved to receive your letter, and to learn that the village was free from the typhus.'

She told me how concerned she'd been when Ambrose insisted on visiting parishioners suffering from the fever, placing himself, as she put it, directly in harm's way. 'But he's strong as an ox, my husband.' Her face lit up with genuine respect, and I wondered once more how she remained so admiring when in private he could be so harsh. 'Thank the Lord he seems healthier than all of us, despite his years.'

'It must have been a difficult time for you all.'

'Especially for Peter. He was so bored without his friends. His nature is changing, as you have surely noticed. It is hard to get a word out of him sometimes.'

'Except perhaps when there is a pretty girl in sight?'

'Indeed.' She gave a rueful smile. 'He dares not flirt like that when his father is around.'

'It is no surprise the girls notice him. He's turning into a very handsome young man.'

'He is a popular boy and his schoolwork is still excellent. We are very proud of him.'

I was burning to tell her my discoveries about Henrietta and the silk, but still I hesitated, fearing to stir up her anger once more. In the end, it was she who inadvertently introduced the topic.

'This vicarage is so dull, do you not think, with these whitewashed walls and plain furniture,' she said with a small sigh, resting from her knitting for a moment. 'I should so love to introduce something to delight the eye. Like those Chinese wall-paintings you described. But Ambrose would never allow it. He'd call it ostentatious, overly indulgent.'

'Marble Hill House is just a showpiece, not a place where one could ever really feel at ease,' I said. 'You are blessed with a comfortable home. But I have to say that those Chinese designs did remind me of something.'

'What is that, dearest?' I looked at the top of her dear head bent again over her work, and almost faltered, fearing to risk antagonising one of the people most dear to me in all the world. But if I stopped now I would never find the truth.

'When we were admiring the wallpaper, it reminded me so much of the silk I showed you, the one with the pagoda design. And would you believe it,' I pressed on, 'we discovered that Henrietta Howard has a gown made of the very same silk.'

She stopped to pick up a dropped stitch. 'I'm sorry, I do not understand your meaning. Why is that so surprising?'

How should I answer? It felt as though I was about to blunder into a thicket, hacking forward without any notion of what dangers it might pose, or where it might end. Would it not be better simply to turn back along the clearer, well-trodden paths of our relationship, rather than pressing on into the unknown? I took a deep breath.

'Mr Garrick told us that Henrietta probably had several children by the king. She fostered two of them with her brother, so they believe that she is their aunt. Can you see the parallel? That is just what we have done, between us?'

Needles clicked loudly in the silence and then, when she spoke, her voice was calm and soft.

'I wish you would not speak of this, Agnes. Have we not agreed? And anyway, I cannot see the relevance.'

'What about the other children? Whatever happened to them?'

'What others?'

'The babies she did not keep. She must have given them away to someone, somewhere.'

Her forehead furrowed with irritation. '*What* babies? Really, your riddling is beginning to try my patience.'

'It is a riddle to me too, dearest sister, one that I have been trying to unravel ever since I found that silk. Our mother left me at the Hospital with a piece of Henrietta's silk gown as a token. I have since learned that silk was woven under the cloak of greatest secrecy, and the merchant dealing with it was under strict instructions to hand over every piece of it and not to show the design to anyone. So who else could have a piece of it, except Henrietta?'

'What merchant is this?' Her eyes snapped up, holding mine in a gaze so piercing it was almost painful.

'The one who went bankrupt, whose silks were in the auction.'

She scoffed. 'It doesn't sound so secret to me, when you were able to buy a piece of it.' She rose suddenly, throwing down her knitting. 'I am tired of this conversation, Agnes. I cannot understand why you are telling me, or where it is leading.'

'Did you know Henrietta Howard?' I blurted.

'Now you're just being silly.'

'I think she might have been your mother, Louisa.'

'For heaven's sake.' She went to the door and closed it, before turning back to me.

'To be perfectly honest I am beginning to fear for your sanity, Agnes. Are you *actually* suggesting that you and I are the illegitimate children of the king's mistress? I've never heard such poppycock. You seem to have become obsessed with this piece of silk and have concocted this fantasy on the basis of some dubious information about a token, of which you have no proof whatsoever. So what if the silk was Henrietta Howard's? That has no relevance to me, or to you, or to anyone else in our family.' She shook her head, exasperated. 'Are we not happy to have found each other?'

I nodded.

'Is Peter a happy, contented boy, growing up in a loving family?'

'Yes, Louisa, he is.'

'Do you have a successful business and good friends in London?'

A tear formed and trickled down my cheek.

'Then please, dearest Agnes, be content with what we have.' She leaned down to squeeze my hand. 'Now, I am going to make some hot milk for Ambrose before we retire to bed. Would you like some?'

I knew of course that she was right: why could I not learn to cherish every happy moment, rather than always searching after that missing piece of the jigsaw? Being part of a family – however imperfect or incomplete – is a very great blessing. And as I was about to discover, one that can so quickly be torn away.

22

Satin: a silk with a glazed surface created using many threads of the warp overlaying the weft.

On my return to London Mrs T. greeted me with an out-pouring of woes: late deliveries of a certain important length of satin, a shortage of silk thread of the correct colour for an urgent job and an irate customer who had returned her gown torn after a single outing, claiming it to have been the fault of shoddy sewing.

Over the past few years I have trained myself not to become flustered by such irritations. In fact there is great satisfaction to be gained through placating a complaining customer, or making a recalcitrant supplier understand that your order *must* be met, and now. Rent must be paid, sup-pliers' overdue invoices to satisfy and, most importantly of all, wages to find.

I spent the following week sorting out the accounts; there is nothing like applying one's brain to the black and white facts that are numbers, ensuring that the books are bal-anced, for sorting out your priorities. Five people – Mrs T. and the four seamstresses – rely on me for their livelihoods, not to mention the legion of children and elderly relatives who depend in turn on their income.

And all the while new customers arrived requesting outfits for the summer season at Bath and elsewhere. On Wednesday, Eva Garrick appeared at our doorstep and we enjoyed a most lively afternoon considering what she might wear – gowns that were both flattering and pretty – to accompany her husband at the various events of his Shakespeare Pageant. Having previously been so much in awe of her, I realised partway through our meeting that she was talking to me as you would a friend, sharing gossip and jokes.

Mrs T. and the seamstresses were greatly impressed when I told them who she was.

'Could she get us tickets to see Mr Garrick on the stage?' they all wanted to know.

As ever, tastes in fashion turned on a penny: waistlines were rising, petticoats disappearing, hoops almost vanished. Sleeve lace must be simpler, necklines lower and more revealing, except for married ladies, of course. A less fussy, more natural look in both line and fabric design seemed an unstoppable trend, but it was a rare sort of customer, the more adventurous types only, who were prepared to embrace it entirely. Some even spoke of the day when stays could be abandoned, though I would eat my hat if this occurred in my lifetime.

'Why would one want to reveal one's untamed curves, darling? Mine are in all the wrong places,' one particularly pompous customer pronounced. Thereafter the phrase 'all the wrong places' was bandied about the sewing room as humorous invective, especially when the seamstresses were trying to piece a particularly demanding fit of bodice or sleeve.

Three weeks passed in almost continuous work, save for a couple of visits from Anna, whose own waist seemed to expand by the day. I designed two gowns for her with high waistlines so that she did not have to wear stays, and made them up in soft cambric.

'At last I can breathe,' she sighed gratefully as I tied the laces at the back, subtly concealed beneath a flattering false cape. 'You're a miracle worker, Charlotte. Why has no one ever thought of designing for expectant mothers before now?'

It set me thinking. Married women spend much of their lives with child, so why should they be expected to conceal their condition or even, as their time approaches, to remain hidden from society? Was their shape something to be ashamed of, somehow offensive to the eyes of men or indeed their fellow women? Surely, the creation of a new life was something to be celebrated?

I determined that the next time a customer came to us asking for a gown to be altered to allow for their expanding belly I would show them my designs for Anna. Of such are small revolutions made, I told myself. Although I rather doubted that it would single-handedly change society's expectations, at least it might make life a little more comfortable for women undertaking the most important task in the world.

Then, late on a Friday afternoon just as we were shutting up shop, she arrived in a state of great distress, her face flushed and eyes reddened from weeping. As I unlocked and opened the door she stumbled into the showroom and fell into my arms. I pulled over a chair and sat her down at once.

'My goodness, what ails you? Not the baby?'

She struggled for breath. 'It's my father . . . I must go . . .'

'Theodore? He is unwell again?'

She leaned against me, clutching at my arms and sobbing afresh. 'Oh Charlotte . . . I cannot bear it . . .'

'Is he . . . ?' I asked, unwilling to say the dread word.

'No, but the doctor says we must prepare for the worst.' She held out a crumpled letter, signed by Theodore's neighbour Mary Marshall. Quickly scanning it, I caught the words: 'We may not have long.'

'Of course you must go to Suffolk at once, and I shall accompany you. That is what I promised,' I said, already starting to plan, in my head, how to persuade Mrs T. to cover for me once more, so soon after my recent absence. But this was a matter of life and death.

At eight o'clock the following morning, just as I was about to leave to meet Anna at the coach stop as we had arranged, there was an urgent hammering at the front door. It was Henri, grey-faced and dishevelled.

'You must come, Charlotte. She is asking for you,' he gasped, grabbing my hand.

'What, who? Now, slowly. Is it her father?'

'No, not him. It is Anna. The pains have started.'

'But it is long before her time.' I know little about childbirth but had heard that if a mother suffered a terrible shock it might bring on a baby too early.

'She has been suffering all night, crying out with the agony. And there is blood, lots of it.' He shuddered. 'She is scared, Charlotte. You know what happened to her mama?'

'But she is strong, Henri. Have you called the midwife?'

'She's just arrived. But Anna wants you. Can you come?'

'Of course, we shall go at once. Just let me get my cape.'

He set off at such a pace through streets already busy with carts and carriages, shoppers and traders that I had to run to keep up with him. Anna's agony could be heard from several doors away. As we entered Wood Street, women were already out on their doorsteps, wringing their hands and whispering their sympathies to Henri as we passed.

Mariette appeared at the doorway carrying little Jean, who was clutching his favourite cloth rabbit. 'We are going to see grand mama, aren't we? We're going to have a lovely day, and then later perhaps we will meet your new sister or brother.'

Henri leaned forward to kiss his son. 'Be good, little one,' he said, adding, 'We really appreciate this, Mariette.'

'Is there any further news of Theodore?' she asked.

He shook his head. 'Not since the letter yesterday that put Anna into such a spin.'

'Then we must pray for both of them,' she said.

The Vendome house is normally such a welcoming place, full of cheerful industry and friendship. But this day the usually bright and convivial atmosphere was cloaked with the heavy weight of anxiety. As we passed the parlour door I saw that Monsieur Lavalle was slumped in his usual chair beside the empty fireplace. He barely lifted his head to acknowledge me.

'It's been a long night for the old man,' Henri whispered.

Breakfast was laid in the dining room, apparently untouched. Not even the normally ravenous apprentices or
the drawboy, it seemed, could summon any appetite. By
this time of the morning we would expect to hear the
familiar thud of the looms from the weaving loft above, but
it was silent. Perhaps Henri had told them to go out for the
day? No one could have the heart to continue their everyday tasks while such a drama was taking place.

As if Anna's cries were not distressing enough, we
encountered cook descending the stairs carrying a bowl of
bloodied red towels. 'The mistress is calling for you, Monsieur Vendome,' she puffed. 'Just going to boil more water.'
We hurried upwards to Anna's chamber.

As we reached the door a formidable figure who I presumed to be the midwife rushed to block our entry. 'Sorry,
master,' she said. 'The birthing room is no place for a man.'

'But cannot I even see her?' Henri protested.

'Be assured we are taking the very best care of your wife,'
she said firmly. 'Please wait downstairs until we call you.'
He stepped away reluctantly, nudging me forward. 'Then
you must allow our friend Miss Amesbury to go in. Anna
has been calling for her.'

'Are you the person she calls Charlotte?'

'I am, madam. Please . . .'

We were interrupted by a most chilling sound, a deep
baying howl like an animal in the deepest distress; the sort
you would hope never to hear from any living being. As the
midwife rushed back into the room, I followed. My dearest
friend was almost unrecognisable: her face contorted and
grey in hue; her body writhing in agony. The sheets were
streaked with red.

'Listen Anna, it's me, Charlotte,' I said, rushing to her side and clasping her hand. 'Squeeze tight if it helps.'

Her eyes turned, wide with fear. 'Save me, Charlotte. I think I'm dying.'

'You are *not* going to die, Anna. This baby will be born soon, and you are in good hands.' The clearest memory leapt into my head: the low, reassuring voice of the nun as she helped me to deliver Peter. 'Breathe slowly and deeply, if you can. Listen to me, follow what I do: in . . . out . . . in . . . out. That's it, keep going like that.'

When the spasm passed I took a cup from the bedside table and offered her a sip of water before the next arrived. Then I took up a clean towel, dipped it into the ewer and wiped the sweat from her forehead.

'Just get this baby out. Get it out,' she hollered, dissolving into pitiful sobs. 'I don't want to die.'

Between each pain I tried to comfort her, telling her that she was doing well, that the baby would soon be born, that she would be right as rain. But as time went by and the midwife's face became increasingly anxious, I began to doubt my words. Anna's cries became weaker, she closed her eyes and her face seemed to blanch yet whiter, as though all the blood in her skin had simply leaked away.

I was beginning to fear the worst when her poor battered body seemed to contort again, and the midwife peered between her legs, shouting. 'I can see the head. Push now, missus. Push as hard as you can. It's nearly here now.'

Anna revived slightly, trying to summon the strength for this last onslaught, before giving up. 'I can't,' she groaned. 'I can't do it.' She closed her eyes again and seemed to drift from consciousness.

'For heaven's sake, isn't there anything you can do to save her?' I shouted. 'She's slipping away.'

My plea seemed to galvanise the midwife into action. She ripped away the bedclothes and, placing her palms at the top of Anna's stomach, began to press downwards with such force that her muscles bulged. Then she moved her hands to either side of the bump, massaging the muscles beneath.

'Come,' she ordered. 'Do this for me.' She placed my hands into position, covering them with her own to demonstrate the pressure required; so fierce that I feared the baby beneath must be squeezed half to death. She returned to the end of the bed and to my horror seemed to thrust her hand right inside my poor friend's body. All the while, she urged me to push now, push again, harder.

'Let the child die if you must, please God,' I prayed silently, sweating from the effort of following her instructions. 'But please, in your greatest mercy, spare the life of my friend.'

I seemed to lose all track of time, but the next thing I knew was the midwife's voice. 'There we go,' she said, holding up a scrap of blue and bloodied flesh, like a tiny skinned rabbit.

'It's a girl.'

She ran her fingers inside the tiny mouth and then proceeded to whack it firmly on the back, several times. The scrap jerked, limp and lifeless. She laid it down and, placing her mouth over the little face, blew into it with her own breath. I gaped, astonished, as with each puff the tiny ribs rose and fell beneath the almost translucent skin. After a few breaths, the skin began to take on a pinker tinge. She stood back and waited for what seemed like an eternity.

And then, such joy! The child coughed and gave a tiny mew, like a newborn kitten.

'Good girl.' Swiftly and expertly swaddling it in a towel, she handed it to me. 'Here, hold her while I try to stop this bleeding.'

It seemed barely credible that such a tiny creature could sustain life. But she continued to mew, so for the moment she was alive. 'Wake up, Anna, please,' I said. 'Wake up! Open your eyes and see. You have a beautiful baby daughter.'

There was no response. I felt for a pulse at her neck and could feel it beating, but only faintly. Desperate now, I splashed water onto her face, gently slapping her cheeks. Her eyelids fluttered, just once, but after that she seemed to drift into a deeper sleep. Now I really feared for the worst.

The midwife lifted what looked like a great lump of liver, wrapping it into a towel and placing it aside. 'Now we should be able to stem that bleeding,' she said. 'But best get the husband to call their pastor, just in case.'

Henri came running as I called for him. 'You have a beautiful baby girl,' I said, showing him the tiny bundle.

'A girl? She's alive?' He peered into the miniature face, no bigger than a puckered crab apple, and tears began to course down his cheeks. 'But Anna . . . ?'

'She has lost a lot of blood. The midwife says we should call the pastor.'

'The pastor? *Bon dieu.*' The expression of utter anguish in Henri's eyes will stay with me forever. He handed the baby back and kneeled by the bed, taking the limp body of his wife in his arms, placing his head on her chest. 'Don't leave me, Anna, I love you so much. And I shall not be able to go on without you,' he keened, looking around with desperate eyes. 'For God's sake, don't let her die.'

The midwife was busying herself pulling away the bloodied sheets, piling them into a corner. 'She's stopped bleeding,' she said. 'That's a good sign.'

'And she is still breathing. We must pray for the best,' I said, kneeling beside him. 'Here, take your daughter, hold her close. The cries might help to bring her round.'

'Open your eyes, Anna my darling, look at what we have.' Henri held the little bundle close to his wife's cheek so that she might hear its tiny whimpers. 'Wake up and say hello to our beautiful daughter.'

He pulled aside the fabric to more clearly reveal the baby's angry red face. Her mewing was growing louder by the moment. This child was determined to live.

'The baby must be fed, Henri. I'll send for a wet nurse, shall I?'

He nodded, gratefully. 'And can you ask for the pastor so she can be christened? I want to call her Anna.'

23

Drugget: a coarse woollen fabric, felted or woven, self-coloured or printed on one side, sometimes corded but usually plain.

Henri, Mariette, Clothilde and I took turns to hold vigil at Anna's bedside twenty-four hours a day. Afternoon blurred into night, and dawn arrived once more. Cook worked tirelessly to ply us with food, exhorting us to 'keep up your own strength to help the missus'. But none of us could summon much appetite.

She brought nutritious broths that we attempted to drip into Anna's mouth with little success. She remained motionless, her face pale as a corpse, the breath barely fluttering in her chest. But her heart was still beating.

Despite her tiny frame, and against all our expectations, the baby continued to live. She was too weak to suck, so the wet nurse dribbled milk into her mouth until, after two anxious days, the little mite began to move her jaws and pucker her lips. At last she was persuaded to suckle; just a few seconds at first, but for longer each time as she grew in strength. We encouraged the nurse to feed the baby in Anna's chamber so that she might hear her daughter's mewling, or somehow sense her presence.

On the third day Anna's condition worsened, her poor abused body alternately racked with the shakes and then becoming hot and restless. The doctor shook his head. 'Childbed fever,' he muttered. 'Often fatal, I am afraid. But we will do our best.' He returned to administer various foul-smelling potions into her mouth and her nether parts, and cupped the skin of her belly to make it blister. Before he left, he recommended cooling her fevers with wet flannels and opening the windows during daytime, allowing sunshine and fresh air into the room.

When Clothilde questioned this advice he said, 'In the old past we used to keep fever patients in darkness and prevent vapours from entering the room. But there is new thinking these days, and I now tend to the view that fresh air is good for them, so long as they are well wrapped and do not become chilled.'

News of Anna's perilous condition spread throughout the community, and Monsieur Lavalle was kept busy downstairs as a procession of friends and family, fellow master weavers, journeymen, members of the French church and even grand mercers with their elegant wives arrived on the doorstep at Wood Street to pay their respects.

Anna's aunt Sarah came, along with her daughter, neither of whom I had seen for several years. Lizzie is a lively soul and a great devotee of the latest fashions; she greeted me with genuine pleasure, but Sarah appeared uncomfortable. She has never really approved of Anna's marriage to a Frenchman and now seemed unconvinced that he could provide her niece with the best care.

'You have engaged a *proper* physician, I hope?' she said, more than once. 'We have a very good man, Lord Harley.

You must have heard of him? He was Lord Mayor a couple of years ago. We cannot do with second best; Anna is so precious to us. His leeching has saved the life of many a fever patient. Let us pay for him to come to you.'

Henri, ignoring her patronising tone, was admirably firm. 'Thank you for your kind offer, Mrs Sadler. But Anna is receiving excellent care from a highly qualified French surgeon with all the latest treatments at his disposal. He has our absolute confidence.' Shortly afterwards she hurried Lizzie away.

Overhearing Henri's conversations with business colleagues was bittersweet. I had never before fully appreciated the respect held in the industry for my friend's talents. After practising for just a few years, her artistry is already much sought after. 'She would be a great loss,' one told him. 'I declare your wife's designs have been responsible for introducing the principles of painting to the loom. And she has surely helped to establish our excellent reputation for English silks around the world.' I repeated the compliment word for word into Anna's ear, hoping that, should she be able to hear me, such appreciation might hearten her and give her strength to fight for life.

Every ounce of my energy was spent either at the bedside or otherwise supporting Henri in any way possible. Each day I would dash back to the shop for at least a few hours to make sure that Mrs T. was coping, lending my hand to any especially urgent tasks if needed. Everything else went on hold. After seven days, as Anna remained in a sort of half-life, her heart beating and chest rising and falling but otherwise lost to the world, a letter came from Suffolk.

'Listen to this wonderful news,' I whispered to her. 'Your father has rallied. He is sitting up in bed, taking food and talking of getting up and going for a short walk tomorrow. And he has been asking about you. He wants to see you, little Jean and the baby too, as soon as you can gather your strength. So you have got to get better for him. Give me a smile, just to show you have heard me, Anna, please. Please?'

Even this brought no response.

⁂

Her fever worsened, but by some means of inner strength, we knew not how, she clung to life.

It was early morning on the first day of June as I set out for Wood Street, and the sun was already burning in the bluest of heavens. Summer had truly arrived. But none of this could lighten the deep, impenetrable darkness in my heart. Life without my best friend was unimaginable. Yet somehow I needed to find the strength to face it.

I had called on God countless times over the past few weeks but even though I support the morality of Christ's teachings, I cannot bring myself to become a regular churchgoer. The sight of so many hypocrites in one place – puffed-up society worthies parading their virtue, when you know full well that their daily lives are full of sin and deception – tends me to queasiness.

Although I loved to sing in the Hospital chapel as a child, the smell of musty prayer books brings back too many memories: of hours on my knees enduring the pain of unforgiving stone while praying to some unseen god for forgiveness from sins I had never been aware of committing.

Sundays at the Manor were no day of rest. We maids would be up at the crack of dawn, lighting the fires that would heat hot stones ready to be lugged in wheelbarrows to the church to warm the cosy box pews where family members would sit in comfort while we shivered on rough benches at the back of the church, frozen half to death in the draught from the doorway.

In church at least I was free from Tobias, but he would always sneak a quick wink at me, or even whisper as he passed, 'I'll be seeing you later, pretty miss.' After the service we would be treated to the sight of him conversing with the vicar, beaming with righteousness even though to my eyes he was the incarnation of the devil.

At Westford Abbots the Sabbath inevitably entails sitting with my sister and Peter in our allotted pew right below the pulpit, trying to prop open my eyes as Ambrose drones on with one of his interminable sermons. He's been known to preach for an hour or even more if the spirit takes him. Sometimes he becomes, as he puts it, 'alight with God's flame', turning fierce eyes upon the congregation and declaiming in a loud and portentous voice about the perils of sin.

There is a certain entertainment to be had in watching the pulpit rock as he flails his arms, setting the spiders trembling in their cobwebs. It is all I can do to suppress the giggles as his face reddens, the blue veins protrude like snakes about his neck and his eyes roll up in their sockets as he hollers entreaties to God for mercy on us weak and evil humankind.

Even long after the service is ended he remains on fire, engaging parishioners in animated conversations at the church door as they attempt to inch away to the warm homes and dinners awaiting them. His mood will continue throughout Sunday lunch at the vicarage. If anyone else tries to introduce another topic he will simply talk over them. We sit in silence listening to a reprise of today's hellfire sermon right there at the table, our plates scraped clean while his remains barely touched.

On these occasions I keep my eyes to my lap, hardly daring to look up for fear of incurring the worst of my brother-in-law's wrath.

So although churchgoing holds no attraction for me, on this clear June day the great white spire of Christ Church towered above me, glowing in the sunshine like a beacon, and something drew my feet towards the wide stone steps that lead up to its porch.

It was here, Anna had once told me, that she'd had her first full conversation with Henri, having spied him descending the organ stairs. She'd taken him for the organ-ist but he'd explained that he was just helping out at this church – not his own – heaving the bellows for the great organ. It was on that day, she said, that she fell in love with his teasing grin and grew certain, somewhere deep in her heart, that he would become important in her life.

I stood at the top of the steps, in the shadow of one of the great columns supporting the porch, so wide that two people could not clasp hands around them, and surveyed the scene before me: the heart of Spitalfields. Ahead were the arches of the market, already lively even at this early hour with traders setting up their stalls. To my left was the churchyard, almost filled with graves even though the church has been built but thirty years. Beyond the low workshops of White Row and Rose Lane lay the green of the tenterground, where silk finishers stretch out the woven cloth, still damp after fulling, hooking it onto frames so that it will dry out flat and square.

All around were streets of tall houses with weavers' lofts built into roof spaces, with wide windows set to catch every glimmer of daylight. From my raised vantage point on the church porch I was almost on a level with those rooftops and could hear the clack-clack of shuttles from the open casements as journeymen settled down to their looms.

Just down to my right along Wood Street lay my friend in her chamber, clinging to life by a thread. The thought compelled me forwards. Although the church door was closed and the round iron handle heavy as a sack of stones, something gave me the strength to lift and turn it. When I leaned on it, the door gave way with a long groan.

I had forgotten how enormous the interior of the church is, larger by far than it appears from the outside. That morning it was luminous, almost dazzling, as the sunshine poured in through the east windows. Soaring columns stretched dizzyingly upwards, supporting rows of barrel vaults on either side, and the detail of the ornate ceiling, picked out in gold, glistened in the light reflected from the white walls. This sight alone is so awe-inspiring that it can make you believe that you are in the presence of something or someone greater than yourself. And perhaps, just perhaps, you are. Certainly, on that day, I felt it.

Despite the racket in the busy streets outside, when I closed the church door behind me all was complete silence, as though I had fallen suddenly deaf. When I cleared my throat, the sound seemed to echo around the vast space. I walked forward, sat down in the back row of the pews and slipped onto my knees.

Dear Lord, I do not usually ask much of you, but please, please, bring Anna back to us, to her family, Theodore, Jane, Henri and the two babies. She is like a second sister to me, and I do not know how we will go on living if she leaves us.

My eyes lifted to the altar, but the statue of Christ on the cross reminded me too much of Anna's ravaged body not more than a few hundred yards away. I closed them again. It may have been a few minutes or more, but the next thing I knew was a hand on my shoulder and a man's voice, deep and gentle. 'Would you like me to pray with you, madam?' I looked up to see a priest, old, white-bearded and bald-headed. Folding his black skirt around his knees, he slid into the pew beside me. 'I sense you are in fear of losing someone.'

How did he know? Had I spoken out loud? Or did his faith give him mind-reading powers? It was unnerving. I sat back onto the pew and reached into my pocket for a handkerchief to dry the tears. 'I thank you for your concern, sir. But I must be on my way now.'

He was unfazed. 'Then I will pray on your behalf, if you will permit me. What is their name?'

'Anna,' I said. 'And her daughter, also Anna.'

It had been arranged that I would take over the bed watch from Clothilde that morning, but just as I entered the house we heard her calling: '*Viens vite.* She is awake.'

Everyone rushed to the bedside: Henri, Mariette, Monsieur Lavalle and even cook. The apprentices were turned away, for there was no room in the chamber once we had all crowded in. Sure enough, Anna's eyes were open, dark pools in the sockets sunk deep in her skeletal face. I thought of the old priest in the church, whispering to his God. Was this his doing?

Henri fell to his knees, clasping her hand. 'Thank the good Lord. You are back with us.'

'Henri?' Her words were slurred and so faint that everyone in the room held their breath. 'My darling. Where have you been?'

'I have been at your side. You have been unwell for days.' Mariette took my arm and squeezed it. Anna tried to push herself up, but Henri stayed her with a gentle hand.

'Lie still, sweetheart. You are very weak and must take some of cook's delicious broth to gain strength.'

She frowned. 'I have been dreaming of a kitten,' she murmured. 'I could hear it mewing, poor thing. I hope it is all right.' The wet nurse came forward with the baby, handing her to Henri who held her up for Anna to see. 'My baby? It's alive?'

The midwife had given the chances of survival beyond a week as 'less than one in four' and yet now, two weeks later, that scrap of flesh looked like a proper baby. She was still tiny as a doll but her cheeks had filled out, and her skin was a normal colour. Her appetite grew stronger by the day and with it her cry, which echoed throughout the house at all hours.

'Look at our lovely daughter, dearest wife. She is still

small but her hold on life is strong. We have named her after you.'

Anna tried to reach out to the child, but she had no strength. I leaned forward and made a crook of her arm, indicating to Henri that he should place Baby there. 'My beautiful girl,' she whispered. 'Oh, Henri, what a miracle.'

She lifted her gaze. 'Goodness, why are you all here in my chamber?'

'We have been here all the time,' I said. 'It is just you who went away, dearest. We feared that we might lose you.'

'Went away?'

'You have been asleep for many days,' Henri said gently. 'But thank the Lord you have woken and come back to us.'

'Where is Jean?'

Moments later cook arrived with the boy, who immediately ran to the bedside, reaching out his fat little arms and crying, 'Maman!' Henri lifted him onto his knee and held him forward so that he could kiss his mother's cheek. The little family was reunited again, complete.

Descending the stairs, my footsteps felt light as air.

When I got home, on my table was a letter from Louisa, enclosing a very competent drawing of the church and the yew trees signed by Peter, and wishing me a happy birthday. It was today, and I had completely forgotten it. But now when it comes around each year, I remember that it is also the day when my best friend returned to life.

24

Mantua: a gown only for the most formal occasions; open-fronted with a train looped up to reveal a petticoat of contrasting silk or lawn, worn with a hooped underskirt (not recommended for younger ladies).

My own life returned to normal, although not entirely. In subtle ways that only became apparent over the coming weeks, Anna's trials had left me altered. Not so much in my body, although it felt so weary much of the time, but in my spirit.

I continued to visit her daily, marvelling at how she had survived two such terrible assaults: the horrific birth and the ravaging fever. Within two days she was sitting up and taking small meals, and by the end of the week she managed to take a few small steps unaided. The good news about her father's recovery cheered her, made her determined to gain strength for him. Her face, although still pale as paper, lit with smiles for every visitor and in time the hint of a bloom returned to her cheeks.

The weather remained calm and bright. We opened the windows of her chamber and placed a comfortable chair so that it would catch the sun. She spent many hours there cradling the baby and sometimes with Jean on her lap, too. Her own milk returned slowly, but the wet nurse remained a constant figure in the house for several weeks and the baby seemed to thrive on this double diet. At just under four weeks old, although still tiny, she no longer felt like a china doll that might break at any moment.

For much of the time she was either feeding or sleeping but sometimes she would open her deep, dark blue eyes for several minutes, gazing at me with a little frown as though trying to work out who I was. I smiled, and her mouth moved almost as though she was trying to mimic my expression. 'Look, she's smiling,' I said. 'Or is it just indigestion?'

Anna leaned over to look. 'She's saying she knows you from somewhere.'

'But she's not entirely sure how I fit into this big confusing world.'

'Well, I can tell you. Henri and I have agreed that we would like to change her name. I know that it is traditional, but I think it might be confusing to have a daughter called the same as her mother.' She paused, looking directly into my eyes. 'So we are going to call her Charlotte.'

'After me?'

'Who else, you dolt?' she said, laughing.

'Oh my dearest, I'm speechless. Thank you. So much.'

'Thank *you*, Auntie Charlotte. Henri told me what a steadfast support you were throughout my illness. He said you were the first to hold her when she was just a little scrap clinging onto life, and in some curious way I feel that makes her partly your child too. I know you are not a churchgoer but we hope you will also agree to be her god-mother, and be a big part of her life in years to come.'

'Of course, I would be greatly flattered,' I said, my voice breaking. 'I haven't told you this, but the day you opened your eyes for the first time after your illness, I had just come from Christ Church.'

'You went to church?'

'To pray for your life. A priest said he would add his prayers to mine.'

She laughed. 'You are full of surprises, Charlotte. I thought you disliked churches.'

'I do, usually. But something drew me in, that day. I felt so helpless, desperate about the thought of losing you.'

'So it's Him up there I have to thank for my recovery, is it?'

'And for the little lady, I suppose,' I said, returning my eyes to the baby's still quizzical gaze. 'Hello, baby Charlotte. We're going to have some fun together, you and me.'

'More than that, my dear friend, I want her to be a strong, independent woman just like you,' Anna said. 'Someone who is confident in herself, and her place in the world.'

Henri came in then, with Jean, and the conversation moved on. Only later, in my own room, did I remember her words. Confident, sure of my place? I must be a better actor than Mr Garrick to have the world so well and truly fooled.

But was that such a bad thing? I recalled what he had recited at Jane Hogarth's Easter supper: *All the world's a stage, and all the men and women merely players.* Perhaps I had learned my part so well that it had become the real me. We are all trying to become the people we would like to be, or what is expected of us. We are all of us, in some small way, acting. My part in this play is *costumière*. I make costumes: clothes worn by people to make them look like the person they want to be. I have gained the confidence, now, to create the clothes that I know people will enjoy wearing, clothing that will make them feel good about themselves.

One afternoon when I arrived back from Wood Street, Mrs T. told me of a new customer who had visited the shop in my absence. 'A right pretentious little madam,' she said. 'Wanted this and that and t'other and all by tomorrow. I told her she'd have to come back another day to see you but if she don't it'll be a fortunate escape. I reckon she'd be more trouble than she's worth.'

'Did you get her name?'

'Lady Margaret Montagu. Posh enough name, don't you think. But her manners were from the gutter,' she scoffed.

A few days later the lady returned to the shop and within moments I found myself sympathising with Mrs Taylor. Lady Margaret, a young married woman of no more than twenty-five years in age, had very fixed ideas: she wanted a day dress in this silk and that design, an evening gown in that brocaded satin and that design. And yet, as we took tea and talked a little more, I began to sense that hiding beneath the haughty veneer was a young woman who did not really know herself at all.

She was not blessed with great beauty: a little too tall, her face too long, her curves what are referred to in the trade as 'understated'. Her complexion was fine, though, and her hands elegant. She had potential. But her ideas were hopelessly old-fashioned: probably those that her mother, an elder sister, or mother-in-law had instilled or even insisted upon. None of the mantua designs she had chosen would do her any favours: they would render her the look of a maiden aunt, overly grand and far too ostentatious for her youth.

I showed her a magazine of the latest fashions that my friend the printer had recently lent me – yes, just as he'd prophesied, these publications had become all the rage. 'A young lady would not be expected to wear hoops or rumps these days, my dear,' I said. 'But look at the elegant shape these *fourreaux* pleats can provide, balanced at the front of the bodice by this charming bow. From the side view it creates such an elegant curve, just as Mr Hogarth described as the essence of beauty.'

An hour went by as I sketched new designs for her to consider. Each time she demurred, deferring to her original ideas. At length I relented, consenting to make up what she had asked for. I took her measurements and she left, satis-fied for the moment. But I knew in my heart that she would not be so pleased when she saw herself transformed into a shapeless, charmless version of her maiden aunt. Most likely many hours of further work would then be required, for no extra payment, making the alterations she would undoubtedly demand. Worst of all, she would be disinclined to recommend us to her friends.

We could not ignore what our customer had asked for, but we changed it subtly in every way: in the shape and length of the skirt, the neckline, the lace ruffles at the sleeves. We added boning to the bodice to give her a shapelier upper line than could ever be achieved with stays, and bold gatherings of the petticoat to emphasise her waistline. Most daring of all, we chose silks of a delicate design and colourway, floral on a plain pale ground, perfect for a lively young woman of her class.

All was completed just a day before the first fitting and I could sense among the seamstresses a collective holding of breath when she arrived. She tried on the evening gown first. It fitted beautifully and already I could see the transformation. But would she like it? There is usually a small frisson of nerves when you turn the looking glass and a lady sees herself for the first time in a new gown, but this time my heart was in my mouth. Lady Montagu moved in influential circles and although she did not appreciate it herself, her opinion was important.

'My goodness,' she breathed. 'Is that really me?'

Indeed it was: a shapely young woman whose face, lit up as it was with a mixture of astonishment and delight, could almost be called beautiful. She posed and twirled before the glass for several minutes, before planting a kiss on my cheek. 'Miss Charlotte, you are a miracle worker,' she proclaimed.

That evening, after a modest meal of bread and cheese with a cup of hot broth, I climbed the stairs to my room, intending to immerse myself in a new novel, a gift from Louisa the previous Christmas that had lain neglected for months. Now I had some time for myself to enjoy it.

When I pushed aside a pile of papers from the table to make space for my tray, a small package slipped to the floor and fell open, its contents glittering in the candlelight. In the dramatic events of the past few weeks, I had forgotten all about it. The terror of nearly losing my best friend had become my uppermost concern and the pagoda silk meant nothing to me now. The birds and trees of the design looked plain and ordinary to my eyes, the scent of lavender barely detectable.

The desperation to find my mother that had gripped me like a kind of madness had gone. Poor thing, she lived in such poverty that she'd been forced to give up two daughters and had probably died young. Who cared how she'd come by the silk? I would probably never find out, but it barely mattered any more.

I am what I am, defined by what I do each day, the people I count as friends, and the ways in which I can help people, I said to myself. *I am good at my job, I run a successful business on my own account, and have no need of a husband. My past is far behind me, and is really of no consequence to me today. I must put aside my search for my mother. What matters now is the future, and that is in the hands of children: Peter, Jean and little Charlotte. They must be my focus now.* It sounds so simple recounting it now but it felt like an important revelation, a major shift in my life. I felt free, at last.

But life has a habit of changing everything. The following morning I received an unexpected visit.

25

Lawn: a very fine linen in plain weave using a fine high thread count resulting in a silky feel.

It was mid-morning, and we were all busy in the sewing room when I heard the bell on the shop door tinkle. I was ankle-deep in gauze and sequins, working on a dress for Amelia Arbuthnot's first ball at the Assembly Rooms in Bath just six weeks hence.

'Let me go, Miss C.,' Sarah said. 'It's probably just the post boy.'

I gladly accepted her offer, but it was just moments before she came puffing upstairs, wide-eyed. 'You have some, erm, interesting visitors, Miss Charlotte,' she said. 'They've asked specifically for you. A personal matter, they said.'

'Interesting? Whatever do you mean, Sarah?'

'They're . . .'

She blushed, and Mrs T. chimed in. 'Spit it out, girl.'

Sarah studied her feet and said, quietly, 'They're dark people, ma'am. Of the skin, I mean. Exotic-looking. But not slaves or beggars, like you usually see those types.' She looked up now, smiling. 'These ones are well dressed and polite. They seemed ever so nice. And they're most keen to see you, Miss Charlotte.'

'A couple? A man and a woman?'

'With a baby, ma'am.'

There was no one among my acquaintance as she had described, but I hastened downstairs anyway, my curiosity burning, thinking that perhaps it was some friends recommended by the Garricks, or the Hogarths. As I entered the room I saw a handsome young couple, plainly dressed but both with a fine, proud bearing. The man was in the uniform of a sailor, the lady in a calico gown with just a touch of lace, and a lawn shawl drawn modestly across her shoulders. In her arms was a large bundle.

I did not recognise them at all, until the young woman said: 'Miss Charlotte? Do you remember me? I am Pearl Matembe.' Her face lit up with the sweetest, most beautiful smile I had ever seen. The young man said, 'My name is Femi. I am pleased to meet you.'

She went on: 'You were so kind to me in the street that day, and I have never forgotten you, Miss Charlotte. And look, here is my baby.' She peeled back the swaddling to reveal the face of a chubby-cheeked cupid, sleeping peacefully.

Surely it could not be? That desperate beggar, clad in rags, who begged me to take her baby? The girl who had left her child on the steps of the Hospital, according to Jane, with my note tucked into its blanket? But yes, now that I looked again, it was that same girl.

'Goodness gracious. Forgive me for not recognising you at first, Miss Matembe, or is it Mrs?' I said, glancing at the boy beside her.

She blushed. 'Oh no, this is my brother.'

'She found me,' he said, simply.

'And it seems your fortunes have turned since we last met,' I said. 'And may I ask, is this that same . . .'

'He is alive because of you, Miss Charlotte. I went to get him back. We just came to thank you.'

'You reclaimed him from the Hospital?'

She nodded, looking down at the baby with an expression of such adoration that my heart overflowed just to witness it. For a few long seconds we all watched the child, mesmerised by his angelic face.

'Well, we don't want to keep you,' the boy said, at last. 'I know you must be very busy.' He gestured around the room, towards the dressed dummies in the window, the rolls of fabric on the counter. 'You have a fine place here.'

I could not let them go so soon. 'I am not so busy that I cannot spare half an hour,' I said. 'Please, will you stay a while? I would so like to learn more about how you came to be reunited.'

We went through to the parlour, and I invited them to sit while I retrieved the jug of lemonade that I had freshly made that morning. They asked polite questions about the gowns hanging from the rails, and I answered as fully as I could. At last the moment felt right.

'Miss Matembe . . .'

'Please, you must call me Pearl.'

'Forgive me, Pearl, but I hope you don't mind me asking. How did you come by this good fortune since we met, being reunited with both your baby and your brother?'

'We do not mind one bit, do we, Femi?' Had I been in any doubt that they were brother and sister, their smiles would have proved it: their grins were such unselfconscious expressions of joy that you could not help but smile with them.

'And since you are the reason why we are here, you most certainly deserve an explanation,' he said.

'When you met me that day I was on the point of giving up, Miss Charlotte, but the food and drink you bought for me gave me the strength to carry on. It is the truth – I had been thrown out of the household where I was working as a maid, and although I searched and searched for Femi, I could find no trace of him.'

'You probably gathered that I am in the navy,' he said. Was he the sailor I'd seen marching with his fellows at Tower Hill docks with my sister that day, I wondered. 'My ship had to sail two weeks earlier than expected but my message must have arrived after she left.'

'I was at my wits' end, living on scraps and sleeping in doorways,' she went on. 'I suppose it is my colour, but no one would take me in. Then the baby came, and I stopped caring about myself; all I wanted was for him to live. I know of some girls who have just thrown them into the river, but it goes against my faith to do such a thing. And that is when I met you.'

'You were such a sorry sight, my dear,' I said. 'It pained me much to leave you.'

'You did not leave me,' she said, hastily. 'The warmth of your kindness remained with me, even when the Hospital turned me away.'

'You took a black ball?'

She nodded. 'I had no idea what it meant, until they explained.'

'But you did not come back to me for help.'

'It took me a few weeks to gather my courage again. My plan was to leave him on the steps with your note and hope that if he was taken in, your name might be enough of a reference. Then I hid behind some bushes to wait. If he was not retrieved by nightfall, I promised myself, I would go back to retrieve him. Happily, within an hour, a well-dressed older lady came by and picked him up. I did not see him again, until a week ago.'

'You were fortunate. That lady was a friend of mine who volunteers for the Hospital. Her late husband was a governor. She persuaded them to take the baby in because she recognised my name. Otherwise, it would have meant nothing.'

'Then you are right, we were very lucky.' She stroked the boy's forehead with the back of a forefinger. 'Afterwards, even though my heart was breaking, I returned to my employers and pleaded for my old job back. I hoped, in time, to save enough to find my son again one day. The housekeeper there had kept Femi's letter, so at least then I knew where he had gone and that, God willing, he would return.'

He took up the story. 'Just as soon as I got off the ship I went to find her, and she told me the story. I'd saved enough to rent two rooms so that we could all live together and get the baby back. I hope to find a job onshore as soon as possible, and Pearl is taking in needlework. Our little family is complete.'

'Femi adores his nephew,' she said, fondly.

'No wonder. He is a beautiful little boy. What is his name?'

'He is Jelani,' she said. 'After his grandfather. It means

244

full of strength. But he has another name too, an English name, Charles.'

'That is a *very* English name,' I said, laughing.

'It is after you, Miss Charlotte,' Femi said.

My cheeks burned. A second baby named after me in as many weeks, a little dynasty. 'I am most honoured. May I hold my namesake for a moment?'

I took the baby into my arms, curious to feel his heaviness after the featherweight of baby Charlotte. 'Hello, little one. What do you make of this world now, after all your adventures?'

It must have been the unfamiliar voice that woke him. His eyes opened, dark brown with curled eyelashes, and fixed me with a steady, serious gaze. As I looked back his lips curled into a smile.

'Look, he knows you,' Pearl said. At that moment, something deep and intense welled up inside me, a powerful memory of the love I had felt for my own baby. A mother's love.

'Thank heavens you were able to get him back.'

'The Hospital seemed suspicious at first,' she said. 'They wanted proof, but fortunately I kept the other half of this.' She pulled a scrap of linen and lace from her pocket. As she held it out I could see that it had been torn in half, and then sewn back again to make a whole, although it took a practised eye to notice since the stitching was so fine.

'It's your handkerchief, remember?' Pearl said. 'You gave it to me to dry my eyes. Forgive me, but in my distress I forgot to give it back. So when it came to leaving him on the steps I tore it in two and left half with him. When I went to claim him, it had been pinned to his record. I was able to show them the other half.'

'You knew about the token system?'

'You told me, that day.'

I laughed. 'Ah yes, so I did.'

'I remember wondering how you knew so much about the Hospital's rules.'

How much did I want to share? They were strangers just half an hour ago, but now they felt more like friends, people I had known for years.

'It is a long story, but all you really need to know is that I am also a foundling.' They gazed at me in astonishment. 'Yes, I grew up in that Hospital. They educated me, they helped me grow. I'm not saying that it was easy, but I am alive because of them, just like little Jelani here.'

'But . . .' she hesitated. 'May I ask, were you ever reunited with your mother?'

'Sadly not,' I said. 'But I have my sister, and my nephew, and that is really all the family I need.'

They wrote down their new address, and we said our good-byes with promises to meet again. I told Pearl that I had noticed the delicacy of her stitching on the handkerchief, and that if I should ever have a vacancy for a seamstress, I would certainly get in touch. Afterwards I went back into the parlour to take a few moments alone before returning to the sewing room.

Just the day before, grateful for Anna's recovery, I had determined to be satisfied with what I already had: my family, good friends, a successful business. But seeing Pearl again so bonny and well, reunited with her child, had brought me face to face once more with that most powerful of emotions: the powerful, complicated and even sometimes contradictory love of a mother for her child, the love that, if thwarted or denied, can quickly become the deepest pain of all. What agony it had been to give up Peter to ensure his future happiness and security, and how much it still hurt, not being able to acknowledge him as my son. How much pain Pearl had endured to make sure her child was safe, and what lengths she had gone to get him back.

Of course, Louisa and Peter were all the family I really *needed*. They made me happy in so many ways. I was fortunate to have them with me. But needing is not the same as feeling. Femi had spoken about their family being complete. Not knowing my mother left me feeling *incomplete*.

I would try just one more time, to find out more.

That night it came to me: might Monsieur Girardieu be able to help? Perhaps if I approached him with a more personal plea, explaining what the pagoda silk had meant to me, he might remember more about it, or be able to give me some clues about how a piece of it came into my mother's hands?

After the shop had closed I hastened to Spital Square. Dusk was falling, and candlelight beamed from the windows of the houses as I passed. But number twelve was in darkness. The shutters were open, but the windows gazed blankly out into the square. I knocked, and waited. And knocked and waited again. Then I walked around to the window and, standing on tiptoe, peered inside.

Even in the half-light from the street I could see all I

needed. The room was empty, cleared of all those papers, those books, all furniture, those sad remains of a once successful business. Monsieur Girardieu and the old lady were gone and with them, so I thought, my last hopes of ever tracing my mother.

26

Tabby: the most basic of weaves, of which there are many varieties: plain, basketweave and balanced plain, also known as chequerboard.

By early August both baby Charlotte and her mother had recovered sufficiently to contemplate a journey to Suffolk.

'Henri is so busy at the moment he cannot take the time to accompany me,' Anna said. 'He will be free to go in September.'

'That is but a few weeks away,' I said. 'He works so hard, a visit to the country would probably do him good, too.' Then she passed me a piece of paper, a letter from her father's devoted neighbour Mary Marshall.

Dearest Anna,

Your father has told me news of his new granddaughter, and I send my congratulations to you all. He and Janey are delighted and cannot wait to meet her.

Theodore is much recovered from his bad turn but the doctor has diagnosed a weak heart (for which there is no cure, alas) and has warned that he must not exert himself. He is certainly not allowed to travel. Of course he has told everyone not to fuss, and continues his usual routines as though nothing is awry. Yesterday, Janey told me he is planning a trip to London to meet the new baby.

I do not wish to alarm you, dearest Anna, but I do hope that you can find a way to discourage this. Perhaps, if you are well enough, you could visit here instead?

'What do you think? Should I wait until Henri is free, or go at once?'

We both understood the message between the lines of Mrs Marshall's letter: Theodore might not have much time left. 'I think you should go as soon as possible,' I said. 'And if Henri is unable to get away and if he agrees, then I shall accompany you. You cannot make that journey on your own, dearest.'

Her relief was evident. I had told her what she needed to hear.

'Thank you, Charlotte. I am sure Henri will agree. We will see to the arrangements as soon as possible, and write to my father. Would next weekend be too soon? We could leave on Friday and return by Wednesday so you only miss a few days' work. Clothilde has offered to look after Jean, but I know that Father and Janey will want to see him as well. Can you bear to share a carriage with a toddler and a crying baby?'

How could I refuse? With much of society fleeing London for the summer season in Bath and elsewhere, trade was always slow in August. It was our usual habit for Mrs T. and the seamstresses to take two weeks' holiday at the height of each summer.

'Let us plan to spend a whole week, Anna. Travelling will be tiring so soon after your illness, but the sea air will do all of us good. Let Theodore have his fill of his grand-children.'

'He'd be glad to see the back of us, after that,' she said, smiling at last.

<hr/>

The journey with two young children in a fully packed coach was as gruelling as we had feared.

It began well enough, with the other passengers cooing over little Charlotte and patting Jean on the head, compli-menting Anna on her beautiful children. It was clear they assumed I was the nanny, and there was no reason to dis-abuse them. The baby, now known to everyone as Charlie, slept for much of the way. When she woke Anna managed to feed her, concealed beneath a shawl so that no one even noticed.

But little Jean is rarely still, except when asleep. For him, having to sit for several hours at a time is torture and before long our fellow passengers were clearly changing their minds about the 'dear little lad'. We tried every trick to entertain him: plying him with food, producing his favour-ite toys and making up stories, but what he most wanted to do was run from one side of the carriage to the other, pushing his way between the cramped knees of the passen-gers, who soon made it clear that this was not acceptable behaviour.

Happily, after a couple of hours of this he would fall asleep on my lap, so heavy that my legs went to pins and needles and my arms cramped with the effort of securing him against the sway of the carriage.

Thus the two-day journey proceeded, punctuated by a stop at the coaching inn in Chelmsford where we all slept soundly, exhausted by the enforced inactivity. At last we arrived in Halesworth to be met by the carter, who transported us along the high ridge that affords such a spectacular view of the wide river estuary. Even Jean was silenced for a short while by the sight. Although it was nearly sunset the fields were still busy with men scything swathes of grain made golden by weeks of sunshine, collecting and tying the stalks and setting the stooks in perfect rows reaching as far as the eye could see.

As we watched the western sky change from blue to pink and orange and finally to deep purple, the stresses of the journey – and indeed all the concerns of daily life – seemed to lift from my shoulders.

On our arrival at the vicarage it was immediately apparent why Mrs Marshall had written with such urgency, and I was grateful that she had spurred us into visiting immediately.

Theodore was a sadly diminished man. Illness had visibly reduced him, by half a foot in height and many pounds in weight. Worse still, the self-assured demeanour I'd always attributed to his quiet certainty of faith seemed to have been undermined: his gait was hesitant, his face lined with anxiety, his voice strangely light and querulous.

David Garrick's recitation about the seven ages of man slipped into my mind. Mr Shakespeare's observations of what he called the 'sixth age' seemed to capture Theodore so perfectly: *his shrunk shank and his big manly voice turning again toward childish treble . . .*

Yet later, as he held little Charlotte in his arms with Jean at his knee, a proud smile filled the hollows of his sunken face and, as he spoke of his delight in seeing us all, his voice recovered some of the warm resonance that had so charmed me long ago.

Anna's sister Janey seemed unaffected by concerns over her father's health: as ever, she bounded like a puppy to greet us, embracing both of us with the joyful lack of inhibition of the child she still is, in her mind, even though she is now twenty years of age. Her smile and cheerful good-heartedness are hard to resist, but as she reached for Jean he wriggled away squealing, running to hide in his mother's skirts.

'Doesn't he like me?' she wailed.

'He'll get used to you soon enough, dearest.' Indeed, within the hour Jean had become entranced by his Suffolk auntie, insisting that she show him around the house and now much neglected garden before engaging her in a serious construction project with the wooden bricks she had managed to unearth.

***

The following day being a Sunday, the household was up at dawn.

Theodore insisted on taking Holy Communion before breakfast, but agreed to let his curate take the mid-morning service so that he could sit with the family in their pew.

'Humour me, let me play the old patriarch,' he joked, gathering his grandson beside him, his daughter and her baby the other side.

What he would not delegate, he insisted, was the sermon. 'They complain terribly about old Marcus,' he said. 'He goes on far too long, and is dull as ditch-water.'

It was clearly a struggle to climb the stairs up to the pulpit, but as he began to speak the energy seemed to flow back into him. Quoting from Corinthians, he said that love for our fellow man, and most particularly for our family, comes without condition: it is kind, does not envy, boast or dishonour others. After elaborating on the theme, he concluded that those of us who have family – and in that he included close friends and community – are the most fortunate people in the world.

'God tells us we must love one another as he loves us,' he said, glancing fondly at Anna and myself, Janey, Jean and little Charlotte in the pew below. 'Reflect His love to your own and you will be doubly rewarded. Cherish your loved ones and value them above all else, because they are those who will bring you the greatest happiness for the rest of your days.'

Bidding farewell to Janey and Theodore was heartbreaking. As Anna suspected, he'd dismissed the notion of coming to live with her in London, although he promised to visit 'very soon'. But his increasing frailty was obvious and though neither of us acknowledged it, we both knew this might be the last time we would see him.

After several blissful days in the fresh air and freedom of the countryside I did not relish the prospect of returning to a crowded, malodorous city. Being in the lap of a loving family and the two demanding but ever-delightful children, among a community where everyone regarded their vicar with such obvious affection and high esteem, seemed to highlight everything that was missing from my life.

The journey went without incident and, to my relief, the shop was just as I had left it. It is never wise to ignore the ever-present dangers of a city where many people have barely enough to live on: premises will be watched for several nights and will be fair game for thieves if reckoned to be unoccupied. Despite having secured all the shutters and locked away from view anything of great value I entered with some trepidation, but happily nothing seemed to have been disturbed.

I took up the bundle of letters and flyers pushed under the door and went downstairs to the kitchen, setting the fire and unwrapping the remaining bread, cheese and apples Theodore's cook had pressed upon us for the journey. Waiting for the milk to boil, I glanced casually through the mail. Among a dozen others was an envelope addressed in Louisa's hand, which I ripped open at once with a glad heart, hoping for – indeed expecting – an invitation, or a promise to visit. After being with Anna's family for a week, I longed to see my own once more.

That this letter might contain the worst news in the world could not have been further from my mind.

27

Taffeta: a fine, crisp plain woven silk with a gloss finish that holds its shape well and is thus suitable for formal gowns, as well as curtains or wall coverings.

My sister's handwriting, never graceful at the best of times, was even more spidery and inconsistent as usual. The letter was dated five days previously; it must have arrived shortly after I'd left for Suffolk, and consisted of these few terrifying words:

> *Dearest Agnes, please come at once. Peter is dangerously ill. Your loving Louisa.*

Even though they were as plain as they could possibly be, I read these words over again and again like a dullard. The milk boiled over with a great hiss of steam followed by the acrid smell of burning. Moving automatically, I lifted the pan and took a cloth to wipe up the stinking mess.

The shock must have made me light-headed, for I found myself clasping the edge of the table and moving towards the chair. I must have sat there for minutes, my thoughts spinning like a top. *Peter is dangerously ill.* What was this danger? Was he still ill, or on the way to recovery? Or was he . . . ? The alternative was too appalling even to contemplate.

At last I pulled myself together: my task was to get to Westford Abbots as quickly as possible. But it was already after six, well past the departure time of the last coach of the day. Although it might be possible to hire a private gig for a very large sum, I had no idea how to go about it. Jane, to whom I would have turned had she been in London, would surely have lent me hers, but I knew for certain that she planned to spend the whole of August in Chiswick. None of my other friends, not even Monsieur Lavalle, were wealthy enough to have their own horses.

There was no choice: I would have to wait for the first coach of the morning. I dragged myself up to the attic with limbs like lead weights, trying to prepare for the interminable hours ahead. Even small, mundane tasks felt like a sacrilege when my future happiness hung in the balance. I lay down, but whenever I closed my eyes terrifying devil-like figures flickered in the shadows of the candlelight, shaking their fists and threatening me with unknown evils. I blew out the candle to deny them, but this made it even worse. In the darkness, chilling scenes crowded my mind: Peter dead, in his coffin, being lowered into the ground. At last, the tears came.

Exhausted by weeping, I sat up and relit the candle. A distant church tolled three o'clock: still three hours to wait, but I could not bear to stay in this room any longer. I rose and dressed in readiness for the journey, packing my case with fresh garments, then went downstairs. I wrote a note for Mrs T., apologising for my continued absence and explaining why I'd had to leave once more. Then I sat by the front door with case and cape at the ready, until dawn finally began to lighten the sky.

❦

It was a relief to get under way after those long, dread-filled hours, treading the route to the coach stop, but as it pulled up I could see to my dismay that the first coach was already brimful with women and children. I would have to wait a full four hours for the next.

'Please sir,' I pleaded. 'It's my son, he is dangerously ill. I must get to him. Let me ride, somewhere, I don't mind where.' On seeing my wretched state he eventually took pity on me. 'You can come up here, miss, if yous don't mind the weather,' he called down, indicating the seat beside him.

'Oh yes, of course. Thank you so much, sir,' I gasped, climbing the ladder up to his box on top of the coach. The seat was narrow, and perilously high above the ground.

'We doesn't usually let the ladies up here, so just make sure you hang on tight, miss.'

With that he flicked his whip and the horses set off at what felt like a furious pace. Although it was probably no faster than the usual speed for a coach, out in the open with the wind dragging the bonnet from my head, it felt quite terrifying.

Before long it began to drizzle, and I was soon soaked to the skin. But I barely noticed the discomfort, nor even cared. Every step of those hard-working horses, every mile covered by those wheels, was bringing me closer. In my desperate, distracted state I began to believe that if I could only get to Westford Abbots my presence would magically restore Peter to good health, and all would be well.

The reality was, of course, very different.

On our arrival, the village felt a dismal and unwelcoming place. Usually there would be a gaggle of villagers waiting to greet their visitors, but this time I was the only person to alight and as I'd had no time to give notice there was no one to greet me. Chilled, bedraggled and soaked to the skin, but so grateful to be here at last, I hurried along the street, itching to run but holding myself in check, not wanting to appear undignified or to fuel further gossip. Fortunately, few people were about in this disagreeable weather, but those hardy souls sheltering under the market cross or huddled in doorways regarded me with suspicion.

When at last I arrived at the vicarage and rang the bell its familiar, usually cheerful clang resounded throughout the empty hallway like a funeral toll. No one answered, and fear clutched at my throat. Where were they? I rang again, and in the silence that followed the yew trees seemed to creak even more sorrowfully than usual.

Suddenly the locks turned with a crack and a crunch, and a stranger opened the door: a dumpy middle-aged woman I'd never met before.

'Yes?' she asked, with an impatient sigh.

'I am Agnes, Mrs Fairchild's sister. She wrote to me, about Peter.'

'She be expecting you?'

'Yes, she is,' I said. 'Please, madam, I beg you, let me in out of the rain.'

Reluctantly, she opened the door wide enough for me to squeeze past and I made immediately for the stairs, but her arm came out quick as lightning.

'Yous must wait in the drawing room, miss, till I get the Mrs,' she said.

'But I must see Peter, at once,' I shouted, exasperated. 'I have come all the way from . . .'

Louisa appeared, flying down the stairs into my arms. Her face was gaunt and grey-tinged; she appeared thinner than I had ever seen her, as though she had not eaten for days.

'Agnes. Oh *Agnes*. My dearest, I am so pleased that you have come. Whatever kept you so long? I wrote over a week ago.'

'Is he . . . ?' I hardly dared say it.

'He is still very poorly,' she said, leading me into the drawing room. 'The fever has been with him for eight days now. He has not eaten anything in all that time and barely opens his eyes nor speaks to us.' Then, in a whisper, 'Dearest sister, I am sorry to have to tell you this.'

I sucked in a breath, for courage. 'Go on.'

'The doctor believes it to be the typhus.'

Again that word, striking terror into my soul. A disease from which few ever recovered. The blood seemed to drain from my heart. 'But I thought that had left the village several months ago?'

'So did we, my darling. But his symptoms are the same. Headache, fever, vomiting and a rash, just as Ambrose witnessed in the victims before.'

I shivered. 'Can I see him?'

'You poor dear, forgive me. You are soaked through and must be starving after your journey. Will you change first, and take a hot drink? We must look after ourselves too, you know, we need all our strength.'

'Who is the new maid?' I asked, lowering my voice. 'She seemed most suspicious.'

'Maggie. She's the widow of old Chapman, who's come in to help. As soon as word got out, both cook and the maid handed in their notice. You can hardly blame them, I suppose. This disease terrifies everyone. Then Maggie turned up. Says she's not afraid of it because she nursed her husband and suffered no personal ill effects, and wants to return the support Ambrose gave them in their own dark times.'

'I trust your husband is well?'

'Indeed. He is out visiting, where else?' There was an unfamiliar note of bitterness in her tone. 'I wish he wouldn't but there's no stopping the man when he's set his mind to something.' She shrugged. 'But I am so pleased to see you, dearest, at last. What kept you?'

'I was in Suffolk, and only returned yesterday. I came at once.'

'No matter, you are here now.' She took my hand and led me upstairs. 'Come, and let us get you changed into something dry and warm. I will get Maggie to bring you something to keep you going until luncheon.'

✿

Peter's chamber was dark as a tomb, the heavy curtains drawn tight against the light, and so stiflingly hot that I struggled for breath. Someone had strewn herbs on the floor, but even they could not mask the stench of sickness.

Having so recently witnessed Anna struggling to survive the gravest loss of blood in childbirth and the fever that followed, I might have been inured to the spectacle of severe illness, but nothing could have prepared me for the sight before me. The handsome boy I had last seen brimming with life and vitality was now diminished to a near skeleton, his skin wrinkled like an old man's, pale as the sheet that covered him. His eyes were closed, his hair matted. The skin of his skull seemed stretched tight over his dear face and his arms, like sticks, lay unmoving by his side. It was hard to imagine how this frail form could sustain life. The vision of a corpse lay before me.

I felt Louisa's hand steadying me, leading me to a chair at the bedside.

'Is he . . . ?'

'Look at his chest.' It was possible to detect just the slightest movement. 'See, he is breathing.'

'I suppose that is all that matters, for the moment.'

'Talk to him, Agnes. I feel sure he can still hear us. I'll leave you together for a few moments, shall I?'

As I took my son's lifeless hand in my own, the bleakness of this small movement brought me to tears and the words stuck in my throat. Even from a young age he would have snatched it away. *I'm a big boy now, Auntie.* But for now I was content just to feel the pulse in his wrist. *Where there is life, there is hope*, I said to myself, stroking his hair and caressing his cheek with the back of my fingers. His skin was hot and clammy, his forehead beaded with sweat.

'Dearest boy,' I finally managed to croak. 'All is well.

Your mother is here now.' *Mother*. It slipped out without my even thinking about it, but I barely cared. How could I maintain the pretence when his life lay in the balance? 'I love you so much, and I am sure you will soon be well again, but you must summon all your strength to fight it. Promise me you will?'

Was that a murmur coming from his lips? I certainly heard something, but there was no further response. Perhaps it was just a noise from somewhere else in the house, or outside. It was impossible to tell.

After a while the smell and sultry heat of the room became overwhelming. 'Oh, I cannot bear this darkness, Peter,' I declared. 'Shall we draw the curtains, just for a few moments?'

I recalled the advice of Anna's French doctor: *Keep the patient warm at all times, but give her plenty of fresh air and sunshine to cleanse the room of feverish vapours.* Pulling the heavy woollen drapes apart, I unlocked the casement latch and threw open the window. The rain had cleared now and sweet fresh air laden with the perfume of flowers in the beds below the window flooded into the room.

'Listen to that birdsong, my darling. The world is beautiful. We shall soon be out there together, enjoying it once more.'

The chamber door burst open. It was Ambrose, with a face like a thundercloud.

'Whatever are you thinking?' he roared. 'Are you trying to kill the boy?'

He strode to the window and slammed it shut then pulled the curtains across, plunging the room into darkness. Bringing his face within a few inches of mine, so that I could smell his sour breath, he shouted: 'Don't you know that in this perilous state he must be protected from the evils from without?'

I said nothing, knowing little about the 'evils without', though I suspected they were unlikely to be backed by any medical fact.

'Furthermore, that he must be kept in close warm air at all times to purge the fevers?'

Fever was something I certainly knew about. 'I understand that the top physicians recommend fresh air and cool bathing these days, sir,' I ventured.

'You *understand*,' he bellowed again, with no regard for the poor suffering boy prostrated on the bed between us. 'And pray, what is the great learning that leads you to this *understanding* of yours, may I inquire?'

I was about to tell him about Anna's safe recovery but realised just in time that any response, however sensible, would only infuriate him even further.

'Listen carefully, Agnes.' He lowered his voice now. 'As Louisa's sister, you are welcome in my house, as always. But Peter is being treated in full accordance with the recommendations of our trusted village physician, who has ensured the successful recovery of many a patient. You will not – I repeat *will not* – interfere, do you hear me? If you disobey my instructions I may find myself in the position of asking you to leave.'

28

Running stitch: a simple stitch, quick to execute, often to hem or outline an embroidery design.

Laced running stitch: threads laced through the loops of running stitch to give a decorative effect.

Ambrose insisted that the three of us must eat together in the dining room that evening, as though everything was normal.

'God has provided us with the fruits of the land so that we may be fit to serve him to the best of our abilities, and who are we to refuse his bounty? Come downstairs at once, both of you,' he commanded. 'For I have a great appetite upon me. The boy will take no harm left alone for an hour.'

The thought of eating anything at all made me queasy, but his orders must be obeyed. He said grace and we ate in silence. Maggie had produced a meal of decent, plain fare: a strong broth soup along with cold meats, pickled walnuts, heavy dark bread and butter. This good wholesome food should have been a blessing, but each mouthful tasted like ashes.

Ambrose seemed determined to draw out the agony for

as long as possible, piling his plate high and chewing with such deliberation that I began to wish he might choke. Sitting there under his baleful eye felt like a punishment, and I could think of nothing but Peter alone upstairs, struggling for breath.

At last it was over, and he rose from the table. 'I'm going out,' he said.

※※※

That night, Peter was overtaken with a high fever and each time he cried out the blood seemed to freeze in my veins. Louisa and I worked together: talking in soft, calming tones, holding him in our arms, trying to make him take sips of water containing the herbal infusion the doctor had provided. We made a good team, doing all we could to keep alive the boy whom we both loved more than ourselves.

He began to babble, unintelligibly at first, but then I heard a name that I recognised. 'He's talking about angels, Louisa,' I said, panic-stricken. 'He's not leaving us, is he?'

She frowned at me, confused.

'He must be at the gates of heaven,' I said, close to tears. 'He can see the Angel Gabriel.'

'Oh dearest, don't worry. It's his friend he's calling for. He's done that before.' She turned to Peter. 'Gabriel's not here at the moment, darling. But we are here, your mother and your Auntie Agnes. We'll look after you, don't you worry.'

After about two hours, his rigours calmed, the heat dissipated. Louisa held a feather to his mouth, where it fluttered slightly. 'His breathing is more regular. He will sleep for a few hours now.' She leaned across and stroked my cheek, tenderly as a mother. 'Go to your bed, my dearest, you have had a very long day.'

I was too exhausted to protest, and it was already past midnight. I fell onto the bed fully clothed and slept soundly until the morning.

※

Shortly after breakfast, Doctor Willingshaw arrived. A tall, imposing man with a powdered wig and extravagant grey whiskers, he strode into the house as though he owned the place.

'Ambrose, my good fellow,' he boomed. 'How is the boy today?'

My brother-in-law spoke with such authority that you would believe he had watched over Peter's bedside all night. 'He suffered the high fever again last evening, and we feared for his life once more, I'm afraid, but he is calm again this morning.'

The doctor pursed his lips. 'In my long experience, there is only so much fever a small frame can survive,' he said, gloomily. 'We shall have to administer further purging, I'm afraid. I have them here.' He patted the large leather case beneath his arm.

'No!' Louisa leapt forward, taking her husband's arm. 'Not again. Please, Ambrose.'

He batted her away like an irritating fly. 'Do you want the boy to live?'

I had to admire her courage. Once again she took his arm, pleading. This time he pushed her harder so that she tumbled back against me and I had to grab her shoulder to save her from falling.

'You will obey me, wife,' he said in a fierce whisper. 'The doctor knows best. If it causes you to be squeamish then I suggest you stay away. Take your sister out for a walk or something, for goodness' sake.' He turned on his heel and followed the doctor upstairs.

As we left the house, there were tears in Louisa's eyes. Even the power of her compassion for the boy whom we both loved so much was no match for her husband's merciless desire for control. We trudged the orchards side by side without speaking, in the mutual acknowledgement that any subject other than Peter was simply too trivial to discuss. Beyond our shared anxiety for his welfare and longing for his safe recovery, there was nothing to say.

The clouds had disappeared overnight and the damp grass steamed in the warmth of the sun. The birds were celebrating loud enough to raise the dead, butterflies flittered on a light breeze and the hedges buzzed with bees hunting for nectar. At one point we spied a small deer and even in the brief moment before it slipped away into the undergrowth I caught a glimpse of its beautiful brown pelt, the bright eyes, the tall ears rimmed with black, the flash of its white tail.

In normal times I would have been cheered by this display of nature's vibrancy and abundance, its complexity and beauty, but today it seemed illusory and unreal, even cruel. Did the world not know that just a few hundred yards away our boy was hovering between life and death? The incongruity was too painful to contemplate.

We had been walking just fifteen minutes and had

reached the corner of the orchard when Louisa spoke. 'It's no good. I cannot bear to be away. Even watching him suffer is better than not being there at all.' Without further words, we turned and set off in the direction from which we had just come.

As we climbed the stairs my heart quailed. What was this treatment Louisa feared so much? The bedroom door was ajar; she hesitated a second before gently easing it open. The sight before us could not have been more shocking; my boy was being subjected to what looked like a barbaric form of torture. Over his pale, naked torso writhed a legion of great black worms as fat as a man's fingers and rivers of red blood streaked from his body, like those paintings of Christ on the cross.

In an instant, Ambrose was looming over us. 'I thought I told you to stay away? How dare you disobey me?' He slammed the door in our faces, and Louisa fell into my arms.

'Oh Agnes, I cannot endure it,' she cried.

I remembered how Aunt Sarah had recommended leeching for Anna. The French doctor had dismissed the idea as outdated and ineffective, but we were powerless to save Peter from his fate.

Any words of comfort would be gratuitous.

That afternoon, after the doctor had left and Ambrose had gone out on his rounds once more, Louisa and I returned to Peter's bedside. We washed away the blood with warm water and I went to lift him so that she could replace the soiled undersheet. How light he was. Even as I held him he did not waken, and I feared that he might have left us. But his heart continued to beat and his chest to draw breath, if only slightly, then enough to sustain life.

Afterwards, as we rested, sitting each side of him, Louisa's eyes began to close. 'Go to your bed, sister,' I said. 'I will call you if there is any change.'

Once I was alone, I took out the book of Shakespeare sonnets that Jane had lent to me after our dinner with Mr Garrick, intending to read some of them aloud to Peter. They were rhythmic enough, their subjects not too controversial or distressing. The sound of my voice might reassure him, or even encourage him to open his eyes, I thought.

But it was too dark to make out the words so I drew back the curtains just a few inches so that if Ambrose returned I could quickly pull them closed once more.

It was then I saw, in a slim shaft of sunlight slipping between the drapes, the glass bowl set on the dresser, covered with a beaded muslin cloth. I lifted the cloth and instantly regretted it, for squirming around in the water were those huge black leeches, fattened from their feast on Peter's precious blood. The very sight of them made my stomach churn. I quickly replaced the muslin cover, sat down and took up my book, trying to erase what I had seen, but their malign presence was already branded into my mind's eye.

It didn't take me long to decide what to do, even knowing that it would incur Ambrose's inevitable wrath. I opened the casement, took up the bowl and threw its contents into the flowerbed below. Those disgusting creatures would make a fine meal for the birds. Then I refilled the bowl from the ewer and replaced it onto the dresser, covering it carefully with the beaded cloth once more, as though it had never been disturbed.

The reckoning arrived sooner than expected. After supper that evening there was a knock at the door.

'Dr Willingshaw, what an unexpected pleasure,' Ambrose said. 'How kind of you to drop by again.' As I said, he always plays the perfect gentleman.

'How is the patient?'

This time, he deferred to Louisa. 'Tell him, wife.'

'Much the same,' she whispered.

'Depending on how he fares overnight, we can administer the treatment again in the morning if necessary,' the doctor said, as he and Ambrose left the room and headed upstairs.

Louisa and I crept upstairs and waited outside the chamber door, listening with ears peeled. I prayed that he would not look under the beaded cloth, but this time my plea fell on deaf ears.

'What is this?' the doctor said. 'Where have they gone?'

I imagined the two men scanning the floor and peering under the bed and the dresser, foolishly searching for the missing leeches.

'They must have escaped somehow.'

'Do you take me for an idiot? They must have been *stolen*, sir.'

'That is impossible, for there has been no one in the house except ourselves, doctor.' Ambrose sounded surprisingly calm. 'But please do not be concerned. Of course if they cannot be found, we will recompense you in full.'

'What on earth . . . ?' my sister mouthed. I grabbed her hand and drew her along the landing into my chamber.

'I'm so sorry,' I whispered.

'What? *You* took the leeches?'

I nodded. 'I threw them out of the window into the flowerbed. I couldn't bear to let him suffer a second time.'

To my great surprise, she gave a little laugh. 'Good girl,' she said.

'But Ambrose . . . ?'

'Do not worry, dearest. I will deal with him.' She squeezed my hand briefly, and we waited until we heard the two men descending the stairs and saying their farewells, followed by Ambrose's footsteps along the corridor to his study, and the door closing.

All the while a powerful knot of fear twisted in my stomach; I was expecting him to storm back upstairs at any moment. But he was too cunning to display his rage so openly.

❊

That night I persuaded Louisa to take some rest, and resumed my vigil at Peter's bedside.

At around midnight I heard the door of Ambrose's study open and held my breath as his footsteps ascended the stairs, expecting him to confront me. But he passed by and went to his own chamber, or so I thought. All was quiet.

And then I heard it. 'What is this, wife? You have turned thief?'

There was an inaudible reply, followed by heavy footsteps and a kind of deep animal growl. 'Do you know what happens when you disobey me?'

A horrible, heavy silence filled the house.

'You must be punished, wife. To cleanse you of your sin.'

'No, Ambrose, wait. I can explain.'

'It is only because I love you.'

'No, please, no.' Her anguished pleading brought me to my feet, running along the corridor. I flung open the door to see a terrifying tableau set before me: Louisa standing defiant as Ambrose loomed over her with his arm raised and fist clenched.

'No!' I shouted, rushing between them.

His fist hit my face with a blow that seemed to lift me right off my feet and I felt my cheekbone crack. The force of it threw me backwards onto Louisa, and we both fell to the floor.

'It was not Louisa,' I managed to gasp. 'It was me. Do what you will, Ambrose, but spare my sister. She's done nothing wrong.'

'You!' His eyes were alight, red embers in the darkened room. 'You?' he bellowed. 'So this is how you repay our generosity, is it, you little bastard?'

As he raised his fist once more I covered my head with my arms, waiting for the pain, but it never came. Beside me, Louisa began so sob.

'Stop your whining, woman,' he said, pacing the floor like a caged bear. And then, in a low snarl: 'Whatever am I going to do with the pair of you?' The footsteps ceased right beside us and my heart seemed to stop. The menace was almost more petrifying than the reality.

'I suppose you know what the Bible says about thieves?'
Silence.

'Speak, girl.'

The pain in my cheek was blinding. 'No, sir,' I managed to mutter. 'I do not.'

'If thy right hand offend thee, cut it off. Think on this, Agnes, and pray for your salvation.'

He turned on his heel and walked out of the room.

After a few moments Louisa raised herself and went to the dresser, dunking a towel into the jug.

'Here, hold this to your eye.' Every dab felt like the jabbing of a thousand needles. She poured water into a cup and handed it to me. Even though my throat burned with each swallow the coldness felt good. My body began to shake uncontrollably, and I burst into tears.

'I am so sorry to have caused this, Louisa.'

'Don't you worry, it will soon pass. Here, dry your eyes.' She passed me her kerchief and put her arms around me until the sobs subsided. 'Now, let us go downstairs and I will warm some milk.'

'He should not be allowed to treat you like this,' I said, hauling myself unsteadily to my feet. She did not respond. How she found the strength to remain so composed under these circumstances I will never fathom. I could only assume that she had become accustomed to it.

Passing along the hallway, I caught a glimpse in the mirror. My cheek and eye socket were already starting to swell. Tomorrow I would have a black eye and a face like a pumpkin.

We rekindled the range, and as we waited for the milk to warm Louisa's courage seemed to ebb away and she began to shiver. A ragged shawl hung from the back of the door – perhaps it had once belonged to their old cook – and I wrapped it around her.

'As soon as Peter is well enough we'll get you both away from here.'

'Get away? Where on earth would we go?'

'To London, perhaps?'

She shook her head. 'I will never leave him, Agnes. I owe him everything, and would be nothing without him.'

'The man was a violent monster. 'He may hurt you really badly, one day. It is too dangerous to stay.'

'It is only when I annoy him,' she whispered.

Annoy? 'Can't you see that it is not your fault, Louisa? You did nothing wrong.'

She turned away to retrieve the pan as it began to boil, and I could feel my anger and frustration rising as she went to pour it, needing two hands to control her shaking. But now was not the right time to press my point. We would talk again once Peter was recovered.

It was approaching dawn and I had fallen into a light doze when he became delirious once more. This time was even more acute than the previous night. He writhed so much that I had to hold him in my arms to prevent him falling from the bed, but his limbs were so thin and fragile that it felt like trying to contain a bird desperate for freedom.

'They're calling for me,' he shouted, over and over again. 'I must go, I must go.'

Who was calling him and where? Was he hearing the angels after all, inviting him to follow them to heaven?

Talking in a low monotone, I tried to reassure him that no one was coming and that he was safe here, I would allow nothing to harm him. But he didn't seem to hear me – at least he showed no sign of it – thrashing and twisting the sheets with his fists, wrenching his head from side to side with such ferocity that I feared he might cause himself an injury. His body burned hot as a fire: if he continued like this for much longer he would surely die.

This time I did not hesitate. Ambrose would tell me to leave in the morning, so I had nothing to lose.

I threw open the curtains and opened both windows as wide as possible to let in the cool night air. Then I took a towel and, wetting it in the ewer, bathed his face, arms, chest and legs just as we had done with Anna. If it had brought my friend out of her fever, surely it must be the right thing to do? I repeated the bathing over and over again, talking to him all the while. After nearly an hour my ministrations seemed to take effect: the moans quietened, the spasms of pain were less frequent. His body felt cooler too, although I could not be sure that this was not simply the effect of the bathing and the chill air.

Now he fell deathly still and I began fear that he was drifting away. But the feather fluttered when I held it above his mouth and when I felt his wrist the pulse was still there, faint, but more regular than before. I closed my eyes, and allowed myself to rest in the chair for a few brief moments.

The next thing I knew was the sound of his voice, a barely audible croak: 'Mother, mother?'

He spoke. What joy! The sickness had muted him ever since I arrived.

'I'm here, my darling boy,' I whispered, squeezing his hand. But his eyes stayed closed and he said nothing more, remaining still and lifeless as before. Had I dreamed it? I closed my eyes and fell back into sleep. Sometime later, I know not how long, it came again.

'Mother, where are you?'

'I'm here, darling. I'm here, right beside you.'

This time my touch was rewarded by the faintest response of his fingers, squeezing mine. His eyelids moved and then, miracle of miracles, his eyes opened wide in their dark sockets. In the dim light of the rising dawn I watched his gaze ranging around the room before coming to rest in my direction.

I beamed at him, giddy with gladness. 'Hello, my darling.'

'Mother?'

Why would I deny it now? 'I am here, dearest.'

'Water,' he murmured. I lifted his head, oh so gently, and brought the cup to his lips. He took the smallest of sips before resting his head back again and closing his eyes once more.

'I love you, Peter,' I said.

'I love you too.' And then my beloved boy gave me the sweetest of smiles before slipping back into a peaceful, healing sleep.

29

Alamode: a thin, plain tabby-weave lustered silk, usually black. Used mainly for mourning and for the linings of expensive garments, as well as the outer fabric, especially for outerwear such as hoods and mantuas.

I was woken by the slam of the chamber window closing shut. The sun was already shining brightly – it must be morning.

'Whatever are you doing? Do you want him to catch a chill?' Louisa said, wrenching the curtains across once more. 'Ambrose will be furious.'

As I raised my head the swollen cheek, almost forgotten in the height of last night's emotions, pulsed with pain once more. 'He's furious with me anyway, what difference will it make?'

'My goodness, that's quite a bruise you've got,' she said more tenderly. 'He won't be happy about you going out looking like that.' Of course. The doctor's leeches go missing and the vicar's sister-in-law appears with a black eye. Such gossip would be the very thing Ambrose feared most.

'How is he?' she asked, placing her palm on Peter's forehead. 'He seems much cooler today.'

'Bathing him with water seemed to break the fever. He even recognised me.'

'He spoke?'

'Just a few words.'

'Do you think . . . ?' At that moment his eyes opened. 'Hello, my darling boy. Are you feeling better?'

He nodded. 'Thirsty.'

She lifted his head and brought the cup to his lips. Before long we were both weeping with joy. Peter had returned to us.

At breakfast Ambrose barely acknowledged me, averting his eyes from my disfigured, discoloured face. Soon after, the doctor arrived once more.

'He seemed pleased with Peter's progress,' Louisa told me, once he'd left. 'But he warned the disease is unpredictable and can relapse at any moment. He advised warmth, darkness and further purging should he show any more signs of fever.'

Over my dead body, I thought to myself. 'No mention of the leeches?'

'No more leeches.'

'Thank heavens for that.'

Ambrose called us all to Peter's bedside and led us in an overlong series of prayers, praising God and the good services of the doctor for his son's recovery. Still he would not meet my eye. I bowed my head and spoke the words along with everyone else, thinking to myself that while God might have played his part, the ministrations of the doctor had been worse than useless. What had really helped to ease the fever at the critical moment was fresh air and water bathing; of this I was utterly convinced.

During the rest of the day Peter made numerous small steps towards recovery, each more encouraging than the last. He slept and woke again, every time a little more responsive than before. We read to him and he seemed to enjoy listening for just a few moments before falling asleep again, but the next time he stayed awake longer, and then longer.

Maggie glanced at my bruised face and turned away without remark before closeting herself in the kitchen, soon producing a nourishing broth of which Peter took a few sips, proclaiming it to be delicious. She beamed with delight: it was the first time he had taken anything but water for nearly a fortnight. Later in the day he took several more sips, and a small square of bread.

He began to ask questions: what had happened to him, why did he feel so weak, why did we have to keep the curtains drawn and why hadn't his friend been to visit him? We tried to answer as honestly as possible without causing alarm.

'But I want to see Gabriel. When can I get up?' he asked.

'Not for a while yet, my darling,' Louisa said. 'You have been very unwell, you know.'

His face fell. 'Then if I've been so ill, why do you both keep smiling?' How could we explain our delight at the return of his youthful impatience? Our boy was back with us, once more.

I dreaded Ambrose's return that evening. Each sight of myself in the glass or window pane was a reminder of that terrifying fist, the shock of that blow. Further punishment would surely come soon enough. Would he threaten me once more, or just send me away under the cover of darkness? I tried to share my fears with Louisa, but she brushed them aside.

'It's done with now,' she said. 'He forgives and forgets easily. It'll be fine.'

I did not feel so reassured, so it was some relief when he begged to be excused from supper. 'I'm all in, wife,' he said. 'It's been an arduous day and I have no appetite. I need an early night.' She fussed over him for a while, taking a tray to his room, but he sent her away.

'He'll be better in the morning,' she said.

Instead we took our own meals to Peter's chamber and ate at his bedside, to keep him company. He even took a couple of spoonfuls himself. We told stories and teased him about his vanity when he asked for a looking glass. The sound of his laughter was like music to my ears.

He slept, soundly and peacefully, throughout the night.

The next day was Sunday. Maggie offered to stay with Peter while Louisa and I went to church.

'You'll be wanting to thank Him for the boy's recovery,' she said, a little pointedly, I thought. 'And the Reverend would be pleased to see you there.'

'But how can I venture out in public looking like this?' I asked Louisa, hoping that my bruises would provide a legitimate reason for avoiding another of Ambrose's rants. But she insisted that we should go together and produced a jar of mercury paste and some cinnabar rouge which she applied with such gentleness and practised ease I realised she must have developed the skill of covering up her own bruises many times in the past. Blended smoothly onto my skin, these ointments concealed the discolouration so effectively that it was barely detectable except from very close quarters. Finally she brought out a hat with a broad, netted brim under which the swelling could hardly be seen.

Ambrose seemed to have recovered from the previous night's exhaustion. Though still pale-faced, he seemed uplifted by the passion of his faith, preaching with great enthusiasm about the power of God's mercy. What about your own mercy, towards your own family, I felt like asking.

He was about fifteen minutes into the sermon, really getting into his stride, when it happened. Without warning, his face contorted and he folded at the waist, grabbing the sides of the pulpit to steady himself. I watched him gulping for breath, trying to force the words from his mouth.

It was a pitiful sight, even though I could feel no sympathy for the man. From our vantage point in the pew below we could see beads of sweat breaking out on his forehead, gathering into a trickle running down either cheek. He made no move to wipe them away as he struggled to continue, but after just a few more minutes his legs crumpled completely and he slid slowly down into the pulpit, out of view. The congregation of some fifty people or more seemed to gasp, as one.

Louisa was on her feet in an instant, but became ensnared in the rush of others running forward to help. The church warden took her arm, holding her back. 'Let us see to him, Mrs Fairchild. I'm sure he will recover in a few moments.'

The usual calm solemnity of the building became pandemonium as everyone dashed about talking all at once, calling for the doctor, making suggestions, shouting for this and that: water, blankets, air. Shortly it became clear that Ambrose could not get to his feet. Struggling to manoeuvre in the confined space and with much grunting and arguing, three men managed to bring his heavy form down the narrow winding stair from the pulpit. Someone produced a door on which they laid him, and carried him away into the vestry, out of sight.

Louisa returned to the pew, her face ghostly pale, eyes darting wildly from side to side.

'What can I do, dearest?' I asked.

'Go home, and look after Peter,' she said. 'I must go to my husband.'

An hour later a procession led by Louisa appeared carrying Ambrose's still prone form on the board, making their way along the path between the yew trees and into the house. They carried him upstairs into his chamber, with the doctor following close behind.

I hid in the kitchen, listening behind the door when he returned downstairs to the parlour. 'I fear it is not good news, Mrs Fairchild,' he said.

Her anguished howl chilled me to the bone. 'Oh please God, not again.'

'Do not despair, I beg you. God may send mercy to our brother in the same way as he has done to your son.'

She ran into the kitchen and collapsed into my arms.

'What if he dies, Agnes? Whatever will I do without him?' she wailed.

You would be happier and stronger and not in so much danger, I wanted to say. The three of us could live together in peace without his constant threats. But at this moment she needed reassurance: 'He is strong, sister, he will survive,' I said.

'It's typhus, Agnes. *Typhus*.'

'Peter has beaten the disease.'

'But Peter has youth on his side. Oh God, please, please don't let him die.' Sobs racked her thin shoulders, wet tears staining her Sunday best gown. 'He is everything to us.'

We sat her by the fire, and Maggie brought tea.

'It ain't right, madam,' she sighed, shaking her head. 'The reverend has worked hisself to the bone to help others. Is this how God repays him?'

We kept the news from Peter for as long as we could, fearing that the shock might send him into a relapse, but he was now much more aware of what was happening in the house around him, and it became impossible to conceal.

'I heard the doctor, but he didn't come to see me,' he said. 'Tell me the truth. It's Father, isn't it?'

'I'm afraid so, my darling. But he is strong and I am sure that like you he will beat it. In a few weeks' time the pair of you will be up to your usual tricks, of that I'm certain.'

His darling face crumpled. 'I don't want him to die, Mama,' he cried pitifully. 'Whatever would happen to us?'

But there was little time for such speculation. Over the next couple of days, Ambrose's condition declined pitifully. The fevers were as violent and terrifying as anything we had seen. Louisa, Maggie and myself took turns keeping vigil. There was endless soiled bedlinen to wash and hang out to dry, visits of the doctor to supervise and meals to prepare, especially since we were trying to encourage Peter to make up for those days of starvation.

The doorbell rang almost constantly with a stream of well-wishers bringing notes of condolence, posies of flowers, fresh-baked loaves of bread, boxes of eggs and other kindnesses. Everyone spoke, without exception, of their deep love and respect for their vicar, and it left me wondering how such a good man – to whom people regularly referred as a saint – could have such a dark, violent side to his nature. However well we believe we understand someone, we can never truly know them or the demons that haunt their innermost thoughts.

A large bunch of roses arrived from the squire and his family, along with a box of luxury foodstuffs: a joint of venison – 'shot on the estate, I'll be bound', Maggie remarked – a small side of bacon, a sizeable cube of chocolate, a pound of butter, two loaves of soft white bread, a hefty round of Cheddar cheese and three bottles of blackberry wine. Louisa bade the messenger wait while she penned a thank you note.

On the second day of Ambrose's illness Peter declared that he was going to see his father. We tried to dissuade him, fearing he could be reinfected by the disease, and pointing out that he was still too weak to walk unaided, for his muscles were so withered that he might stumble and fall. But he refused all help and with jaw set in grim determination, raised himself from his bed and took his first slow and tentative steps along the landing. Once he reached the chamber where Ambrose lay, only half-conscious of his surroundings, he took a seat by the bed and took his father's hand.

'Can he hear me?'

'Of course, darling,' Louisa said. 'Although he may not reply.'

'I love you, Father.' The boy's voice trembled, and I could see my sister fighting her own tears. 'You must get well. I did, so you can too.'

❊❊❊

Louisa and I were so utterly exhausted that we frequently fell asleep in our chairs. Even during Anna's trials I had never felt so tired, nor could I remember a period when I had not lain flat in my bed for so many nights. But nothing, not even the doctor's purging, leeching or cooling him with damp towels – to which Louisa acceded reluctantly – seemed able to abate the course of Ambrose's illness.

Late one evening he began to call out in his delirium, much as Peter had done. His words were clear. 'Get my curate.'

'He will be abed, my dearest,' Louisa said. 'We will call for him in the morning.'

'No!' he bellowed. '*Now*. Get my curate. Go now.'

Dull-faced, she went for her cloak. 'He's going, Agnes, and he knows it. Why else would he call for the curate in the middle of the night?'

Ambrose was right. We gathered to witness the prayers the curate spoke with great tenderness, blessing the now silent form of his revered vicar. Afterwards, we sat at the bedside to watch and wait. In the early hours of the morning, his heart stopped and the breath stilled in his chest.

This man, larger than life, filled with such powerful faith and selfless duty towards his fellows; this man who had saved my sister from the gutter and helped rescue me from servitude, and yet who harboured beneath this apparently beneficent exterior a contradictory character of terrifying violence and cruelty, was no more.

I was so tired I barely knew what to think or to feel. Louisa and Peter were distraught, of course, and I did my best to comfort them, but with his passing a great weight seemed to be lifted from my shoulders. The atmosphere in the house, too, seemed calmer, easier, more straightforward. We spoke openly and without fear, we came and went as we wished, within the constraints of mourning, of course. We ate when we chose, and what we chose, and rested when we felt like it.

In a curious way our family bonds felt stronger without him.

30

Crepe (also spelled crape): a silk or wool fabric with a distinct-
ively crisp, crimped appearance, usually woven in black and
used for mourning wear.

I have often looked back on that time, those days following
Ambrose's death, wondering whether in the grief and turmoil that such a tragedy brings I could ever have imagined
the astonishing turn of events that took place so shortly
afterwards.

The village was thrown into mourning, of course. Louisa
took to her bed and sobbed for a full night and day, and
there was little that Maggie or I could do to comfort her. I
feared for Peter, too, his body still weak from his own trials.
Although he had previously recovered at least some of his
appetite, he began to refuse food once more. He rose and
dressed each day but would soon run out of energy, burning
out quickly like a fire lit with fine twigs.

Several times I found him weeping. 'I miss him, Auntie.
He was always there, you know.' Even through his tears, he
managed a damp smile. 'I didn't always agree with him,
especially all that hellfire stuff he used to preach, and I was

sometimes afraid of him, but whatever will we do, now that he's not here?'

'He loved you very much,' I said. It was true, I supposed, although my heart blenched at the thought that Peter might also have been on the receiving end of Ambrose's peculiar kind of love. How many times had he too felt the hard edge of the man's fist? I was surprised that he'd shown no curiosity at all about my bruise, nor even given it a second glance, until I began to understand that perhaps in this household such things were just too commonplace for remark.

Yes, their lives would change, with that I had to agree, but I tried to reassure him that his father would have made a will providing for the two of them. Even though they would probably have to leave the vicarage at some point, it would not be at once, and I would make sure that they were never without a home. Already in my head I was planning, working out how to rearrange the attic rooms in my shop to create a second bedroom.

The funeral took place on the third day. The bishop came from Chelmsford to take the service and so many travelled from far around to attend that there was standing room only in the church, crowds spilling out beyond the porch and into the churchyard. My sister followed the coffin, pale and dignified in her widow's weeds, and Maggie lent me a veil and a black crepe gown that I hastily altered to fit my slighter form. Another family brought a black silk jacket for Peter that had been worn by their son after his father's demise.

Death had stalked this village for so long that they were well provisioned for mourning.

Throughout the previous tumultuous days I had been in regular correspondence with Mrs T. and although she continued to reassure me that everything at the shop was 'perfectly under control' and exhorted me not to 'fret yourself', I would have to return to London before long or the business might start to suffer from my absence.

But abandoning Louisa and Peter in the rawness of their grief was out of the question, at least for the moment. There were numerous official meetings to be had. The day after the funeral, Ambrose's solicitor called in to read the will. The three of us, with the curate acting as witness, were invited into the drawing room, nervously awaiting the pronouncement which would determine how they might live the rest of their lives.

The first revelation was that despite his meagre stipend, Ambrose's frugal habits had enabled him to save the extraordinary sum of just over a thousand pounds. But what followed was less encouraging: the list of those to whom in his munificence he bequeathed sums of money and small items of property was lengthy, and I began to wonder whether anything would remain for his family. The church was to receive fifty pounds, his curate twenty, Maggie a further ten, and numerous other people and organisations with whom I was not familiar.

My name did not appear on the list, nor had I expected it. In fact it was only afterwards, when my sister mentioned it, that I even noticed. 'I'm so sorry, darling Agnes, but I am sure he loved you even so. We shall find something for you anyway, to remember him by.'

In truth, I had no desire to be reminded. The omission only served to confirm what I have always known; that Ambrose only tolerated my existence in their lives out of commitment to my sister, and because I had provided him with the son he had always so desired.

The solicitor came to the end of his reading, and looked up with a smile. 'Your husband was the most generous man, Mrs Fairchild,' he said. 'Many of these benefactors are poor people, with little else to their names. These bequests will make a great difference to their lives. But fear not, there is still the sum of eight hundred pounds, which should provide amply for yourself and your son so long as you are prepared to live modestly. If you would like any help with how to invest it to the best advantage I shall be happy to put you in contact with my advisor.'

Next day we received news that threw the household into a further fluster. The bishop had invited himself to tea.

'However shall we manage without cook to make her famous sponge cake for him?' Louisa cried.

'I can produce a passable fruit scone.'

'He hates any dried fruit, it gives him heartburn. Whatever else can we provide?'

In the end, Maggie produced a surprisingly good honey and cinnamon cake and I made scones without the fruit, served with quince jelly and clotted cream, which the bishop pronounced to be delicious. After tea he asked for 'a few words alone with Mrs Fairchild'.

'Whatever is he telling her?' Peter said, once we had withdrawn to the kitchen. 'Why aren't I allowed to hear it?'

The darling boy! I could have wept for him. Even in his tender years he was already developing a sense of manly protectiveness, a feeling of responsibility for their future now that Ambrose was gone. His childhood was at an end.

Louisa emerged looking drawn and anxious.

'Come, let us sit at the table and you must tell us everything,' I said. She glanced at Peter, then at me. 'We all need to know, Louisa. You must not hide anything from us, so that we can deal with this all together, as a family.'

And so it transpired that as I suspected they would soon have to leave the vicarage, the only home Peter had ever known, once a new vicar was appointed.

'It's so unfair,' he said. 'Why do we have to?'

'Just think about it, dearest,' she said. 'If every family was allowed to stay in the vicarages around the country, the church would just have to build more and more of them, and they have no money for that sort of thing. It makes sense if you think about it.'

'I suppose so.' He scowled. 'How soon do we have to leave?'

'He cannot tell us exactly. Gabriel's father will stand in for general services in the meantime and there will be a locum to take communion, but as the bishop says, the village deserves not to wait too long without a vicar. It may be a few weeks, two months at the most.'

'A few *weeks*?' He was trying to be strong but I could see his chin tremble. 'What then? Where shall we live?'

'You will never be without somewhere to live, that I promise,' I said. 'Perhaps you could come to London?'

'London?' His eyes widened, and then a shadow fell over his face. 'But how can I leave Gabriel?'

'That is a topic for another day, dearest,' Louisa said.

'Now, let us eat some more of your auntie's delicious scones, for they will not be so good tomorrow.'

The bishop's visit stirred my sister into a frenzy of activity. The following day I woke to hear her moving furniture. 'Whatever are you up to, Louisa?' I called.

'It has to be done soon enough, if we're to move out within a few weeks.'

Pulling on my bed gown and slippers, I followed her voice to Ambrose's study. I had never before crossed the threshold into this formerly forbidden territory, and even now felt a small tremor of fear as I opened the door. It was a small dark room lined with shelves bowed under the weight of many heavy tomes. In the centre was a large mahogany desk almost entirely covered with books and papers. It reminded me of the merchant's chaotic show-room.

Louisa was crouched on the floor beside a heavy wooden chest that she had pulled away from the wall – the noise I'd heard – so she could raise its lid.

'Goodness, this is going to be a marathon task,' I said, looking around. 'Why don't we wait until after breakfast, dearest, and I will help you?'

She sat back on her heels, pushing a stray strand of hair beneath her cap. 'The bishop says I must sort through my husband's papers immediately and send him any that I consider to be confidential, or of special interest to the diocese.'

'Whatever can he mean?' I asked, gesturing around the

cluttered room. 'Surely these are just Ambrose's books and writings?'

She shrugged. 'Who knows? My husband never spoke of his work to me. I just hope there aren't any hidden surprises.'

'We could just send all of it to the diocesan office, perhaps? That'd save a lot of work.'

'And risk allowing them to see something Ambrose wanted kept private? No, I owe it to him to sort things out first.'

'Then let me help you, dearest,' I said. 'For a start we could sell some of those books. I'd imagine they're worth a few pounds.'

After breakfast, we began. While she went through the voluminous boxes of papers and notebooks, I sorted the books into three stacks: a large one for 'sell', a second for 'diocese' and a third, much smaller, for 'keep'. Each time I consulted her she dithered, saying 'keep' more times than most until I reminded her that wherever she lived next might not have space for a library. After a while she simply delegated the decisions to me, which speeded up the process greatly.

We laboured for several hours. It was dusty work. 'Let us take a break, sister, I need some fresh air,' I said, pulling spider filaments from my sleeve.

'Good idea. If you get the kettle on I'll come once I've finished this drawer,' she said.

After fifteen minutes she had still not emerged. I returned to find her sitting in Ambrose's favourite chair, with a small brown cardboard-bound notebook in her hands. Tears were falling onto the pages, smudging the ink.

'Louisa, whatever is it?'

She handed the notebook to me. Ambrose's handwriting was scrawly and hard to decipher, but after a few moments my eyes became accustomed and I began to see that it was a kind of diary. I skipped over several short entries of little import – 'call on Mrs Berrisford', 'order prayer books', 'write to the bishop' – until I reached the longer one.

Dear God, it has happened again. I love her dearly but she does irritate me so with her wittering and her feminine concerns that there comes a point when I cannot help myself. An evil demon seems to take over, controlling my voice and uttering such cruel words that my beloved cowers and cries.

Then somehow, dearest Lord forgive me, the crying seems to enrage the demon so greatly that it forces me to raise my arm to her. It is as though I have acted in a dream, for afterwards, when I then see her on the floor, her cheek reddened or her lip split, I can scarcely believe that it is my doing.

She does not chide me nor complain, for where else could she go? But each time seems more violent than the last and I genuinely fear that it will one day cause her mortal injury. I love my wife, and would cut off my right hand if I felt that might stop it.

Dear Lord, have I not served you well? Have I not brought many to recognise your ways, shown many kindnesses to my fellow man? Please, I beg of you, grant me your forgiveness and guide me to greater understanding so that I may control this demon.

I pretended to continue reading for a few seconds, for the words were spinning in front of my eyes, my thoughts in turmoil. My first reaction was of astonishment, and then anger: how dare he write these words, so knowingly, so coldly? And how dare he try to deflect the blame away from himself onto some 'demon' acting beyond his control?

It was your fault, I felt like shouting. *No one else made you do it and it was in no one else's power to stop it unless you acknowledged responsibility for your own actions.* But I held my tongue. After all, my dearest sister, still weeping at my side, was the one who had suffered the most. She should not have to answer for his sins.

'The dear man, he knew it was wrong,' she sobbed. I said nothing. How deluded she was; she would probably never accept the truth that he was, at heart, a violent bully. 'He always apologised afterwards – perhaps not in so many words, but by being especially kind to us both.'

'*Both* of you?' I shouted, sickened. 'He hit *Peter*, too?'

'Oh no, my darling. But Peter knew. How could he not, being in the same household? He was always there to comfort me, the dear boy.'

Now, my legs began to tremble. I threw the notebook to the floor as though it was somehow contaminated with evil and stumbled to a chair. Ambrose was eight feet below the ground, but his malign legacy persisted. For years I'd believed that this vicarage was the perfect, stable place for my son to be raised, that he was growing up happy and well loved. But now I was discovering the conspiracy of silence into which he had unwittingly been drawn, the extent of the lies he had learned to tell, the walls of collusion that he and Louisa had created to protect the man who controlled them with fear.

Louisa began to laugh. Was it hysteria? 'Dearest, whatever is the matter?'

'Don't you see? He has left me a wonderful message.' She took the notebook up from the floor where I'd thrown it, and held it to her heart, her face illuminated with genuine happiness.

'It must be a great relief, my darling,' I said. 'To be free from fear at last.'

'You don't understand.' She opened the notebook and turned to the tear-stained page. 'Look at what he wrote: *I love her dearly.* He really did love me, Agnes. I always knew it but, forgive me, there were times when I doubted him.' She turned her face upwards and crossed herself. 'Thank you, Lord, for this sign. May he rest in peace.'

Only now did I start to grasp her meaning. Deluded she might be, but it was important for her to believe – and this diary was the proof she needed – that despite his violent outbursts Ambrose had genuinely loved her, that he was truly contrite about his actions and had sought God's guidance to try to prevent it happening again. Here it was, in black and white. Now she could say goodbye to him cherishing the best of her memories, rather than dwelling on the worst.

I leaned across, took her hand and squeezed it. She squeezed back. How I loved my sister, in that moment. In the silence that followed I sent up my own prayer of thanks to whoever might be listening. She was safe, Peter was well and Ambrose was dead, no longer a threat to anyone.

31

Appliqué: ornamental needlework in which pieces of fabric are sewn onto a larger piece to form a picture or pattern.

The house was deep in mourning, we dressed in black each day and visitors continued to arrive at the doorstep with flowers and long faces. Some of them, the ladies in particular, even wept.

But I was happy, perhaps happier now than I had been for many months, waking each morning with a smile. So happy, in fact, that I had to stop myself humming as I went about my tasks, for fear of being considered disrespectful. Once we had sorted out the vicarage, from here onwards the three of us could live the lives we wanted without interference or fear.

Nothing could break our family bonds now.

Louisa and Peter would be able to live quite comfortably on the money that Ambrose had left them. I even began to consider how we might be able to live together – perhaps Mr Boyson might be able to offer us larger premises for the shop, or a smaller house nearby where all three of us could live. I felt confident that now Ambrose was gone there would be no more talk of rent rises, and we could resume our normal friendly relations.

Fate had brought us the opportunity to build ourselves a wonderful future and each day of tedious work, sorting, packing and boxing up all of their belongings, brought us closer to that new life. At least, that was how I saw it.

But progress was infuriatingly slow. Peter was reluctant to relinquish a single toy, shirt or pair of outgrown boots. Louisa took hours deciding whether she could live without a certain much-chipped mixing bowl, or a pair of gloves even though they were split between the fingers. Having been accustomed to living frugally in two small rooms, it astonished me how they had accumulated so many belongings. I supposed that if you have the space, you tended to fill it.

The weather was still warm and dry and I longed to get into the fresh air, but Louisa was reluctant to leave the house. 'It would not be thought seemly for me to be seen taking my leisure so soon afterwards. What if someone calls and I am not here to receive them? Besides, I cannot face meeting anyone in the street. If they offered condolences I would surely start cry.'

'Then do you have any objection if Peter and I go out?' I said. 'He needs the sunshine for his health, and a short walk would help to improve his strength. It cannot be good for him to be cooped up in this dusty house all the time.'

He accepted without hesitation. 'Can we call on Gabriel, Auntie?'

I glanced at Louisa. 'Yes, of course. But remember, dear one, you are still in mourning and must comport yourself appropriately – no silly games. There will be time enough in the future for that.'

Gabriel's mother is a woman of many words. She offered us her condolences at great length, saying how sorry everyone was, what a good man Ambrose was, how everyone in the parish respected him greatly, how we would miss him so much, it would be hard to find anyone who matched his dedication, the church would not be the same again, and so on. She turned her attentions to Peter, embarrassing him with her prattling about how well he looked, thanking the Lord for his good mercy in sparing him, and what a terrible disease it was and how unfair that their small village should have had to suffer so.

'Peter and I are going for a short walk in the orchards,' I said, at last finding a moment to interrupt her as she took a breath. 'Would Gabriel care to join us?' Her son arrived at the doorstep and on seeing Peter bounded out with a shriek of delight, clasping his friend in such a fierce embrace they both fell to the ground and began wrestling like puppies.

I walked a few discreet paces behind but close enough to eavesdrop on their chatter as the two boys pulled ahead, arm in arm.

'What was it like?' Gabriel asked.

'It?'

'Having the typhus.'

'Oh, that. Weird, horrible. Like being in a dream most of the time.'

'Still, I'm glad you're well now. Oh, I should have said first, I'm sorry about your father.'

'Yeah.' They walked in silence for a short while.

'At least you didn't cry at the funeral.'

'It was odd. I didn't feel anything much then. It's now we're packing everything up it makes me sad.'

'Packing, why?'

'We've got to leave the vicarage.'

'What? You're moving?'

'Yes, silly. We have to let the new vicar come and live here.'

'But you'll stay in the village, Peter? You can't move away, because . . .'

'We might move to London, Mother says. To live with my aunt.'

'But that's miles and miles away. I'd never see you.'

'I know. But I think I can persuade her to look for somewhere nearby.'

'Yes. Tell her you have to stay. I'd miss you.'

'I'd miss you too, Gabe.'

※

Each evening Louisa and I would review our progress and make plans for the following day. We opened a bottle of the squire's blackberry wine and took to drinking what we called a 'nightcap', although it was usually some hours before bedtime. The wine was delicious: sweet and tart at the same time, full of the sunshine that had ripened the fruit and mellow like the autumn in which the berries had been plucked from the hedgerows. Although neither of us said it, the wine was all the more enjoyable for the freedom in which we could drink it.

I told her of the boys' conversation that afternoon.

'They are such good friends,' she said. 'It would be sad to break them up. But as the days go by I wonder whether staying in Westford Abbots is such a good idea.'

'Why so, dearest? I thought you loved this village?'

'Indeed I do, or rather did. But would we forever be considered the grieving son and widow, wearing black and living in the shadow of everyone's undying loyalty for Ambrose? In the face of his reputation it will be hard enough for the new incumbent to gain the respect of the congregation without the daily reminder of his family still living in the village.'

'But do you also not have friends here you would be sad to leave?' I knew, of course, that although she had many acquaintances, hardly any were close enough to be regarded as friends.

She shook her head. 'Oh, I don't know. I cannot bear to think about it at the moment, dearest. It is all too sudden.' She took out her handkerchief, dabbing the corners of her eyes. 'Leaving this place seems like accepting that he will never come back, that we will have to live the rest of our lives without the only man I have ever loved.'

The genuine depth of her feeling for a man whom I'd considered brutal, self-absorbed and more wedded to his God than to his family never ceased to amaze me.

Slowly, Louisa began to regain her emotional strength. She smiled from time to time – I even overheard her and Peter laughing, a joyful sound. Life was returning to the family like a bright sunrise after a long dark night. Even though

THE DRESSMAKER OF DRAPER'S LANE

in public we were expected to be in mourning, at home we were beginning to enjoy the freedom to be ourselves. The ruler of all things had gone, and we could decide what to do and when to do it. I began to see what life might be like with the three of us living together as a family.

Yet with each passing day I became more restless. September was just around the corner, when ladies returning from their summer seasons would turn their thoughts to new gowns, cloaks and hats for the winter. Mrs T. was very capable and I trusted her implicitly with the cutting out, sewing and finishing, but she did not have the way with customers that I had developed over the years; how to appear in accord with their ideas while actually suggesting another style, or design of fabric that would suit them far better. Neither did she have any aptitude for pricing, tending to quote too low for the true value of the job, leaving little or no margin for profit.

It is a trade based almost entirely on word of mouth. The businesses that thrived were those most persistently attentive to the whims of fashion and the fluctuations of fabric prices. I could not let that slip. The livelihoods of five people were dependent upon me, as well as my own.

At last, I felt compelled to tell Louisa that I would have to return to London the day after the morrow, while reassuring her that I would come back to Essex in two weeks' time to finish the packing and, when it came time, to help them move.

It was on the afternoon of my last day that it happened. She'd asked me to make sure all of the cupboards and drawers in the 'guest room' – my usual chamber – were completely emptied. The wardrobe is a great heavy thing in dark oak, wide and capacious with double doors and a deep drawer beneath. The cupboard itself was empty so I went to open the drawer, but it was warped and refused to budge. Fearing that I might pull off the handles by wrenching too fiercely, I gave a knock to each side with the heel of my palm to straighten it.

At last, with an ease that sent me reeling backwards, the drawer opened. It was empty save for some fronds of dried lavender that must have been placed there many years before to ward off moths. In the corner was a torn piece of plain tissue paper that I assumed was rubbish. But when I went to crumple it in my hand I felt a sudden pain in the heel of my palm, so sharp that I cried out, thinking I'd been stung by a sleepy wasp. As I dropped it, a piece of cream worsted fell free from the paper, with a needle threaded through it. A bead of blood was already starting to form on my palm.

The shock of the needle prick and the sight of the red blood must have shifted something in my mind, like layers of curtains being pulled apart to reveal a distant landscape, a landscape of memories that had remained concealed, or perhaps suppressed, for many years. The reminders had always been there, of course; the sharp pain in my palm when I first took up the pagoda silk, the faint smell of lavender, my dreams of brilliantly coloured birds and the gnarled old apple tree in the vicarage garden that had always seemed especially magical. But until now these had come only in brief, disconnected fragments.

For all of my early years I was in the power of others, bounded by rules and in daily fear of being punished for breaking them, sometimes severely. Even in my first few days at the vicarage I must have understood that, benign though he appeared to be, Ambrose held the keys of power over my sister, and thus of my own future happiness. I was allowed into the family on his terms. Perhaps it was that overriding, gut-wrenching dread, the dread of my mis-demeanours being discovered, of being cast out of paradise, that had caused me to bury those memories so deeply.

Now, all of that fear had gone and as I sat back on my heels, sucking my bloodied hand, the fragments began to coalesce, merging into a scene so powerful that in my mind's eye I could recollect every detail, even all these years later.

It was on one of those days after my arrival in Westford Abbots for the very first time, long before I knew that I was expecting Peter, long before our arrangement for his adop-tion, long before I became a seamstress. I had just turned sixteen and oh, the joy of having my own room, a comfort-able bed to lie on, a choice of books to read and all the time in the world, even in the afternoon, to read them. Louisa popped her head around the door.

'Ah, there you are. You look content.'

'More than I have ever been in my whole life,' I said, without a shadow of exaggeration. 'I could not be happier.'

'I have to slip out to take some things to the church for Ambrose. You stay with your book, dearest. I'll be away for only an hour, promise,' she said. 'Then we shall take tea.'

On reaching the end of my chapter I decided to stretch my legs. Looking out of the window over the garden, the fruit already starting to ripen on our favourite old apple tree in the corner, I felt myself fizzing with exhilaration and wonder at my good fortune. What remarkable circumstances had rescued me from the oppression of Tobias's attentions and the arduous duties of a housemaid, and led me to this beautiful place in the heart of my new-found family? And here I was, enjoying for the first time in my life the comforts of my own private chamber.

I went to the dressing table – a dressing table! – and sat on the stool, turning my head this way and that in the mirror, fancying myself as a beautiful society lady. In my head I spoke to an imaginary maid: 'I shall wear the shot green silk tonight, Mary, with the emerald necklace and earrings his Lordship gave me. They complement my eyes so well, he says.'

Miming her ladyship's actions I reached into the drawer, pretending to take out a jewel box and opening it, cradling the jewels in my hand before arranging them around my throat and fixing the clasp at the back of my neck.

Now I was ready for the gown and went to the wardrobe. Hanging inside I discovered what must have been Louisa's winter garments: a few dresses in plain wool and linen and a long woollen cape, but no gown of shot green silk. Extreme inquisitiveness had brought me trouble many times in the past, and now it led me astray once more. I opened the heavy drawer beneath and discovered various folded shawls, two muffs and a box of gloves. The smell of lavender was sweet to my senses.

Sitting cross-legged on the floor I began to try them on, first the muffs and then the gloves. I had never had any of my own, you understand, and just wanted to know what they felt like. In winter, we housemaids would simply pull our sleeves around our hands, or wrap them in the ends of our shawls. The sensation of each individual finger clothed in its own tube of leather felt so luxurious that I almost wished it were winter already.

When I went to put them away I discovered something else that had previously been hidden beneath the gloves. It was a small piece of pale cream worsted, about a foot square. As I drew it out into the light I could see that someone was attempting to craft a sampler. In the centre, slightly askew, was a cross-stitched square inside which a few letters and numbers had been outlined in pencil, ready for the embroidering. At each corner of the square were tacked four pieces of colourful silk figures, ready for being appliquéd onto the wool ground to create a decorative frame.

From my experience of sewing I knew that the would-be creator of this sampler had set themselves a very ambitious task, because appliqué needs a neat edge, and silk frays in a heartbeat.

Just then I heard the front door downstairs, and Louisa's cheery call: 'I'm back, Agnes. The kettle is on.' Guilt-ridden and fearful of my misdemeanours being discovered, I hastily began to shove everything back into the drawer. But as I did so a needle that had been threaded into the back of the sampler pricked the palm of my hand, and the blood blotted a bright red stain onto the plain cream wool. I sucked at it and tried to rub it away, but the spot remained stubbornly bright.

Now all these years later I held in my hands that very same sampler, still unfinished. But what now caused me to gasp was the design of those pieces of fabric tacked to the sampler ready to be appliquéd. There was the exotic bird, the twisted tree, the fiery dragon and the silver-roofed pagoda. It was *that* silk, the Chinoiserie brocade woven for Henrietta Howard, the precious royal silk that our mother had somehow got hold of and used as a token when she took me to the Foundling Hospital.

Sitting at the foot of that same wardrobe I understood at last why, on that day we brought the bundle home from the auction, that silk had felt so familiar and had both fascinated and unsettled me all at the same time. It was burdened with powerful emotions from that long-ago day, of curiosity, guilt and fear. But questions now flooded my mind: whose sampler was it? Louisa was no seamstress, which would account for the uneven cross-stitching. Where had she obtained the silk? Had it been left to her by our mother, or discovered after her death? Now, surely, was the time to ask.

As I wrapped it back into the tissue paper I noticed a small brown mark of dried blood on the pale worsted.

In the hours that passed after discovering the sampler my resolve began to falter. Was it fair, so soon after Ambrose's death, to risk asking Louisa to reveal distressing memories? Yet how could I delay, when this sampler must hold the key to the mysteries I had for so long desired to understand?

I was due to return to London the following day to make

sure that all was well at the shop, and though I planned to return again the following week, this might be my last chance to discover the truth.

That evening after Peter retired Louisa and I went to the drawing room, as usual. I have always loved this space, so light and peaceful, with windows on two sides giving an outlook into the garden. A golden afterglow of sunset filled the room and we threw open the windows to breathe in the sweet evening air, so welcome after our dusty tasks.

She brought in two wine glasses and the second bottle of the squire's blackberry wine.

'Here's to my dearest sister,' I said. 'To your love and your courage. I'm sorry I have to leave you tomorrow, but I'll be back just as soon as I can.'

'Thank you, dearest. Having you here at my side has meant everything to me.' She smiled, and in that smile I could see signs of her former sweet self, now that the strain of the past few weeks was beginning to lift.

Still I hesitated, reluctant to disturb this pleasant scene; just the two of us in amicable company, knowing that Peter was safe and well in the room above and – God forgive me – without fear of Ambrose and his unpredictable moods. But the hidden presence of the sampler seemed to nip at my shoulder. Now that it had emerged from its long hiding, its secrets must be told.

I went to retrieve it from the dresser drawer where I'd hidden it. 'I found this when I was turning out the wardrobe in my chamber,' I said, as casually as possible, handing it to her. 'Is it something you want to keep?'

The shock of recognition was clear. Her face drained and her fingers shook as she placed her glass on the side table. She looked up at me and then back at the sampler again.

'Perhaps I could help you finish it?' I said, trying to keep my voice calm and steady. 'Those Chinese figures are very beautiful, are they not? I recognised them at once; they're from the same silk I showed you that I'd bought at the auction with Anna. Do you remember?'

A long silence followed, save for the harsh alarm call of a bird in the garden warning of a cat, perhaps, or an approaching jackdaw? She took a breath and for a moment I hoped she might be about to speak, but she sighed and fell quiet again.

'Louisa?'

At last, she looked up and sat back in her chair. 'My dearest, I hoped you would never have to know.'

'Know what, sister?' Now my heart filled with dread, and I wished I'd left the sampler hidden. Sometimes it is better not to know. But it was too late to take it back.

'It is a dark and difficult chapter of my life that even now it troubles me to recall.'

'Then stop, dearest. I don't want you to be further hurt. Let's forget I even mentioned it.' I went to take the sampler from her hand but she pulled it back, gripping so fiercely I feared she might prick herself on that same needle.

'When you showed the silk to me at the shop that day I feared the whole edifice of our deceit might come tumbling down. But you seemed to forget about it, and when you raised it again, I persuaded you not to pursue it.'

Edifice of deceit? A cold hand crept into my chest. Had I been deliberately deceived?

She took up the bottle of wine and refilled her glass before passing it across to me.

'I can see that the time has come for you to know the truth.'

32

French knots: a favoured decorative stitch used to create accents in a design. The size can be increased with additional turns of the thread around the needle.

'Do you recall me telling you how I was taken from my mother and placed with an aunt? And how Ambrose took me on as a maid?'

'Then after a few years you became his housekeeper, and later he asked you to be his wife?'

Louisa nodded and paused a second, forehead furrowing as she searched for words. 'But those years were not as straightforward as I painted them.'

'My dear, what happened?'

'This is the shame I hoped never to reveal to you, nor anyone else.' She spoke so quietly that I had to lean forward to hear her. 'You see, before I met Ambrose I had already set my heart on another man.'

I could breathe again. If this was the extent of her secret, it was of little consequence. 'It is no shame for a woman to have many suitors, dearest. Why do you say so?'

'He was not a suitor, Agnes. He was a client.'

'A *client*? What kind of business were you engaged in?'

My question was genuinely innocent; I had no inkling of what she meant.

Her cheeks flooded crimson as the wine stain on her lips. 'I was a streetwalker.'

Of course I knew the term but it did not register, not at once. 'You walked the streets?' I said, stupidly.

'I was a whore, Agnes.' She spat out the words, staring at a point past me, grimacing as though the memory caused her physical pain. 'A common whore.'

I shook my head, still struggling to understand. Surely this was all wrong? How could my respectable sister ever have been a street girl?

'Please don't think badly of me, Agnes.' She dropped her head into her hands. 'I had no choice. My aunt and uncle forced me into it, to pay for my bed and lodging. I hated it, of course. It was degrading and dangerous and I pleaded with them to set me free, but I was trapped because they handled all the transactions. They made good money from me.'

I took a gulp of wine, shaken by the horror of her revelation, the cruelty of it. Our mother had entrusted her child to the safe care of this couple and they had repaid this trust by making her walk the streets. 'I would never think badly of anything you do, dearest sister. You must not be ashamed, for you had no choice. I know how that feels. Remember how I was forced myself, by that vile man at the Manor? I had no choice either.'

She nodded.

'Anyway, that is all in the past. We are both strong, and we have both survived.'

Now she began to speak, the words rushing over

themselves like water from an overflowing well. 'But there is more, Agnes, for I found myself with child. I had already known this man for several months and he paid my aunt and uncle well in return for my exclusive services. He treated me so tenderly that I imagined myself to be in love with him. Although he was a good deal older, he was so handsome, so wealthy and a widower, and he seemed so fond towards me that I began to entertain the hope that he would make me an honest woman, poor deluded fool that I was. Why would a respectable merchant want to marry a slut?'

'You were never a . . .' I started.

'But that is what he called me when I eventually plucked up the courage to tell him of my condition. He flew into a great rage and sent me from his house, forbidding me ever to return.'

'Who was this terrible man, Louisa, who treated you so?' She ignored me, talking on.

'A kind of madness gripped me, dearest, for the terrible shame of it I suppose. One day I simply headed for Blackfriars Bridge, thinking that I might kill myself. But I didn't have the courage, not then or even later. I could not return to my aunt's house so I sold my body on the streets for a few more weeks – until my condition became so obvious that no man would have me – and managed to save enough to rent a hovel, which is where the child was born. I was starving and desperate, but even then I could not bring myself to end our lives.'

My ribs ached from holding my breath. 'Whatever happened to the baby?'

'Someone told me about a new place that had been set up to the west of the city, the Foundling Hospital.'

My neck began to prickle, as though something unseen and terrifying was creeping up behind me, too terrible to face. 'You took *your* child to the Hospital?' I gasped. 'Just like our mother did?'

She nodded. 'It was just a few weeks after that I learned of the vicar who was seeking a housemaid and went to apply for the post. And that is when I began the sampler, once I was settled there. For something to remember her by. But I am no seamstress, as you know. It defeated me and I never had the heart to finish it.' There was a half-smile on Louisa's lips, her gaze far away, deep in the memories.

'She was the dearest thing, a perfect child. I called her Agnes,' she whispered, kneeling forward on the carpet before me and reaching up to cup my cheeks with warm, soft palms as though I were something infinitely precious.

'Don't you see?' she whispered. 'It was *you*. Agnes Potton.'

There was a roaring in my ears, so loud it was almost painful, and I began to shake, unable to listen any more, unable to bear her touch. Pushing her roughly away, I began to pace the floor, rubbing my face in my hands, trying to wash away the confusion. My cap became dislodged and I threw it to the floor. Nothing made sense.

'That's right, my darling.' She stood up now and walked towards me, her face beaming, reaching out for me. 'I am your mother.'

Her smile was too bright, false and almost menacing, like a jester. The air felt heavy and viscous, thick with deception, hard to breathe.

'No!' I yelled, arms flailing to fight her off. 'You're lying.' What kind of warped trick was this? 'This cannot be right. You are my *sister*. And you are only seven years older than me. How can you be my *mother*?'

She stopped a few feet away. 'You are right,' she said, 'about the lying. I have been lying to you ever since we met, dearest. But I am not lying now, that I promise. All that is over with. What I am telling you now is the absolute truth.'

Recoiling in disgust, I pushed her roughly out of the way, hurrying out of the room. Where to go? Gasping for air, I ran out into the garden, across the damp grass to the old apple tree, perhaps something, anything, solid and familiar.

'No, no. It can't be,' I shouted. 'Don't let it be. I don't want it to be like this.' But the tree gave no comfort: as I clasped my arms around its trunk and pressed my cheek hard against the rough bark, it left my skin scraped and raw.

Blinded by tears now, I ran back to the path. Ahead of me was the gate, and beyond that the great solid form of the church silhouetted against the darkening sky. But it offered no sense of peace or solace; that was Ambrose's realm, a place reeking of hellfire and, ultimately, of death.

I began to pace once more, not knowing which way to turn. Along the path on either side of me stood the old yew trees, dark shadows against the sky. They had often appeared sinister or even threatening, especially when they creaked in the wind. But now, in the still of evening, the only sound was the gentle goodnight twitters of sparrows nesting in their dense branches, and their presence seemed to calm my thoughts.

What times had they witnessed, these great ancient

trees, in their centuries of growing? What displays of human joy and tragedy, what ordinary lives, what extraordinary events? My feet slowed. The sky above me was a deep, luminous blue, speckled with early stars. It was not cold, even now, but the air was damp and laden with dew and I shivered, pulling my shawl close around my shoulders.

There were footsteps on the gravel behind me, the warmth of a hand on my shoulder and a gentle whisper: 'Dearest, I am so sorry.'

'I don't understand,' I said, still dizzied with confusion.

'Come, let me help you up.' She cupped my elbow. 'Let us go inside, and we can talk calmly and sensibly.'

She led me indoors, sat me down, poured more wine and bade me take a sip, then another. She took her seat and waited quietly. I could not meet her eyes. That face had been so dear to me, every movement and every gesture so familiar, yet she was a stranger now. How could she *possibly* be my mother? We were so alike, two peas in a pod, everyone said. Of course we were sisters.

I finished the glass and she filled it again. But even the burn of the wine slipping down my throat could not ease the ice in my heart.

'But you are only seven years older than me,' I said again.

She looked into her glass, as though it held a secret. Then, eventually, she looked up.

'I lied to you, Agnes. I was fifteen when I gave birth to you.'

I gaped at her. 'You are *fifteen* years older than me? How is that possible? You look so young.'

'At any other time, your words would be flattering,

dearest. But I am afraid that it is the truth. Remember? I said there would be no more lies.'

The anger was rising in my chest once more. 'So *why*? Why did you tell me so many lies?'

'I never wanted to, Agnes. Had it been my own choice . . .'

'Then why? WHY?' My shout reverberated around the silent house and I remembered that upstairs my son was sleeping. I lowered my voice. 'Why didn't you tell me this long ago?'

She took a deep breath. 'It was part of my agreement with Ambrose. So that you would never guess that I was your mother.'

In that moment I hated her, wanted to bawl at her, hit her, anything to stop her saying those words, the very words I had wanted to hear all of my life, now violated by their terrible deceit and poisoned by that brute Ambrose. She was *not* my mother. How could she be? How could she *ever* be?

Through the tumult in my head I could hear her voice continuing quietly and calmly. 'You must understand, dearest. I was but a child myself, ignorant and terrified of having to spend the rest of my life on the streets. Giving you away was the hardest thing I have ever done, and the grief of it nearly broke me. Even to this day the memory of it is etched on my heart. All I ever wanted was to have you back again.'

'Why did you not come looking for me, then?'

'Ah, I so wished to, my dearest. You cannot know how much I wished it. I felt your loss like the loss of a limb and I often dreamed that you were back in my arms. But I was in no position, a lowly maid with no home of my own. The years went by and I had to resign myself to never seeing you again. I rose through the ranks and became Ambrose's housekeeper, as you know. Even then, how would I keep a child?'

Her dilemma was all too familiar to me. I should have felt sympathy, but anger still burned in my heart.

'It was when he asked for my hand in marriage that I summoned the courage to tell him about you and to bargain with him, asking if we might search for you. It took him several days to give me an answer. He agreed with my proposal, but on one condition. As a man of the church, he said, he could not allow it to be known that his wife had borne a child out of wedlock. It would cause too much scandal. So he made me vow that, should we ever trace you – and I suppose he never believed that we would – you would be known as my sister, a sister born just seven years after me, so that no one would suspect the truth. Imagine my despair: how could I think of agreeing to such a dreadful deception? But I was in no position to argue. My only thought, every moment of every day and night, was that I might once more be able to hold you in my arms, and this was my only chance of finding you again.'

So this was the so-called 'edifice of deceit'. My mind still struggled to make sense of everything she was telling me. I felt untethered, unstable, like walking on quicksand, disconnected from the world. Even this room with its familiar furnishings and memories, both happy and troubled, now felt strange, as though I were seeing everything for the first time.

Louisa knelt at my feet once more, taking my hands, her

upturned face desperate now, beseeching. 'My darling, please forgive me. Sister or daughter, it makes no difference to my love for you.'

She had lied for so long that my place in the world and everything in my life was being turned upside down. 'How can I forgive you, when I can no longer tell what is the truth and what is not any more?' I shouted.

Her eyes shone with tears. 'My darling, I would never have lied to you if I'd had my own way. It was the cost I paid for being able to have you by my side again. Like the arrangement between us for . . .' She pointed towards the room upstairs.

Peter. My heart seemed to falter in my chest. My beautiful son. Of course I understood only too well the pain of giving him up and would have travelled the earth to find him again, even given my life for him had it been asked for. And of course I would have accepted almost any condition if it meant the chance of being reunited with him again.

But my anger still burned. How could she have deceived me for so long? 'Why tell me now, Louisa?'

'It was you who asked, remember? You who found the sampler. Besides, now that Ambrose . . .'

'Is dead?'

She nodded. 'There will be no more lies. I promise. Now we can be entirely honest with each other for the rest of our lives.'

'And what about Peter? Are we going to go on deceiving him, just as you have with me?'

She blanched and sat back on her heels. 'I knew this would arise, and have given it much thought. But how do you think he would feel if we told him you are really his mother, and I his grandmother? I know that we have promised there will be no more lies, but is that the right thing to do, just now, after all that has happened and all the upheavals we're facing?'

Her words gave me pause; of course she was right. He would feel betrayed just as I was, upset and angry at having been deceived all these years, his world turned topsy-turvy even as he was still grieving for Ambrose and facing the loss of his childhood home.

'Perhaps we can explain it to him one day in the future, when he is a grown man and better able to understand,' I said.

She wiped her eyes with the corner of a sleeve and managed a watery smile. 'I know it will take time for you to accept what I have told you. All I can say is that I have always loved you and you will always mean everything in the world to me. You are my only, precious daughter. I pray that you will in time find it in your heart to forgive me.'

Slowly my anger began to dissipate, and I found myself able to think more clearly and calmly. We took more wine and talked on and on, late into the night, exploring the many avenues that had hitherto been closed on account of Ambrose's insistence. She described the intensity of her joy on discovering that I was still alive and had been found and then, even more overwhelming, our first meeting here in Westford Abbots.

When it was discovered that I was expecting, she had been forced to accede to Ambrose's insistence that they should adopt the child, and even further layers of deceit had to be woven. The alternative he presented her with was to send me away, never allowing her to see me again.

'He so wanted a son, and I'd always felt it was somehow my fault for failing to provide him with one,' she said. 'I knew only too well what kind of life you would have faced without our support, and besides, I could not bear to lose you again. But I promise we shall have no more lies between us now.'

Like small, slow drops of a gentle balm, her words began to melt my heart.

'I had never been happier,' she went on. 'I would wake each morning and pinch myself. I had a perfect sister and a beautiful son, but even this bliss was tainted by the pain of knowing that I could never tell either of you the truth. Ambrose made me swear that I must never, ever let slip anything that might undermine his reputation, which is why it came as such a shock when you showed me that silk, dearest. I was terrified that if you persisted in pressing for the truth, he might throw you out and I would lose you forever.'

'I was so sure the silk would lead me to my mother,' I said. 'When I discovered that it had been woven for the king's mistress I even allowed myself to believe that I had royal blood in my veins.'

She laughed. 'The truth is much duller, I'm afraid. My mother – your grandmother Agnes – really was the lost soul I told you of. She lived in squalor and drowned her sorrows in gin. I never knew my father – and I suspect that neither did she. My aunt was harsh towards me, but the truth is I would probably have died in that hovel had she not taken me in.'

'I went looking for her, you know.'

'Looking for who?'

'The woman you told me was our mother. I went to Stepney Green and searched the graveyard. I even met the vicar and he let me look at the birth, marriage and death records. But I couldn't find any Pottons.'

'That is because my aunt insisted I take their family name, so Potton is my uncle's surname.'

'Then what was your mother's name?'

'Cooper,' she said. 'I was born Louisa Cooper. In Stepney Green, though I doubt my mother ever took the trouble to register me.'

'But her death might be in the records, and she may have been buried there?' It was a common name and I might have read it on a gravestone, but I had no memory of it.

'Perhaps we could go back one day,' she said. 'It could have been a pauper's grave and even unmarked, but her death might be in the records, somewhere.'

'Of course, if you wish,' I said. 'At least we would know what we were looking for.'

'Forgive me, dearest, for sending you on such a wild goose chase.'

I glanced over at the table where the sampler still lay exactly as she'd left it what felt like a lifetime ago.

'No, it was the silk Anna bought at the auction that sent me on the chase,' I said. 'I felt sure I had seen it before, and now I know why.'

'I was so shocked when you showed me,' she said. 'I

couldn't believe it. Just seeing it again brought everything back, and I was terrified you would uncover my deception.'

'So wherever *did* you get hold of it?'

'From the customer I told you about, the merchant. He'd boasted of confidential royal commissions and even showed some of them to me, so I knew where they were stored. When he sent me away, I managed to stuff a few samples beneath my petticoat before I left. My plan was to black-mail him with them somehow or at least sell them for the silver in the thread.'

Louisa . . . the merchant . . . that silk . . . the royal com-mission. The connections were bewildering. A sudden shocking thought flashed into my mind. 'Was his name Girardieu?' I stuttered. 'The one who threw you out?'

She glanced at me, sharply. 'Do you know him?'

'He's the merchant who dealt with the commission for Henrietta Howard, whose silk was sold at auction. Anna and I went to visit him in Spital Square. But he's gone now – I went back to check and the house was all dark and closed up.'

'Ha! Gone bankrupt. He deserves it.'

The realisation crept into my head only slowly, a small whispery voice growing louder and louder until it became a shout. 'Monsieur Girardieu was the man you were with when you . . .' I faltered. 'When you got pregnant? He was the father of your child?'

She nodded.

'You are sure?' Nausea swilled in my stomach.

'He was my only client.'

Nothing was real any more. It felt as though I was standing apart from myself, looking at another person, a daughter who had not only discovered her mother – although it would take some time to think of Louisa in that way – but also a father?

That day, when Anna and I had visited Monsieur Girardieu, I'd felt a curious sense of recognition, even affiliation. Now I knew why. I'd found my father. Even met him, shaken his hand. In any other circumstances I might have been ecstatic, but in that moment felt only a sense of revulsion at the way he had so cruelly discarded Louisa and their unborn child.

'Did you ever see him again?'

'Of course not. He disowned me, remember? Told me never to darken his door again. Left me destitute and back on the streets, with child.' She paused a moment. 'Although I do sometimes wonder whether you have inherited from him your interest in fabrics, your flair for design and colour.'

'I hope to be more fortunate in business than he was,' I said, finding a smile at last.

'You know how proud I am of your success, Agnes, I always have been. You are such a talented young woman, running a successful business on your own account.'

'I could never have achieved any of it without your help, you know.'

'All I've ever achieved is being a housewife, a supporter of my husband's good works.'

'And a mother,' I added. 'You have been a very good mother to Peter.'

She flushed. 'It means a lot to hear you say that. I have always been conscious of you looking over my shoulder, making sure that I raised your son as you would have done, had things been different.'

'Of course you have. You have done a marvellous job.'

'I want to be a good mother for you too, my darling, if you will let me.'

On an impulse, I blurted it out. 'Come and live with me, Louisa, so we can be a proper family, the three of us. It makes such sense. Peter would love London, once he got used to the idea. In time, we could find him a good apprenticeship.'

'He still wants to become a sea captain, thanks to you,' she said, smiling. 'Perhaps we could find him something less dangerous?'

'My place is small but maybe with your money from Ambrose we could afford to rent somewhere bigger. At least, we could ask old Boyson, see what he has to offer? And right now my business is going really well. It has grown so much I could really do with some extra help. What do you think?'

'How can I be of any help? I am no seamstress, Agnes, as well you know.'

'I urgently need someone to keep my finances in order. I've seen your household accounts and they are neater than any I've ever managed even in years of trying.'

'But I am so ignorant of that world. You would need to teach me the ways of business, dearest.'

'Of course I would. It would be fun.'

'Then, if you are sure, I cannot imagine anything better than the three of us, living together as a proper family.'

As we embraced it began to dawn on me that despite her revelations, nothing had really changed. If anything, the bonds between us had become even more powerful, more all-consuming. I had always held my sister in such high regard, felt the need to please her, to comply with unspoken expectations. But now there was no sibling competition. Her love for me was as unbounded and unconditional as that I felt for Peter. Whatever our mistakes or misdemeanours we would always put each other first, for the rest of our lives.

There was more, although it took some days afterwards to appreciate fully. That familiar, silent ache of feeling that something was missing, that deep knot of anxiety that had persisted for so many years, had melted away. I had found my mother.

Perhaps now, after all, I could really know myself.

A note on the history that inspired
The Dressmaker of Draper's Lane

Miss Charlotte first appeared as a minor character in my 2017 novel *The Silk Weaver*, and came to play a far more important part than I had initially imagined for her. Many readers have since remarked on what an interesting individual she was: an unmarried independent woman running her own business in the days when this was most unusual.

Before long I knew that Miss Charlotte's story was asking to be told. Anna and Henri, protagonists in *The Silk Weaver*, would play an important part in her life just as she had in theirs. I needed no encouragement to return to the setting of eighteenth-century Spitalfields, in East London, not least because it is where my own family's silk weaving business began in the early 1700s.

In those days, to run a business and employ others it was necessary to undertake an apprenticeship and become a member of a company such as the Haberdashers or Mercers or Drapers, and to gain the Freedom of the City. This avenue was rarely open to women, and certainly not those from poorer classes, because of the cost. But there was a real-life precedent: Ann and Mary Hogarth (sisters of the great artist William) ran their own millinery shop, which in those days meant providing not just hats but the full range of men's and women's clothing. It has been suggested that the sisters were apprenticed to their mother, another Anne, who inherited the business from her own mother and father.

This turned out to be a neat coincidence: William Hogarth was one of the first governors of the Foundling Hospital in London and his wife Jane was a volunteer, helping to monitor the work of the foster parents with whom the foundlings were lodged until they turned five years old. Jane appears in *The Silk Weaver* and returns to play an important role in this book, too.

Perhaps the most poignant of the exhibits at the Foundling Museum are the tokens left by mothers as proof of identity in case they were able, at some point in the future, to reclaim their child. Many of these tokens are pieces of fabric, among which are a few examples of silks. This, of course, appealed greatly to my own interest in silk, and the fact that – as readers of *The Silk Weaver* will know – the character of Miss Charlotte's friend Anna was inspired by the life of the famous eighteenth-century silk designer Anna Maria Garthwaite.

Another neat link became apparent when I visited Hogarth's House in Chiswick – what William Hogarth called his 'country cottage' – and realised that it was only a few miles from Marble Hill House, the Palladian jewel built on the Thames at Twickenham for Henrietta Howard after her 'retirement' as the king's mistress. Henrietta was a great fan and collector of Chinoiserie, the exotic designs introduced into England through imported Chinese porcelain. In the dining parlour at Marble Hill House today

– now run by English Heritage – is a reproduction of the hand-painted Chinese wallpaper that hung there in her day. Also displayed in the house is the portrait of the young Henrietta that so struck Miss Charlotte when she visited.

A further fascinating connection followed: the Hogarth house is neighbour to Chiswick House, another wonderful Palladian mansion built by Lord and Lady Burlington. They were instrumental in introducing David Garrick, the actor, theatrical manager and great Shakespeare proponent, to his wife, the Viennese dancer Eva-Maria Veigel. Hogarth painted a charming portrait of the couple, who were part of Henrietta Howard's circle of intellectual and artistic friends, and so would have been perfectly placed to organise a visit for Miss Charlotte to Marble Hill House. They were also great fun to write!

If you are interested in following up any of these links, here is a list of the key websites and sources:

The Foundling Museum, London: www.foundlingmuseum.org.uk

Marble Hill House, Twickenham: www.english-heritage.org.uk/visit/places/marble-hill-house

Hogarth's House, Chiswick: www.williamhogarthtrust.org.uk

The Fashion Museum, Bath: www.fashionmuseum.co.uk

Dennis Severs' House at 18 Folgate Street, Spitalfields: www.dennissevershouse.co.uk

John Styles, *Threads of Feeling, The London Foundling Hospital's Textile Tokens 1740–1770* (The Foundling Museum, 2010)

Janette Bright and Gillian Clark, *An Introduction to the Tokens at the Foundling Museum* (The Foundling Museum, 2014)

Cecil Willett Cunnington, *Handbook of English Costume in the Eighteenth Century* (Faber & Faber, 1964)

Gillian Pugh, *London's Forgotten Children: Thomas Coram and the Foundling Hospital* (Tempus, 2007)

Tracy Borman, *King's Mistress, Queen's Servant* (Vintage, 2010)

David Bindman, *Hogarth* (Thames and Hudson, 1981)

Kirstin Olsen, *Daily Life in 18th-Century England* (Greenwood Publishing Group, 1999)

ACKNOWLEDGEMENTS

I am indebted to my editors at Pan Macmillan, Caroline Hogg and Alex Saunders, and my agent Caroline Hardman of Hardman & Swainson, for their clear-eyed advice and support in helping *The Dressmaker of Draper's Lane* make its way into the world.

I'd also like to thank all those readers of my previous novel, *The Silk Weaver*, for their kind comments and encouraging me to return to my characters and their life in eighteenth-century Spitalfields. Your wish is granted!

As ever, my family, David, Becky and Polly Trenow, have been amazingly supportive, as have my wonderful friends. Finally, I'd like to give a special mention to Pete and Sarah Donaldson and their staff at Red Lion Books in Colchester, the much-deserved Independent Bookshop of the Year regional award-winner in 2018.

If you want to find out more about how I wrote *The Dressmaker of Draper's Lane*, please go to www.liztrenow.com. You can also follow me on Facebook (www.facebook.com/liztrenow) and on Twitter @liztrenow.

The Silk Weaver

1760 Spitalfields

Anna Butterfield's life is about to change forever, as she moves from her idyllic Suffolk home to be introduced into London society. A chance encounter with a French silk weaver, Henri, draws her in to the volatile world of the city's burgeoning silk trade. Henri is working on his 'master piece', to become a master weaver and freeman; Anna longs to become an artist while struggling against pressure from her uncle's family to marry a wealthy young lawyer.

As their lives become ever more intertwined, Henri realises that Anna's designs could give them both an opportunity for freedom. But his world becomes more dangerous by the day, as riots threaten to tear them apart forever . . .

Inspired by real historical events and characters, *The Silk Weaver* is a captivating, unforgettable story of illicit romance in a time of enlightenment and social upheaval.

Read on now for an extract . . .

PROLOGUE

Anna rests her head on the cushion and traces her finger along the stems of daisies and the nodding heads of blue-bells embroidered onto its calico cover. The silken threads, though worn and coming loose in places, still hold their colours and gleam in the sunshine.

'Bluebells and daisies,' she sings to a familiar nursery rhyme tune. 'Bluebells and daisies. They all grow here, they all grow here.'

They are seated together on the old chaise longue in the window of the vicarage sitting room. This is where her mother likes to work at her embroidery, although she has to hold the frame further away than normal because her belly is so huge and round these days. She says that it is because she is growing a new brother or sister but Anna cannot believe it possible that there could really be a child inside her mother's body.

She is bored. Because of this baby bump they cannot go for their usual walks together across the heath or down to the marshes to collect wild flowers for pressing, as her mother says it gives her backache. Neither can they do much gardening, which Anna also adores. She loves getting her hands dirty making soft beds in the black earth into which they scatter tiny seeds. She cannot believe that these little specks will grow into beautiful flowers next year, but her mother promises they will, just like she's promised about the baby.

'Wait and see, my little one,' she says. 'Have patience and you will find my words are true.'

Although she is only five, Anna has already learned to name many wild flowers and some garden varieties, too. The ones she finds easiest to remember are those which perfectly describe the flowers themselves and seem to roll off the tongue: love-in-a-mist, snapdragon, foxglove, hare-bell, forget-me-not, wallflower, ox-eye daisy. Others she finds more difficult to pronounce and has to say over and over again before they come out right: delphinium, convol-vulus, asphodel, hellebore.

She returns her attention to the cushion. How different these two flowers are: the perky little daisy with its open face of tiny white petals around a yellow nose; the closed heads of the bluebells – more purple than blue, she thinks – hanging from a stem that seems barely able to carry their weight.

'What flower would you like to be?' she asks her mother. 'A daisy or a bluebell?'

'A bluebell, because it smells so sweet.'

'I'd rather be a happy daisy than a droopy bluebell,' Anna says. 'Besides, daisies flower all summer, and bluebells are only here for a few weeks.' She hums the little rhyme to herself a few times and kicks her feet.

'When will you teach me how to sew flowers like you do?'

'Sit up, and I will show you right now,' her mother says.

She puts the needle between the thumb and finger of Anna's right hand, guiding it with her own fingers. Then she helps Anna's other hand hold the frame flat, just like she does.

'We are doing a simple chain stitch for the stem,' she says, guiding the hand with the needle so that it pierces the calico just so. The needle disappears, pulling the green silk behind it, and then is pushed through from the back, emerging, as if by magic, just beside where they made the previous stitch. They do it again, and a third time, and Anna can see how the stem is growing before her very eyes.

But when she insists on trying without her mother's guiding hand, everything goes wrong. The stitches go everywhere and the needle loses its thread. She throws it down in a temper.

'I hate sewing,' she grumbles. 'Can we do drawing instead?'

Just then, her mother's body seems to go rigid, and she gives a sharp gasp. 'Run to the church and fetch your father,' she says through clenched teeth. 'Quick as you can. I think the baby is coming.'

Even years later, Anna cherishes the memory of that day and that inconsequential conversation with her mother. Perhaps it was important because this was the last time that she had her mother to herself, before Jane arrived. But what she remembers most, as clear as if it were yesterday, is the cushion with its embroidered flowers, and the silks glimmering in the sunshine.

LONDON 1760

I

There are many little civilities which a true gentleman will offer to a lady travelling alone, which she may accept with perfect propriety; but, while careful to thank him courteously, avoid any advance toward acquaintanceship.
— *The Lady's Book of Manners, 1760*

The carriage pulled to a sudden halt, and for a moment Anna dared to imagine that they had arrived.

But something was wrong. In the distance could be heard a great deal of commotion: deep-voiced male shouts and the screech of women's voices. They could see nothing from the windows and no one came to open the door. The four travelling companions sat without speaking, trying not to catch each other's eyes. Only the silent sighs of irritation and tiny tics – the tapping of toes, the drumming of fingers – suggested that this delay was out of the ordinary.

After a few minutes the gentleman of the middling sort cleared his throat impatiently, took his cane and knocked briskly on the ceiling of the carriage – *rat-a-tat-tat, rat-a-tat-tat*. There was no response. He leaned out and hollered upwards.

'Coachman, why are we stopped?'

'We'll be on our way shortly, sir.' He did not sound convinced.

They waited a few moments longer, until the gentleman huffed and sighed again, stood up and let himself out of the coach, telling his son to stay with the ladies. Anna heard him exchange words with the coachman, and five further minutes passed. When he climbed back inside, his cheeks were so flushed she feared he might be about to suffer a choleric turn.

'Nothing to worry about, ladies.' His tone was falsely calm. 'May I suggest, however, that you pull down the blinds.'

The carriage began to jerk backwards, forwards and sideways with such violent movements that the four of them were thrown about like butter in a churn. It seemed that the coachman was attempting the almost impossible task of turning around a coach and four on this narrow highway.

The shouting outside became louder. It was hard to make out any words, but at times it took on the rhythm of a chant, angry and menacing. What sounded like stones seemed to clatter on the cobbles around them and, even more alarmingly, against the carriage itself. One of the horses whinnied sharply as if in pain. The hollering came closer now, and Anna could make out a single syllable repeated again and again. It was shocking how such a plain, everyday word could sound so very threatening in the voice of an enraged crowd.

The coachman was hollering too, urging the horses to push on, pull back, hold hard. Everyone inside the coach remained tensely silent as they tried to brace themselves against the jolts. Both gentlemen stared fixedly forwards; the lady turned her face downwards towards her lap, her eyes sealed tightly as if in prayer.

Although she too was trying to remain outwardly composed, Anna could hear her own heart hammering in her chest and her knuckles, clutching onto the strap above the window, shone white in the gloom of the interior. She began to wonder whether this sort of thing was a regular occurrence in the city; she had heard there were demonstrations and mobs that could become violent, but never thought for a moment that she might directly encounter one.

Finally the carriage set off again at a great lick, but with the blinds still drawn it was impossible to see in which direction they were now travelling. 'My dear sir, please tell us what was happening,' the lady said, looking up at last, her breathing ragged. 'Do I understand that our coach was the object of the commotion?'

'Have no fear, my dear lady,' the gentleman said smoothly. 'We were in no danger. There was an obstruction in the road. The coachman has decided to try another route into the city.' The colour of his face had returned to normal, but Anna didn't believe a word.

'But why would they be shouting about bread?' she ventured. 'And why would they choose strangers as the focus of such an attack?'

'It is not for us to presume.' He pursed his lips and would not be drawn further, so the four lapsed into another heavy silence.

Now, she began to worry about their delayed arrival. Cousin William was due to meet her at the Red Lyon public house, but how could she get word to him that they were well over an hour late? She had eaten nothing but a slice of bread and a small lump of cheese since breakfast and her stomach was rumbling so loudly that she feared that her companions would hear it, even over the clatter of wheels on the cobbled street.

At last the coach pulled to a halt and she heard the shout, 'Spitalfields Red Lyon, Miss Butterfield.'

She climbed stiffly from the carriage and waited while her luggage was unloaded from the rear and placed beside her. In just seconds, the coachman shouted a cheery farewell and they were gone. The carriage and its passengers had become a haven of safety and protection and as she watched it turn the corner and disappear from view she felt abandoned and a little afraid. She was on her own in this great city.

Around Anna and her cases flowed a seemingly unending stream of people. Some walked at a leisurely pace in twos and threes, absorbed in conversation, while others, apparently engaged on urgent errands, scurried quickly, dodging between the groups.

She found herself entranced by the cries of the street pedlars. A woman waved a bunch of sweet-smelling herbs in front of people's noses, shouting, 'Buy my rosemary! Buy my sweetbriar! A farthing a bunch to sweeten your home.' Some cries even sounded like poetry: 'Pears for pies! Come feast your eyes! Ripe pears, of every size, who'll buy?'

In her village, people would stop to gossip with travelling

salesmen – it was one of the best ways of discovering what was going on in neighbouring villages, who had died, who had married, who had borne children and how the hay, corn and fruit harvests were faring. But here in the city it appeared that everyone was too busy to chat.

Every kind of produce seemed to be for sale: boxes and baskets, brushes and brooms, Morocco slippers, matches, saucepans, wooden spoons and nutmeg graters, doormats, chickweed and groundsel for bird seed, oysters, herring, ropes of onions, strawberries, rhubarb and all manner of other fruit and vegetables and, most enticing of all, delicious-smelling hot loaves, baked potatoes and meat pies that made her stomach rumble all the more.

Apart from the traders and a few beggars, no one was taking the slightest notice of her. A lone woman waiting on the roadside in the country would have received several offers of help within a few moments. Here, it was as if she were invisible, or something inanimate like a statue or an island around which the human river was forced to navigate. Among this mass of people her presence was of no consequence at all. *I could disappear*, she thought, *and no one would ever be the wiser.* It was a curious feeling, both frightening and freeing all at once.

And the noise! The clatter of drays and carriages across the cobbles, the shouts of hawkers and women hollering at their children. In the hubbub it took a little while to make sense of any words, and now Anna began to realise why: much of it was not in English.

She looked around. Across the road, although it was not yet dusk, a crowd of drinkers had gathered at the Red Lyon

Inn, spilling into the street, tankards in hand, engaged in conversations animated with much raucous laughter.

Behind her, high brick arches fronted the pavement and, through them, she could see a cavernous interior dense with tables and other wooden structures. It looked like a market, but Anna had never seen such an expanse of stalls. Just two dozen filled the square at Halesworth, even at Michaelmas, yet there looked to be well over one hundred here. Although trading had ended for the day and the stalls were now empty, pungent smells of herbs and vegetables, stale fish and rotting meat wafted across the road.

Minutes ticked by on the cracked-faced clock above the market. Her stays were tight, her stomach empty, she had a raging thirst and she was beginning to feel light-headed. She shifted her weight from toe to heel and from foot to foot as she had learned during long hours at church, and prayed that William would come soon.

Time passed and she fell into a kind of reverie. The next thing she knew, she seemed to be on the ground, vaguely aware of someone kneeling by her side and cradling her head, with another person standing close on the other side, fanning her with his cap. It took her a few moments to understand where she was.

'Oh dear, I am so sorry to be a nuisance,' she mumbled, starting to push herself up.

'Do not be troubled,' the young man said. 'We are keeping you safe.' He spoke something unintelligible to his companion who disappeared, returning shortly with a cup of water which she sipped gratefully.

'Are you having a home?' the young man asked. 'A family? Or a friend, perhaps?'

'I am come to stay with my uncle, Joseph Sadler of Spital Square,' she said, her wits now slowly returning, 'and my cousin William was to meet me here.' The young man spoke some further incomprehensible words to his friend, who left them again.

A glorious thought slipped into her confused mind: perhaps they were speaking in tongues, just as the Apostles described? She'd always considered it an unlikely story – just an allegory, like so many tales in the Bible – but something rather like it did indeed seem to be happening to her. She smiled to herself. *The Lord does indeed move in mysterious ways.*

A crowd had gathered now, but with this young man's arms around her she felt curiously unafraid. She could see that he was clean-shaven and gentle of demeanour. His eyes were the deepest brown, like horse chestnuts freshly released from their cases. Although wigless and not, as far as she could see, dressed as a gentleman, his dark hair was neatly tied back, and he spoke to her tenderly and smiled often, to reassure her. There was a sweet, musty smell about him; not unpleasant but strange, nothing she could recognise.

The second boy returned, panting, 'He come.' Not wanting her cousin to find her on the ground, and since she was now feeling considerably recovered, Anna tried to stand. The two young men gently put their arms around her waist to help her up.

At that moment a loud shout came from the edge of the crowd. 'Make way, make way. Let me by.' As William appeared – for indeed it was he, a tall, thin-faced young man in a powdered wig – his face darkened.

'How dare you? Take your hands off the young lady at once,' he bellowed, and a fist whipped past Anna's nose into the boy's face. He grunted and fell away, nearly taking her with him but for the strong left hand of William holding her arm painfully tight. He aimed another punch at the second boy, who fell in an untidy heap at their feet. The crowd gasped and drew back.

'Now get out of my sight, cabbage heads,' William bawled, lashing out with his boots as the crowd tried to drag the boys to safety, 'and if I ever catch you touching an English lady again, I'll string you up by your webbed feet.'

'Do not be so harsh, Cousin,' Anna whispered, shocked by his violent response. 'They were helping me. I had fainted from the heat.'

'Dirty frogs,' he growled, barking instructions about the baggage to a man with a pushcart. 'You should never have allowed it. You have much to learn about how a young lady should comport herself in the city.'

'Yes, I expect I do,' Anna said, in what she hoped was a conciliatory tone. He grabbed her arm again and began to drag her along the road with such haste that she had to trot to keep up.

'Hurry along, Anna Butterfield. We have been waiting for hours. I cannot imagine why you did not send word of your arrival earlier. Had you done so you would not have caused this trouble. You are most terribly late and supper has gone cold.'

Fortunately it was but a few minutes – at William's pace – from the Red Lyon to Spital Square. They stopped outside a house with a wide shop frontage: bow windows either side of a grand front door set with bottle-glass, and double pillars that supported a porch to shelter callers from the rain. On a board hanging below the porch was written in elegant gold script: *Joseph Sadler & Son, Mercers to the Gentry.* They were here at last.

She turned to go up the steps, but William grabbed her arm once more and pulled her onwards, opening a smaller side door that led into the darkness of a long entrance hall. They passed two doors on the ground floor – probably leading into the shop area, she assumed – up some stairs to a wide landing, and through yet another door into the dining room.

Uncle Joseph stepped forward first, welcoming her with a formal handshake and a smile that disappeared as soon as it had arrived, as though it were an infrequent and unexpected visitor. He was a daunting figure: tall and portly, whiskered and bewigged even at home, high-collared and tail-coated, with a well-rounded stomach held tight under his embroidered silk waistcoat. He must once have been a handsome man but good living had taken its toll. His jowls drooped and wobbled like a turkey's wattle.

'Welcome, dear Niece,' he said. 'We hope you will be happy here.' He waved his hand proprietorially around the sumptuously furnished room, in the centre of which a deeply polished oak table laden with silver glistened in the light of many candles.

Anna dipped her knee. 'I am indebted to you, sir, for your generous hospitality,' she said.

Aunt Sarah seemed a kindly sort with a smile that, unlike her husband's, appeared quite accustomed to her face. She kissed Anna on both cheeks. 'You poor thing, you look weary,' she said, standing back to regard her up and down. 'And your clothes . . .' She gave a little sigh and her eyes turned away as if the sight of Anna's dress was too terrible to contemplate, even though it was her Sunday best. 'Never mind. You shall have supper now and a good rest after your long journey. Tomorrow we can see about your wardrobe.'

She has the same voice as my father, Anna thought, with the slight lisp that seemed to run in the family. She was his younger sister, after all, but it was difficult, without staring, to divine precisely which features they shared. The lips, perhaps, or the eyebrows? Certainly not the stature. Sarah was very much shorter and more rounded while her father was angular and long of limb, proportions which Anna had inherited and which, she knew, were no advantage for a woman. But the familiarity of her aunt's features helped Anna feel at home.

Cousin Elizabeth made an elegant curtsey.

'Please do call me Lizzie, Cousin Anna. I am so looking forward to having an elder sister.' On her lips the lisp sounded sweet, even endearing. 'A brother is no use at all,' she added, with a poisonous glance across the table. William returned a scowl which, in truth, did not seem to have left his face since their first encounter.

Lizzie would be around fourteen years of age, Anna calculated. A pretty little thing, she observed, round-faced like her mother but much slighter, all auburn ringlets and cream lace, six years younger than her brother and four years younger than herself. Sarah had borne several other children, she remembered, but these were the only two who had survived. She recalled her father sighing over his sister's letters: 'Another child gone into the arms of our Lord. Alas, poor Sarah. If only they could live somewhere with healthier air.' In church, he would name Sarah's lost babies out loud, beseeching God to care for them in heaven.

Anna understood from this litany of sadness that childbirth was something to be dreaded, perhaps more than anything else in the world. Yet how could it be avoided, she wondered, when one grew into a woman and became settled in the proper manner?

They sat down and Joseph poured goblets of a liquid the colour of ripe plums. 'Claret', he called it. As her uncle raised his glass with a toast 'to the arrival of our dear cousin, Anna', she took a tentative sip; it was sharper than communion wine but tasted delicious. She ventured another and yet another until she found herself becoming quite warm and relaxed.

'You poor things, I cannot imagine the trials you have been through these past few months,' Aunt Sarah said, handing around a plateful of cold meats. 'I do hope that dear Fanny's last few weeks were not too difficult?'

The warm glow disappeared as a vision of her mother appeared in Anna's mind: ghostly pale and skeletal, propped against the pillows and struggling to contain paroxysms of coughing, gasping for every breath and unable to speak or eat for the congestion in her chest.

It had been a long and lingering illness: a slow decline followed by apparent recovery, bringing new hope, only to be dashed by further decline. Throughout it all, Anna and her sister Jane had nursed their mother, trying as best they could to shield their father who, as the village vicar, had plenty of problems of his own: difficult parishioners, the demands of his diocesan masters and the need to shore up the ruinous fabric of the church.

The exhaustion of caring for her mother and running the household had kept Anna from dwelling too much on the tragedy ahead. When it finally came, Jane took to her bed and wept, so it seemed, for several weeks. Nothing could console her except for the sweetmeats she consumed by day and the warmth of her sister's embrace in their shared bed by night.

Their father, Theodore, though hollowed-out and grey in countenance, continued about his daily work, the only difference being that he retired earlier to bed than usual. Once or twice, in the dead of night, Anna would hear heartrending sobs through the wall and longed to comfort him. But she resisted the impulse, sensing that he must be allowed to embrace this misery without needing to keep face for anyone else.

As for herself, the anticipated collapse into despair never really happened. She rose each day, washed and dressed and did her chores, made meals for the family, organised the funeral tea and tried to smile when people commented on how well she was coping. But inside she felt empty, almost indifferent to her own misery. Grief was like sleep-walking through deep snow, its landscape endless and unchanging, every step painful and exhausting. The world seemed to become monochrome, colours lost their hue, sounds were muffled and distorted. It felt as though her own life had been taken, along with her mother's.

Dragging herself away from these painful recollections,

she turned back to the dining table, and her waiting aunt. 'Thank you, madam, she was peaceful at the end.' As she said it, she crossed her fingers in her lap. It was an old habit from childhood, when she believed it might save her from God's wrath when lying. But then she uncrossed them as she realised that her words had a certain truth: the lifeless form laid out on the bed had indeed looked peaceful, now that all pain had gone.

'And my dear brother, Theo? How is he coping with his loss?'

'His faith is a great comfort, as you can imagine,' Anna ventured, although she knew well that the opposite was true: his faith had been sorely tested these past few months.

'It is a cruel God, indeed, who takes with one hand while purporting to offer solace with the other,' her uncle said.

'Each to their own, my dear,' Sarah muttered.

'It is an interesting conjecture, all the same.' William's eyes glittered, alert for the challenge, his thin lips in a sardonic twist. 'Just what *is* the point of God, when all's said and done?'

'Shush, William,' Sarah said, sliding a glance towards Lizzie and back again to her son. 'Save such debates for your club fellows.'

A silence fell over the table. Anna took a couple of rather larger sips of claret. 'I do hope you will forgive me for my tardy arrival. The coach was held up by a commotion, and we had to find another route into the city,' she said.

William looked up sharply. 'What kind of commotion? Where was this?'

'I do not know exactly where, I am afraid. It was as we

entered the city, and we could not see anything from the coach on account of having to draw down the blinds. There was much shouting – something about bread, I thought I could hear.'

'Sounds like another food riot,' William said. 'Probably those Frenchie weavers again, like last month. They're always revolting. Have you heard anything, Pa?'

Joseph shook his head, jaws working on the generous spoonful of meat and potato he had just stuffed into his mouth. 'If they didn't waste so much money on Geneva, they would have plenty for bread,' he muttered. 'And it would help if those Strangers would stop stirring things up.'

William took out his watch, put down his knife and spoon with a hurried clatter and pushed back his chair. 'Forgive me, I am late for the club,' he said, grabbing his jacket and bowing slightly in Anna's direction. 'We will meet again tomorrow, dear Coz. In the meantime do try to stay away from cabbages. They can cause the most odorous indigestion.'

Anna puzzled over this until, later, she recalled his 'cabbage heads' jibe. Why he should be so vitriolic towards two innocent and indeed most helpful young men was a mystery, but so much of this new world was unfathomable that it made her feel quite dizzy to contemplate.

After the meal Lizzie was deputed to show her the rest of the house – the upper floors at least, for the ground floor was entirely devoted to Uncle's business and the basement, she presumed, was the domain of the servants. The building stood four storeys tall and, although deep from front to back, it felt less spacious than her own dear vicarage and nothing like so homely. She admired the opulent silk hangings, the elegant furniture, the painted wainscoting in each of the main rooms and the shutters on every window, but the overall effect was to make the place darker and more formal.

Next to the dining room, at the front of the house above what she presumed to be the shopfront, was a wide, elegant drawing room with a cast-iron fireplace and marble surround. Out of the window, Anna could see the street and the small square of grass with a few young trees which, she thought to herself, no doubt afforded the house its grand address. And yet the building was attached on either side to others so that it was difficult to see where one started and the other ended. *Land must be very scarce in this cramped city*, she thought to herself, *that even in such prosperous areas they cannot afford to be separated from their neighbours by even a few feet.*

'Do you have a garden?' she asked.

'It's just a patch of mouldy grass and a tree,' Lizzie replied quickly. 'I can show you tomorrow.'

'I love to sketch natural things.'

'There is little to inspire an artist,' Lizzie said. 'Although I know where we could see flowers and fruits in great abundance.'

'Where is that?' Anna asked.

'At the market. All sorts, from farms and Strangers' gardens and from foreign countries too, piled high in their thousands. It is a wonderful sight.' Lizzie laughed suddenly.

'I do not suppose that is what you had in mind for a painting?'

'Not really,' Anna said, pleased to be talking of lighter matters after so many serious hours. 'Although I should love to see it.'

'Mama will not let us enter the market; she says it is common. "'Twould not be decorous for a young lady."' Lizzie mimicked her mother's tone, crinkling her pretty features into a grimace. 'I think that's silly, don't you? But I shall ask if we can visit our new church tomorrow, so we can pass by.'

Anna demurred. It would be unwise to appear disloyal to her aunt at such an early stage. 'I could turn my pen to architectural scenes instead, but I do find the perspective of buildings such a puzzle, don't you?'

Lizzie's face fell, her smiles gone as quickly as they arrived. 'I would love to be able to draw, but my tutor is so scornful of my attempts that I scarcely dare to try.'

'Then I shall teach you,' Anna said.

'Oh yes,' Lizzie said, instantly recovered. 'I should like that very much.'

After her tour of the house Anna begged leave to retire.

'Of course, you must be exhausted,' her aunt said. 'But I must warn you that your chamber is up many stairs, and it is rather plain. We are short of rooms because the ground floor is given over to the business. We hope to move shortly, to an address more suited to Sadler and Son's status, do we not, my dearest?' She smiled at her husband but his face remained impassive. 'Lizzie, why don't you show Anna to her room? Her luggage is already there and I shall send the maid at once with water.'

They climbed a narrow wooden stairway to the very top floor, which Lizzie called the 'old weaving loft'. It had been converted, she said, now that Uncle Joseph had finished with the weaving and turned to selling finished silks for his living. The room, next door to one shared by the cook and Betty the maid, was indeed small and plain, with a wooden chest of drawers, a side table with a bowl and ewer, an upright chair and a bed that, although simple, looked marvellously inviting to her weary limbs.

After Lizzie had clattered back down the stairs, Anna opened the casement, took a long breath of warm night air and sighed deeply, releasing the muscles of her face that had grown painful from holding a polite smile.

She climbed under the covers, but sleep was slow to come.

The bed was short, the horsehair mattress lumpy and the blanket smelled unaired. But if not as comfortable as her feather bed at home, she was at least warm and safe. What more could she want for?

It was certainly warm in this attic on a hot July evening. Little breeze stirred the air, even up here on the top floor. The noise from the street was astonishing – did people in the city never rest? It seemed hardly to have abated since she first stepped from the coach this afternoon: brays of laughter from boisterous gangs of young men, the shrill calls of women and wails of children, the howling of dogs and keening of cats, the clanging of coaches and the hammering of handcart wheels on the cobbles. In her village all would be quiet at this time of night except for the rhythmical boom of the breakers when the wind was in the east.

What an adventure it had been. Despite the sorrow of leaving and the heaviness in her heart which had not lifted since her mother's death, she could not help being a little excited.

'Life has much to offer a talented young woman such as you,' her father had said as they sat together that last evening. 'There is so much to see and so much to learn, much in the world to savour and enjoy. But you will not find it here in this little community. You must go and seek your fortune in the city.'

'Like Dick Whittington, I suppose?'

'Indeed,' he laughed. 'And if you become Mayor of London, then you must invite us to your grand residence. But remember you can come home whenever your black cat leads you here.'

Even though the first day on the road had been perfectly straightforward and without incident, every small event came as a surprise for a novice traveller. She had been instructed to refrain from conversing with the other passengers for fear of encouraging intimacy, but it was so rare to spend time in the company of strangers that she could not prevent herself from scrutinising them, as covertly as possible to avoid appearing rude.

All ages of human life seemed to be represented in the cramped space of the stagecoach. Next to her on the bench was a stout gentleman who studied his newspaper in a self-important kind of way, harrumphing with disapproval at what he read and digging her in the ribs whenever he turned the page. After a while he fell asleep, tipping alarmingly sideways onto her shoulder before stirring and sharply pulling himself upright, only to repeat the process every few minutes.

She could not see the faces of the two women on his other side but knew they must be herring girls from Yarmouth, unmistakeable from their odour and redness of hand. On the opposite bench, two stout housewives from Bungay occupied sufficient space for three and chattered unceasingly all the way to Ipswich. Each jiggled a small child on one knee and a baby on the other.

The children whined incessantly before falling asleep with dribbles of snot streaming unchecked from their noses, while the chubby cupids took it in turns to cry: piercing, disturbing sounds in such close proximity. In between wails these babes would bestow cherubic smiles upon any who caught their eye, and all would be forgiven until the next bout of yowling. When it went on for too long, their mothers would yank down their tops and stuff the wailing infants' faces into the exposed folds of disconcertingly white flesh.

A withered elderly gentleman had levered himself into the narrow space next to the two ladies and, when he too fell asleep, Anna feared that he might be silently squeezed to death, with no one the wiser until all had disembarked.

To reserve her stares and pass the time, she took out the pocket Bible her father had pressed into her hand at their parting. Her faith had evaporated during the long nights of her mother's agony, and had never returned, but the familiar phrases of the epistles were comforting. As she opened the scuffed leather cover she saw for the first time that he had inscribed inside the frontispiece, in his vicar's spidery hand: *To my dearest Anna, God keep you and hold you.* Tears prickled behind her eyelids. *When will I see the dear man again?* she thought. *How will he cope, with just Jane to care for him?*

Although she was only five at the time and had witnessed little of her mother's labour, she understood that her sister's birth had been long and arduous. When she finally arrived, the baby was blue and limp. Defying all expectations, her sister survived and slowly gained strength and weight. It was not until much later they discovered that the difficult birth had left long-lasting effects: Jane's right side was weak and she walked with a limp, dragging her foot painfully behind her. And although sweet-natured, she was slow in her mind, struggling to understand those things that others found simple, and never managing to learn reading and writing.

How will she manage the household without me, strange little creature that she is? Anna thought to herself. *Will she understand Father's needs? Will she stay well? And will she find company and friendship with other girls in the village, now that I have gone?* How she missed them both, already.

When they finally reached the staging inn at Chelmsford, the portly gentleman took her hand to help her disembark.

'May I help with your overnight case?'

'Thank you very much,' she replied, grateful that someone had taken even a slight notice of her. 'This is this one. I suppose the portmanteau and hatbox will stay on the coach for the onward journey in the morning?'

'That is the usual custom, if you have informed them.'

He picked up her shabby canvas bag and his smart leather case and walked with her across the yard towards the front door of the inn. 'Pardon me, madam,' he said, 'please do not think I am too forward if I offer a nugget of advice?'

'Dear sir, any advice is most welcome, for I am unfamiliar with the customs of the road,' she said.

'Then may I recommend that you might ask for your meal to be served in your room? The tap can become somewhat rowdy and may not suit your gentle temperament.' As if to prove his words, a roar of voices accosted them as he pushed open the door. She hesitated on the threshold but he took her arm and gently led her between the crowded tables through a fog of tobacco smoke towards a serving hatch. He shouted over the hubbub to a surly-looking woman Anna assumed to be the innkeeper's wife and, shortly afterwards, a scruffy boy appeared and showed them upstairs. As they parted on the landing, Anna said, 'You have been most kind, sir.'

'May you rest well, madam,' he said, with a slight bow.

The little exchange had so cheered her that she barely noticed how small and sparsely furnished was the room, how grey the bedsheets from too many launderings. When it arrived, the cold mutton was greasy and the potatoes pocked with black eyes, but she was so hungry she cleaned the plate without a thought. The candle stump they supplied quickly burned out and she found herself facing a long, disturbed night, trying to ignore the bedbugs as they celebrated the arrival of new flesh, and listening to the tap room below becoming ever more lively.

When she slept, finally, she dreamed of returning home to find all unchanged, the vicarage full of activity and laughter as it once had been, the fires lit, the family foursome intact. She fell into her mother's embrace, smelling the mingled aromas of laundry soap and garden herbs that, to Anna, spelled love and security.

When she woke in the early hours and realised where she was the tears came at last, wetting her pillow with long, racking sobs that seemed to shake her whole body. How could she think of leaving that beloved place? But how could she return to it, when she would never again feel her mother's warmth?

Yet next morning her mood seemed to rise with the sun. She was sorry to discover that the kindly gentleman was not joining them again, but stepped aboard the coach full of optimism at the prospect of another day of travel, even venturing a smile at the only other passenger, a smartly dressed lady. After twenty-four hours of barely speaking to another person she would have welcomed a conversation, and was disappointed when the lady immediately took out her spectacles and opened her book.

She turned to her own thoughts, excited at the prospect of seeing at first hand all that she had heard about the great metropolis, and of making the acquaintance of her uncle and aunt, and her two cousins. After being confined to the house caring for her mother for such long, dutiful months she yearned to spread her wings and see the big city, and they had generously offered her this opportunity.

In the early afternoon, they stopped at a village to pick up two gentlemen who appeared to be father and son, and the coachman invited the ladies to disembark for what he called 'a fine view of the city'.

At first, Anna could make out only the River Thames, reflecting the sun like a silver snake along the valley beneath a reddish-brown pall of smoke. As her eyes adjusted to the distance, she could discern ribbons reaching out towards them and in every other direction. After a few moments she came to realise, with astonishment, that these were streets of houses, in their hundreds, even thousands. The numbers of people all these buildings might contain was barely imaginable. In the densest part of the city before them, along the river's edge, barely a speck of green could be seen; not a tree, not a field in sight.

How will I ever survive in such close proximity to so many others, all breathing that smoke-filled air? she wondered. Her village had but three hundred souls, with fields and woods occupying all the land to one side, sand dunes and the great empty sea to the other. *What will I find to paint, in a place with no flowers or trees, no butterflies or birds?*

❧

Turning restlessly in the attic bed, she felt empty and emotionless, as though travelling at such an unaccustomed pace had caused a part of her soul to be left behind. She had waited so long for her 'big adventure' to start. But now that she was actually here, everything seemed so strange and unfamiliar, even frightening, that she longed to be back in the comfortable familiarity of the countryside.

In Love and War

Three women, once enemies. Their secrets will unite them.

The First World War is over. The war-torn area of Flanders near Ypres is no longer home to troops, but groups of tourists. Controversial battlefield tourism now brings hundreds of people to the area, all desperate to witness first-hand where their loved ones fell.

At the Hotel de la Paix in the small village of Hoppestadt, three women arrive, searching for traces of the men they have loved and lost. Ruby is just twenty-one, a shy Englishwoman looking for the grave of her husband. Alice is only a little older but brimming with confidence; she has travelled all the way from America, convinced her brother is in fact still alive. Then there's Martha and her son Otto, who are not all they seem to be . . .

The three women may have very different backgrounds, but they are united in their search for reconciliation. They must accept what the war took from them, but also look ahead to what life might bring in the future . . .